The First Blast of the Trumpet

The First Blast of the Trumpet

by

Marie Macpherson

www.penmorepress.com

The First Blast of the Trumpet
by Marie Macpherson

ISBN-13: 978-1-946409-50-8(Paperback)
ISBN :-978-1-946409-51-5(e-book)

BISAC Subject Headings:
FIC014000 FICTION / Historical
FIC026000 FICTION / Religious
FIC044000 FICTION / Women
FIC121000 FICTION / World Literature / Scotland
FIC098020 FICTION/World Literature/England/16th & 17th Century

Address all correspondence to:

Penmore Press LLC
920 N Javelina Pl
Tucson AZ 85748

DEDICATION

This is dedicated to the one I love—for keeping faith

ACKNOWLEDGMENTS

I would like to thank all those friends, family and colleagues whose help, comments and moral and practical support have contributed to the production of this book.

Among the many reference sources consulted, I am indebted to the following whose thorough research has proved invaluable—but I accept full responsibility for my interpretation of their facts.

Transactions of the East Lothian and Field Naturalists' Society; Ishbel C. M. Barnes, *Janet Kennedy, Royal Mistress;* Jamie Cameron, *James V;* Carol Edington, *Court and Culture in Renaissance Scotland;* Roderick Graham, *John Knox—Democrat;* Stewart Lamont, *The Swordbearer;* Rosalind K. Marshall, *Mary of Guise*; *John Knox;* Marcus Merriman, *The Rough Wooings;* Pamela E. Ritchie, *Mary of Guise in Scotland*

For practical help, thanks are due to the staff at the John Gray Centre, Library and Museum.

Finally, words are not enough to express my thanks to Matt Macpherson for his unfailing support and patience.

Contents

Part Five

Cast of Characters

* Denotes fictional characters

House of Hepburn

Elisabeth Hepburn—daughter of 1st Earl of Bothwell; Prioress of St. Mary's Abbey, Haddington

Margaret Hepburn—Meg, sister of Elisabeth; married Archibald Douglas, 6th Earl of Angus

John Hepburn—Prior of St Andrews Priory, later Bishop of Moray; uncle of Elisabeth

Janet Hepburn—Prioress of St. Mary's Abbey; sister of John Hepburn

Patrick Hepburn—1st Earl of Bothwell; married firstly, Joanna Douglas; secondly Margaret Gordon

Margaret Gordon—1st Countess of Bothwell; mother of Meg & Elisabeth

Adam Hepburn—2nd Earl of Bothwell; son of Patrick Hepburn & Margaret Gordon; married Agnes Stewart

Patrick Hepburn—3rd Earl of Bothwell, dubbed the Fair Earl; married Agnes Sinclair

Joanna Hepburn—daughter of Patrick Hepburn & Joanna Douglas; half-sister of Elisabeth; widow of Lord Seton; founder of St Catherine's Convent

Agnes Stewart—Nancy, 2nd Countess of Bothwell; natural daughter of Earl of Buchan; former mistress of James IV & mother of Jenny; widow of Adam Hepburn & mother of Patrick

Patrick Hepburn—Prior of St. Andrews, later Bishop of Moray; uncle & tutor to Patrick, 3rd Earl of Bothwell

Harry Cockburn—stable lad at St. Mary's Abbey

* Katherine Hepburn—Kate, orphan of indeterminate parentage; mistress of James IV

* Betsy Learmont—nursemaid to the Hepburn family

* Isabelle Campbell—orphan adopted by Elisabeth Hepburn

*Jamie Campbell—brother of Isabelle

House of Douglas

Archibald Douglas—5th Earl of Angus, dubbed 'Bell the Cat'

Archibald Douglas—6th Earl of Angus, grandson of the 5th Earl; married firstly Margaret Hepburn; secondly Margaret Tudor

Elizabeth Drummond—widow of George, Master of Angus; mother of Archibald, 6th Earl of Angus

Janet Douglas—Jinty, sister of Archibald; married firstly John Lyon, 6th Lord Glamis; secondly Archibald Campbell of Skipness

George Douglas of Pittendreich—brother of Archibald, 6th Earl of Angus

Elizabeth Douglas—sister of Angus; wife of John, 3rd Lord Hay of Yester

Margaret Douglas—daughter of Archibald Douglas & Margaret Tudor; married Matthew Lennox; mother of Henry, Lord Darnley

Janet Douglas—Jessie, Mistress of the King's Wardrobe to James V

House of Stewart

James IV—King of Scots 1488-1513; married Margaret Tudor; sister of Henry VIII of England

Margaret Tudor—widow of James IV; married secondly Archibald Douglas, 6th Earl of Angus; thirdly Henry Stewart

Janet Stewart—Jenny, natural daughter of James IV & Agnes Stewart; half-sister of James V; married Malcolm, 3rd Lord Fleming

James V—King of Scots 1513-1542; married firstly Princess Madeleine of France; secondly Marie de Guise-Lorraine

Sir David Lindsay of the Mount and Garleton—tutor to James V; poet, playwright

John Stewart—2nd Duke of Albany; grandson of James II; Regent of Scotland 1514-1524

Marie de Guise—widow of Duke of Longueville; married James V

Mary, Queen of Scots—daughter of James V & Marie de Guise

Margaret Erskine—mistress of James V; wife of Lord Robert Douglas; mother of James Stewart by James V

James Stewart—natural son of James V & Margaret Erskine

Matthew Stewart—4th Earl of Lennox; descendant of James II; married Margaret Douglas; father of Henry, Lord Darnley

Henry Stewart—son of Andrew Stewart, 1st Lord Avondale; distant cousin of James V; later 1st Lord Methven; 3rd husband of Margaret Tudor

Antoine D'Arcie—Duke of Albany's French lieutenant in Scotland

House of Hamilton

James Hamilton—2nd Earl of Arran; Governor & Regent of Scotland 1543-1554

Jean Hamilton—Jeanie, his daughter; pupil at St. Mary's Abbey

James Hamilton of Finnart—dubbed the Bastard; natural son of 1st Earl of Hamilton

Catholics

David Beaton—Abbot of Arbroath; later Cardinal of Scotland

Katherine Beaton—his sister; nun at St. Mary's Abbey

Lady Marion Ogilvie—mistress of David Beaton

Sister Maryoth Hay—nun at St Mary's Abbey; sister of John, 2nd Lord Hay of Yester; aunt of John 3rd Lord Hay

John Hay—3rd Lord Hay of Yester, dubbed 'the Wizard of Goblin Ha'; husband of Elizabeth Douglas, nephew of Sister Maryoth Hay

Andrew Forman—Archbishop of St Andrews

Dr John Winram—Sub-Prior of St Andrews

* Sister Agnes—French nun at St Mary's Abbey

*Father Dudgeon—Parish Priest at St Mary's Collegiate Church, Haddington

Reformers

John Knox—son of Margaret Sinclair & William Knox; godson of Elisabeth Hepburn

William Knox—older brother of John

George Wishart—former priest; protestant reformer

Widow Ker—housekeeper to John Knox

James Balfour of Pittendreich
Henry Balnaves of Halhill

John Cockburn of Ormiston

Hugh Douglas of Longniddry

William Kirkcaldy of Grange

John Leslie of Parkhill

Norman Leslie, Master of Rothes

James Melville of Halhill

John Rough—Ayrshire preacher

Ladies at Court

Janet Kennedy—mistress of James IV & Archibald 'Bell the Cat' Douglas, *inter alia*

Isobel Kennedy—daughter of Janet

Mariota Hume—widow of John, Earl of Crawford

Elizabeth Hamilton—widow of Matthew, Earl of Lennox

SCOTLAND

Map of Central and Southern Scotland
1500-1548
Aberdeen
Angus
Ethie
North Sea
Dunkeld
Arbroath
Scone
Perth
Firth of Tay
Argyll
Cupar
St. Andrews
Fife
Falkland
Elie
Firth of Forth
Stirling
Aberlady
Tantallon
Dumbarton
Haddington
Leith
Pinkie
Dunbar
Linlithgow
Hailes
Coldingham
Glasgow
Edinburgh
Berwick
Crichton
Bothwell
Yester
Nunraw
Arran
River Tyne
Kilwinning
Kyle
Jedburgh
Flodden
River Tweed
Firth of Clyde
Hermitage
Carrick
England
Thrieve
Solway Moss
Whithorn
Solway Firth

HOUSE OF HEPBURN

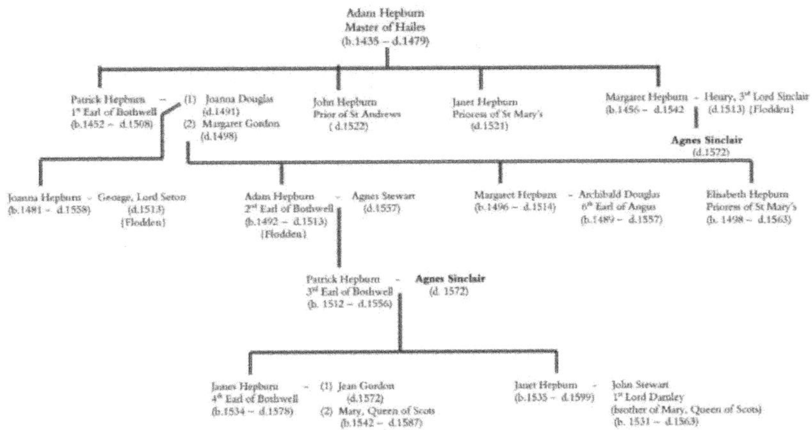

King
of Sc
(b.1

M
2n
(b

glas

Jean Hamilton
(d.1596)

(b. 1542 – d.1587) Lord Darnley
(b. 1545 – d.1567)

HOUSE OF HEPBURN

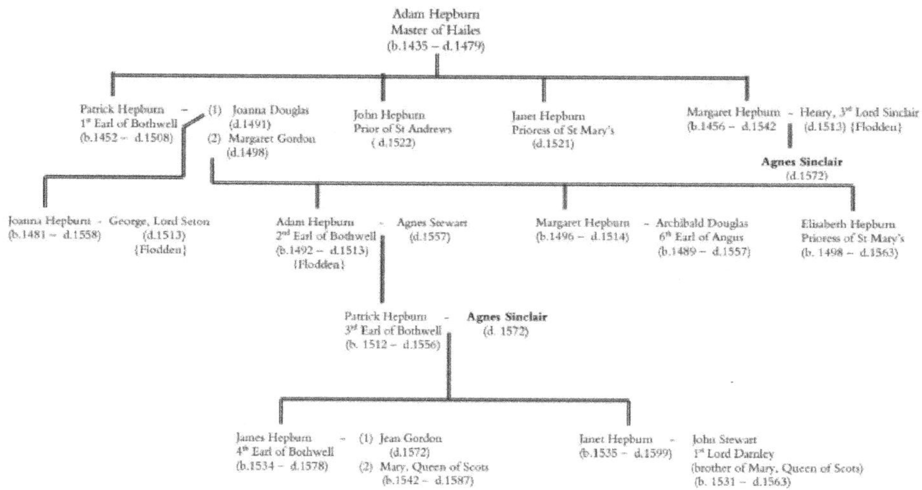

PART ONE

Chapter One
Hallowe'en

The night it is good Hallowe'en
When fairy folk will ride;
And they that wad their true love win
At Miles Cross they maun bide.
— *The Ballad of Tam Linn,* Traditional

Hailes Castle, Scotland, 1511

'There's no rhyme nor reason to it. Your destiny is already laid doon,' Betsy declared.

She hunkered down on the hearth to jiggle the glowing embers with a poker and then carefully criss-crossed dry hazel branches on top. Huddled together on the settle, the three girls drew back as the fire burst into life, the crackling flames spitting out fiery sprites that frolicked their way up the chimney. Betsy wiped the slather of sweat from her flushed face and scrambled up to plonk herself down beside them by the ingleneuk.

'Doom-laden, did you say Betsy?' Elisabeth queried, her head dirling at the thought. 'So where's the use in making a wish?'

'Wishes–and hopes and dreams,' Betsy added, 'are what keep us going. You make a wish in the hope that it'll come true, but you'll never flee your fate. Now then, my jaggy thistle, when the flames die down, cast your nut into the fire and wish on it,' she instructed. 'And mind, be wary what you wish for.'

Elisabeth delved her hand into the basket and pulled out two nuts coupled together.

Betsy nodded slowly and said, 'Ah, a St John's nut. That's a good omen.'

'That my wish will come true?' Elisabeth's ferny green eyes glinted in the firelight.

'Nay, lass, but it'll guard you against the evil eye. Don't fling it but keep it safe as a charm against witches.'

With a doubtful glance at her nurse, Elisabeth slipped the enchanted nut into the pocket of her breeches and chose again. 'I will never marry,' she began, pausing to savour the astonished gasps before throwing her nut onto the red-hot embers, 'unless for love,' she added.

'Don't be all blaw and bluster, Lisbeth my lass,' Betsy chided. 'It's a wish you've to make, not a deal with the devil. And in secret, otherwise it'll no come true.'

'Then I'll make it come true,' Elisabeth retorted.

Betsy shook her head. 'You'll have no say in the matter. You maun dree your weird, as the auld saying goes.' Then, seeing Elisabeth's quizzical frown, she added, 'You must endure your destiny, my jaggy thistle, whatever it may be. And never, ever tempt fate by having too great a conceit of yourself. Forbye, if you marry for love, you'll work for silver.'

'We'll see,' Elisabeth replied, quietly determined that *she* wouldn't share the lot of those lasses sacrificed at the altar for the sake of family alliances and financial gain. Leaning forward, her brows drawn tightly together, she glared at the hazelnut, willing it to do her bidding. The nut twitched around the embers before splitting open and spitting out its kernel.

'Sakes me!' Betsy muttered.

'What does it bode?' Elisabeth tugged impatiently at Betsy's sleeve.

'That your peerie heid and nippy tongue will lead you into bother, my lass,' Betsy cautioned.

'And that no man will touch a jaggy thistle such as you,' Kate chimed in.

Elisabeth twisted round, ready to repay her cousin's stinging remark with a sharp nip, until her older sister Meg drew her arm away.

'Even the briar rose has thorns, mind,' Elisabeth snapped instead. 'Bonnie you may be, Kate, but blithe you're not.'

'Tsk, tsk,' Betsy chided. It made her heart sore to hear her three wee orphans, her bonnie flowers of the forest, bickering. She shook her head as her jaggy thistle, the sharp-witted, spiky-tongued Lisbeth, lashed out at her fair-haired, pink-cheeked cousin Kate, who, like a pawkie kitten, kept her claws hidden until provoked.

Ignoring their squabble, gentle Meg leant forward and cupped her chin in her hands to gaze wistfully into the fire. She lowered her hazelnut gently into the embers where it sizzled and sputtered, before slowly fizzling out. 'Oh, dearie me,' Meg moaned, biting her lower lip to stem the tears.

Betsy patted her knee. 'Don't you fret, my fairy flower for thon signifies a quiet, peaceful life.'

'Does it, Betsy? Truly?' Meg's blue eyes, the shade of the fragile harebell, glistened with grateful tears. Fey, frail Meg had no desire to marry but secretly craved the contemplative life of a nun, sheltered from the hurly-burly of the world behind a protective wall. Let not matrimony and maternity be my destiny, she prayed.

'My turn now,' Kate announced. Ever pernickety, she'd been rummaging through the basket, picking over the nuts until finding one to her liking. Smooth, flawless and perfectly round.

Elisabeth looked at her askance. 'We ken fine what the gowk will wish for,' she taunted. 'And since it's no secret, it'll no be granted.'

Kate's eyes blazed in the firelight. 'Make her stop, Betsy.'

While Elisabeth and Meg were daughters of the late Patrick, 2nd earl of Bothwell, Kate's parentage was vague. An orphan of one of the minor scions of the family—though tongues wagged she was a love-child—the 'lass with the gowden hair' had been warded by the earl and brought up with his own daughters at Hailes Castle. Mercilessly teased by Elisabeth for being a gowk, the cuckoo in their nest, Kate aspired to improve her lowly position through marriage.

Now Kate studiously inspected the bed of embers, taking her time deciding where to place her nut. They all bent forward to watch as it skittered about, before being spat out onto the hearthstone. Instinctively they drew their feet back.

'You'll have to throw it back in at once for your wish to come true,' Elisabeth said.

Betsy glowered at her but was too late to stop Kate. She'd already picked up the sizzling nut—and dropped it again with a piercing yelp of pain.

'Cuckoo! Cuckoo! Feardie-gowk!' Elisabeth goaded her.

'Sticks and stones may break my bones, but names will never hurt me,' Kate recited and sucked on her smarting fingertips to soothe them.

'You were the clumsy kittok for dropping the nut and now your wish is forfeit,' Elisabeth shot back.

'I don't believe you,' Kate whined. 'You're only saying that because you don't want me to marry Adam. Well, you'll see. I'm no common kittok. I shall be a great lady one day. I shall be the countess of Bothwell.' She flicked back her golden hair and glared at her tormentor.

'Over my dead body, you brazen besom,' Elisabeth muttered under her breath. Kate may have set her heart on their brother, Adam, the young earl of Bothwell, but Elisabeth had set her teeth against it. She couldn't abide the thought Kate becoming her brother's wife and a titled lady, for she suspected that, beneath her simpering mannerisms and ladylike demeanour, skulked a scheming wench.

'While no-one will waste a glance on a rapscallion like you,' Kate was taunting, 'a gilpie no a girl.' She tilted her head to look down her snub nose at Elisabeth, clad in her brother's cast-off riding breeches, her copper hair tousled and unkempt.

Seeing her jaggy thistle about to snap, Betsy clamped her hand across her mouth. Only when Elisabeth nodded to indicate that she'd keep her gab shut, did Betsy let go.

'Wheesht, wheesht, my fairest flowers,' Betsy crooned, 'this is no a night for bickering.'

Kate stood up abruptly. 'These daft games are tiresome,' she said, wrapping her shawl tightly around her shoulders. 'I'm away to bed.'

'Afore the witching hour? On your own?' Elisabeth said, feigning a deep menacing growl.

Kate glanced round, horror-stricken by the sinister shadows cast by the flickering tallow candles, before stammering, 'Well, why not? I ...I...'

'There's no telling who or what you'll meet on Hallows Eve,' Elisabeth continued in her spooky voice, fluttering her fingers in front of Kate's anxious face. 'When ghosts and ghouls and bogle-men walk the earth.'

'Don't you be scaring the living daylights out of her,' Betsy scolded. 'Don't fret, Kate, you'll meet your match soon enough. Come, now, and sing us the *Ballad of True Thomas*.' She leant forward to stoke the fire with more logs. 'Coorie in, my bonnie lassies, and listen.'

With a hostile glare at her cousin, Kate tossed her fair curls and began crooning softly. Though Elisabeth would rather die rather than admit it, she loved listening to Kate's linnet-sweet voice.

> "True Thomas he pulled off his cap,
> And louted low down to his knee.
> All hail, thou mighty Queen of Heaven!
> For thy peer on earth, I never did see."

The girls listened spellbound to the legend of Thomas the Rhymer, lured by the Queen of Fairies to Elfland where he disappeared for seven long years, although it felt like only three days to him. Before he left, the fairy queen gave him two gifts: a tongue that never lied and the power to see into the future.

'Betsy, have you the second sight?' Meg's quiet whisper broke the mort-cloth of silence that had fallen over them after Kate's eldritch song.

Betsy Learmont came from an old border family descended, so she said, from this very Thomas of Earldoune, half minstrel, half magician, famed and feared for his sorceries. She stared into the fire for a few moments before answering. 'I jalouse we all have in some way or other. We've all been given a sixth sense, a third eye, some cry it, that sees beyond the veil, but more often than not, most folk pay it scant heed. For where's the use in being able to peer through the dark veil smooring the future with no power to change it? And those who are truly foresighted would say it's more of a curse than a blessing.

'But at certain times of the year, like tonight, All Hallows' Eve—or *Samhain* as the auld, Celtic religion cries it—the thin veil between this world and the next is drawn back. Nay,' she said, shaking her head at Meg's raised eyebrows, 'not your Christian paradise. Nor thon limbo where the souls of unbaptised bairns and pagans linger for eternity, but the twilight world between heaven and earth where the fairy folk and the unquiet dead dwell.'

'The unquiet dead?' Meg uttered with a yelp.

'Wheesht!' Betsy put a warning finger to her lips, 'To mention them risks rousing them.' She lowered her voice to a faint whisper. 'The restless shades of folk that have been murdered or have taken their own lives, who roam the earth, seeking out unwary bodies of the living to possess.' Her chilling words sent a shiver through the girls. 'On this witching night, our own spirits can leave our bodies, too. That's why you're able to see the spectre of the man you'll marry.'

As she said this, the blustery wind soughed down the chimney, gusting smoke into the chamber and rattling the shutters. The girls drew their thick woollen shawls more securely over their heads and huddled in closer together against the cold draughts. As the mirk and midnight hour approached, Betsy set about making hot pint. She plunged the scorching poker into a kettle of spiced ale sweetened with honey until the toddy sizzled and simmered merrily, rising to the top in a smooth, creamy froth.

'This will give you good cheer and good heart,' she promised and handed the girls a cup each.

While they blew on their courage-boosting draught to cool it down, Betsy scraped some soot from inside the chimney to rub on their faces as a disguise to fool the malevolent spirits of the unquiet dead. It was nearly time to ring the stooks.

'I'll just bide here by the fire.' Kate shivered. 'It's gey cold and dark to be wandering about.'

'You mean you're too feart,' Elisabeth taunted. 'And what will Adam think when he hears that the future Countess of Bothwell is a feardie gowk?'

Ignoring the jibe, Kate smeared her fire-flushed cheeks with soot and then wiped her clarty hands on Elisabeth's breeches.

Before the jaggy thistle Lisbeth could retaliate, Betsy deftly stepped in to hand them each a branch from the fairy tree. 'These rowan twigs will ward off evil spirits,' she said. 'Hold on to them for dear life. Or else.' As she lit the taper in the neep lantern, its ghoulish grin of jagged teeth glowed in the dark.

Elisabeth lifted it up and pulled a face at it. 'This will scare the living never mind the undead.'

'Mayhap, now mind and go widdershins round the stooks, not sunwise,' Betsy said, before adding, 'and beware of tumbling into thon ditch, my jaggy thistle.'

The snell blast as they stepped out from the shelter of the castle walls caught their breath. Hearing the wind whistling and howling like a carlin through the trees, the girls hesitated. Top-heavy pines swayed back and forth in the wind, threatening to fall over and crash down on them. Trees stripped of their leaves were transformed into blackened skeletons with gnarled, wizened fingers pointing in menace. Leaves whirled and reeled madly like hobgoblins at Auld Clootie's ball. Clouds scudded past the furtive moon, casting unearthly shadows. Striving to make no sound that would alert evil spirits, the girls stepped lightly, but the crisp, dry leaves crackled and crunched underfoot.

By the glimmer of the neep lantern, they skirted round the ditch filled with fallen leaves until they came to the crossing point. In the cornfield, the harvest straw gathered into sheaves stood like rows of drunken men leaning into each other for support.

Kate clung tightly to Meg but kept looking round, convinced that they were being followed. She stopped to brandish her rowan switch and yelp, 'Aagh! What's that?'

'Wheesht! You'll wake the unquiet dead with your screeching,' Elisabeth growled.

'Look over there.' Kate was pointing with her twig. 'Isn't thon a bogle-man?'

All three huddled together to peer at the eerie shape frantically waving its tattered limbs as if in warning.

'Thon's a pease-bogle, you daft gowk.' Elisabeth sneered as the scarecrow keeled over in the strong wind.

Stopping beside the nearest haystack, they bickered about which way to circle it.

'Betsy said mind and go widdershins,' Meg said, her teeth chittering.

'The devil's way?' Kate said. 'Against the sun? Will that no bring bad luck?' Quivering, she grasped Meg's arm.

'Not at Hallowe'en,' Meg said to reassure her. 'For on the witches' night we'll vex Auld Nick mair if we go sunwise, says Betsy. Now shut your een and hold your arms out in front. Circle three times and on the third turn your sweetheart's spectre will appear.'

‘I… I… I’m no sure I want to do this.’ Kate glanced round, fearful that some malevolent spirit was stalking them.

‘We’ll do it together,’ Elisabeth suggested, for she, too, was feeling uneasy.

Meg, who had no wish for a spouse in any form—body or spirit—held the lantern while the two girls, eyes tight shut and arms stretched out like sleepwalkers, began to circle the stook. Willing herself to see the image of the one she loved, Elisabeth squeezed her eyelids tight against her eyeballs until colours flashed and flared in her head.

As they circled for the third time, leaves disturbed by a field mouse or vole rustled nearby. An owl or bat whooshed past her, and then a high-pitched scream rang out, chilling her blood. Two shapes came out from the shadows of the trees and stumbled across the cornfield towards them. As they loomed nearer, Elisabeth drew back, alarmed to see two bogles, the whites of their eyes gleaming in blackened faces.

‘Beware the unquiet dead!’ a deep menacing voice rumbled.

‘Or the quiet undead!’ another echoed.

When one of the ghouls darted forward to reel her in, Elisabeth turned tail. She flung aside her rowan switch and stumbled over divots towards the ditch.

Suddenly the burn bubbled up and a torrent swept her off her feet. As she was tossed and spun in the murky water, shadowy figures whirled around her. She tried to grab hold of a hand, but the rotting flesh fell away from the fingers. A severed head spun towards her, its fronds of hair streaming out behind, its face stripped of flesh. With greenish-black pus gushing through the empty eye sockets and its jaws locked in an eternal grimace, the skull leered at her. The burn water thickened and darkened to blood red, brimming into her lungs. As the whooshing sound in her ears died down, she opened her mouth to gulp down air.

From far away she heard an unearthly voice murmur, 'She's coming to herself.' Arms lifted her up and propped her against a dyke.

Elisabeth snorted to clear the stench of decaying leaves in her nostrils, but as she wiped the glaur from her eyes she let out a yelp. Behind the jagged-toothed neep lantern, another ghastly head, with soot-stained mouth and bone white teeth, was yawning wide. She jolted backwards and then forwards, her forehead whacking the fiend's nose with a loud crack.

'Ouch!' The bogle's hand darted to its face. '*Nemo me impune lacessit*. You're well named, my jaggy thistle. Who'd dare meddle with you? Your snite is worse than your bite. And there was I, ready to bewitch you with a kiss.' He dabbed at the streaks of sooty blood trickling from his nose and muttered, 'Pity.'

Meg who was kneeling in the mud to massage her sister's ankles with fingers cold as the grave, said, 'She hasn't broken anything.'

'What about me?' the ghoul wailed. 'Not only my nose but my poor heart is sore.'

'She's well enough if she can skelp him like that,' Kate hissed. But then, seeing the other bogle-man approach, she widened doe eyes at him to whimper, 'Forbye, this spanking wind is whipping the skin off my cheeks.'

'Come, then, afore it flays the hide off you.' Adam, the fiendish earl of Bothwell, held out one crooked arm to Kate who needed no further coaxing to link her arm through his. But her face darkened to a glower when he offered his other arm to his sister Meg, whose bony frame was trembling with cold. Meanwhile the wounded ghoul was helping Elisabeth to her feet.

'You... you... scared me half to death, Davie Lindsay,' she scolded.

'Better not let the cold kill the other half then.' Lindsay pulled her into the shelter of his cloak but the stink of soot from his blackened face began to prickle her nostrils. As she screwed up her nose to stifle a sneeze, he pressed his finger hard against her top lip. 'Squeezing is better than sneezing, my jaggy thistle. And kissing can wait. But keep in mind whose spirit you've seen tonight, otherwise the devil knows who you'll marry.'

'Two
A Cursing

The eldest she was vexed sair,
And much envied her sister fair.
Into her bower she could not rest,
Wi grief and spite she almost brast.
— 'The Ballad of The Twa Sisters', Traditional

Hailes Castle, January 1512

Elisabeth lay on top of the bed, cradling a hot stone wrapped in cloths to soothe the dull ache in her womb. The curse of Eve, her monthly bleed had begun and though her eyelids were heavy and she craved sleep, she dreaded falling into the terrifying dwam.

'No wonder you were scared,' Betsy had said. 'Didn't I warn you about the fairy hole? You were lucky—the wee folk could have dragged you away. But I fear the fairy blast may have dinted you with the falling sickness. Keep the St John's nut with you always to spare you from it.'

At Hallowe'en Elisabeth had tumbled across a threshold, from girlish innocence to the darker, mysterious realm of womanhood. Ever since then it felt as if the unquiet spirits had possessed her, making her tetchy and tearful—not like herself at all. Reliving that moment when Lindsay had bundled her tightly in the folds of his cloak tingled the tiniest hairs all over her skin. Was that what was meant by falling in love? Head-over-heels. Tapsalteerie. Whigmaleerie.

She lay back, eyes closed, to relive their first encounter four years ago at the Tournament of the Wild Knight. On that wondrous day, ten-year-old Elisabeth had rubbed her eyes as a strange, oval cloud appeared high above. Everyone was looking upwards expectantly. The egg-shaped cloud cracked and was slowly creaking and cranking until it opened to let out a huge bird that spread out its elaborate wings to hover above them before gliding down to earth. While the crowd clapped and cheered, Elisabeth pushed her way past legs and skirts to where the bird had landed. Her eyes grew huge and her lips rounded into an O. Never in her short life had she seen anything like this. Feathered and festooned in gold and emerald plumage was the most glamorous woman: tall and wide-hipped, with skin the colour of a burnished chestnut and lips as plump as plums.

The flight of the Moorish Maiden was the highlight of the grant tournament and the thrilled spectators crowded round to congratulate Master of the King's Revels, Sir David Lindsay, on his breathtaking spectacle. Brimming with excitement, Elisabeth swooped at him, demanding to soar and fly like the Lady Bird. With a great whoop, he'd picked her up and whirled her round and round, her petticoats billowing outwards. She'd screamed in delight as the world swung round, a whirligig of gaudy colour. Gaily coloured tents and pavilions adorned with banners of silver and gold and flying pennants had flashed past her eyes in a trice.

Back down to earth, she'd staggered around drunkenly for a while, her head still reeling with dizzy exhilaration.

'Steady now, steady.' Lindsay held her firmly to stop her from keeling over.

'Nay!' she cried out, holding up her arms, 'Mair birling! Mair birling!'

'Are you pestering our court jester?' her brother Adam chided, before turning to wink at his friend. 'Our jaggy thistle is thrawn and never takes nay for an answer. She'll never let you stop, even if you make her puke.'

'Indeed?' Lindsay laughed and picked her up again, whirling her round until giddiness made him wobble and lose his balance. He set her down gently, keeping her steady until her head stopped spinning.

After blinking a few times, Elisabeth focussed her eyes on him and solemnly put the question. 'Davie Lindsay, will you marry me?'

'Since when did maidens do the speiring?' His grey eyes were twinkling but, on seeing her face about to crumple, he knelt down on one knee and took her hand.

'Your proposal may be most precocious, Lisbeth, but it's the best I've had all day.'

'Most precious? Truly?' she replied.

'Aye, and precious too,' he nodded, his face serious. 'Now, no flashing those green eyes at anyone else or you'll make *me* green. With envy. You're promised to me, mind.'

Now older and less naïve, Elisabeth questioned whether Lindsay's pledge had just been a ruse to quieten a tousie ten-year-old lass? Had he been sincere when he'd tried to steal a kiss at Hallowe'en? Or only teasing? She was startled out of her dwam by the shrill screech from the next room that sent needle-sharp shards of pain shooting through her skull. Her cousin's strident shrieking was loud enough to awaken the dead.

'Not only is that shameless whore a bastard,' Kate squawked, 'but the mother of one. Hurled out of the royal bed by the king who's had his fill of her, thon flaggartie slattern smickers at Adam. How dare she? Does he ken where she's been fyking? Does he ken she's already had the king's bairn? How could he! For all he kens Nancy may be carrying another royal bastard.'

So Meg had broken the bad news, Elisabeth thought. At the end of January Adam was to marry—not Kate as she'd wished—but Agnes Stewart, a former mistress of the king. Nancy as she was known, was not only the natural daughter of the earl of

Buchan, but mother to one of James IV's several ill-begotten daughters. Kate felt severely wronged by the brazen harpy who had swooped down behind her back and carried off her sweetheart.

Elisabeth got up and stood in the doorway to watch. Hell hath no fury like a woman scorned and Kate seethed, angrier than a cowped wasps' byke.

'And yon cow-clink is to become the countess of Bothwell! It cannot be! Meg, you're his sister. You must make Adam change his mind,' she hissed.

'But how?' Meg stammered, her face pinched tight with fear,. 'What can I do? He never made a promise to you, did he?' She flapped helplessly around her cousin, like a mother hen trying to calm her chick. Kate gripped her by the forearms and dug her sharp nails into her shilpit flesh.

'Nay, but he's your brother and you saw how he flirted with me. You can't say he was only trifling with me. He cannot marry yon ... yon strumpet. I won't stand for it.'

Kate's eyes, swollen from salty tears, bulged in her puffy face as she shook frail Meg back and forth until her bones creaked.

Elisabeth could abide no more. 'Leave her be, you skirling shrew!' She pounced on Kate and hauled her away from her sister who reeled backwards, stunned by her violent tirrivee. 'If Adam has made up his mind to wed Nancy, then he will—and he'll do so because he loves her,' she went on, further stoking Kate's blazing fury.

'Love? How could he love that tawdry trollop?' Bitter tears had stained Kate's cheeks and her perfectly groomed golden hair spilt untidily over her shoulders. For a split second, Elisabeth felt sorry for her—slighted love was sair to bide—until Kate's face warped into an ugly mask of rage and she poked an accusing finger at her.

'He's been dintit, smitten, and it's your fault. You never wanted me to marry him, Lisbeth. You've put a hex on him, you witch—some spell of Betsy's, some potion in his ale. You must have done something to beglamour him, you cankart carlin. How else could he...'

Kate clenched her fists, as if desperate to lash out at something. Or someone.

'How dare you cry me a witch, you cuckoo in the nest,' Elisabeth snapped. 'I had no hand in it. Forbye, what would my brother want with a vauntie-flauntie like you who thinks that, just by batting her eyelashes, men will come flocking? Much good your joukerie-pawkery has done you. Och, dearie me,' she drawled, 'my heart's all aflutter. I fear I may fall into a swoon.' She raised a limp hand to her forehead in mockery before dropping it to wag a finger. 'That may draw their attention, but it won't hold their interest.'

Kate turned to Meg who was massaging her sore arm. 'Hark at her. The jaggy thistle is jealous because I can attract admirers.'

'Even a festering corpse can draw maggots,' Elisabeth retorted.

'Just like you to be mean and nasty,' Kate retorted and tossed her head. 'Forbye, plenty of suitors dangle on my every word.'

'Aye, but that's all they do,' Elisabeth shot back, 'dangle like flabby worms on the end of your fickle hook, while sonsie Nancy kens how to reel them in.'

In a fit of frenzy, Kate launched herself at her tormentor. Elisabeth grabbed her wrists and, as they wrestled, the blood whooshed in her ears. The flesh on Kate's face seemed to dissolve, unveiling the skull beneath: Elisabeth blinked and stumbled backwards onto the settle. She gave her head a good shake and, when she dared to look again, Kate was bleating and rubbing her wrists. Her face was puffy and tear-stained but not macabre. Elisabeth stood up warily and swayed unsteadily towards her. She sniffed a few times and then ran her fingers over the greasy blotches smearing Kate's cheeks. 'What's that muck on your face?'

'Goose fat,' Meg volunteered before nipping in between the two adversaries to keep them apart. 'Betsy says it's good for the complexion.'

'Much good it has done you, gowk,' Elisabeth sneered and wiped her hands up and down the front of Kate's woollen gown.

Arching her back, Kate hissed and spat like a cornered wildcat and her eyes narrowed to demonic slits. 'If I were a witch, I'd cast the evil eye on all you Hepburns, the whole clan.'

Meg's pale face drained to a deathly pallor. 'Oh, Kate, you should never cast such a cantrip.' She reached out to restrain her cousin who waved her hand away impatiently.

'I'd curse you standing,' Kate declared. 'I'd curse you sitting. I'd curse you in bed... I'd curse every hair on your head to be nit-infested, every bone in your body to crack and every breath that you breathe to throttle you till the last gasp.' As she let fly with the cursing, her whole being blazed: her face aflame, her lips frothing with bile, her eyes dirling with blood-red fury.

Meg closed her eyes, murmuring a prayer and making the sign of the holy cross. Elisabeth fumbled in her pocket for her charm against the evil eye and rolled the St John's nut between her fingers. Kate faltered for a moment before bursting forth with a final blast.

'The devil swarbit on you, Lisbeth! Just wait. You'll see. I'll have my revenge.'

Chapter Three
The Wedding Feast

Was never in Scotland heard nor seen
Sic dancing nor deray.
– *Christis Kirk on the Green,* Anonymous, 15th Century

Hailes Castle, 31 January 1512

'No expense has been spared, I see,' Prior Hepburn said as he warmed himself by one of the two huge log fires blazing at either end of the Great Hall. His appreciative glance took in the bare flagstone floors strewn with heather and the rough stone walls bedecked with seasonal red-berried holly and green-leaved ivy. More importantly for the gluttonous Prior of St Andrews, the oaken trestles buckled under the weight of the nuptial feast. The aroma of roasted meats and fowls was stirring up his digestive juices. Conducting the marriage ceremony of Adam Hepburn and Nancy Stewart had been hungry work indeed.

The prior cast his keen blue eyes over the lavish spread: gigots of venison and wild boar, all kinds of roasted birds and a sheep's head, its skull stuffed with boiled brains. He rubbed his podgy hands and smacked his fleshy red lips, drooling in anticipation of cramming his belly. Already ensconced at the trestle, his sister jiggled her head in approval. Even stouter than her brother, Dame Janet, the Prioress of St Mary's Abbey, goggled greedy eyes at the honeyed cakes and sweetmeats piled up on plates in front of her.

'They say the king himself paid for the bride's gown,' she said, reaching out for a bonbon. 'And her daughter Jenny is to be stabled in the royal nursery with all the rest of the king's bastards.'

'Small recompense for services rendered,' the prior sneered. 'As the foremost earl in the land, Adam could have skimmed off the cream of Scotland's maidenhood, yet he chooses the brock from the king's table.'

Dame Janet waggled her ornate headdress. 'It's a sorry trait in the Hepburn men to be dintit with royal quines. Adam's grandfather, whom he was cried after, laid siege to Mary of Guelders, James of the Fiery Face's widow, and afore that Patrick Hepburn of Hailes was champion of Queen Joan, widow of the first James. And even Adam's father, our brother Patrick, God rest his soul,' she said, crossing her breast, 'had to share his own wife with king James.'

'Don't be casting up that old clishmaclaver.' Prior John's violet eyes flashed with anger. 'Whatever wagging tongues may say it was not the *countess* of Bothwell whom the king dabbled with but the flighty *Lady* Bothwell. Thon wanton, Janet Kennedy, was mistress of Bell the Cat Douglas, amongst others. When he gifted her the barony of Bothwell she had the brazen cheek to mislead everyone by styling herself *Lady* Bothwell. Nay, our brother's wife, Countess Margaret, was a fine, modest woman who had to thole that scandal. May *her* soul rest in peace.'

'Pardon me, brother.' Dame Janet rolled her eyes in mock apology. 'Well, let's be thankit that Adam hasn't fallen for Queen Margaret.'

The prior snorted. 'What full-blooded Scotsman would? The English Tudor rose has lost her bloom already and grown blowsy and stout.'

Glancing at her brother, Dame Janet opened her mouth to retort, thought better of it and clamped it shut again. 'Let's hope Adam kens what he's taking on,' she remarked instead.

‘Nancy Stewart is a spirited lass. Men may be drawn to her, as bees to heather bells, but her like are rarely content with just the one loun. Young Adam will not be the last, I fear. She'll be lowping the dyke afore long.’

The prior frowned at her. ‘They’ve only just taken their vows.’

‘And when did that ever stop folk?’ Dame Janet shrugged her plump shoulders. ‘Forbye, it’s only the plain truth I’m telling.’ Turning her gaze toward the door, her bulbous eyes swelled even more. ‘See what toothsome dainties we have here,’ she commented nudging her brother.

The three girls hesitated on the threshold of the Great Hall. With her head held high, Kate surveyed the guests with a defiant look. Dressed to rival the bride in a gown of rich, ruby red velvet, she stood with one hand on her thrust-out hip as if in challenge. Let Adam Hepburn have his slattern: she would show everyone what he’d missed.

Dame Janet grinned. ‘Thon one looks set to become a brazen besom.’ She turned to her brother who was leering at Kate’s well-developed bosom straining the laces of her bodice, testing the limits of decency. ‘Pop your een back in for a moment, brother,’ she scolded. ‘Thon bonnie flowers you’re ogling so randily are your nieces.’

Bashful and self-conscious, Elisabeth kept her eyes down as she fiddled with the white fur trimming on the sleeve of her mistletoe-green velvet gown. Meg—nun-like in a plain robe of palest cream wool—shimmered like a will o’ the wisp between the two rivals. While the comely Kate flaunted herself in her low-cut bodice, Elisabeth felt awkward. Tall and gawky, with bones poking out at all angles, Lisbeth was indeed a gilpie of a lass, more comfortable in her brother’s cast-off leather breeches and jerkins than laced into confining corsets and restrictive skirts.

Though her figure was beginning to fill out, putting more flesh on her bones and softening the sharp edges, she still felt too spiky. Like a skittish colt, she had frisked and fretted while Betsy mercilessly brushed the tangles out of her unruly hair until it rippled, a mane of burnished copper, down her back. Alarmed at how immodestly high the tight lacing of the bodice pushed up her meagre bosom, Elisabeth had swaddled herself in a shawl.

'How swiftly time flies! How quickly they have grown.' The prior became pensive. He hadn't seen them since they were babes, not since he'd fallen out with his older brother.

Dame Janet's attention was elsewhere, drawn to one of her favourite dainties. As she sank what remained of her teeth into the delicacy, her eyelids quivered in ecstasy. She then sucked her fingers languorously, one after the other, to savour every last globule of grease. Meg and Elisabeth, their eyes like collops, exchanged glances.

Dame Janet smacked her lips. 'Just how I like them: soft, squidgy and sweet. Tastier than a strumpet's teats. Taigle your tongues round these, my lassies, for your hair to curl and your juices to flow.'

They screwed up their noses at her tempting treat of stag testicles slowly poached in a honeyed sauce while the sight of a guest scooping out the greyish skirlie from the grinning sheep's head was making Elisabeth feel quite queasy.

Prior John crooked his pinkie. 'Let's take a keek at you.' His saturnine eyes scrutinised them closely before alighting on Elisabeth. He gave a long, low whistle. 'By Christ's blood, if this one isn't the very image of her mother. She has her eyes.'

He dabbed at the beads of sweat glistening on his brow with a silk napkin. Leaning forward he thrust out a hand to pull down Elisabeth's shawl for closer inspection, but she grasped it even more firmly and glared boldly at him.

'Ha! Shielding your modesty, are you? No harm in that. How old are you now, my bright young virgins?'

When Dame Janet informed him that Meg had just turned seventeen and Elisabeth was nearly fourteen, he exclaimed,

'Already? And what of their future? What provisions are being made?'

The prioress shrugged her plump shoulders. On his father's death, this had been Adam's responsibility, she explained, but the young earl had been too taken up with his own marital matters to make plans for his sisters.

Hepburn flashed an angry rebuke at the prioress. 'Then it's high time we stepped in, sister. And the sooner the better.'

While the trestles were being cleared away, Elisabeth scanned the hall for the groomsman. Ever since Hallowe'en she'd been like a hen on a hot girdle. How could she have dunted Davie Lindsay on the nose! What must he think of her? A daft, foolish lassie, no doubt. Or away with the fairies as Betsy believed. There he was, talking to one of the king's men. She picked up a goblet of wine and quickly downed it to stop her heart from racing. The tight lacing on her gown constricted her breathing and her hands were clammy with perspiration.

While waiting, she checked her sleeve where she'd hidden the magic talisman Betsy had given her. Then she shrugged her shawl downwards, lowering it just enough to expose her shoulders. Hands clasped, she worried at her hangnails until Lindsay dismissed the servant. With a final pat on the talisman, she took a deep breath and started towards him.

At that moment, Kate swished past her to strut in front of Lindsay. 'Sir David, the very man. I have a favour to ask of the groomsman,' she said coyly.

Watching Kate bat her eyelashes and simper in the way that seemed to please men but which stuck in her craw, Elisabeth seethed. If he put his arm round Kate's waist, if he whirled her round the floor, she wouldn't be able to thole it. Whatever Kate was requesting, Lindsay was shaking his head in response. Good. He'd snubbed her and now she was moving on to more lucrative quarry: a swarm of admiring young studs.

Summoning all her courage, Elisabeth stepped forward and tapped Lindsay on the shoulder. 'Will you dance with me, Davie?' she asked, trying to control her wavering voice.

He looked her up and down, his expression puzzled.

'What? Can this be my jaggy thistle? Why, I hardly recognise you in your finery.' Then, wagging his finger, he gently chided her. 'You may have blossomed into a bonnie flower of the forest but your manners are still rough-hewn. Did they never teach you that it's unseemly for a lady to ask a gentleman to dance?'

Elisabeth's cheeks flamed as crimson as Kate's gown and her courage ebbed away. Another mistake. She was about to slink off but he took her hand and squeezed it firmly. 'Stand firm, my jaggy thistle, and mind your motto: *Who dares meddle with me*?'

He picked up her shawl that had slipped to the floor, but instead of draping it round her, he flung it over his own shoulder. 'If my lady does not spurn my advances,' he gave a knowing wink, 'I shall be honoured to be her knight this evening. And I claim this shawl as my token.' He bowed low with an exaggerated flourish.

As they waited for the musicians to strike up, Elisabeth blurted, 'Please forgive me for cracking your nose, Sir David. I didn't mean to.' She began to fiddle nervously with her fur-trimmed sleeve where she'd hidden the sprig of mistletoe that Betsy assured would bring good luck in love. Stretching up on tiptoe, she swiftly pecked him on the cheek. Lindsay took an exaggerated step backwards in surprise, his eyes crinkling with laughter.

'What's this? A kiss under the mistletoe! Why, what a little pagan you are! First you invite me to dance, and then you kiss me like a wanton hussy. What next, I wonder? But once smitten twice shy.' He tapped the bump on his nose.

Helpless desperation gagged her sharp tongue and she felt as jiggly as one of the jellies on the banqueting table. Why hadn't she paid more attention to how Kate flirted?

Lindsay leant in closer. 'You have much to learn, my guileless thistle,' he whispered, brushing her cheeks lightly with his lips. As the music struck up, he gripped her tightly round the waist and whirled her into the throng of dancers. Giddy and breathless, her cheeks glowing, her flesh tingling at his touch, she willed this whigmaleerie to go on forever and ever.

'Stop the music! Stop the music!'

The reeling throng of dancers gradually wound down, bodies bumping into each other as they came to a chaotic halt. Who had dared to give such an order?

The lackey that had been speaking to Lindsay earlier was swaying unsteadily on a trestle table and waving his arms in the air. 'Harp and carp, Davie Lindsay! Harp and carp! You're the groomsman and it's high time for the bedding. Get on with it, man.' His speech was a slurred drawl but the guests congregating around the shoogly table clapped and cheered.

Raising her voice above the clamour Kate remarked, 'Who does yon flunkey think he is, giving orders like that? Why doesn't somebody pull the drunken oaf down?'

Dame Janet's fingers dug into her bare arm. 'Have you not heard of the Guiser, my lass?' Kate winced as the prioress yanked her in closer. '*That's* who *thon* is. It's the king's fancy to dress up as a commoner and stravaig about the land to fyke freely with any lasses that catch his een. One of the royal privileges. He thinks he's well buskit. As if anybody could be fooled. Thon foxy red hair and long neb stick out a mile,' she snorted.

'That is King James?' Kate's round eyes widened, first in astonishment, then in admiration. 'But Sir David telt me he wouldn't attend the wedding.'

'His grace likes to think he's fooling us all and we maun feign to be fooled.'

The lackey king's voice rang out. 'The time is ripe. And so is the bride. And I'm as impatient as the groom to...' he smacked his lips and cackled lewdly, 'loosen her snood.'

'Why would they be needing a bedding?' Dame Janet trilled, her shrill voice cutting through the hubbub. 'The whole world and its mother ken that the bride's cherry has been picked long ago.'

The lackey chuckled. 'You speak the truth, my lady prioress. And if the king himself were here he could vouch for the bride's bedchamber skills.'

Dame Janet placed her hand on her bosom, rolled her goggle eyes dramatically and sighed. 'It's a great pity His Grace has not deemed it worthy to grace us with his presence.'

'Aye, but he has.' The lackey pulled off his cap triumphantly to reveal the sparse, pale-reddish hair of King James himself. 'And he's come to measure the groom's knack and see if it's up to regal standard. By royal command stand proud, my Lord Bothwell, and let the bedding begin.'

As the drunken crowd around her hooted and howled, Meg looked bewildered. 'I don't understand. What does he mean?' she asked.

Dame Janet leant over and grinned, baring the jagged remains of her blackened, rotting teeth and belching fumes of claret in her face.

'You chaste young damsels have been living a life more sheltered than in my cloister, I fear. Time to school you in the ways of the world. He means that after the prior has blessed the bed, the groomsmen and bridesmaids will lead the newly-weds to their chamber where,' she broke off with a vulgar, coarse laugh, 'they'll be stripped naked and hurled together on the bed. Then they shall dance the reel of Bogie until we're all satisfied that the deed is done.'

'Aye, until *Consummatum est!*' Prior John pronounced irreverently his lips contorted into a repulsive leer.

'Hark at the lecher,' Dame Janet said. 'It's the part of the nuptials he enjoys most. Never mind joining them together in the sight of God, my brother can hardly wait to drool over their bodily union.'

'Adam and Nancy are to be gawked at? By this drunken, rowdy mob?' Meg gasped. 'But that's shocking.'

'Aye, by the whole clamjamfray.' Dame Janet said and patted Meg's hand. 'There's no need to be so mimsy-mou'ed, my lass. Sonsie Nancy is no modest maiden. She kens a thing or two about tail-toddle. Aye, and you'll have to learn about it ere long.'

At her aunt's warning, Meg's horrified face swiftly drained of any colour, becoming even paler than her gown.

'Cast your een at all the fawning lickspittles, falling over themselves to bend the knee to their monarch,' the prioress sneered.

In the midst of them all was Kate who had revised her opinion of the insolent fool. She fussed with the neckline of her bodice, tugging it down lower to reveal even more of her charms.

Meanwhile, the monarch was becoming impatient. 'What's the delay, Davie? You cannot tell me the bride is unwilling.'

'Forbear with me, Lisbeth,' Lindsay said and draped the shawl round her shoulders. 'I maun obey His Grace's bidding. The king's pleasure aye comes before my own.' His breath soft and sweet against her cheek as he whispered softly, 'Wait for me, I'll be back as soon as I can. You promised me a kiss, mind.'

'A song! We need a song,' the king was shouting. 'To cantle up the bride and groom for the marriage bed.'

Kate stepped in front of the drunken rabble and began to sing, her strong soprano soaring high above their discordant chorus:

'Fye, let us all to the bridal,
For there will be lilting there;

For Jockie's to be married to Maggie,
The lass with the gowden hair.'

Meanwhile, Meg was leaning against the doorjamb for support. Turning her ashen face to Elisabeth, she whispered, 'Oh, Lisbeth, I pray I never have to wed. I couldn't thole their jibes and jeers on my wedding night.' Shrinking into herself she shielded her womb. 'I fain would stay a virgin. How I wish mother were still here with us.'

Seeing the pained look flicker across Elisabeth's face, she clutched her arm.

'Oh, Lisbeth, I didn't mean ... You mustn't think I was casting it up to you.'

But Elisabeth had no such thought for she knew well enough that there was not a spiteful bone in Meg's delicate body. Winding her shawl round her sister's shuddering shoulders she led her away.

Chapter Four
Annunciation

I have thee luvit loud and still,
Thir yearis two or three.
— *Robin and Makyne*, Robert Henryson, 15th Century

Hailes Castle, 25 March 1512

Betsy had opened the shutters wide to air the chamber, fusty and stale with wood-smoke after the dark, damp winter. By the fireside, Meg sat curled up in the Orkney chair, a gift to her father when he was appointed Lord of Orkney and the Shetland Isles. With short, stumpy legs and a high oaten straw back with a hood to keep out chilling draughts, the chair suited Meg perfectly. Weary after rising early to attend Mass of the Annunciation at the nearby abbey, she supped Betsy's milk brose. Never mind that it broke the Lenten fast, Betsy insisted she needed it to restore her strength after all that knee bending.

Meg shivered as Elisabeth burst in, leaving the door wide open. Still dressed in her breeches and riding jerkin after her morning ride, she prowled up and down, anxious and edgy. Her fidgeting usually kittled up Kate, but she seemed not to notice. She sat idly with her embroidery in her lap, staring into the middle distance as if in a dwam, quietly humming to herself.

Elisabeth scrambled onto the window bunker and poked her head out of the window of the west tower. Far below, the waters of the River Tyne tumbled through a ravine before flowing more calmly in front of the castle. Further along the riverbank to the west, masons were clambering up and down the scaffolding erected for the construction of the new belltower at St Mary's Abbey, but her eyes were drawn northwards. Across the Tyne and beyond the rise lay Garleton Castle, the Lindsay family seat.

'Dicht yourselves, my bonnie lassies,' Betsy said as she came in hirpling. Her lopsided gait, caused by a childhood ailment, had left one leg shorter than the other. Giving Lisbeth a playful skelp on the seat of her breeches,' she added, 'for you have an important visitor.'

Wabbit at the thought of company, Meg snuggled deeper into her chair, while Kate, a secret smile flitting across her face, picked up her sewing and began stitching tiny crosses. Elisabeth sprang from the window seat and bounded to the door like an exuberant puppy, colliding unceremoniously with their visitor. Thrown off balance, she backed into the room again, flustered at the sight of the king's herald resplendent in a red tunic with the lion rampant emblazoned in gold. Every day since Adam's wedding, Elisabeth had ridden out by Garleton Castle, hoping for a chance encounter with Davie Lindsay, but she'd always been disappointed. Had it all been a dream she wondered? But now here he was—large as life.

Graciously refusing Betsy's offer of refreshment, Lindsay bowed courteously to them all. In vain, Elisabeth tried to read the expression on his face but, in his rôle as professional courtier, Lindsay was inscrutable. Not a glimmer of a smile or even a wink as he requested permission for a private audience with one of the ladies. Black affronted at her untidily braided hair Elisabeth pointlessly brushed at the mud on her breeches.

She was about to step forward when Lindsay strode past her and held out his hand—to Kate, who gazed up at him demurely from under her eyelashes. Her backward smirk as she flounced out of the room on Lindsay's arm ruffled Elisabeth's temper. Why did he want to speak with Kate? What could he possibly have to say to thon gowk?

'Surely he's not going to ask for her hand?' she said, desperation in her voice.

'Wheesht, wheesht, my lass,' Betsy said to calm her. 'He's on the king's business, so he told me. He wouldn't be wearing thon tabard otherwise.'

'But what has the king to do with Kate?' Elisabeth grumbled, gnawing at her hangnails until slapped down by Betsy. She thrust her hands under her oxters and stomped up and down the room. When at last Kate appeared, she paused dramatically in the doorway before making her announcement in a newly acquired, haughty tone.

'I have been chosen to be one of the queen's ladies. And I am to leave for Edinburgh immediately. Betsy, you shall help me to gather my belongings' she commanded and pranced off, leaving Betsy to hirple behind, muttering and rolling her eyes.

Meg heaved a sigh and leant forward, hand on her chin to gaze into the fire. 'What a grand privilege for Kate! To be invited to the court of the Thistle and the Rose! Oh, Lisbeth, do you mind the poem that was written for the queen's arrival into Scotland?

'Aye, all thon rigmarole about the mighty English king's daughter being *a princess most pleasant and preclare*, praising her beauty and regal bearing,' Elisabeth snorted. 'Telling us she was the fairest of the fair, when she wasn't even bonnie.'

Meg sighed. It was true. Even she had been disappointed when they had met Margaret Tudor at the Tournament of the Wild Knight. 'Aye, I mind it was the Moorish lady that took your fancy, Lisbeth. While all the ladies of the court scanced at her for being a coarse blackamoor, you kept saying you'd never seen anyone so sonsie.'

Elisabeth nodded wistfully at the memory. With her glossy chestnut skin, shimmering corbie-black hair and teeth as white as caller oyster pearls, Black Ellen, as she was cried, was majestic. In contrast, Queen Margaret was a dowdy dunnock.

'Short and squat and skrinkie-faced with froggy eyes. And a mouth like this.' Elisabeth pursed her lips together and pushed them out in grotesque imitation. 'Not a princess but a puddock.'

Meg gave a little chuckle. 'Just as well she didn't hear what you said about her otherwise, she'd have had your eyes out.'

'Even if she had, she'd never ken what a puddock was.'

'Oh! I'm sure one of her toadies would have enlightened her grace,' a male voice broke in.

Startled, Elisabeth swung round. Lindsay was leaning against the doorjamb, arms crossed, the corners of his mouth crinkled into a mischievous smile.

'Well, whoever wrote that poem about her was telling barefaced fibs,' Elisabeth maintained though her cheeks were reddening.

'Have you no poetic soul, my dear lass?' Lindsay said.' I'll admit that eulogy is not one of the makar's best. William Dunbar has written much better verses than those.'

'Like the *Twa Marrit Women and the Widow*?' Elisabeth giggled while Meg gave her a cautionary look. Nancy Stewart, now their sister-in-law, had often dropped tantalising hints about this bawdy poem but always refused their pleas to recite it for them.

'Tsk, tsk, it's not for the ears of two maiden lassies like you,' Lindsay chided. 'Once you're both old hen-wives, perhaps.'

'By then it'll be too late,' Elisabeth retorted. 'Surely we need to ken now so as to...'

'Seek out the sleekit tricks wives use to deceive their husbands?' Lindsay suggested.

'Nay. To learn how to be a lady. Like Kate.' Elisabeth pouted and, thrusting her hips forwards, tucked her hands into the pockets of her old breeches.

'That,' he began, slowly eyeing her up and down, 'could take some time.'

'Oh, stop scarting and nipping, you two,' Meg cut in. 'You're wearing me out.'

Lindsay winked. 'Just sharpening our tongues for a bout of flyting.'

Meg yawned wearily and said, 'Then take our jaggy thistle out for a walk, Sir David, and douse her feisty temper.'

With a Kate-like toss of her braids, Elisabeth flounced out of the chamber with Lindsay in her wake. She led him down to the postern gate and watched him scramble down the steep riverbank before challenging him. 'Where have you been, Davie Lindsay? You gave your word that you'd come.'

'So, my jaggy thistle is still prickly, with no kind word for her sweetheart. O cruel maid, does it not please you that I am here now?' He slipped his arm round her waist but she wriggled free.

'Only to speak with Kate, it seems.' She refused to look at him and kept her arms firmly folded. 'How long would I have had to wait otherwise?'

'I beg forgiveness, my dearest Lisbeth, but it's not so easy to escape from court. The king's affairs aye keep me busy.'

When he tried to sweep a stray lock of hair from her eye, she shied away.

'So, no hope of claiming that kiss, then? Pity.' And, with a nonchalant shrug of his shoulders, he turned round and walked off.

Elisabeth wanted to scream in frustration. Her childish peevishness was driving him away and she had no artful tricks to lure him back. She ran after him and clutched at his arm.

'Don't go, Davie. I'm sorry. Look, you can kiss me now.'

She squeezed her eyelids tightly together, puckered up her lips and waited. Aware of a slight movement from him, she screwed up her face more enthusiastically. Instead of feeling his lips pressing against hers, she heard a peculiar, strangulated sound. Baffled, her eyes flew open to see Lindsay's shoulders quivering and his face red and contorted as he choked back tears.

'Are you unwell?'

'Nay... Aye... I mean nay. I'm s...s... so sorry.' He pressed his hand hard against his mouth. 'It was just that you put me in mind of a puddock. The way you ...' he managed to blurt out, before doubling up in a fit of laughter.

Elisabeth's cheeks burned, affronted at his cruel mockery. 'Then, it's your loss. For all you ken, I might have been turned into a princess.'

Before she could stomp off, he grabbed her round the waist and pulled her in close. Catching her unawares, he kissed her firmly on her parted lips. Not a short peck or a swift smack, but a long, lingering kiss full on the mouth. He hugged her tightly, squeezing out her life-breath and making her heart race. When he let her go, her head was reeling: the whole world spinning and wheeling like the day he'd birled her round and round. Tapsalteerie. Whigmaleerie.

'Now, that,' he insisted, 'is a kiss.'

Instinctively her arms flew up and clasped his neck in a stranglehold.

'Are you so offended you that you now want to throttle me?' Lindsay burbled, breaking free from her grasp. Only when he felt her relax in his embrace, did he kiss her again. 'Aye, there's a chance that this puddock may turn into a princess.'

Reluctant though he was to leave her, he'd have to go. Kate wouldn't take kindly to be kept waiting, Lindsay explained. Elisabeth gazed at him in a daze before suddenly taking off up the slope. At the top she dropped down onto her front and yelled, 'Watch this!' She began tumbling over and over downhill, until recovering her balance just in time to avoid splashing into the river. She was scrambling to her feet when something caught her eye. She bent down to pick it up cupping it in her hand and ran towards him.

'Has my kiss transformed my jaggy thistle into fluffy thistledown, to be wafted away on a slight breeze?' Lindsay said. 'My powers of enchantment are more potent than I thought.'

‘I’ve made a wish, Davie,’ Elisabeth struggled to suppress a cheeky grin. ‘I cannot tell you what it is, but I’ve cast a cantrip that, if you ever kiss another lass, you’ll turn into this.’ As she lifted away her top hand, a tiny pond frog with jigging feet sprang from her palm. ‘And then,’ she wagged a warning finger at him, ‘I swear I’ll cut off your legs.’

The next morning, as they witnessed Kate riding off in triumph with Lindsay, Elisabeth scowled while Betsy’s face clouded for a different reason.

‘Poor Kate. Our wee rosebud thinks she’ll be living a life of idleness and luxury but she’ll have a rough furrow to plough. Margaret Tudor, the puddock queen, as you cry her, is soon to be brought to childbed. The monarch himself has summoned Kate. To keep the royal bed warm, I reckon.’

Chapter Five
Holy Orders

Blame nocht thy Lord, sae is his will;
Spurn nocht thy foot againis the wall;
But with meek heart and prayer still,
Obey and thank thy God of all.
— *The Abbey Walk*, Robert Henryson, 15th Century

St Mary's Abbey, Haddington, May 1512

Prior Hepburn raised a goblet to his wine-stained lips with one podgy hand and stuffed bread into his mouth with the other. Watching him eat swiftly and methodically, Elisabeth nudged Meg to whisper from behind her hand. 'Take a keek at thon moudiewort—like a greedy mole shovelling dirt with its paws.'

Meg, who was picking at her food, anxiously awaiting whatever important news he had to tell them, stifled a nervous giggle.

Dame Janet glowered at her gluttonous brother chomping on roast capon and swilling it down with large draughts of claret as if it were his last meal. 'You'll dig your own grave with your teeth. A crammed kyte makes a crazy carcase, mind,' she warned, while her stubby teeth nibbled incessantly at a plate of candied fruits.

The prior belched, wiped his lips with a linen napkin and then winked across at Elisabeth. She looked away, embarrassed for she could still taste the soggy kiss from those lips, fleshy and tender and fringed by his bushy beard, when he'd greeted her. But it was the prior's eyes that were disconcerting. Of the most intense, violet blue they brooded, all seeing, all knowing, beneath beetle-black brows.

While the prior dallied with the serving lass, the girls followed Dame Janet along to her inner sanctum where she hoisted her great bulk onto the deep, goose-feather mattress. She sank into the soft down pillows with a groan.

'Ah that's better. Now the weight is off my feet. Soft bedding's good for sair banes.'

Though it was unlikely that, being upholstered in so much flesh, her bones would feel anything, Elisabeth thought. She gazed in wonder at the ornately carved four-poster bed hung with rich brocade curtains and piled with fluffy pillows. Embroidered tapestries lined the walls and finely woven rugs covered the floor. The light from the fat beeswax candles suffused the chamber with a rich warm glow. Such luxury in a nun's cell was surprising. The furnishings were far more sumptuous than anything at Hailes Castle, where coarse rushes and dried heathers covered the floors and foul-smelling tallow tapers glimmered in the passageways. Hailes lacked a mother's touch.

Meg was examining an intricately embroidered cushion depicting a fabulous golden bird, with wings outstretched to escape the flames of a fire, that had caught her eye.

'Thon's a bird of paradise. If you like it, take it,' Dame Janet said, before adding quietly, 'for your sister will be getting all the rest.' Then, turning to Elisabeth who was admiring a wooden kist, she said, 'That's made of the rarest rosewood. Go on. Open it.'

The large carved chest was cedar-lined and delicately scented with juniper sprigs to ward off moths and preserve the abundant collection of gowns in silk, satin and velvet. In her youth Dame Janet had worn these underneath the nun's habit—her small rebellion against being forced into the abbey, she explained with a conspiratorial wink at Elisabeth. Now that her ample frame had outgrown them, the prioress proclaimed her defiance by adorning herself with worldly baubles, powdering her face with white lead and rouging her lips.

'But all this is more magnificent than a bride's plenishment!' Elisabeth exclaimed.

Dame Janet chuckled. 'Aye. Nothing but the best for one of Christ's consorts.' She was untangling the expensive necklace and bracelet buried in the podgy folds of her neck and wrists to show her when the door was flung open.

Prior Hepburn ambled into the chamber and said, 'If you ladies have tired of fashion and furnishings, it's time to discuss more important matters. Your brother Adam has been sluggish in settling the plans for your future, but no more time must be wasted, my bonnie lassies.'

He settled into a chair and began massaging his paunch to ease his digestion. 'It has been decided that one of you is to be married and the other will enter the nunnery.'

The girls exchanged worried glances before Elisabeth spoke up.

'It will be the answer to Meg's prayers to take the veil, uncle, and I would fain be wed. To a man of my own choosing,' she added hastily.

Scowling at her, Prior John raised a hand. 'It's not your advice, I'm seeking, lass but your obedience. You'll do as you're bid. Both of you.' His blue eyes darkened. 'Now tak tent. A marriage to the heir of the earldom of Angus, one of the foremost titles in Scotland, has been arranged.'

Elisabeth furrowed her brow. 'You don't mean Archie Douglas? The grandson of kenspeckle Bell the Cat Douglas?' she splurted. 'Some might say he's one of the brawest lads in the land, but he's also one of the wildest. I wouldn't marry him if he were the last man on earth.'

From the depths of her feather bed Dame Janet sniggered quietly, 'Fain be wed indeed.'

Prior John narrowed his eyes. 'And neither you shall, Elisabeth. As I was saying, this most favourable marriage has been arranged—at great effort and even greater expense on my part—for your sister, Margaret.'

Meg's fingers fluttered to her lips as she let out a tiny, startled squeak.

'And since you, too, would fain be a bride, Elisabeth,' he went on, your wish shall be granted. You shall become a bride of Christ, here at St Mary's where you'll be ordained in due course.'

Elisabeth sprang to her feet. 'But, uncle, I fear you've mixed us up! It's Meg who wants to be a nun, not me. She says her prayers every day. In Latin! She never misses on Sundays and holy days—unless she's poorly. Meg is the holy one. She has the temperament of a saint.'

'While you have the temper of a fiend, that much is becoming clear.' Dame Janet had hoisted her weight onto her elbows. 'Pay heed to your uncle! You'll have to learn to curb thon nippy tongue when you come here. Or be made to take a vow of silence.'

Like a startled hare, Elisabeth looked from one to the other. 'But I have no wish to be a nun. Ask Adam. He'll tell you.'

Dame Janet's cheeks wobbled as she gave a hearty laugh. 'Did you ever hear such a thing? She has no wish! As if her wish was of any account. And don't think your brother has any say in the matter, either. He may be your guardian but he's not your keeper and you're certainly not mistress of your fate. Gey few women, if any, have that privilege. I, for one, had to bend the knee. And your eldest sister, Joanna, was married off. To Lord Seton no less, and none the worse for it. Now Meg is to be wed, and your fate, my dear lass, is to be a bride of Christ, like me. And there's an end to it.'

'But... but...' Elisabeth was floundering until a thought floated past her like a piece of flotsam. She grasped at it greedily. 'I have no call from God. He hasn't chosen me.'

Dame Janet sneered. 'That's of no import. Neither was I privy to the voice of God. Not that you'd listen if the Almighty bawled in your lug, my lass. You've a mind of your ain.'

The prior nodded. 'Aye, she's a lass of mettle, and that's no fault in a Hepburn, but now my lass it's time to do as you're bid. You've been ganging your own gait for too long.'

Elisabeth cast him a sidelong glance to snipe, 'Is that what's meant by Holy Orders?'

Meg, who had sat in stunned silence throughout, spoke up. 'It's not in Lisbeth's nature to take the veil; it would suffocate her. I will gladly change places with her.'

When they all turned to gawp at her, Meg looked shamefaced. 'Not that I would wish Archie Douglas as a bridegroom on anyone, far less my own sister.'

'Your sacrifice is admirable, my dear niece, but in the best interests of the Hepburn family, your future has already been decided. You're an obedient lass, Meg, and will do as you're bid. As for our jaggy thistle, perhaps more gentle persuasion is needed.'

A forced smile stretched across the prior's sensuous lips as he heaved himself to his feet and beckoned for Elisabeth to follow him into the garderobe. In the small intimate closet, he began to rub his fingers up and down and then across the wooden panels until one clicked. He pushed it open and led her into a low-roofed, sloping passage, built to allow Dame Janet's bulky frame to be carried along in a chair to services in the chapel, he explained. He opened a door and led Elisabeth up a turnpike staircase to the newly constructed belltower.

From the top, Elisabeth gazed around in wonder. The sun, still high in the luminous evening sky, lit up the fertile fields, magnifying the lush green of the growing grain and the grass of the grazing fields. As the prior waved his arm, proudly pointing out granaries, mills, breweries, and orchards, he scared a couple of cooing doves roosting on the parapet. They flew off, clumsy and slow in contrast to the swifts, swooping and swerving as they scooped up clouds of midges.

'All that you can see, my dear Elisabeth, and more, belongs to the abbey.' He fell silent for a few minutes to let her consider the value of the view. 'I've been endowing the lands of Haddington for some time in the knowledge that you'll inherit this post one day. As prioress of the abbey, you'll be a rich and powerful lady.'

Elisabeth winced as his podgy hand squeezed hers. She stared ahead, fearing to look at those spellbinding eyes that threatened to weaken her resolve. She wouldn't make it easy for him to win her over. The promise of land and riches would not tempt her away from her love for Lindsay.

He sensed her stiffening like a stookie. 'I was hoping to keep certain facts from you, but your thrawn reluctance leaves me no choice.' He dropped her hand abruptly. 'You may not wed, my dear lass, for the simple reason that you have no tocher. No dowry has been settled on you, because you were, to put it kindly, born on the wrong side of the blanket.'

Shading his eyes from the sun's glare, the prior avoided her stare. Clearing his throat he went on, 'Your mother, God rest her soul, was taken in adultery—during one of your father's long absences—and you are the fruit of that union. When she died, my brother Patrick agreed to bring you up as his own, so as not to shame your mother's memory, but he didn't settle on you the same rights as his legitimate daughters, including Meg.'

'But, uncle,' Elisabeth began and tapped him patronisingly on the arm, as if speaking to a doited half-wit, 'Kate is the love bairn, not me. She's the cuckoo in the nest.'

The prior chortled. 'Aye, the saying is true enough: It's a wise child that kens its own father—and mother, forbye. But don't be dirling your head about Kate. She'll have more to do at court than sing for her supper. It's *your* fate that is being decided.'

Elisabeth's head was indeed whirling. She'd often mocked Kate for being ill-begotten. Surely it couldn't be true that she, too, was a love child? A bastard?

Her voice dropped to a whisper. 'Then who is my father?'

'Your father,' he began and then broke off. In the silence she could hear his breath whistling between his teeth. 'Your father was a buttery-lippit blackguard who was slain in a border foray. That's all you need to ken.' As his breathing became more laboured, beads of sweat broke out on his brow. 'But don't fret, you're not alone. You join a merry band of distressed gentlefolk who have to make their own way in life. As the fourth son, without land or wealth, I couldn't make a suitable match: the only path open to me was the Church. And like you, I was reluctant, for I had no calling and would have fain followed a worldly career. But needs must.

'When I was offered the priory of St Andrews with all its benefices, I didn't hesitate. Your Aunt Janet has also made a comfortable life for herself, as you can see. As prioress, she manages this property with all the monies pertaining to it, but she'll not live forever and there *must* be a Hepburn to control these lands.' He drew her in close, his intense blue eyes scrutinising her face.

'My dear niece, you may not have a vocation in the spiritual sense, nevertheless, it is your duty to take over as prioress of this abbey one day. With your strong will and quick wit you're truly deserving of what I have to offer. If you go against my wishes and wed, you wed with nothing.' His stout arms squeezed her so hard that she struggled for air. 'And to a nobody, for no lord or high-born gentleman would consider marriage to you without a tocher.'

That could not be true. Surely Davie Lindsay wouldn't care whether or not she had a dowry, but would he overlook her ill-starred birth? Would he be as generous as Adam had been with Nancy and love her despite that?

‘This news will have ca’ed the feet from under you, no doubt,’ the prior continued, ‘but in time you will understand the significance of what I am saying and the value of what I am giving you. All this,’ he declared with a sweep of the arm, ‘is my legacy to you, my dearest niece. This abbey is your birth right. Accept it with good grace.’

He leant forward and smacked his fleshy lips against her forehead, leaving a damp sticky stain.

Six
Matrimony

It, that ye call the blest band that bindis so fast,
Is bare of bliss, and baleful, and great barrat wirkis.
— *The Treatise of the Twa Marrit Women and the Widow*,
William Dunbar, 15th–16th Century

Hailes Castle, August 1512

Meg carefully lifted her mother's bridal gown from the kist and shook it out to show Nancy. A headless wraith, the dress swished and rustled as she held it up against her. Even though the fragile oyster silk was greying with age and the lace trimming was yellowing, she wished to wear it to her own wedding—to feel that her mother was with her, watching over her, and to help her thole the dreaded ordeal.

'Betsy isn't keen. She says that getting wed in my mother's bridal gown bodes ill.'

'Havers,' Nancy said. 'If you believed every auld wives' tale, you'd never get out your bed. Wear what pleases you. Forbye, a solution of vinegar will whiten the lace and any tears can be mended when it's taken in.'

For the dress swamped Meg, whereas it was a perfect fit for Lisbeth. 'That's another sign that she should be the bride, not me,' Meg said mournfully. 'I'm terrified of being bairnt, Nancy, that I'll share my mother's fate.'

Her slim hips weren't suited to childbearing, she fretted, and that her frailty would make her vulnerable to the fever that took away their mother soon after Lisbeth's birth. Childbed had been her deathbed. Writhing in Betsy's arms and being made to put her hand on her mother's icy forehead was etched on Meg's memory. How she had howled. Why, she asked years later, had such a young bairn been made to touch her mother's corpse? So as to prevent her spirit from troubling her, Betsy explained. Well, it hadn't. Ever since then her mother's quartz-white face had haunted Meg's dreams. Now that another nightmare was about to begin, she was panic-stricken.

'Nay,' Nancy disagreed, 'your destiny lies in your ain hands if only you'll grab it. Dinnae be living your life in dwam.'

Meg envied her. Ripe and ready to drop with her second child, Nancy had little inkling of her distress.

'Have you ever ridden astride a horse?' Nancy asked. 'Losing your cherry would be easier, if you had.'

Meg shook her head. Only Lisbeth dared to do so: another reason in her favour.

'Never fash. The first time may be a bit sore and you may bleed a little,' the well-seasoned Nancy reassured her, 'but no more than you do every month.'

The first time! And her deflowering would be made public—in front of a gawping crowd! It was unbearable. Meg felt her guts tie in knots at the thought.

'I'm not hurting you, am I?' Nancy had taken a brush to her hair. '

'No,' Meg whispered. Quite the contrary. The way Nancy groomed her hair with long, languorous strokes was soothing. She didn't tug or yank at the tangles but teased them out with gentle fingers that tickled her neck and shoulders. Meg closed her eyes, luxuriating in the warmth of her touch. Would Archie Douglas make her feel like this? From the smirks and sneers of his boorish brothers, she guessed that her groom had been initiated into the secrets of the bedchamber, but in their brief betrothal they'd never been alone together, never mind dally in anything more intimate.

'A man comes to the boil fast—too fast, oftentimes, while a woman needs gentle coddling before she starts to simmer.' Nancy's lips were soft against the crease of her neck. 'At least your brother has learnt that, otherwise I'd never have agreed to wed him. As for King Jamie, well...' she rolled her eyes, 'you lie with the king not for pleasure but for reward.' She jiggled the expensive jewel-encrusted gold bracelets on her arms. 'Pleasure you maun seek by other means.'

Meg's eyes widened as Nancy knelt beside her. She ran a finger over her lips and gazed at her with deep, sensuous eyes the colour of rich heather honey. No wonder Adam had fallen for the voluptuous Nancy.

'A kiss is sweet, isn't it, but have you never fondled your lips —down below?' Nancy whispered.

Meg blushed and shook her head. 'Down below' was a gash, an open wound, which bled once a month. Betsy had given her a lotion to smear 'down there' before the dreaded conjugal act, but she felt ashamed about touching herself to apply it.

'Well, my dearest sister, time to learn the secrets of *The Twa Marrit Women*.'

'*The Twa Marrit Women*!' Meg gasped. 'You've heard it?'

'Heard it? I could have written it! If I could scrieve!' Nancy's remark made them both shake with laughter till their cheeks were sodden with tears.

'That's better,' Nancy murmured. 'You need to loosen your corsets—in all ways.'

After pouring them each a generous goblet of wine, Nancy heaved her bulk onto the bed and patted the space beside her. They lay together quietly sipping their wine, until Meg's eyelids began to droop. When Nancy pulled her in closer, Meg nestled into her soft, comfortable body to rest her head on Nancy's heavy breasts. Drowsy with wine and lulled by the steady beating of Nancy's heartbeat, Meg's mouth slackened and she began to doze.

With her free hand, Nancy caressed her neck, moving in little circles down to her slight breasts. Taking her time, she lowered her hand and tweaked at Meg's nightgown. As Nancy leisurely stroked her thighs, Meg purred contentedly but when her hand brushed against her Venus mound, her eyes flew open.

'Trust me,' Nancy murmured. As her hand crept higher and began to fondle her secret-most places, Meg quivered. 'Come. Touch yourself. There's nothing to fear. Close your eyes and feel how soft your quim is,' Nancy coaxed, guiding her hand to touch the soft folds of skin. 'As tender as your lips,' she purred. 'Now frot gently with your finger until it throbs.'

She moved her hand away to let Meg take over. 'Keep going,' Nancy urged. 'Till you feel the love sap flowing in your womb. A man's seed will shrivel in a dry bed. It needs your moist milk to flourish and thrive.'

Tentatively at first, Meg began caressing the cleft between her thighs while Nancy gently caressed her nipples. A deep flush spread over Meg's skin, sending a delicious warm glow through her belly. As waves of painful pleasure surged through her, she arched her back moaning and gasping like a shameless strumpet.

'That's it,' Nancy urged. 'That's the way, lass.'

As Meg lay back exhausted in the crook of her arm, Nancy lightly brushed away the strands of damp hair clinging to her brow and nuzzled her earlobes to whisper, 'Now you ken how to warm up yourself for Archie. Forbye, you have no need to wait for him. You can pleasure yourself any time you feel like it.'

On the last night of her maidenhood Meg lay as still as a corpse trying not to cough and disturb Lisbeth who was snoozing peacefully beside her. Though Betsy's sleeping draught had deadened her limbs, it had failed to calm her reeling mind. Her ordeal was as nothing compared to the cruel torture of the early Christian martyrs and saints, she scolded herself, but that brought cold comfort. If only she could change places with Lisbeth. If only she could enter the convent, she would be a virtuous and faithful bride of Christ.

She was not the only one who had considered such an exchange. Archie's mother, Lady Douglas, who'd been expecting more smeddum from a future countess of Angus, made no secret of her contempt for her son's shilpit betrothed and had suggested a marriage to her younger sister instead. Sturdier in character and constitution, Elisabeth was clearly the hardier stock, but Prior Hepburn would have none of it. Furthermore, the arrangement had been signed and sealed and could not be rescinded without serious loss of honour. Meg's long-held desire for a loving partnership was dashed. Her marriage was a business deal; her wedding the signing of a contract between two powerful families.

Fearing they were being fobbed off with the runt of the litter, Lady Douglas had been unrelenting in negotiating the dowry. She should not fret unduly, Prior Hepburn reassured her, ofttimes marriage was the making of a lass like Meg. A man would soon bring her to life, put the roses into her cheeks. Once wedded and bedded, the bonnie bluebell would bloom.

On the morning of the wedding, the bride, head bowed, her face hidden by a veil waited outside the grand oaken door of St Mary's Church, while her groom, Archibald Douglas, announced the terms of the dowry.

After the *Sanctus,* the couple knelt in front of Prior John to exchange vows and receive the marriage blessing. As Archie lifted the veil from the bride's face, Prior John's upraised hand stopped in mid-air. His face blanched.

'What the deuce do you take me for?' he thundered. 'The Abbot of Unreason? Who dares to play hunt the gowk with me?' he blustered, his brow bulging with veins as purple as his robes. 'I'm no fool. I shall not marry this woman to this man.'

For, standing in front of him, on the verge of exchanging vows and rings with Archie Douglas was not Meg, but Elisabeth.

'Compose yourself, Hepburn,' Archie's grandfather, the fearless Bell the Cat, barked. 'There's no jape being played here.'

That morning, weakened from a rasping cough, Meg could hardly stand, never mind walk up the aisle. To postpone the wedding would risk giving the Douglases an excuse to call it off and so, in great haste, the seamstress had altered the dress again—this time to fit Lisbeth who had agreed to stand as proxy for her sister—but only at the wedding, not at the bedding, she insisted. Secretly Elisabeth could hardly wait to see the look on her uncle's face when the veil was lifted. And he did not disappoint.

'The devil dryte on you, Douglas,' Prior John hissed. 'You never thought to tell me! For a while I thought... I thought...' His voice trailed off.

Amongst the lady guests, tongues wagged and heads waggled knowingly. Meg was poorly because she was already with child and suffering from the sickness of the early months. No one was shocked. On the contrary, was that not a good sign, proof that she was fertile?

Regaining his composure, Prior John carried on with the ceremony, though he paid particular attention to the wording of the marriage rite in case there was some other joukerie-pawkery going on under his nose. Elisabeth's mischievous smile and those fern green eyes with hazel glints peeking out from under long eyelashes, so disconcerted him that he almost faltered over the irrevocable words, 'I now pronounce you man and wife.'

Chapter Seven
Education

Howbeit that nuns sing nichts and days,
Their heart knows nocht what their mouth says.
—*Ane Satire of the Three Estates,* Sir David Lindsay, 16th Century

St Mary's Abbey, Winter 1512-1513

Sister Maryoth's thin lips clamped together in a disapproving grimace at the novice who could recite neither the *Ave Maria* nor even the *Pater Noster*, nor, indeed, any prayers at all. Elisabeth knew next to nothing about Scripture: she had never said her beads and had no idea how to behave at holy Mass. Christmas and Easter were the only occasions she had attended the chapel. Unlike Meg, whose faith was a comfort and solace to her, Elisabeth skipped Sunday Mass, preferring to go hunting and hawking with the Hepburn men. Why bend the knee themselves, these border brigands would say, when they gave money, land and benefices to the sisters of St Mary's to do their praying for them?

Had she even been baptised? Sister Maryoth wouldn't be surprised that, with thon heathen Betsy as her nurse, the novice was still a pagan. She heaved an impatient sigh. Being one of the few literate nuns at the abbey, she'd been given the task of turning this wild child, this spawn of Satan, into an obedient, compliant novice, who—and the thought stuck in her craw—would be prioress one day. A position that, as Dame Janet's scribe and keeper of the financial records, she believed she deserved.

The cell where Elisabeth was incarcerated was as cold as a tomb, with no coverings on the flagstones and no warming fire. Inky patches of damp spattered the walls. The bed was a hard wooden board covered with coarse woollen blankets that itched the skin like fleas.

'This is how we all live,' Sister Maryoth declared. 'You're to be treated no differently from the other sisters.'

No fear of that. Stupefied from lack of sleep, Elisabeth dragged her feet to the chapel three times a day. Matins in the early hours—so early it seemed to be the middle of the night—was particularly tortuous with Sister Maryoth pinching her arms to keep her awake. Genuflecting, crossing herself, telling her beads, reciting *Pater Nosters, Aves, Glorias* and *Credos* daily, forever and ever. *Amen*. Interminable Latin chants that made no sense to her. Nor did Sister Maryoth make any attempt to explain them but seemed to take a perverse pleasure in listening to her mangled attempts. And, if she made a mistake, it was a venial sin. Whatever that was.

Sister Maryoth's particular devotion was to St Mary, the patroness of the abbey, and she spent hours praying to the miraculous statue of the Black Madonna and Child. During the great flood of 1358, when the Tyne overflowed its banks, a devout nun had snatched up the statue, threatening to throw it into the water, unless Our Saviour and his Holy Mother saved the abbey from destruction. At that very moment, the surging waters shrank back and the river once again flowed peacefully within its banks. What proof of the power of faith!

Since then, pilgrims had come with their humble offerings to beseech the Mother of God to intervene on their behalf to her Son. At the Lady Altar, where candles burned night and day, screwed-up scraps of paper scrawled with prayers from petitioners were strewn at her feet and an assortment of tattered rags, trinkets and amulets dangled from her arms.

'To be worthy of your calling, you must first learn the joy of suffering,' Sister Maryoth informed the novice.

Which meant kneeling on cold flagstones while the Holy Mother and Child gazed down with glazed eyes, indifferent to her torment. The tale of the statue's miraculous appearance was often recounted. While cherubim and seraphim may have flown the Holy Family's house from Nazareth to Loreto in Italy, their Black Madonna had sailed from the east in an oyster shell to her chosen resting place near the abbey. Whoever dared suggest that the icon had been carved from a blackened log washed up in the River Tyne was derided as a heretic. Over the years, the original paint had flaked off and attempts to restore it rendered the Madonna more like a vulgar old courtesan than the Mother of God.

Hearing Elisabeth whinge about her aching knees was music to Sister Maryoth's ears: proof, if any were needed, that she was unsuited to be a nun and unworthy of becoming prioress.

'I do what I can,' Sister Maryoth whined in reply to Prior John's questions about her progress, 'but the girl has no calling. Not one iota of religious feeling. She can't understand the difference between superstitious nonsense and religious rite. Marriage would smoor her high spirits.'

'That's not for you to judge,' the prior retorted. 'If she is to take over as prioress one day you must persevere with her.'

Bowing her head in submission, Sister Maryoth pressed her lips more tightly together to suck down the bilious envy welling in her craw. You cannot make a silk purse out of a sow's ear, she wanted to say, but if telling him was to no purpose, perhaps showing him would be. She would bide her time.

She did not have long to wait. One morning at matins she caught her charge gazing with longing at the dusty motes dancing in the sunbeam that lit up the gloomy nave. Used to a life outdoors, Elisabeth suffered greatly from being cooped up in the suffocating, cloying confines of the cloister but that should not excuse her, Sister Maryoth scowled. She was about to scold the irreverent novice for being distracted from her prayers, when a divine flash inspired her. After the service she took her aside.

'Since I can abide your wretched moans no longer, and from the goodness of my heart,' she said with a false smile,' I shall permit you to go out riding.'

Elisabeth gawped at her in disbelief as the holy sister stipulated two conditions: a strict time limit of one hour and with the stable lad Harry Cockburn as escort.

'However,' Sister Maryoth added, placing a conspiratorial finger to her thin lips, 'this must be our secret. If your aunt and uncle hear of it, they'll put a stop to it forthwith.'

Chapter Eight
A Courting

Or, what is love, or to be lo'ed?
Fain would I learn that law.
—*Robin and Makyne*, Robert Henryson, 15th Century

The Garleton Hills, Spring 1513

Squinting, Elisabeth followed Lindsay's finger pointing out all the landmarks visible from the crest of the Garleton Hills. To the east, the shimmering Craig of Bass was circled by squawking seabirds, and to the west, the lion couchant of Arthur's Craig guarded the sloping silhouette of Edinburgh Castle, skirting the skyline above the smoky haze of Auld Reekie.

The whole of central Scotland may be laid out before them but admiring the scenery was not Elisabeth's priority. Aware that Sister Maryoth could just as capriciously curtail the privilege she had so generously granted, she was edgy and impatient. After riding out from the abbey to Garleton, she'd left Harry Cockburn at the kitchen door. The lure of bread and ale and the company of saucy scullery maids, who teased and flirted with him mercilessly, would keep him occupied during the precious hour she was allowed alone with Lindsay.

'And do you see straight ahead there?' Lindsay pointed across the wide bay of Aberlady and over the Forth estuary. Though the sky above them was clear, a shower of rain was falling on the twin paps in the Kingdom of Fife. 'Thon's the Mount of Lindifferon, lands I inherited from my mother.'

'And does Garleton also belong to you?' Elisabeth asked.

'Aye, it does. Do I see that busy brain of yours calculating how much I'm worth?' He squeezed her shoulders. 'I'll take you to the Mount one day, so you can see for yourself.'

'Do you promise? Cross your heart? Before they make me take my vows.'

As Lindsay pulled her into his arms, she nestled closer against his chest, pressing against him to intensify the needle-sharp prickles of raw pleasure zigzagging up and down her spine.

'Och, a wee pagan such as you could never be a nun,' he replied, planting kisses, soft as a dusting of pollen, on the top of her head.

Elisabeth wasn't so sure. She wriggled round to face him and wrinkled her brow to ask, 'Davie, would you marry a lass without a tocher?'

'That would be foolish. For what other reason would a wise man wed?'

'Oh,' she replied. Disappointment flooded her eager heart.

Lindsay tilted her chin and gave her a stern look. 'I speak in jest, my jaggy thistle. Do you question my honour as a gentleman? Why, of course I'd marry the lass I loved, whether she had a dowry or no.'

Blushing, she lowered her eyes before daring to ask, 'Do you love me, Davie Lindsay?' She looked up, anxiously awaiting his answer.

The jaggy thistle's forthright question had taken the seasoned courtier aback. He hesitated before replying, 'Aye. That I do, you wee scamp.'

Her face lit up but swiftly clouded again as she put another question. 'And if we were wed, they couldn't force me to take my vows, could they?'

'Nothing would please me more, Lisbeth. When the time is ripe I shall ask Adam for your hand.'

'It's not Adam's permission we need,' she said quietly, 'but my uncle's. And if we go against his wishes, I'll no be given a tocher.'

He frowned. The fact that she had no dowry didn't disturb him so much as the idea of provoking the legendary wrath of the formidable Prior Hepburn. If he ever found out about their clandestine courtship, Lindsay was under no illusion that he would have him gelded at the very least. He pressed his thighs together tightly at the thought.

But there was another way, Elisabeth explained. They could elope.

Lindsay raised an eyebrow. 'Elope? What a fanciful notion! So, you'd like to be whisked away like some gypsy ganging over the march.'

'And then we could be handfasted,' Elisabeth replied, her voice rising in excitement. 'It's an ancient border custom, Betsy told me. We need only exchange promises in front of two witnesses. No need even for a priest.'

Lindsay chuckled. 'What! You want us to plight our troth in the middle of the forest. Like tinkers and common folk!'

'I'd rather be an honest gypsy who gives her heart freely than a nun languishing in a cell, locked up against her will,' Elisabeth retorted and pushed him away rather too brusquely, judging from his raised eyebrows. Why couldn't she learn to curb her reckless reactions? She scolded herself. Not without cause they cried her the 'jaggy thistle'. She let out a deep breath and lowered her eyes, gazing at him sideways from under her eyelashes affecting the kind of plaintive, appealing expression that Kate employed—often to great effect.

'Enough of making calf's eyes at me, Lisbeth, it doesn't suit you.'

Offended, she tossed her head and turned away, her elbows folded in a huff, but he pulled her back.

'Lisbeth, listen to me. I understand your plight, but I would be loath to steal you under cover of darkness like a roving gypsy. We shall be wed in the proper way.' The naked yearning burning in her eyes caused his heart to lurch, and he regretted having to douse her hopes. 'When the time is right. But these are difficult times, my dearest love. There are grave matters concerning the safety of the realm to deal with before I can begin to think of my own personal happiness.'

'What about my happiness? Our happiness. Don't you care about that? Don't you care about me?' she snivelled, wiping her nose on her sleeve.

'That I do, my cherished one. More than you can know. But first and foremost I'm a servant of the king and he has entrusted me with a special mission. The king's will aye comes afore my own.'

'I care not a fig for the king.' She began beating her fists against his chest in frustration, salty tears of disappointment stinging her cheeks. He grabbed her by the wrists to stop her flailing hands.

'Listen to me, Elisabeth.' His harsh tone made her take heed. Stubborn to the point of being thrawn, his jaggy thistle could vex him beyond his patience at times. 'This is no time for starry-eyed romantic fantasies. Henry of England is threatening our borders. The country is about to go to war.'

'All the more reason for us to wed before you go,' she blubbed. 'Please, Davie, don't let them send me back to the abbey. What if something should happen to you?' She licked away tears with the point of her tongue. 'At least if we were handfasted, I'd be your relict, wouldn't I? And I would have a home in Garleton, if...' she trailed off.

Relict indeed. He pulled her in close and gently rubbed her back. His lips fluttered like moth's wings against her cheek.

'I'll speak to the king himself. He has a soft heart and will intervene for us. Don't fret. As soon as this is all over, we shall be together. Forever.'

Heartened by Lindsay's promise, Elisabeth picked up Harry at Garleton to ride back to the abbey. As she skipped through the cloister her gaiety was crushed by a dour voice saying, 'Dame Janet has been looking all over for you. You're to come at once.'

Sister Maryoth had been skulking in the shadows and had snuck up behind her silently, without warning. With her soundless steps, her aunt's secretary had mastered the uncanny knack of appearing from nowhere. A chill seemed to accompany her spectral presence—even her breath was cold. Harbinger of doom rather than herald angel, Elisabeth thought. Sister Maryoth may have been renowned for her piety, but she couldn't abide her mim-mou'ed holiness.

With her head to one side and a smile as warm as a late spring frost, the nun delivered her message and then, just as she was about to flit away, she added, 'I trust you enjoyed your little jaunt.'

Something about her insinuating smile disturbed Elisabeth. She marched back to the stable where Harry was rubbing down her horse in the stall. He looked sheepish and uncomfortable.

'Have you been blabbing, Harry?'

His face flared redder than a rowanberry as she glared at him.

'Naw... naw... nothing,' he stuttered. 'I'd never do that.'

'For if you clype on me, I'll tell on you—for wenching yon scullery maid, Elisabeth warned.

'I give you my word, Dame Lisbeth,' he stammered, 'that I will never, ever betray you. I'd cut off my right arm before I did that.'

Taking her time to change out of her riding breeches and into her habit, Elisabeth braced herself for her visit to the prioress. Dame Janet was propped up on huge goose down pillows, languishing in her soft feather bed. Her chubby fingers dipped incessantly into a bowl of comfits that she sucked slowly, one after the other. Since she could neither chew nor stomach strong meat, she would complain, sweetmeats and honeyed liqueurs were her only sustenance.

'Sister Maryoth tells me yon stable lad has a fancy for you. She's seen how his eyes gobble you up. Harry Cockburn may be a strapping lad with a fine set of limbs but you must not let that turn your head. You're over flichtersome, lass. Glowering at the moon, you don't want to be falling in the midden.' Dame Janet chortled, her thick rouged lips slowly parting to display stumps of teeth in wrinkled gums.

Elisabeth breathed a sigh of relief. She'd worried that they'd found out about her furtive meetings with Lindsay.

'But just in case you're tempted,' Dame Janet continued, 'I've a few words to say about this blissful state of marriage that most women hanker after. This sacrament created by the Church fathers to sanctify the messy business of procreation. Go forth and multiply, they tell us,' Dame Janet mimicked her brother's sermonising voice, 'not just once—or even twice –but every year of your life while you're still broody. When not bleeding you're breeding.

'It may seem a lofty and worthy aim to produce souls to keep God company in his lonely heaven, but that's never in a man's mind when he dances the reel o' Bogie with his wife every night. Every man is in thrall to his pistle, with never a thought to what their womenfolk have to thole: a few spurts of pleasure for them means untold grief and agony for us. Our punishment for Eve tempting Adam to commit the first sin, so they tell us.' She snorted with unconcealed contempt. 'It ill behoves the Almighty if he made such a weak, fushionless creature as Adam in his own image.' She paused for a moment to ponder this possible blasphemy and then popped in another comfit, smacking her lips together with a satisfied slurp.

'Seeing his gross error, Almighty God showed more gumption when he created woman, yet he has scant regard for our sex. All very well to spare the Virgin Mary the indignity of being bedded, but she still had to bring forth the bairn in a byre with the kye and the yowes. I ask you, if God in his wisdom deemed such a nativity good enough for his beloved son and her mother, what chance is there for the rest of us? Even the beasts in the field suffer less than a woman in childbed.

'That's if you don't part with a bairn before it's time. Or you may carry it in your creel, only for it to be stillborn. And many's the bairn that has failed to thrive, and countless more have lived for a few months or a few years before being struck down by some affliction. God's little angels we cry them, doomed to strum harps for eternity. Humph.' She took a sip of cordial and then wiped her sticky lips delicately with an embroidered napkin.

'All too often the price to be paid for bringing a child into this world is its mother's life. Her death then leaves a wheen of mewling orphans and a feckless, grief-stricken father. And even if you are spared, you'll be troubled with ailments that even Job himself wouldn't thole. Then, as soon as one has been weaned, another will be sown in the womb. You'll aye be heavy-footed and old before your time. Your man may find you comely enough now, but when you're baggy-eyed, with your firm young skin hanging loose in a paunch, he'll look elsewhere for his comfort. They all do.' She nodded knowingly, though years of over-indulgence rather than childbearing had bloated the voluptuous figure of her youth.

'Marriage does not mean, as you might think, my dear niece, freedom and independence. Not for nothing is it called wedlock. You have no wish to be cloistered but consider what other choice awaits you: to be beholden to a mere man. In pledging her marriage vows, a woman must promise to love, honour and obey her husband. Like a slave to its master, a wife is expected to do her man's bidding, whether she wishes or no. Tell me, what would you prefer? To be kilted to some puddock prince, or to be a bride of Christ and, one day, prioress of this abbey?'

The air in the chamber, stuffy from the heavy scents of pomanders and cloying confectionery, and the heat from the stoked-up fire, was making Elisabeth drowsy. She sat on her hands, waiting impatiently for her to finish. Dame Janet's words flowed over her, as meaningless as the Latin Mass. Nothing to do with her, for she knew better. Not once had her aunt mentioned the achingly delicious tingling that left Elisabeth weak-kneed and soft-limbed with desire.

'Why did you no tell Meg of this?' she asked.

Dame Janet scowled at her bold question. 'Do you think she'd have gone up the aisle willingly if I had? Meg is one of those doomed to bear the burden of carrying on the human race. I'm telling *you* so that you ken what a fortunate escape you've had.'

'But what if you love someone? Surely that must make marriage worthwhile?'

Dame Janet's piggy eyes, scarcely visible in the folds of flesh, glared at her. A grotesque parody of female beauty with her powdered face and plucked eyebrows, she bore a striking resemblance to the crude icon of the Black Madonna.

'Marriage for you has never been an option. As for love!' she harrumphed. 'Love only happens in fairy tales, my lass. Who in your ken has ever married for love? However,' she leant forward as much as her bulk would allow, to confide, 'if you itch, then by all means scratch. If you fancy a tumble in the hay with the stable lad, make sure you're not bairnt. Och aye, there are ways and means,' she nodded. 'Betsy's the one to ask.' Dame Janet readjusted her great weight on the bed. 'Tak tent of what I've telt you, lass.' Exhausted by her sermonising, the prioress yawned deeply, sank back into her pillows and closed her eyes.

Elisabeth had no intention of going to her grave a dried-up, withered old virgin, never knowing the sweet pleasures of being cherished by a man. *That* was what it meant to be alive. The passion of Christ, the celestial consort, was no consolation for forgoing the passion of a warm-blooded man. Pining prostrate on cold flagstones in front of a wooden-hearted Madonna was for the likes of pious Sister Maryoth. Elisabeth would not bend the knee. Taking the veil would not be her fate. She would flee the coop and escape from this dovecot of fasted women.

Chapter Nine
Rumours of War

By Flodden's high and heathery side,
Shall wave a banner red as blood,
And chieftain's throng wi meikle pride.
—*The Ballad of Thomas the Rhymer,* Traditional

Hailes Castle, 15 August 1513

Every able-bodied man between the ages of sixteen and sixty with victuals for forty days had been summoned to muster at the Boroughmuir on 18th day of August, but not the earl of Bothwell's men. They had been spared traipsing into Edinburgh only to tramp back out again and would join the main army on its way past Hailes to the south.

Lindsay had ridden non-stop from the city to deliver the king's marching orders to Adam, one of the chief commanders of the campaign, and now surveyed the makeshift camp set up between the River Tyne and the high road. Men in ill-fitting hauberks and brigandines scurried about hither and yon like ants whose nest had been disturbed. Canvas tents had been set up and fires burned where blacksmiths sharpened swords and shod horses' hooves. At the risk of being dishonourable, Lindsay couldn't help but voice his private concerns.

'This is more than folly, Adam, it's sheer madness.' He wiped his brow, dusty and sweaty from his ride. 'I worry for the king's wits. And I'm not alone. Bishop Elphinstone, among others, is against this ill-advised campaign, and that old seasoned warrior, Bell the Cat Douglas, has spoken his mind agin it.'

And received no thanks for it, but an unmerited insult from his monarch that, if fearful, he should go home. Black-affronted, Douglas had done just that and taken his grandson Archie with him but leaving his two sons for honour's sake.

All this strife because of James IV's promise to their 'Auld Allies', the French, to come to their aid if attacked by the English. When Henry VIII landed an army on French soil, Louis XII's wife Queen Anne had sent a love letter and a turquoise ring to James, appointing him as her bounden champion. The chivalrous king could not deny the request of a lady in dolorous plight to march into England for her sake.

Such a pompous utterance, displaying more ill-judgment than chivalry, dismayed Lindsay who suspected the 14,000 French crowns on offer was more of an enticement. This *coup de foudre* was in danger of ending up as an ill-fated *coup de grâce*, but neither reason nor unreason swayed James's decision. Not even the apparition of St Andrew at St Michael's Kirk in Linlithgow that had warned the king against leading an army into war and dallying with women. Nor the phantom herald that had appeared at the Mercat Cross in Edinburgh on the stroke of midnight and listed the names of all those earls, lords, barons, gentlemen and sundry burgesses of the city who would appear before his Satanic Master within forty days. Despite his highly superstitious nature, James paid no heed to these doom-laden portents. Nothing, it seemed, would dissuade him from his misguided mission. Lindsay was in despair.

'Nor should it,' Adam affirmed. 'There have been too many of these auld wives' tales for my liking, Davie. Why, you may even have set up these tricks yourself, sleekit showman that you are,' he quipped, jabbing his finger at the heraldic crest on Lindsay's embroidered tabard.

'Queen Margaret Tudor, too, has been afflicted with fearful dreams of his bloodied corpse pierced with arrow.'

Adam snorted. 'That's no surprise. Not only is she Harry of England's sister, but a jealous wife, riled by her husband's rally to a rival queen's cause.'

'You misjudge her,' Lindsay replied, 'for all her faults, the queen is concerned that the royal succession rests on an eighteen-month-old infant. This reckless undertaking puts the monarchy in jeopardy. It's not worth the 14,000 crowns the French are contributing.'

Adam laughed. 'Never mind auld wives' tales: you sound like my own wife!'

For Nancy, too, had doubted the king's reasons for going to war. All for some high-bendit notion, he was prepared to sacrifice us all, she'd warned. 'To save a damsel in distress. Hardly. She's twice-marrit and twice his age. Huh. James's head swivels too easily—thither and yon and back again. It's no wonder he can't see straight. I should ken better than most! I've borne him a daughter. God forbid that Jenny should have her father's flichtersome wits.'

Anxious about her daughter's safety at court in Edinburgh, Nancy had begged Adam to fetch her, but he'd shrugged off her concerns. After all, she was the king's responsibility. If Jenny were his own flesh and blood, would he be so uncaring, she'd reproached him, her tawny eyes flashing and her Stewart temper riled. Despite Lindsay's reassurance that the court had already fled to a secret refuge where Jenny would be far from danger, Nancy had banished Adam from the marital bed. Brooding in her chamber she'd refused to come and admire the muster.

Now, scanning the display of arms with a critical eye, Lindsay could hardly blame her. 'A woeful wappinschaw,' he groaned.

Adam placed a hand on his shoulder. 'Have faith, Davie. Since Harry Coppernose is in France with the bulk of his army, we have the edge over the English. Our artillery is among the finest in Europe. Why, our guns are bigger for a start.'

'But they're too heavy and slow,' Lindsay pointed out. 'They can only fire one shot a minute, while the English guns can fire three. I have it on good authority.'

Adam wagged his head. 'You may be the diplomat, Davie and no doubt your spies are well-informed, but I'm the soldier and I can tell you we not only have more men but they are better armed.'

Lindsay surveyed the straggly line of untrained farmhands, surly stable lads and half-hearted quarter-men struggling with eighteen-foot pike staffs and questioned his friend's judgment. 'Your men seem ill at ease with thon long lances, Adam. How are they going to use them?'

'To topple riders from their horses—in the way the French commander, D'Aussi, has advised.'

'And can they?' Lindsay replied, looking doubtful.

Adam dismissed his concerns with a wave of his hand, reluctant to tell him that, though D'Aussi may have given his advice, he had neglected to give them any training.

'I wish I had your confidence, Adam.' Lindsay rubbed his chin.

'I put my trust in hard steel, Davie,' Adam replied with a cheery slap on his friend's shoulder. 'And the 14,000 gold crowns from the French coffers,' he winked. 'Besides, what do you know about warfare, master poet? Away and prepare your pen to write a triumphal ode to commemorate our glorious conquest of the English.'

An ode to victory was the last thing Lindsay felt like writing: he dreaded that it would be an epitaph he'd be penning. With a heavy heart he mounted his horse and rode off.

St Mary's Abbey

At the abbey, Prior Hepburn was giving his sister their marching orders.

'If the invaders reach this far, retreat to the fortalice of Nunraw. It will be easier to defend. Begin making plans now. In the meantime, lock all gates here at the abbey. No-one is to enter or leave.'

'Lisbeth, for one, will champ at the bit for having her wings clipped,' Janet mumbled, savouring a bonbon of exotically sweet *marche de pan*.

Hepburn frowned. 'What do you mean?'

Her mouth slackened, dribbling tiny morsels down her chin. Too late, Dame Janet realised she had blabbed. 'You ken how our peerie-heided niece would rather flee about the countryside than mind her lessons. She's a lass who craves fresh air and exercise,' Dame Janet gabbled, adding, 'Forbye, she's not alone. The stable lad aye goes with her.'

His face had turned as purple as a bishop's robe. 'What? You let her go out riding with Harry Cockburn? How could you be so lax?'

Dame Janet popped in another sweet. 'She's safe enough with Harry.'

'An uncouth stable lad, with nothing between his ears, and a brainless quhillie-lillie between his shanks! I despair of you, Janet. With all this talk of war, bands of brigands will be scouring the land, looting, pillaging and raping. Sheep, cattle, women. It's all the same to them.'

'And do you think that locking her up in a nunnery will keep her safe and out of reach of marauding men? Why, it's the first place they'll come to.' Prioress Janet sniggered gleefully, as if relishing the thought. 'Unless we all slash off our noses and lips, like the nuns of Coldingham, to slake the lust of barbarous invaders.'

This prospect sent shivers up the spine of Sister Maryoth who was lurking with her ear to the door. She jumped back, caught off-guard when the door suddenly burst open.

'Bring my niece,' Prior Hepburn thundered. 'At once.'

Sister Maryoth pressed her hands together. 'It grieves me greatly to tell you,' she said, trying to suppress a smile cracking her face. 'But the novice Elisabeth has eloped.'

Chapter Ten
Handfasting

Lovers beware and tak gude heed about
Whom that ye love, for whom ye suffer pain.
—*The Testament of Cresseid,* Robert Henryson, 15th Century

Hailes Castle, 18 August 1513

'Damn and blast! Where do you think you're going?' Adam bellowed, waving his arms furiously. The horse galloping full pelt along the riverbank had scattered the disorderly lines of the wappinschaw to all the airts before slowing down.

'Adam, you mustn't go to war,' Elisabeth blurted. She leapt down from her mount and flung herself at her brother. 'I had a dream.'

'Not another one.' His scorn mixed with angry annoyance, Adam tapped his foot impatiently as he listened to her garbled account of her recurring nightmare: bodies swirling round in the flood, the severed head, the leering skull that had left her with an abiding sense of foreboding, throttling her so that she could scarcely breathe.

Elisabeth laid a hand on his arm. 'So, you see, Adam, you mustn't go.'

'Not another doom-monger,' Adam groaned. 'A creditable performance, Lisbeth, but hardly credible.'

Her eyes opened wide in alarm. 'What other portents have there been?'

'Ask him, he'll tell you.' Adam pointed towards the stables where Harry Cockburn was rubbing down a steaming stallion. 'For I wager the hellish herald and the spirit of St Andrew are but figments of our court jester's fertile imagination,' he scoffed.

Elisabeth looked puzzled until Lindsay came out of the stable leading a fresh horse. She rushed up to him. 'Davie! Is that true? Have there been other omens?'

Lindsay placed steadying hands on her shoulders. 'There are aye portents when folk in peril try to make sense of the unknown, Lisbeth. Fear plays strange tricks with the mind.'

'Aye, and if we listened to every old wife and her havers, we men would never go to war,' Adam snorted.

'That would be no bad thing,' Elisabeth maintained. She tore herself away from Lindsay to grab hold of Adam. 'Don't you see, my dearest brother? Your lives are in mortal danger?'

'Women know nought about warfare.' He frowned, trying to prise off her fingers clinging limpet-like to his arm. 'Now I must see about getting these men back into some sort of order and getting you back to the nunnery. Where's thon Harry Cockburn? Till I slap his sappie head for putting you in peril.'

'You're not going with them, are you, Davie?' Lindsay's non-committal shrug of his shoulders told her otherwise. 'If there's a war, men will be killed and wounded. You and Adam might be…' she trailed off, recalling the horrific images of her nightmare. She trembled at the thought that she might never see Lindsay again. This might be their last chance. She stretched up on tiptoe to whisper in his ear. 'What about us, Davie? Have you spoken with the king?'

Lindsay shifted uncomfortably, for he'd not yet kept his promise. 'It would be imprudent to pester his grace with our personal plight when he has more important matters on his mind.' When her face drooped, he went on, 'Come, now, my thrawn thistle. Stand firm. Until this war is over…' he broke off, taking time to mull over a plan. She was to bide at Hailes with

Nancy and her bairn and, as soon as it was safe to leave, he would send for her. Not to Garleton, for that was undefended, but to Edinburgh, where Lindsay had some rooms in a tenement in St Mary's Wynd, just off the High Street.

Elisabeth's face lit up. 'It'll be no fib that I'm off to St Mary's! To Edinburgh! If you think that's for the best, Davie.' Becoming pensive again, she said, 'But mind what I said about handfasting. Let's do it before you go to war. Please, Davie. Then surely they cannot make me go back to the abbey.'

The alarm in her voice and dismay on her face moved him. He hugged her tightly to his breast and burrowed his face in her hair. He'd done his best to put a stop to this senseless battle. He yearned to forget all thoughts of war and death and ignore the king's feckless orders that were making life more uncertain than ever. All he desired was to keep her safe. His spiky Lisbeth, always determined to grasp the thistle, was ready to follow him to the four corners of the earth. He may never see his love again. 'Why shouldn't we pledge ourselves to each other, my jaggy thistle?' he replied.

Overjoyed by his reply, Elisabeth ran to her brother with a request—to stand as witness to their handfasting. Adam had shaved off his bushy beard—for greater ease in slipping his metal helmet on and off—and cut his hair *en brosse* to keep it lice-free and to prevent the enemy hauling him by the hair. Clean-shaven and bristle-haired, he looked like a newly hatched baby bird, naked and vulnerable, and no longer the fierce, bearded warrior. He brushed her unruly hair back from her face and tilted her chin up to look her in the eye .

'Nay, forgive me, lass, but I cannot. You're courting trouble with Davie Lindsay, Lisbeth. He'll not make you happy.'

'How can you say that?' Elisabeth replied, tears welling in her eyes. 'He's a man of honour and your best friend. And I love him.'

'That you love him, I'm in no doubt, but, as your brother and guardian, it's my duty to shield you from harm. For I fear that you'll never be first in his heart. I ken Davie Lindsay too well. Two loves already possess the royal herald.'

'What? He has other paramours?' she yelped, but then how could she be so naïve as to imagine that she would be the first and only love of Lindsay, an experienced courtier and man of the world.

'Nay, Lisbeth, he has no mistress that I know of. Nay, Davie Lindsay is first and foremost the king's man. He would lay down his life for his master. And his second passion is poetry. Every spare second you'll see him scribble, scribble, scribble. You'll aye play second fiddle to the makar and that will never suit you. For, my jaggy thistle, you can be a demanding and wilful lass. Forbye, he's o'er old for you. Davie's already a man of six and twenty and you're a maid of only fifteen summers.'

'Sixteen,' she corrected him. 'Why, Margaret Tudor was barely thirteen when she wed King James. And he was already thirty.'

'The marriage of the thistle and the rose was a union of two countries, not loving hearts. And that English rose has turned into a thistle, a constant thorn in the king's side. Jaggy thistle though we cry you, you're still a rosebud, not yet full blown. Now, I'll get Harry to take you back to the abbey. Mind the Hepburn motto: Keep tryst, my jaggy thistle.'

While Adam went off to find Harry, Elisabeth ran with her tearful tale of woe to Nancy who was in her chamber nursing baby Patrick.

'Men,' she muttered, comforting her peevish son. 'I hope my sulking isn't souring my milk. They may boast that they ken all about war, but they ken naught about love. Let's see if he'll agree to the terms of my truce.'

Adam would be allowed back into her bed, but only if he gave the couple his blessing. When he readily agreed, Nancy gave Elisabeth a broad wink and whispered, 'See how easily these warriors surrender in the battle of the sexes.'

Betsy was more difficult to win round. Elisabeth had taken for granted that she would share her joy but her nurse kept shaking her head and muttering, 'She's away with the fairies. It's far worse than I thought.'

Their handfasting in the Great Hall of Hailes was not a joyous occasion, Elisabeth thought with Betsy beating her breast, struggling to keep back the tears and Adam drumming his fingers against his thigh, impatient to be off to enjoy his own coupling with the merciful Nancy. Nevertheless, the lovers plighted their troth, promising to be faithful to each other for a year and a day when they would be lawfully married. From his pinkie, Lindsay eased off a gold ring, a gift from King James, and placed it on the fourth finger of her right hand.

'And in a year's time, when we are truly wed, I shall give you a wedding ring and place it here,' he said tenderly stroking her middle finger.

'I vow never to take this off until then,' Elisabeth murmured.

Following Betsy's instructions, they licked the thumbs of their right hands and stuck them together to seal their solemn vow. Betsy then gave them each a blue ribbon tied at the ends in a lover's knot.

'*Keep Tryst* is the Hepburn slogan,' Elisabeth said as she looped her ribbon round Lindsay's neck.

'And *Endure Fort* is ours,' Lindsay replied, following suit. 'You'll have much to bear in the coming months, my thistledown. Mind our motto and stand firm whatever happens,' he urged before lowering his head to kiss her.

They were about to raise a cup in toast to the newly betrothed couple, when baby Patrick toddled up to his father, whimpering and tugging at his elbow. Adam stooped to attend to the infant who did not recognise this smooth-cheeked stranger. He howled and flailed his chubby arms and knocked the goblet out of his hand. The sight of the wine spilling out and staining the flagstones blood red was too much for Betsy who let out a long, low wail.

That evening, as she was brushing the white petals from Elisabeth's hair and preparing her for the bridal bed, Betsy crumpled.

'Oh, my wee lassie! My wee thistledown,' she moaned. She threw her pinny over her face and rocked back and forth, on her stool, making an eerie, keening sound.

'Betsy, you're giving me the cold creeps. Why the dirge? This is not a wake! And this is my nightgown, not my shroud!'

For the handfasting ceremony Elisabeth had donned the only gown she owned, the one she'd worn at Adam's wedding. Of mistletoe green. How could she tell the hapless Lisbeth that it was bad luck to be married in the pixies' colour? Or, that the spilt wine was another ill omen? Instead, Betsy thrust something wrapped in a damp cloth into her hand.

'Here, take this. Stap it in your quim afore bed.'

Leaving Betsy to her lamentations, Elisabeth went to the privy. She unwrapped the cloth and screwed up her nose. A ball of sphagnum moss soaked in red wine. How was she expected to stuff that inside her? And what would Lindsay think?

However anxious and expectant she was, her groom lay fully clothed and fast asleep on top of the bed. Not too old, perhaps, but too tired? She crawled up to him and tried to nudge him awake but he only snored more loudly and turned onto his side. She lay down and curled her backside into his groin, bringing one of his arms round her belly and the other round her breast.

'I'm not leaving this bed still a maiden,' she whispered, feeling him stir behind her.

'You're just a lass, Lisbeth,' he croaked, his voice groggy with sleep. 'It isn't fair to love you and leave you. Nor do I wish to harm you. There will be time enough.'

'This is the time. This very night. Teach this nun to be a wanton, for then the convent will spurn me. Unless, of course, you're a monk and have taken a vow of celibacy—or a larbar, Davie Lindsay,' she snickered mischievously.

'What? Where did a lass like you learn such a word? Who's been teaching you the wicked ways of the *Twa Marrit Women*?' He rolled her over to face him. 'Do you ken what it means?'

Her hazel eyes twinkled. 'An impotent old man.'

'Older than you I grudgingly admit being, but impotent I am not. Rest assured on that.' He pushed himself up onto his elbows, a satirical smile quirking the corners of his lips. 'Larbar you cry me? I'll show you I'm no eunuch. And certainly no monk.'

In the chilly hours of dawn they were awakened by the martial sounds of men-at-arms bawling, armour clanking, drums banging, horses snorting. Lindsay was about to slip out of bed—he couldn't bear to say farewell —but the touch of her hand caressing the sensitive skin between his waist and hips melted his resolve. He moaned softly and turned to her. For their first time, he'd been cautious, not wishing to cause hurt but she had opened up to him like a flower. No longer the jaggy thistle but a pink-tipped gowan unfolding its delicate petals to the sun.

Now the noises of war and nearness of danger sharpened their arousal and they clung to each other in a desperate attempt to wring out every last ounce of pleasure, before coming together in a climax of doomed ecstasy. As if making love for the very last time, Lindsay thought gloomily as their passion subsided and they fell back to lie spreadeagled side by side. He clasped her tightly to his chest and buried his head in her bed-tousled hair.

Once Lindsay had gone, Elisabeth had lain hugging the pillow, tearfully trying to salvage what she could from their brief honeymoon. After their initial nipping and scarting, he had slowly and gently stroked her skin with feather-light fingertips until she thought her very bones would melt. Only then, when he sensed she was ready, did he lay claim to her. The initial shock was breathtaking but, whispering soothing words and guiding with skilful hands, he'd brought her to such an intensity of pleasure that made her cry out. So as to memorise every blissful second she squeezed her eyelids shut and chronicled every kiss, every caress, every stroke of their lovemaking. This way she hoped to staunch the self-pity and frustration that threatened to engulf her.

Bleary-eyed and dazed, she dragged herself up to the battlements of the west tower where Adam was dandling his crabbit son in his arms to soothe him. He gave her a knowing wink.

'And this,' he said, holding up the snotty-nosed toddler, girning for sleep, 'is what you can expect from your dallying.'

Rubbing her teary eyes, Elisabeth attempted a weak smile.

'Look yonder, Patrick!' Adam had caught sight of the cloud of dust that signalled the approach of the main force coming along the high road from Edinburgh. The snivelling infant seemed unimpressed by the cavalcade of weaponry which his father began to tot up: the five cannon and two culverins of the Seven Sisters cast by Robert Borthwick, the king's master melter, drawn by thirty-six oxen; the numerous wagons of cannonballs and powder casks.

'The Seven Sisters?' Elisabeth sniggered. 'With thon long-nebbed barrels are they not brothers?'

Adam fired her a withering look. 'Doubtless they are most definitely female to the cannoneers deafened by their bellowing. Forbye, even without the muckle mouth of Mons Meg, we cannot fail to win with this vast array of armoury.'

As Elisabeth clasped her hand to her mouth to stifle her unseemly mirth, the ring on her finger caught her eye. Of the rarest Scottish gold, Lindsay had told her, from a mine in the Leadhills. Twirling the ring she noticed engraved letters—King James's initials—encircled by the *memento mori*—a skull and crossbones. Her stomach lurched uneasily and she felt slightly sick. Let there be no more omens, no more portents she prayed.

Curious to see her shiny plaything, little Patrick reached out chubby fingers to grab it until his father pulled his hand away to wave at the procession. How could this warrior's son not fail to be amazed at his first sight of military might? Nobles and knights in full armour, their metal breastplates and helmets gleaming in the morning sun, rode on horseback. Behind them marched the remaining soldiery; mercenaries and conscripts with pikes and staffs, and finally, straggling at their tail, bondagers and byre-men—untrained, unkempt and some unshod—wielding pitchforks and scythes as if they were sauntering to the harvest. Spotting Harry Cockburn amongst the stable lads she gave him a cheery wave.

Bringing up the rear lumbered the camp followers. Carts and haywains laden with cauldrons and kettles, pots and pans, sacks of meal and sundry victuals trundled past, drawn by scraggy nags. Barefoot children, chasing scabby-coated curs, scampered alongside the carts driven by their mothers dressed in sweepings from battlefields. Though some of the women wore canvas jackets tied with military belts and buckles, most were clad in garments cobbled together from ragged remnants: motley cloaks and shawls patched out of tattered flags and banners filched from the fallen of past forays.

Elisabeth's heavy-lidded eyes sprang open. She pulled herself up. Women going to war! There was something she could do after all! She could help to load weapons, fetch food and water, cook and even tend the wounded.

Adam put a restraining hand on her shoulder as if reading her mind.

'Nay, Lisbeth, you'll have no truck with them. Those women are nothing but whores and scavengers. They earn their living swyving with the soldiers first and then ransacking their butchered carcases afterwards.'

When the time came for Adam to lead his troops off to battle, he looked up at the ramparts where the remorseful Nancy was holding up Patrick and waving his tiny hand for him to bid his father God speed. Elisabeth was giving her brother a last hug when Betsy hirpled up to him.

'Afore you go, take this my brave laddie.'

She pressed a polished stone into his palm and curled his fingers round it. 'To protect you from harm.' Her eyes clouded over. 'And mind, beware the burn.'

Elisabeth looked puzzled.

'Water,' Betsy replied, her misty eyes seeing beyond the present. 'It's a prophecy of True Thomas. He foretold the flooded field and the hidden burn.'

'I swear to you, Betsy, we will brook no hidden burn, for we are Hep-burns, are we not! Time to keep tryst,' Adam laughed gaily. Grasping the talisman tightly, the warrior waved his fist in the air, a signal for the drums to start beating and the men to follow.

Chapter Eleven
Confrontation

Ane false intent under ane fair pretence
Has causit mony innocent to die.
—*The Puddock and the Mouse*, Robert Henryson, 15th Century

Hailes Castle, August 1513

Hilter-kilter down the brae she somersaulted, head over heels, tumbling over tussocks and divots, before landing in the mire at the foot. High overhead black birds circled the air. Corbies. Birds of ill-omen, the ravens flapped their deathly wings like black flags. She splayed her hands and feet to try and stand up, but she kept sinking in the bog. Underfoot the land was sodden and swampy, fed by a reddish brown burn burbling half-hidden among the bracken.

Wheeling round and round, the crows' shrieks became more strident before they plunged headlong downwards. Across the burn a thin mist obscured shadowy figures, waving their arms, whether in greeting or warning she couldn't tell. She kilted up her skirt to wade into the burn but her feet kept slipping on slimy pebbles.

Suddenly the burn bubbled up and a torrent swept her off her feet. As she was tossed around in the murky water, body parts whirled past. A jagged limb, the hand with the rotting flesh and, worst of all, the severed head spinning towards her, baring its teeth. She opened her mouth...

'Where is he?' Prior John was louring over her, his fiercesome eyes blazing as he yanked the blankets off her bed.

Still woozy from her horrifying nightmare, Elisabeth cowered into a tight ball. Was she still dreaming? She wiped the sleep from the corners of her eyes.

'Where is thon sleekit tod slouching?' The prior had drawn out his dirk to stab at the blankets and knelt down to search under the bed. He hauled himself up and kicked open the lid of the kist. He pulled out clothes with one hand and thrust his dirk into them with the other. Breathing heavily, he slammed the lid shut with a juddering bang.

'I trust you're not plucking at any crow to scouk your obligation, my lass. If this is some girlish fancy, another bee-heided ploy on your part to flee your fate, then make no mistake, as soon as I lay my hands on that rapscallion who has dared to defile you, I'll send him off with more than a flea in his ear. This is what I will do to him.'

Elisabeth braced herself, hugging her knees closer to her chest as he loomed over her, his hooded eyelids shading his violet eyes, his full red lips spluttering.

'I will gladly put my hands on his thrapple like this...' She gasped as his clammy hands ringed her neck and his thumbs pressed firmly on her gullet, 'until he is choking for breath. Then I shall cut off his pistle and stuff it into his gob to gag the cringing coward's whimpers. After that, I shall ram a rod up his sliddery arse and slice him in two. His belly I will slash in front of his eyes, gralloch him like a deer and pull out his gizzards.

'I will then take great delight in wrenching him limb from accursed limb and cast his remains to the howling beasts. That's what I shall do to the man who has dared to cross me and make off with my precious jewel. If he has any sense, he'll get himself killed in the fray. An arrow straight through the skull from some merciful archer.'

Snorting and grunting like a fierce bull in full charge, the prior's primal wrath was magnificent to behold. Elisabeth's mouth was dry: she swallowed hard. How had he found out? Who had told him? The prior leant over her, his breath hot and steamy in her face as he waggled his head in disbelief.

'It can't be true my niece would run off willingly with such a wastrel as yon stable lad.'

'Stable lad?' She felt herself go limp with relief. 'You mean Harry Cockburn?' Nervousness made her titter. 'That gangly, tongue-tackit lad?' Whose spotty baw face turned as red as his hair every time she looked at him. 'Oh, uncle, how could you think for one moment that we were running away together?'

'Nay, but I was led to believe...' he broke off.

She knelt forward and grasped his hands. 'Dearest uncle, you must understand. I had to say farewell to Adam. Before he went off to battle. And Harry offered to take me.'

'Aye, that is what I was afraid of.'

She beamed him a smile of pure innocence 'Uncle! How can you think so ill of him! Harry would defend me with his life.'

The prior's dark eyes narrowed in suspicion. 'That's as may be, but I am taking steps to ensure that neither he nor any other man gets close to you. While you, my taiglesome lass, will now have to learn to graith the harness. You'll be confined to your cell to cleanse your body and soul in preparation for receiving the sacrament of Holy Orders.'

Chapter Twelve
The Miracle of the Flood

Hail, mother and maid without macle
Bright sign, gladding our languishing
By might of thy miracle.
—*Ane Ballat of Our Lady*, William Dunbar, 15th–16th Century

St Mary's Abbey, 8 September 1513

The statue of the Black Madonna swayed ungracefully on the bier at the head of the procession meandering its way down to the river. Too stout to walk the short distance from the abbey, Prioress Janet swung heavily in a litter strung between two ponies that picked their way gingerly over the uneven ground. Trudging behind, Prior Hepburn wished that he, too, could have been borne in a litter. Soaked through by the constant drizzle, his lavishly embroidered vestments weighed heavily on him.

Every year on the Nativity of the Blessed Virgin Mary, he celebrated a Mass of Thanksgiving to the patroness of the abbey. The 8th of September was also the anniversary of the Miracle of the Flood that had occurred in 1358. Then the calm waters of the Tyne had become a raging torrent that had destroyed houses and bridges, swept away newly harvested sheaves from the fields, drowned kye and livestock and carried off huge oaks and trees down to the sea. A great many folk lost their lives trying to save their meagre belongings. Save for the intervention of a pious nun from St Mary's Abbey, who implored the Mother of God to come to their aid, much worse could have befallen them.

Every year Prior Hepburn used the anniversary to remind his flock that even worse may befall those who neglected to pay their tithes. However, Dame Janet had balked at his veiled threat.

'Not this year, brother,' she told him. 'The women cannot pay on time.'

'Then I shall threaten to excommunicate them with bell, book and candle,' the prior replied. 'That will strike the fear of hell and damnation into their souls.'

Dame Janet's head wobbled from side to side on her fleshy neck. 'Much good your curses will do you. Show some mercy, brother. The women have been left to gather in the harvest while their menfolk have answered the king's call to arms. These braw lads may be paying for the safety of the realm with the ultimate sacrifice—their lives—and it will be solace and consolation their women are seeking from the clergy, not hell and damnation. You'd do better to pray for victory in the coming battle—that's what the folk want to hear—and for another miracle. A sign that heaven is on our side would not go amiss.'

The mood among the crowd—mostly women, children and old men—on the Abbey Bridge was tense. Hunched against the rain, they silently watched the procession come to a halt by the water's edge where the statue was slowly lowered to the ground. Robed in the rough brown habit of a novice, Elisabeth knelt down before it, clasped her hands in prayer and bowed her head in an attitude of humility. Dame Janet tugged at the prior's chasuble.

'Behold, brother. It seems our niece has taken heed of her lesson.'

'Aye, she plays her part well. Perhaps she has the makings of a nun after all.'

While Prior John blessed the Black Madonna with oil of chrism, a strong-armed curate swung the golden thurible back and forth on a heavy chain. The smouldering incense used to smother the stench of the unwashed and enshroud the ceremony in mystery, was making Elisabeth's eyes stream and catching in her throat. Choking back a desire to retch, she bent down to pick up the statue. To the strains of the choir chanting *Salvemus,* she lurched towards the river. The Black Madonna seemed to be growing heavier and heavier by the second and her arms ached as she struggled to keep it aloft. Raindrops streamed down her face like tears as she strove to utter the magic prayer:

'Holy Mary, Mother of God, help us in our hour of need. Protect thy house from the waters. Save us from peril ... or else...'

The crudely painted, egg-shaped face of the Madonna swirled before her eyes, its enigmatic smile distorting into a ghastly grimace. Go on, I dare you, it taunted. The booming sound in her ears grew louder and the world began to spin round. In a bid to be rid of this unholy burden, she pitched forwards onto her knees and cried out, 'Or else Thy Divine Image shall be cast into the waters.'

'What, in the name of the Virgin most holy, was the wee pagan doing now?' Sister Maryoth muttered. With supernatural effort, she picked up the skirts of her habit and shot forwards. She made a frantic lunge for the statue as it rolled down towards the river where it teetered teasingly for a moment on the brink before tumbling in with a scornful splash.

The crowd gasped as the statue sank, their choral 'Oooh' of horror changing to 'Aaah' of relief, as it bobbed up again out of the murky depths. Desperate to save the icon from a sacrilegious dunking, Sister Maryoth flung herself into the water and floundered towards it. Stumbling on the stony riverbed, she steered the icon towards the side where choirboys were waiting to haul it out. Spluttering out slimy river water, the sodden saviour of the Madonna crawled out of the sludge onto the marshy bank.

'Trust Maryoth to fling herself body and soul into the task,' Dame Janet remarked, 'Baptism by total immersion. John the Baptist himself will be waggling his sainted head with pride. Will this impress the faithful, do you think?'

Prior John, however, was not amused. 'It's bad enough with those two competing to making a bauchle out of me without your barbs, Janet,' he carped.

But his sister's perceptive comments made him reflect. The prior turned to address the crowd. Like a giant bird of prey he raised his arms draped in the heavy embroidered chasuble and proclaimed. 'Let us give thanks to God the Father and his Holy Mother for granting his humble servants another miracle. Behold how the Black Madonna floats on water! This sign from Our Lady of the Flood pledges victory over our enemies. On the field of the coming battle we *shall* prevail,' he declaimed triumphantly.

Chapter Thirteen
Flodden

And wond'rous weel they kept their troth;
This sturdy royal band
Rush'd down the brae, wi' sic a pith,
That nane could them withstand.
—*The Ballad of the Laird of Muirhead,* Traditional

St Mary's Abbey, 13 September 1513

The sound of raindrops drumming non-stop against the window shutter woke her early. Elisabeth groaned. Since the day of the miracle of the flood, the rain had never ceased. The constant downpours not only seemed to be confirming her guilt but were conspiring to make her punishment more difficult. Three times a day she had to get down on her hands and knees and wash the chapel floor. Already the skin on her hands was chapped and raw from wringing out the cloth in a bucket of cold water and the scabs on her knees never had time to heal. More rain, more pain.

Splashing through the puddles on her way to the chapel, she noticed more beggars and paupers than usual sheltering in the courtyard. Heaps of tattered rain-soaked blankets stirred and, from deep within one huddled pile, a child whimpered.

At Mass that morning, Prior Hepburn was raising the sacred chalice for the Eucharist when a bedraggled, glaur-ridden figure came staggering up the aisle to the high altar. Elisabeth's heart sank at the muddy trail left by his tattered footcloths.

Sister Maryoth rose from her knees. 'How dare you break into our service! This is a house of God. We are at prayer.'

The lad slumped down at the altar steps and burst into sobs. 'Aye, and all your prayers will be needed on this woeful day. Scotland is lost. Our king and countrymen—all wede awa'!'

The nuns fluttered round him, anxious for news of their kinfolk. The noblest lairds of the land had fallen on the fatal field of Flodden, among them the gallant twenty-one-year-old earl of Bothwell, cut down while leading the bold men of East Lothian into the fray.

'My nephew! Slain? The king's army routed?' Hepburn's florid face grew pale. 'May God have mercy on their souls.'

Some of the nuns followed his lead and began to pray but, when one of the older nuns began keening, others joined in this more ancient custom, their doleful lament drowning out any religious prayers.

'And who brings these terrible tidings?' The prior questioned. He peered at the lad, unrecognisable in tattered clothing slathered in gore and glaur, before bawling, 'The cream of the country perishes but you survive? How is it that you escaped? Or did you flee the field afeart, Harry Cockburn?'

The prior lumbered down from the altar and began kicking the miserable stable lad lying crumpled in a heap on the steps. He ordered Sister Maryoth to fetch the abbey watchmen. Too old for warfare, these men were keeping their pelts dry and slaking their drouth with ale in the kitchen.

'Coward and sneak thief that you are, Harry Cockburn! Scum such as you don't deserve to live. I'll have you scourged until the skin flakes from your back like the bark of a birch.'

Grabbing Harry by the scruff of the neck, Hepburn threw him to the watchmen who tied his hands behind his back and marched him back down the aisle. While Sister Maryoth led the little procession out of the chapel, the prior shuffled back up the altar and flicked through the pages of the Holy Missal. The

Mass in Time of War for the salvation of the king's servants and the extinction of his enemies was no longer right and fitting.

'*Requiem eternam.*' He growled the opening words of the Mass for the Dead.

Over the next few days, clusters of stragglers and camp followers who had come seeking food and shelter lay sprawled around the abbey courtyard and cloister. Their forty days' supply of victuals had been used up long before the battle, leaving their menfolk too weak and hungry to fight. As she passed among them handing out weak ale and bread, Elisabeth tried to glean any scraps of information about Adam or Lindsay, but there had been too much carnage, too much butchery for the slain to be identified.

Their stories were heartrending. Men who had removed their boots to keep their footing as they charged down the slippery brae had slipped and fallen. Others had tripped over their unwieldy pikes to be trampled to death in the marsh by those coming behind. Yet more had drowned as they stumbled to wade across the burn.

'There was a burn?' Elisabeth gave a jolt. Hadn't Betsy warned Adam of a burn?

Tragically, that was their undoing. In their plan of attack, the leaders hadn't foreseen the marshy stream hidden among reeds at the foot of the brae.

'And yet the rout was foretold,' a woman with a bairn suckling at her breast declared, 'but they paid no heed. Did it never cross their minds why the accursed field was named Flodden edge? And now the burn is running crimson with their blood.'

'It was thon French general's fault.' Hauching phlegm in her throat, a sturdy woman dressed in ill-fitting breeches, spat out a slimy gobbet to show her contempt. 'Arming our menfolk with waffly bits of stick. For, if thon fancy French spikes didn't shatter in the rumption, the English billhooks smashed them all to smithereens. Waving a handful of thistles would have been wiser. At least they could have stung their arses.'

Her vitriol unleashed a communal catharsis of grief among the women who began to pour out their harrowing descriptions. How could they begin to identify their loved ones scythed down in battle? They'd had to leave the butchered carcases of their loved ones strewn about Flodden field, to be feasted on by flocks of corbies and gnawed at by curs and rats.

Elisabeth pinched her wrists to keep from fainting and swallowed hard to keep the brash from rising in her throat. And when they described how crows pecked out the eyes from cloven heads and gorged on minced brains, her hand flew to her mouth. Did they howk out Adam's bonny blue een?

And what about the king's herald? Was there any news of him? In his red and gold tabard, Lindsay would have stood out on the battlefield, but the women shook their heads wearily. The chaos was such that many were still unaccounted for. Could he have been taken prisoner? Nay, they jeered. Knowing that the English would grant no quarter, the Scots had fought to their last breath. Few, if any, had surrendered.

When the camp followers had tried to bury their dead, the triumphant English had chased them from the field, mercilessly stripping the bodies naked of anything valuable. These sluts and whores, as Adam had cried them, began beating their breasts with guilt and remorse that their menfolk hadn't been given a decent burial. The Abbess of Coldingham had shown some Christian charity by allowing the fallen to be buried in the abbey graveyard, but only the corpses of the few identified as highborn. Those of the common soldiers were left as fodder for the corbies.

'And King James? What of him?' Elisabeth feared the reply, for she was sure that Lindsay would have shared his fate. He would never, ever have left his monarch's side. Reports were contradictory. That the king had fallen under his own banner; that Lord Home had carried him off the field, wounded but still alive; that the English had taken him prisoner. So the flame of hope still burned in her breast.

But not in that of Sister Maryoth whose brother, John, Lord Hay of Yester had been slain. The sisters took it in turns to press their ear against the door of the chapel, listening to the sounds of wailing and lamentation from within. Consider how his sacred flesh was scourged to shreds, Sister Maryoth howled, how his divine head was crowned with thorns, the blood gushing down his heavenly face. Consider how the nails impaled his hands and feet.

In penitential sackcloth, Sister Maryoth was following the stations of the cross, Christ's final journey to Golgotha. The coarse cloth chafed at her skin while around her waist she'd fastened a heavy chain that cut into her flesh, forming angry looking weals. After dragging herself on her knees to pray at each station on the *Via Dolorosa*, she flopped, face down onto the cold flagstones to contemplate the horror of the crucifixion.

These acts of self-mortification she endured for her brother's sake. As a martyr who had sacrificed his life at Flodden he should go straight to heaven, but Maryoth dared not presume divine will. Offering up her suffering, however, should ensure a plenary indulgence for his soul's immediate release from purgatory or, at the very least, a considerable reduction in his sentence there. Hell was not an option.

The sisters witnessing this display swithered from being awe-stricken at her extreme piety to being worried that she'd lost her wits. Her lamentations, however, left Elisabeth cold. Her own scullion hands and skinned knees were testament to her thrice-daily penance. What a pity Sister Maryoth had not put her self-indulgent breast-beating to better use by giving the chapel flagstone a good scrubbing while on her knees.

Two days and nights Sister Maryoth fasted and kept vigil until very early on the third morning, while the rest of the convent slumbered, she fell into a swoon. Flashes of light zigzagged in front of her eyes and illuminated her soul with a revelation: that the slaughter of the flower of Scottish manhood was not the fault of the foolish and misguided King James. No, Almighty God was taking revenge: casting his Son and Mother into the waters of the Tyne had been an act of blasphemy.

Coming out of her trance, Sister Maryoth prayed to the Black Madonna for divine disclosure. What had possessed this wild child to commit such a sacrilege? An evil spirit or, heaven forfend, Satan himself? After all, Elisabeth had been brought up by that old witch, Betsy Learmont. What black arts had she taught her? The Prince of Darkness was amongst them and God in his wisdom had entrusted his humble and obedient servant Maryoth with the task of purging this evil from their midst.

Chapter Fourteen
Ordination

Then would I say: 'If God me had ordained
To live my life in thraldome thus and pain:
What was the cause that He me more constrained
Than other folk to live in such ruin?'
—*The King's Quair*, James I, 15th Century

St Mary's Abbey, 9 November 1513

Arrayed in the virginal white of a novice with a wreath of embroidered flowers crowning her chestnut hair, Elisabeth approached the altar and genuflected. Prior Hepburn smiled indulgently.

'Her recent loss seems to have purged our bee-heided niece of all her daft notions.'

'Aye,' Dame Janet replied. 'Now that her fiery temper has been smoored, you'll find our niece more willing to accept her fate.'

Elisabeth's fire had indeed been quenched. A few days before, at the Requiem Mass on All Souls' Day, Prior Hepburn had read out the roll call of the fallen at Flodden. To help her *endure fort* Elisabeth had fumbled for the talisman she'd hidden underneath her sark. Looped onto the blue ribbon were the king's ring and the St John's nut, its kernel pierced with a needle. On hearing Adam's name she pressed it against her heart but was shocked and numbed when she caught the name

—Sir David Lindsay. Her heart shoogled. Lindsay had been slain. Her spirit was broken.

'Dies Irae, Dies illa. Day of Wrath, that dreadful day,' the choir had chanted, '*Lacrimosa dies illa.*'

Now, at her ordination, the prior was well pleased at how meekly his niece had surrendered to his will. Nevertheless, anointing her on the forehead with holy chrism, he was not so pleased to see that her downcast eyes were red and swollen and her face pinched and pale. He must have a word with Maryoth not to be so harsh.

After Elisabeth had pledged her vows, he presented her with two gifts. From a velvet-lined box he took out a string of rosary beads made from freshwater pearls with an exquisite silver crucifix that glinted in the candlelight. He draped it over her wrist and placed in her hands a *Book of Hours*, expensively illustrated with a jewel-encrusted cover and gold clasp. The newly ordained nun could only nod her thanks.

The sacrificial lamb was led into the sacristy where Sister Maryoth tore off the wreath and put away the pearl rosary beads and the gaudily engraved *Book of Hours* for safekeeping. Then she set about cutting the novice's hair. She grabbed it in tufts and hacked at it clumsily, cropping it back almost to the scalp, all the while muttering prayers and incantations under her breath to fend off evil.

'Lord, she is not worthy. Lord, forgive me for this shameful offering. Cast out the horned Prince of Darkness from this child of Satan,' Maryoth mumbled and then halted. 'What's this?' Her hand had become entangled in the blue ribbon round Elisabeth's neck. 'A holy scapular?'

Having no idea what a scapular was, Elisabeth gripped hold of it and nodded.

Sister Maryoth sneered. 'That I very much doubt. For a heathen such as you, it's more likely to be a lucky charm,' she said and tugged at the ribbon, snapping the love knot and sending the ring and the nut clattering onto the flagstones.

Elisabeth dropped to her knees, splaying her fingers to search for them but as she crawled about, Maryoth stamped on her knuckles and then crunched the nut underfoot. The ring had rolled away unseen.

'As for this.' Sister Maryoth dangled the blue ribbon as if it were a venomous viper. 'The only way to be rid of this devil's tail is to burn it.' With that, she held it over a candle, watching intently until it shrivelled to cinders. The vicious look in her narrowed eyes betrayed a desire to dispose of her rival in the same way.

Meekly the newly shorn lamb obeyed the order to strip off her white lace gown and stood shivering in the cold vestry, hugging her tender breasts. Elisabeth closed her eyes as the dun-coloured habit was pulled down over her head, prickling her scalp and scratching her skin. Even when the callous sister tugged the hempen cord and knotted it tightly until it dug into her waist Elisabeth did not flinch.

For now that she had lost Lindsay and her only connection to him had been severed, nothing mattered any more. She didn't even have the St John's nut to protect her from the evil eye. Covering her shaven head with the wimple and securing the ties, Sister Maryoth thrust a heavy wooden crucifix, crudely carved with the figure of the dead saviour into her hands.

'You are a bride of Christ, now. Kiss your holy spouse, Sister Elisabeth.'

Chapter Fifteen
Birth

> The Lord God formed man of the dust from the ground
> and breathed into his nostrils the breath of life;
> And man became a living soul.
>
> —*Genesis* II:7

St Mary's Abbey, 30 November 1513

Her head bowed under her cowl against the skelping wind, Elisabeth scurried across the courtyard to the chapel. The regular gaggle of beggars sheltering in the porch, squinted suspiciously at the straggly line straying into their patch. Cripples on homemade crutches hobbled alongside the feeble and infirm being hauled on makeshift litters of ragged sheets, while other, less fortunate souls, had to shauchle along on their hands and knees, dragging their scruntit bodies through the grime and glaur.

'There's o'er mony for the money,' the beggars grumbled uncharitably, though they had no need to fret. For the pilgrims, who'd trudged through hail, wind and sleet, hadn't come to poach their alms but to press their lips to the holy relic.

After the humiliating rout at Flodden, doubts about the miraculous powers of the Black Madonna had been spreading like a plague of boils amongst his flock. To rekindle their faith, Prior Hepburn was sending a precious bone of Saint Andrew to the abbey. To touch it may, or may not, procure a cure in this world, but would certainly guarantee a plenary indulgence—

total remission of their time in purgatory—in the next, so he promised. The parish priest, Father Dudgeon, had argued for the relic to be displayed in the larger collegiate church of St Mary's since it could accommodate more of the faithful. Prior Hepburn had refused. The precious relic would be shown in a pavilion in the grounds of the abbey for, if any miracle did occur, he wanted the glory to go to his convent.

Waiting their turn to venerate the relic, the pilgrims huddled together against the snell wind, teeth and tongues chattering. Which fragment of the sainted apostle's body would it be? His upper-arm bone or kneecap, perhaps, or even a finger from the cathedral's collection? When word came through that the tiny silver reliquary contained not a forefinger, a thumb or even a pinkie, but a tooth, the pilgrims choked back their disappointment. Size should not matter as they puckered their lips to kiss the magic box containing the blackened stump of a molar.

Sister Maryoth's lips also puckered—in disgust at the sight of all those filthy mouths covered in suppurating sores defiling the sacred relic. She sniffed deeply into the pouch scented with rose oil to stave off the stench, before turning her wrinkled nose to where the professional paupers were squabbling and jostling for position. As keeper of the priory purse she organised the alms distribution, an act of charity she begrudged, for it tugged at her heart strings to undo the abbey purse strings and dole out to unworthy scroungers. Gathering the nuns round her she dispensed coins and warnings.

'Keep your distance, sisters, or you risk being infested with lice. Do not be fooled by thon feckless leeches who elbow their way to the front. So as to wheedle alms the sleekit sluggards rub their sores with buttercup sap to keep them pus-ridden.'

Elisabeth kept her head down to avoid the louring looks, not only from Sister Maryoth but from the knot of tight-lipped women with whimpering weans on their hips and pinched-faced toddlers clinging to their skirts. Shivering in sullen silence, these widows of Flodden were black affronted at having to ask for charity. They carefully counted up the meagre offerings being doled out and grumbled that it was a lot less than the tithes exacted from them at harvest time: the lives of their menfolk worth hardly a groat.

She was emptying the last of the coins from her pouch when a sudden squall sent the beggars scurrying for cover and the sisters scuttling back to the abbey. Feeling faint from fasting for the feast, Elisabeth lagged behind the others when she felt a hand tug at her cloak. A young lad, no more than four or five years old was hopping from one bare foot to the other to keep them from the freezing ground. His pleading eyes loomed huge above sunken cheekbones as he held out his hand.

'Poor wee Willie,' a woman muttered. 'His father fell at Flodden and his mother's baggit with another bairn.'

'Aye, she's in travail at this very minute,' her companion said. 'She'd no money for a skeily-wife and the howdie is doing all she can. But they've sent over to Hailes for Mistress Learmont.'

'Aye, Betsy Learmont has the knack. She'll see her through.'

Betsy was here! Elisabeth gave Willie a coin and asked him to take her home. Let Maryoth in her mercy chastise her for carrying out an act of charity.

She followed the lad through Giffordgait, past rundown hovels that became more and more dilapidated as they neared the Nungate Bridge. Smoke from peat fires hanging heavily over the turfed roofs blurred her vision, making it difficult to avoid stepping into what could be either mud or dung or both. The recent rain had enriched the sharp, sour stench rising from the gutters swilling with sewage. Scraggy hens squawked and squabbled on sodden midden heaps until scattered by a pack of feral dogs. The lad stopped at the broken-down door of a butt-and-ben, squatting at the edge of the Tyne in the shadow of the magnificent collegiate church of St Mary's on the other side of the river.

The door scraped open and Elisabeth had to stoop to enter. The reek from the mutton-fat tapers stung her eyes, blinding her for a few moments. When her eyes had adjusted to the murky light she saw the lad on his knees, blowing onto a log to rekindle the flame under the cauldron of tepid water suspended on a swey. Muffled sounds came from the corner where a woman with a cloth stuffed into her mouth was writhing on a pallet of chaff. The howdie, a local woman who helped out in childbirth, was leaning over her, trying to wipe the sweat from her brow as she tossed her head from side to side. At the other end, Betsy was busy wringing out blood-soaked cloths. With her eyes smarting and her nose itching, Elisabeth strove unsuccessfully to stifle a sneeze.

Betsy whirled round. 'Sakes me, Lisbeth, what are you doing here? This is no place for a young lass. Away you go.'

'I heard the lad's mother needed help,' Elisabeth replied.

Betsy sighed. 'Well, lass, you might as well make yourself useful. You mop her brow while Annie boils up the brew.' She handed the howdie some dried leaves wrapped in muslin.

'Why is she gagged like that?' Elisabeth whispered. 'To stop her screaming?'

'Nay, lass, it gives her something to bite on other than her own tongue,' Betsy explained. 'It helps her to thole the birthing showers, the spasms that push the bairn out. But I fear her travail's been over long. She's losing strength.'

When the howdie untied the gag and tilted her head forward, the woman let out a shriek.

'Wheesht, Maggie, wheesht! Have a wee sip of this if you're able,' Betsy urged. 'It'll help ease the bairn through.'

When the woman grimaced with pain convulsed by another contraction, Betsy fumbled around in the large pockets of her skirt and produced a poke, a small muslin bag containing a powder. She whispered to the howdie, 'The raspberry leaves aren't working, something more drastic is needed.'

She shook some of the powder onto her palm and cautiously dabbed Maggie's tongue with tiny specks. Too powerful a dose of deadly nightshade could be just that, she explained to Elisabeth. Deadly. The miniscule dose Betsy administered would, she hoped, put the mother to sleep and leave her to get on with prising the reluctant babe from the womb. Within minutes Maggie stopped struggling, closed her eyes and went limp.

'Now we can get on with it.' Betsy thrust her head between the woman's thighs and, after much twisting and turning, she yanked out what looked like a haunch of mutton.

The howdie sighed and clasped her hands. 'Ah, the canny moment. Praise be to the Virgin!'

Betsy carefully untangled the cord that had twisted round the baby's neck and bit it off, spitting it out into a bowl. Elisabeth's stomach somersaulted.

'What have we got Betsy? Lad or lass?' the howdie asked.

Betsy examined the infant and frowned. 'A wee laddie,' she said brusquely, more concerned about the faint bluish tinge round the tiny puckered lips. Wiping away the traces of birthing blood and mucous with a cloth, she threw him over her shoulder and thumped his back a few times, but the infant stubbornly refused to take his first breath.

'Has this one taken a scunner to life already? Well, perhaps that's for the best,' Betsy murmured, preparing to swaddle him in his shroud.

'No, Betsy, you can't just let him...' Elisabeth exclaimed. Though the messy, beastly process of birth was curdling her stomach, the thought of letting the bairn die revitalised her.

'Here then, lass, take the wean and blow into his mouth. I'm jiggered. There's no puff left in me. Now don't be feart to give him a fair good blast.'

Betsy passed the infant over to Elisabeth who gawped in panic at the wizened face, thrawn and twisted from the efforts of being born. With his eyes tightly shut, fists clenched and lips pursed, he seemed to be defying life. Tentatively she covered the baby's lips with her own and puffed gently into his mouth. Again, she blew—more strongly this time—filling his tiny lungs with her own breath until she sensed a slight movement in his chest.

'That's the way, lass.' Betsy leaned over and trickled some liquid into the bairn's mouth. He wrinkled his nose and, as the strong spirit hit his gullet, he gave a plaintive cry.

'That's something at least. I was afeart the cord might have throttled him. He'd better not get a taste for the *aquavitae*, mind. He's better off with this,' Betsy said and lay him at his mother's breast where his toothless gums instinctively latched on to her nipple. Woken by her infant's cry, the mother laid a hand on Elisabeth's arm.

'Sister,' she mumbled, 'will you shield him from the fairy blast? Will you be my bairn's godmother and make sure he's christened soon? Afore the fairies spirit him away?'

'Aye, that she will, Maggie,' Betsy answered for her. 'I'll see that she does.'

Once she'd fallen asleep with the bairn suckling at her breast, Betsy brought out the flask again.

'I reckon we need this ourselves now. Not only to wet the bairn's head but to quicken our own spirits. Here's good health and long life to us all.' After taking a long, satisfying swig, Betsy wiped the rim and passed the flask to the howdie.

'And you too, Lisbeth. For though his mother may have borne his body into this world, you breathed life into him and stirred his soul. And from now on, you and thon laddie will aye be thirled together. For as long as you both shall live.'

Elisabeth raised the flask to her lips but instantly recoiled. Throughout the laborious birth, she'd struggled to quell her queasiness, but now just a whiff of the sharp spirit brought waves of nausea welling up from the pit of her stomach. Holding her hand firmly to her mouth, she rushed outside to retch agonisingly into the gutter.

Chapter Sixteen
Baptism

The bairnie she swyl'd in linen so fine,
In a gilded casket she laid it syne,
Mickle saut and light she laid therein
Cause yet in God's house it hadna been.
—*The Ballad of the King's Daughter*, Traditional

St Mary's Abbey, 8 December 1513

At the baptismal font Elisabeth handed the bundle snoozing in her arms to Betsy.

'I ken you'll keep him safe, Betsy. I dread letting such a frail new born drop into the font.'

While Elisabeth held the candle and chrism cloth, Betsy gently pulled back the swaddling shawl for Prior Hepburn to christen the bairn. He'd also agreed, in the absence of anyone else, to stand as his godfather. He peered at the crinkle-faced bairn and then with practised hands, vigorously massaged his ears and nose with his own saliva. Betsy winced as he dabbed his forefinger with salt before winding it into his tiny mouth. To open the portals of evil to the odour of sweetness and sanctity, the prior explained.

Betsy cringed. What kind of religion decreed that this wee mite was a child of darkness and sin, the devil's bird, until a gob of spittle and a splash of water transformed him into a blessed son of God? she wondered. Where was the joy in such a faith? And when the prior asked, 'Dost thou renounce Satan and all his works?' she shook her head. What a daft question for a week-old wean. Betsy unwrapped his swaddling and handed him naked to the prior who anointed him with chrism oil before dunking him in the baptismal font, splashing them all with holy water.

'In nomine Patris, et Filii, et Spiritus Sancti ... '

After the third dunking his watery eyelids flickered but still he made no sound. Brusquely Betsy snatched the infant and rubbed him dry before wrapping him in the chrism cloth. When at last he gave a plaintive whimper, her chest heaved with relief.

'That was chancy. Better than nothing, I jalouse,' she muttered, swiftly withdrawing the pin she had sneakily inserted beneath the chrism cloth. For if the bairn hadn't cried out, it would have been a bad omen, that he wouldn't be long for this world. While the holy water may have exorcised the devil, the pinprick had cast out the evil eye.

Meanwhile, the prior was blessing their new godson three times to bring him into the Christian fold. '*Ioannes Cnoxus*,' he said, christening him in Latin. John Knox.

PART TWO

Chapter Seventeen
Absolution

Next in the dance followit Envy,
Filled full of feud and felony,
Hid malice and dispite.
—*The Dance of the Seven Deadly Sins*,
William Dunbar, 15th–16th Century

St Mary's Abbey, 18 December 1513

The sudden ray of sunlight through the slit window struck the gold leaf and sent glittering shafts skipping around the cell walls. Elisabeth rubbed her eyes. The *Book of Hours* with its lavishly illuminated illustrations was wondrous to behold, but she could make no sense of the mystifying squiggles that made up the text. Even if it were not written in Latin, she still wouldn't be able to understand it. If only she could read.

She loosened the hempen cord digging into her waist and chafing her skin. Peering at the illustration of the Annunciation, she could readily sympathise with the Virgin Mary's plight. When she'd been locked in her punishment cell, doing penance by praying and fasting she hadn't needed to ask for monthly cloths. That, the washerwife had pointed out, was one of the benefits of fasting. It staunched the accursed monthly bleed. And another, she'd added with a conspiratorial wink as she gathered up the linen for washing, was gaining Sister Maryoth's favour for it would be a sign of devotion in her eyes.

Only it wasn't, and the spiteful sister had forced Betsy to confirm her suspicions, that Elisabeth's soul was full of sin and her womb great with child.

Absorbed in her thoughts Elisabeth didn't hear Sister Maryoth slithering into her cell. Her uncle was on his way, the harbinger of doom warned with no attempt to hide her glee.

'Cantle up your spirits, my precious jewel,' Prior Hepburn said forcing a smile, 'and confide in me. I am your confessor.' His puffy face was puckered with concern and he spoke in the wheedling tone he used in the confessional to encourage the penitent to unburden his heart. Elisabeth hesitated, caught off-guard by his solicitous manner. She grimaced. Stomach cramps were making her feel queasy, but her uncle's cloying sympathy was just as nauseous.

'He took you by force, didn't he?' he said, taking her hand. 'Thon sleekit skite, Harry Cockburn did indeed violate my precious jewel! Why didn't you tell us the truth? I should have libbed him when I had the chance. But have no fear, I'll scour the land till yon poltroon's found.'

He squeezed her hand tightly to stem his fury at the loss of his prey. While transferring Harry to the deep pit dungeon at Hailes Castle, those drunken old watchmen had let him slip through their slack hands and denied the prior the pleasure of a scourging.

Elisabeth inhaled deeply. Now was the time to tell the truth. Now was the time to confess that her father's child was not the dim-witted Harry, but Sir David Lindsay. What would it matter now that he was dead? She couldn't let the lowly stable lad take the blame and bear the brunt of her uncle's wrath. Harry didn't deserve that.

Behind the prior's back, Sister Maryoth was smirking quietly to herself, silently giving thanks to God that her scheme had come to fruition. She had paid the washerwife to be on the alert for tell-tale signs, and now Elisabeth's broadening girth could not hide the truth. Soon her prayers would be answered, leaving the way open for her ambition to be fulfilled. Prioress Hay of St Mary's Abbey! Dame Maryoth! While the prospect made her quiver with excitement, she must not let herself be seduced by the sin of pride.

When Elisabeth whimpered like a helpless kitten and allowed the prior to drew her to him in a comforting embrace she sensed panic in Sister Maryoth's eyes.

'We shall be sorry to lose our dear sister Elisabeth,' she blurted, 'but of course it would be unseemly for a future prioress to bear a child. Forbye, virginity is a prerequisite of our order and chastity our most important vow.' She narrowed her lips to prevent them from breaking into a gloating, self-righteous smirk and cast her eyes downwards.

So that's what she was scheming. Her feigned humility didn't fool Elisabeth. By showing mercy and forgiving his niece, the prior would be jeopardising Maryoth's ambition.

'Don't be too hard on Harry, dearest uncle,' Elisabeth began. 'He's a simple soul.'

'Not so simple that he doesn't know what to do with his pistle,' the prior growled.

'But Harry thought that I hankered after him and that, when I tried to push him away, I was only teasing and jiggling him. But he's a strong lad and, well...' Elisabeth turned away to hide her blushes.

'Wheesht, my precious pearl, it's not your fault. I'm sure you didn't lead him on.' As Hepburn pulled her into his arms, his wiry beard scratched her cheek. She tried not to wince.

'I didn't, uncle. He truly believed I was giving him the glad eye because,' she paused to glare over her uncle's shoulder, 'Sister Maryoth told him so.' There. *That* would take the starch out of her wimple.

Sister Maryoth's smooth oval face clouded over. 'By the Holy Virgin, Mary, the Mother of God,' she began, clutching her rosary with two hands, 'I would never encourage such... such... lechery.' Her eyes widened. 'How can she say such a thing? After I took pity on her and let her go out riding! None of us could be her chaperone, so who better than Harry? I was only doing what I thought best, and this is how she repays me.' She drew a square of linen cloth from her sleeve and snivelled into it.

'Steek your gab, sister.' The prior leapt up to jab a finger at her. 'It's a pity silence isn't one of your vows. My niece has been ravished and it's all the fault of your wagging tongue. That you could suggest such a lout as yon stable lad could even look at my niece! To kittle him up so that he'd be bold enough to pluck her precious cherry!'

Sister Maryoth tried not to flinch as flecks of spittle splattered her face. The prior looked round, caught sight of Elisabeth's gilded *Book of Hours* and grabbed it from the shelf. Not the Bible, but the next best thing.

'Whatever is said within the walls of this chamber is sacrosanct. Do you hear?' He waggled a menacing finger at her. 'Nothing that is discussed here will—on pain of your life—nay—on the loss of your immortal soul, be spoken of anywhere, to anyone, at any time. And, to make sure that you do...' he said, holding out the book. 'Swear an oath.'

Prior Hepburn stomped along to his sister's chamber and shook her awake from her post-prandial slumber. Dame Janet wiped the sleep from bleary, blackened eyes to listen to her brother's sorry tale.

'What's done is done,' she said, her mouth gaping wide in a lazy yawn. 'And a corbie is no whiter for being washed. And after your threats, brother, I doubt we'll see young Harry in these parts again.' She leant over to choose a bonbon from the box by her bedside so as to sweeten her mouth stale with sleep.

'Our niece is more sinned against than sinning,' the prior declared. 'And since I have the power to absolve her, she is now as pure as the day she was born.'

'Like Christ's Holy Mother? You're surely not saying there was no stain of original sin on Lisbeth's soul as well? Immaculate virgin and mother most chaste? That's quite a claim,' she remarked with a little chortle. 'So, we're to have our very own virgin birth in our midst, brother? Now that will indeed be a miracle.'

Her plump shoulders shook with laughter, but the prior scowled. 'Your flippancy is unseemly at such a time.'

'Tell Maryoth, to bring me Betsy,' Dame Janet ordered.

As she led the forlorn-looking nurse to the prioress's chamber, Sister Maryoth's fingers plied up and down her rosary to ward off the witch's evil miasma. With her folklore and superstitions and arcane knowledge of female problems, Betsy was at worst a godless heathen and at best a follower of the auld, Celtic religion. A witch in other words, though she'd never dare to utter this aloud.

'Away and tell your beads elsewhere, Maryoth. This is not for your ears.' Prior Hepburn pointed to the door.

Hostility oozed like black bile from the holy nun as she passed the ungodly pagan on her way out. The prior waited a few moments, opened the door again and, satisfied no-one was eavesdropping, said, 'Betsy, you're the canny woman, so tell us, what can be done about this?'

Thoroughly miserable, Betsy shook her head. 'It's no the bairn's fault it's misbegotten. If only I'd found out earlier when it was still a tottie wee mite, I'd have no qualms about scouring it out. But Lisbeth is at least four months gone. Forbye,' she said, raising her eyebrows, 'is it no against God's law to redd out a wean? Even if the mother's life is at risk and she's struggling to feed another four or five, the unborn bairn must be saved, so the priests say. A canny wife like me could be put in the jougs for helping out a mother at her wits' end.'

'Well, Betsy, rest assured that will not happen,' the prior promised. 'And the Church has the authority to overlook a minor indiscretion when the greater good is being served.'

Shifting in her seat, Betsy shot him a sideways glance. 'You mean turn a blind eye when it suits them?'

Chapter Eighteen
Visitation

The heartly joy God give ye had seen
Was shown when that their sisters met!
—*The Tale of the Uplands Mouse and the Burgess Mouse,*
Robert Henryson, 15th Century

Tantallon Castle, Yuletide 1513

Etched against the darkening sky, the jagged outline of Tantallon seemed to be ablaze as a shaft of low winter sun flashed through the murky rain clouds to set the castle's red stone on fire. Elisabeth sat bolt upright in the saddle, bringing her horse abruptly to a halt.

Betsy trotted up alongside on her pony. 'What's wrong, my lass?'

'It looks ... eerie.' A shiver of apprehension ran through Elisabeth.

Betsy nodded. 'Aye, I ken fine what you mean. It gives me the cold creeps, too.'

Their ponies clattered over the drawbridge and through the portcullis into the fortress perched precariously on cliffs overlooking the Firth of Forth. The huge iron gate of the impregnable Douglas stronghold clanged shut behind them. The last rays of the setting sun had long passed away and the deep shadows of towering walls cast a gloom even more terrifying than absolute darkness. Elisabeth had been looking forward to spending Yuletide with her sister at Tantallon, but now, gazing up at the high walls, she felt more trapped than she'd ever been in the convent.

Swaddled in a fox fur cloak, Meg scampered across the frost-covered courtyard to greet them, a vulnerable little dormouse against the backdrop of the castle walls.

'You've come at last!' she cried, flinging herself upon them.

'How could we turn down the invitation of such a grand lady! Countess of Angus, no less.'

Elisabeth squeezed her sister tightly. Even through her woollen cloak and velvet dress she could feel her bones, as spindly and fragile as a wren's. Though never big and buxom, Meg seemed to have shrunk and, despite her newly elevated rank and expensive garments, was looking unhappily gaunt and woebegone.

'Thanks be to God someone is glad for me. Not everyone here is overjoyed.' Meg cupped her mouth with her hand and glanced upwards at the shuttered windows. 'My mother-in-law is sore affronted that she missed her turn to be countess.'

Flodden had not only carried off Lady Douglas's husband, George, master of Angus, and his brother, but had cheated her out of her title. And then, while they were still in mourning, her father-in-law, the fifth earl, had died only a few days before, leaving the title to Archie.

'We aye thought that Bell the Cat must have at least nine lives! But losing his two brave sons in such a stramash broke his heart. And Lady Douglas is seething that one of the auld man's mistresses—Janet Kennedy who claims he married her—has crawled out of her scutter hole, demanding a share of his estate. She's threatened to put a hex on the hizzie!'

'Aye, her long neb has been sorely put out of joint,' Betsy remarked. 'She'll no be using it now as a kirnstick to curdle cream.'

The girls burst into giggles but when the frosty air caught their breath and Meg started coughing, Betsy hustled them inside. As they warmed themselves in front of the log fire, Elisabeth pulled open her cloak to reveal her bump.

'A bairn? You're going to have a bairn?' Meg seemed wonderstruck. 'But, Lisbeth, how can that be? You're a nun! You've just taken your vows! You've never lain with a man!' She paused, 'Have you?'

Elisabeth took a deep breath before relating her tale. When she'd finished and Meg asked where Davie was now, she had to bite her lip. 'He was slain. Along with Adam.'

'May their souls rest in peace,' Meg murmured, crossing herself. 'Oh, my poor, dear Lisbeth, what are you going to do?'

'Never fash, my bonnie lasses. It will all work out fine,' Betsy replied, although quite how, she wasn't sure. Regular doses of raspberry leaf tisanes had failed to bring on her courses, and Elisabeth hadn't been able to keep down the hot toddy of juniper berries simmered in aquavitae long enough to do its work. The roots of the lesser meadow rue, usually a proven remedy, had only loosened her bowels. Hot mustard baths and even the vigorous ride from Hailes had failed to slacken her womb. More invasive procedures Betsy would not consider for her dear thistledown. Nature would have to take its course.

'But Lisbeth, you'll never be able to bring up a bairn in a convent,' Meg said. You'll have to leave. And come here. Aye, that's it! You can come here to have your bairn!' She leapt to her feet, clapping her hands together. 'Perhaps this is God's will!' Her forget-me-not blue eyes flashed and two little crimson spots brightened her cheeks. 'Are we not told that the Lord works in mysterious ways? It's true! This is one of his wonders!'

So far Meg had failed in her obligation to produce an heir. Her fault, Lady Douglas had accused, for being either frigid or barren, or both. But how could she conceive when Archie tumbled into her bed, stinking of drink and lust after evenings carousing with his brothers? She couldn't bring herself to practise Nancy's lessons but lay waiting, rigid as a poker. Then, if he hadn't fallen into a stupor, he would begin jabbing into her. Not an act of love, but a painful, humiliating assault that left her sore and sobbing while he snored away, insensible and insensitive.

And now the newly entitled earl of Angus had abandoned her altogether. He spent all his time at court dancing attendance on the widow queen, leaving Meg a virtual prisoner in this fortress. Every night she went down on her knees, pleading with the Mother of God to bless her with a child and now her prayers had been answered. Not in the way she would have expected but, nevertheless, a baby had been sent. Borne in her sister's womb.

She squeezed Elisabeth's hands. 'Lisbeth, you are indeed heaven-sent. God in his mercy has ordained this! I'll tell them that I'm with child. And when the bairn's born, I'll bring him up as my own. You have no need to fret.'

For the first time in many dark months Meg felt alive. The little cherries on her cheeks ripened into apples and, as she began making plans for the confinement, Betsy took hold of her hands.

'I've no wish to douse your hopes, my lass, but I fear you're winding yourself into a pirn. When did you last lie with Archie? And when did you have your last bleed?' she asked.

Meg's mouth drooped; her eyes dimmed. Months ago would be the answer to both questions.

'And you ken why, my lass,' Betsy said softly. 'There's no meat on you. You're just a rickle of bones.'

Meg picked up the brightly coloured bird of paradise cushion gifted by Dame Janet and pressed it to her stomach. 'Look at my belly now! And I'll make myself eat. If you'll feed me up, Betsy, I swear I'll eat for two!'

Throughout their stay Meg kept hoping and praying that the child would be a lad. Would that be tempting Providence? A son would raise her esteem in the eyes of the Douglas clan. Her mother-in-law wouldn't be so swift to look down her long neb if she produced an heir. Judging by the tenacity with which the unborn infant had clung to his mother's womb, despite all her attempts to scrape him out, Betsy was convinced it must be a lad in there.

Worn down by Meg's constant pestering, Betsy agreed to divine its sex. She checked the three-week-old hen's egg for hairline cracks and then tapped it against the side of the bowl. She was about to separate the yolk from the white when she sucked in her breath: a double yolk. Tutting to herself, she shook her head.

'What will it be, Betsy. Lad or lass?' Meg dared to ask, crossing her fingers behind her back.

'One or tother. Or both.' Betsy was bewildered. She'd have to try another test. While Elisabeth lay stretched out on the settle, she held a knotted string over her womb, watching its progress intently as it swung back and forth and round and round. After putting her ear to her belly, she straightened up and tapped her chin.

Seeing her nurse's bewildered expression, Elisabeth gave a nervous laugh. 'I hope you're no going to tell me there are two in there, Betsy!'

Betsy frowned 'Ah, well, now you might have hit on something there. Twin babes, now, that might explain... but I don't think so, for I can only hear one heartbeat.'

'Twins! O Betsy, that would be wonderful.' Her eyes feverishly radiant, Meg clasped her hands together. 'A bairn each for Lisbeth and me! That *would* be a miracle!'

Chapter Nineteen
Epiphany

Thus made they merry while they micht nae mair
And 'Hail, Yule! Hail!' Cryit upon high.
Yet efter joy ofttimes comes care
And trouble efter great prosperity.

—*The Tale of the Uplands Mouse and the Burgess Mouse,*
Robert Henryson, 15th Century

Tantallon Castle, 6 January 1514

Elisabeth scuttled along the passage, chilly as a tomb and dimly lit by torches flickering in sconces. Her shadow fell now before, now after, and every so often she spun round to see if she was being followed. Wheedled into playing a game of tig, it was Elisabeth's turn to be het and she was cheating. Jinty, as they cried Janet, the baby of the Douglas family, was about her own age but acted much younger. Airy-fairy Jinty, with her skellie eye that could make her look fey or sleekit or both, scampered about Tantallon, playing pranks and enlivening the dour castle with her high-pitched shrieks. She would only ever sit still, listening enthralled to Betsy's tales.

Weary of their game, Elisabeth had gone beyond their agreed boundary of the northeast wing, hoping to give Jinty the slip, but after all the twists and turns she was now lost. She should have brought a candle or left a trail but that would have given the game away, so now she groped her way uncertainly along the gloomy tunnels. The sounds of raucous laughter and shouting brought her to a halt. The Great Hall. She'd need to retrace her steps to avoid that den where the Douglas men gathered to carouse.

'Och, a bonny wee heir for Archie! An heir for the earl of Angus!' the drunken chorus were yelling:

> 'Then durst no man come heirhand the king
> But the surname of the doughty Douglas
> Which so royally in this region did ring.
> Ding doun Tantallon.'

The Douglas menfolk, famed for breaking all bounds in conduct, hadn't allowed mourning for their grandsire to spoil their Twelfth Night festivities. And now they had joyous news to celebrate. An heir was expected! At long last the countess of Angus was with child.

Elisabeth peeked round the door. Up in the gallery, the last minstrel standing was valiantly plucking out a tuneless melody on the lute and warbling words of either joy for the conception of a new laird or lament for the death of the old one. Down below, several bodies lay slumped across a trestle strewn with flagons and beakers, their heads buried beneath the scattered remnants of a feast. Others had collapsed onto the floor, among the dogs rooting around the rushes for discarded bones and scraps. Those still on their feet threw back their heads to empty their tankards and then howled their war cry, 'A Douglas! A Douglas!'

A movement in the corner caught her eye. A pair of maggot-white hurdies were thrusting between the thighs of a serving wench pinned against the trestle. Elisabeth drew breath and slid away, hoping to sneak past unseen but her way was blocked.

'Who the deuce have we here, Geordie? Friend or foe? Or spy!' A Douglas henchman grabbed her by the wrist. 'By Christ's holy blood! A nun! If you've come to say grace, sister, save your breath. We're all hell-bound heathens here. And if you've been cast out of the nunnery, come and join our pagan revels instead.'

Elisabeth tried to snatch her arm away. 'I'll make my own way back.'

'Not in our castle, you won't.' Archie's brother, George, had risen unsteadily to his feet and was staggering towards her. His large beefy chest bulged out of his shirt slashed to the waist and his belly spilled over his loosened breeches. He scratched at the wiry black hairs on his chest and leered at her. 'We'll have no strangers wandering around willy-nilly.'

'I'm no stranger. I am sister to the countess.'

'Ah, Meg's wee sister. And a holy one at that. Welcome to our infernal heaven on earth.' He dragged her into the hall and bellowed to his cronies. 'Do you ken that clerics deem women the very devil? And nuns the most wanton whores of all! Is it not every nun's desire to be ravished?' He thrust his leering face so close that she could see his red-veined eyes and smell his stinking breath. 'We'll make sure you don't go to your grave wondering. It would be a great pity if only wriggling worms wammled their way into your virgin's womb.' He twisted his forefinger suggestively.

'Aye, and we'll all be up and ready to tirl her at the pin,' one of his henchmen shouted.

'Steek your gabs you crankous crew. You'll all get your turn,' George yelled.

He wrenched her round and crushed his lurid claret-stained lips down on hers. His tongue forced its way through her teeth, slithering like a slug round the soft, secret places of her mouth. When she tried to bite down on it, he quickly withdrew and whispered hoarsely in her ear.

'So, you want something meatier to nibble on? Get down on your knees, wee sister,' he growled and thrust her roughly to the floor. While he fumbled clumsily with the laces of his breeches, Elisabeth clutched the wooden crucifix hanging on the cord round her waist and ran her fingers over the lifeless figure.

'Don't waste your fondling fingers on the dead Christ,' George said. 'Here's something quick and lively that'll respond to your caresses. The answer to your maiden prayers.'

She waited until the flaps of his breeches were hanging loose before lunging forward to stab the crucifix as hard as she could into his groin. George grimaced in pain, letting out an inhuman yowl as he crumpled to the floor. She scrambled up from her knees and looked round in alarm, fearful that the barbarous Douglas horde would round on her for humiliating their brother. The din was deafening as they whooped and howled, thumping the tables and clanging their pewter tassies together.

'That's some blessing she's given you, Geordie,' a henchman cackled. 'That'll steek your pistle for a fair spell.'

While George writhed about, nursing his throbbing genitals, Elisabeth held the crucifix aloft to proclaim: 'Begone from me, ye cursed. May ye be hurled into the everlasting fires of hell! And the devil take you all.'

She fled out the door and stumbled over the crouching figure of Jinty, her shoulders heaving with silent laughter.

'Our Geordie is het now! All het up! Look at him lowping and whauping! Once his cock whangs up again, you'll be in for a walloping!' Jinty sniggered, her eyes rolling disconcertingly in different directions. She grabbed hold of Elisabeth's hand and hauled her through the maze of dark passages.

Hearing footsteps, they would press hard against the wall, holding their breath until they passed. Stopping at a narrow door, Jinty creaked it open. While she trotted up the winding stair as nimble as a goat, Elisabeth had to heave herself up on the rope handrail to the topmost turret where she leant gratefully against the wall to catch her breath.

‘I brought Meg up here once,’ Jinty said, stretching up to look out over the parapet, ‘for I thought the sea breezes would blow away her cough, but it only made her worse.’

Elisabeth could understand. Icy droplets from the splashing waves pierced her lungs like shards of glass. The five-storeyed tower of Tantallon was built on the edge of a cliff that fell away to the sea far, far below. Even the lofty west tower at Hailes was not so steep. The fierce waves licked eagerly at the cliff face, rising higher and higher, as if stretching up to pull her down. To stop her head from swirling, she focussed her eyes on the Craig of Bass encircled with a halo of swooping seabirds.

‘This is the best spot in the whole castle,’ Jinty gazed longingly over the parapet. ‘I could stay here forever. It’s the only place I feel free.’

‘You’re not afeart of heights?’ Elisabeth asked.

Jinty spread out her arms like wings. ‘Nay! I would fain fly off here and soar across the seas, gliding on the wind like one of those gulls.’

Listening to her baring her soul, Elisabeth marvelled that the Douglas clan could produce such lyrical poets and such uncouth boors. Jinty had the poetic soul of her uncle Gavin, the poet and cleric, but not, thank goodness, her brother George’s foul-mouthed tongue.

Chapter Twenty
Clishmaclaver

Wise women have ways and wonderful guidings
With great ingenuity to bejape their jealous husbands.
—*The Treatise of the Twa Marrit Women and the Widow,*
William Dunbar, 15th–16th Century

Holyrood Palace, Spring 1514

Perched on a stool in the darkest corner of the sewing room, Kate listened to the court ladies chattering at their needlework. A minstrel plucking out tunes on a lute accompanied their tittle-tattle. Singing smutty lyrics *sotto voce*, he kept leering and winking at Kate. Stitching a tapestry cushion or tatting a lace collar was the pretext for the ladies who gathered together for their daily dose of gossip, as much a sport for them as hunting was for their menfolk.

Everyone was fair game and they were merciless in dissecting their present prey: the widow Queen Margaret, and the young earl of Angus. The queen's flaunting infatuation with a married man provided a tailor-made seam for them to work on. The fact that she'd given birth, only months after the Flodden rout was being embroidered with salacious insinuations about the possible parentage of Prince Alexander.

'I, for one, would wager that Angus has sired the bairn,' Lady Crawford affirmed. 'The king and queen weren't on the best of terms and hadn't bedded as man and wife for a long while.'

‘There was no dirrie-dantoun with her and Archie Douglas, I doubt the queen would have cuckolded the king.’ Lady Lennox retorted.

Of similar age and status these two senior ladies had been countesses until the deaths of their earls at Flodden. However, shared widowhood hadn’t brought these life-long rivals any closer together.

As wife of a Stewart and a niece of James III, Lady Lennox considered herself the senior lady and took her role as self-appointed guardian of the royal morals seriously. In her view Marion Crawford, one of the borders Homes and notorious rogues, was an ill-gabbit gossipmonger who revelled in muckraking. Their verbal jousting provided entertainment for the bored court ladies.

Lady Crawford, whose game lay in contradicting Lady Lennox at every turn, shot back, ‘Forgive me, but I’ve been a lady of Queen Margaret’s chamber many a year and I swear that the Tudor wanton has lain with Cheeping Archie for her pleasure. She’s a Tudor, mind, with Tudor appetites and tastes, and couldn’t do without a man in her bed for long. Innocent bride she may have been, but the king's grace soon had her prenticed in tail-toddle.’

Their scandalous prattle kept Kate from falling asleep on the wobbly stool. She’d spent yet another night huddled in a blanket by one of the huge ingleneuks in the kitchen for she had nowhere else to go. For years she’d stomached Elisabeth’s taunts for being a cuckoo in the nest and so she’d leapt at the chance of coming to court, not, as it turned out, to serve as one of the queen’s ladies, but one of the king’s concubines. At first she’d been scandalised but, when James promised to reward her with a dowry and a wealthy husband, she had reconsidered. Besides, it had done Nancy Stewart no lasting harm to her reputation or marriage prospects—perhaps even enhanced them and so Kate had given in. But then the king had perished before fulfilling his promise to provide for her future and his widow had certainly no intention of honouring pillow pledges. Queen Margaret had flung her out of his private quarters, along with all his other paramours he'd lodged there. Since then, penniless, without spouse or protector, Kate had been living like the burgh mouse in Robert Henryson's fable, in perpetual fear of the house cat.

She'd never condescend to return to Hailes to be treated as an unpaid skivvy by her gloating rival, Nancy. Nor would she accept the invitation of Adam's older sister, Lady Joanna Seton, a Flodden widow, who had founded a convent in Edinburgh. Enter a nunnery! That would indeed be a living death sentence. She'd rather live a twilight life, lurking in the gloom of the palace, sleeping wherever she could, living off scraps from the table and fending off unwelcome attention from lowly lackeys and lewd lute players. She hadn't changed her clothes for months and her own smell repulsed her. Her bonny golden hair had become dull and matted and unsightly plooks had broken out on her sallow skin. How would she be able to attract patronage in this state?

As Kate shrank back, hoping to blend in with the tapestry behind her, Isobel Kennedy, another discarded mistress groomed by her mother for the king's bed, drew up a stool beside her.

'Hark at the clapperdins,' she murmured, 'weaving their venomous tales and spreading their muck. Yesterday they were squabbling about whether King James was slain at Flodden or is now crawling to the Holy Land on a pilgrimage to do penance for his sins or has guised himself as a beggar. Anyways, we cannot pin our hope on his return. Our only way out of this midden is to find a widower, or an auld lecherous greybeard, whose scrawny arms will welcome a lithesome lass to warm his lonely bed and produce an heir or two.'

'You'll have no trouble in finding a patron,' Kate assured her. With her beguiling Celtic looks—raven black hair and porcelain pale skin, Isobel was a beauty like her mother.

With no reply forthcoming from Lady Lennox, Lady Crawford had tossed aside her rumpled linen square. She had no patience for fine needlework and her loose, erratic stitching often had to be unpicked. Preferring to needle her rival, she said, 'If Angus did indeed sire the child, then the prince may be a Douglas bastard.'

Lady Lennox looked up from the panel she was embroidering with neat, even stitches and waved her needle menacingly in the air as if considering where to jab it. 'I'd hold my ill-scrapit tongue if I were you, Marion. Thon red-headit bairn was never a Douglas. A talebearer is worse than a thief. What you're saying is slander.'

'Och, it's just harmless blethers. Life is dreich enough without a scouthering scold like you dousing our merriness,' Lady Crawford scoffed.

'Nevertheless, Margaret Tudor may be too shrewd to be baggit with another man's bairn,' Lady Lennox affirmed, 'but what's she thinking of, dallying with a Douglas? Troublemaking rabble-rousers with their swords aye drawn at the ready, the Red Douglases will stop at nothing to advance their kin. Ding doun Tantallon. Thon old saying is true,' Lady Lennox gave a knowing nod for their slogan aptly described the inbred audacity of the Douglas clan to overstep the mark. 'It's as clear as the neb on his face that Angus is after a share of the throne. The sheer effrontery of the blackguard.'

'Unlike others who would stake their claim,' Lady Crawford remarked.

Lady Lennox ignored this jibe. Angus was an upstart while her family the Lennox Stewarts had a rightful claim to the crown, but she wasn't going to demean herself by pointing this out to the ill-informed Marion. Instead, she went on, 'Forbye, Archie Douglas already has a young wife.'

'And a bairn on the way,' Lady Crawford reminded her. 'Though that won't please her grace...' she'd started to say before someone nudged her.

As the other ladies fell silent, Isobel elbowed Kate. The royal herald sir David Lindsay had entered the sewing room unannounced and scanned the chamber as if looking for a familiar face.

'Since losing his beloved lord and master,' Isobel said, 'the grief-stricken herald wanders like a wraith about the court. Many are concerned he's lost the will to live but what he needs is a wife. Come on, Kate. Up on your feet,' Isobel said and stood up to give a deep curtsey.

Lindsay bowed politely in return, and then caught sight of Kate cowering on her stool behind her. He peered at her closely before holding out his hand to raise her up.

Chapter Twenty-One
Hunt the Gowk

Black Douglas, and wow but he was rough!
For he pull'd up the bonny brier
And flung it in St Mary's loch!
—*The Ballad of the Black Douglas*, Traditional

Tantallon Castle, Spring 1514

The dreich, damp castle of Tantallon, high on a crag above the Firth of Forth and blasted from all sides by the four winds, was aggravating Meg's frail health. Racked by fits of violent coughing, she stayed bundled up in bed to keep warm. The freezing sea mists weren't doing her any good, Betsy said, alarmed at seeing flecks of blood in the phlegm Meg whooped up. It grieved her to see her fragile harebell wilting and waning. The climate inland at Hailes would suit her better, she suggested, but Lady Douglas reared her long craig, bridling at her suggestion.

'This is her home now,' she said tartly. 'Meg is the countess of Angus and here she will bide. The next earl will be born, as all the others afore him, here at Tantallon.' And she herself would take care of her. Had she not brought up a wheen of bairns to adulthood?

When the physician diagnosed the croup, Meg implored Betsy to take Lisbeth away to Hailes. Her own health didn't trouble her so much as that of the unborn baby but Elisabeth was loath to leave Meg at the mercy of Lady Douglas.

'Don't fret. She'll not harm me. Not while she thinks I'm carrying an heir. Forbye, it will only be for a few weeks, Lisbeth, and when you come back it will be time for our confinement.'

'And how will we keep your mother-in-law out of the birthing chamber?' Betsy asked. 'She'll want to be there to make sure her grandchild is delivered safely.'

Meg spluttered, coughing up rheum that Betsy gently wiped from her cracked lips.

'Tell her I've got some kind of catching disease and that it wouldn't be safe for her to be there.' With great reluctance Betsy and Elisabeth made ready to leave for, despite Meg's brave effort to reassure them, they doubted whether she could keep up the pretence on her own.

As soon as they had ridden away from Tantallon, Lady Douglas laid down the rules that her daughter-in-law must follow.

'You must eat, otherwise you'll never be strong enough to bear my grandchild,' she insisted, serving up rich dishes to put flesh on her bones. But Meg had no appetite for the rich puddings of honey and thick cream that curdled in her stomach. Whenever she tried to swallow, her gullet constricted and, if she regurgitated, Lady Douglas's long nose twitched in undisguised disgust at the sickly mess.

Some days Meg could hardly raise her head from the pillow and her head reeled when she had to get up to use the chamber pot. Jinty was her only sympathetic visitor. Not only to gobble up the sweet puddings spurned by Meg, but to chatter cheerfully about the new arrival, a playmate for her to fuss over. But when Jinty was caught cramming a slice of pie into her mouth, her mother banished her from Meg's chamber.

Mystified that Meg's belly was not swelling as it should, Lady Douglas summoned the physician from Edinburgh. The black-coated doctor hovered like a raven sizing up his prey before landing his talons onto her stomach and then, with chilled pasty hands, he kneaded her belly like dough, pressing it hard down against her spine. When he forced her legs apart to probe deep into her, she cried out as his dirt-encrusted claws scratched the tender inner folds of flesh. He then took Lady Douglas to one side to ask if there had been any unusual flux.

'Nay,' she replied confidently, for nothing escaped her hawkish eye.

Sensing that the fiercesome mother-in-law might withhold his payment, the doctor refrained from airing his concern that the bairn might already have died in the womb. He could hear no tiny throb of a heartbeat. The remedy in that case would be to cut her open but not without great risk to the mother's life—and to his own reputation if she died. Then the child must be very small, he opined. To boost the baby's growth, he prescribed his own receipts for strengthening cordial and tonics. If nothing else, they could do no harm.

This judgement did not please Lady Douglas. Never mind that a puny heir would bring disgrace on the Douglas family, it would make it more difficult to procure a divorce for Archie, as non-consummation could not then be claimed. Now that her son was high in the widow queen's favour, it would be a pity if anything should stand in his way. She would dispense her own remedy.

Meg screwed up her face at the evil-smelling potion Lady Douglas made her drink, for it stung the tiny, bleeding sores that had broken out on her gums. The only saving grace was that it made her fall into grateful oblivion; painless darkness, where figures, formless but familiar gathered in the shadowy underworld. Was that her mother hovering over her? Had she come at last? Whether she was dreaming or dying she neither knew nor cared.

When she woke up, she was alone. No-one was keeping watch by her bed. Her breathing came more easily. No coughing. No fiery darts jabbing into her chest. No pain anywhere. She raised her head from the pillow and sat up for the first time in weeks. The fever must have passed.

She felt an urgent need to use the chamber pot and stumbled out of bed, but weeks of being bedridden had weakened her muscles. Her legs trembled before giving way beneath her. She crawled towards the pot and squatted, holding onto the bedpost to keep from toppling over. Though giddy and light-headed, she didn't feel sick. Using the bedpost to haul herself up, she got to her feet, swaying slightly. The fuggy stench in the darkened sick room caught her throat. Fresh sea air would cleanse her lungs. She would climb up to the high tower.

A pall of perspiration swathed her brow as she groped her way barefoot along the dim stone passageway and her nightdress slapped like a sodden dishrag against her skin, making it cold and clammy. The shivering started, slowly at first, and then increased, until her teeth were chattering and her very bones were trembling.

Shrieks and screams and the pitter-patter of feet running hither and yon echoed throughout the castle. She stopped, holding her breath to listen. Further along the passage she glimpsed a hazy figure, its head hidden beneath a gossamer veil. A guardian angel flitting in and out of the shadows: or the spirit of her mother in her bridal veil—one of the unquiet dead.

'Wait for me!' Her strangled cry brought on a coughing fit but fearing to lose sight of the spectre, she struggled on. Rounding the corner, she came to a halt. Flickering torches cast eerie shadows down the sides of a broad staircase. There was no sign of the angel. Looking down the steep flight of stairs made her dizzy and she grasped hold of the rope banister for balance. She glanced around anxiously. Something shimmered beside her, flimsy and light like an angel's wing, and hovered in the air before gently falling over her head. She heard a stifled giggle. Startled, she let go of the post and staggered around blindly, trying to tear off the veil.

'Hunt the gowk!'

Happit in the veil, Meg took an unseeing step sideways and teetered on the edge before being hurled forward into space and timelessness. A spine-curdling scream dinging around Tantallon was the last mortal sound she heard.

Chapter Twenty-Two
Requiem

I doubt that March with his cauld blasts keen,
Has slain this gentle herb that I of mean,
Whose piteous death does to my heart such pain
—*To a Lady*, William Dunbar, 15th–16th Century

Hailes Castle, May 1514

'This won't hurt,' Betsy said as she vigorously rubbed her oil-smeared hands together before warming them over a candle flame.

Half-lying on the bed, her eyes looming owlishly over her bump, Elisabeth watched warily as Betsy then ran her oily hands gently over the swollen dome of her belly, so far hidden by the loose folds of her habit.

'You're not casting a hex on me, Betsy, are you?' she said with a nervous laugh.

'No fear of that, lass, I'm just making sure that the bairn's not tapsalteerie.'

Tapsalteerie! Whigmaleerie! The thought more than Betsy's massaging fingers made Elisabeth's stomach lurch. That wasn't natural, was it, to be upside down? Did it mean the bairn was accursed?

'Nay, nay, my lass. Far from it. Them that are born heels-over-gowdie are well-favoured in life's morning march and are gifted with the healing power, so they say. But we need to coax the bairn into flipping over to come head first into the world! It will save you a lot of grief, too. So speak kindly to him. Tell the wee man to do a somersault.'

'The wee man?' Elisabeth gave a start. 'How do you ken it's a boy?'

'Och, lads are aye likely to be more carnaptious and contrary,' Betsy chuckled.

As Betsy kneaded her distended belly, Elisabeth could feel the baby kicking. What to say to this wee mite about to start out on life's journey? Her voice a faint whisper, she assured him that, once he left the safety of her womb, her sister Meg would love him as her own and bring him up as heir to the Earldom of Angus. He'd be a grand gentleman one day.

There was no word of Meg's death until Lady Douglas arrived at Hailes to hand over her corpse to Betsy—as if it were a packet that had been delivered to the wrong place. Tears of sorrow and anger welled in Betsy's eyes as took Meg's scrawny, lifeless body tightly swaddled in a linen winding sheet with only her pale, waxen face showing, and laid her on a trestle.

'I'm returning her home for burial. She doesn't deserve to be entombed as a Douglas. We were greatly deceived,' Lady Douglas sniffed. 'She was never with child. When the physician cut her, there was no bairn.'

Betsy scowled. 'You sliced open our beloved Meg?'

'Aye, to save the bairn if possible: we'd done all we could for her. She was afflicted with the flux and couldn't keep anything down. And when the fever burned through her, she was too weak to fight it. She just went down.' Her hand fluttered as she spoke. 'Falling like a rowan leaf in autumn. We even brought in a learned physician from Edinburgh.'

Betsy failed to be fooled by Lady Douglas's grief. 'And how many weans has this surgeon brought forth from his ain womb?' she asked and began, slowly and reverently, to unwind the linen sheet.

Lady Douglas shot out a hand to stop her. 'There's no need for that. The physician has already prepared her for burial.'

The two women glared at each other over Meg's dead body.

Betsy narrowed her eyes. 'Has he indeed? Well now, I'm going to make sure she's laid out properly. By one who loves her.' Paying no heed to Lady Douglas, she went on unwinding the sheet. Seeing the ugly purple bruises blotching Meg's translucent skin, she breathed in sharply.

'That was the bloodletting,' Lady Douglas said quickly. 'The skin turns black and blue when it's pierced for the leeches to suck the blood—so the physician explained. Not that you'd know anything about that,' she sniffed. 'He learnt his skill at the College of Surgeons in Edinburgh founded by King James himself,' she went on proudly. 'Where the latest advances in medicine and chirurgianrie are taught and homespun remedies scorned.'

'Chicanerie did you say?' Betsy asked innocently.

Lady Douglas stretched her long neck so that she could look even further down her nose at the uncouth nursemaid. 'You may be nearer the truth than you ken, for he said that Meg was so desperate for a bairn that she fooled herself into believing she was with child. It sometimes happens in barren wives. Fussing and fretting can dry up their courses and bloat the belly, duping the body like a gowk storm whirls the mind.'

'Gowk storm indeed!' Betsy spluttered. It wasn't the want of a child that addled her wits.'

Lady Douglas narrowed her eyes at the insolent nursemaid. 'We, too, were duped. Meg was never robust. Had we kent the truth about her poor health we'd never have agreed to the marriage. Perhaps it's turned out for the best. Any bairn she might have conceived would doubtless have been a weakling.' With a final sniff of her long neb, Lady Douglas got up to leave. 'Tell anyone who asks that Meg died in childbed and that the bairn was stillborn. No more need be said.'

Left alone with the wilted remains of her hapless harebell, Betsy lit candles round the trestle to examine Meg. She doubted Lady Douglas's explanation. Such discoloration on a corpse could only be caused by a battering or, fortune forbid, high doses of arsenic. Not that anyone would take heed of a lowly nurse's suspicions. The crudely stitched gash in her side where Meg had been ripped open made Betsy gasp and she had to steel herself with a generous dram of *aquavitae* for the task of laying her out.

After washing the bruised body, Betsy anointed her bonnie flower with fragrant oil, keening softly all the while to keep from weeping. For no tears could be allowed to fall on the corpse or the shroud, otherwise her spirit would have no rest. There would be time enough for tears after the burial. She wrapped her lovingly in her grave clothes, her mother's oyster satin wedding dress worn by Lisbeth at Meg's proxy marriage. Uncanny it was that all three of them had worn the same dress in such different circumstances. Weird, how fortune's wheel turned.

As she took a comb to Meg's fine fair hair, it came away in clumps: another sign of arsenic poisoning. She cut off two locks, one for Elisabeth and one for herself—there would be none for Archie Douglas—covered her hair with a linen snood tied firmly under her chin to keep her jaw shut and laid her head on the bird of paradise cushion. She crossed Meg's hands, one over the other, and placed a small dish of salt on her breast to prevent the stiffening of her body. After waving a lighted candle over Meg three times, she strewed her corpse with sprigs of May blossom for her final journey. Finally, Betsy kissed her dear Meg's icy forehead.

'Fare thee well my fairy flower, my bonnie harebell,' she murmured, pressing her eyelids tightly to stem the tears.

Elisabeth had been hovering outside the door, impatient to say her farewells but Betsy bundled her away and shut it firmly behind them. A woman about to give birth should never look on an unburied corpse in case the deceased's spirit claimed possession of the bairn's body. Elisabeth's eyes opened wide. So Meg's spirit hadn't yet gone to rest? She gazed about her and whispered into the air.

'Swear to me that you will tarry here to haunt them, Meg. Swear to me you'll never let them rest in peace.'

Meg was buried in the family crypt at Hailes alongside their mother and brother. No one from the Douglas side, not even her husband Archie, attended Meg's funeral: he was too busy arranging his nuptials to the dowager queen, Margaret Tudor.

Chapter Twenty-Three
De Profundis

Ave Maria, gratia plena Dominus tecum
benedicta tu in mulieribus
et benedictus fructus ventris tui.
—Latin Prayer

Hailes Castle, Spring 1514

In the dawning hour, a surging pain seized Elisabeth, as if a blazing hot poker had been plunged into her entrails. She sat up and bent double to hug her cramping womb. In a trice Betsy was up and about. She hung a cauldron of water on a swey over the ingle and counted out torn strips of linen. After setting a basin and a chamber pot by the bed, she boiled up a fusion of herbs that tasted as foul as it smelled. She pressed Elisabeth's lips together to force it down and, seeing her stomach begin to heave, held out the basin.

'It's easier to thole on an empty belly,' she assured her. 'That's one end cleared. A good scouring out now will be easier to deal with than later.'

Drained and wabbit, Elisabeth wanted only to sink back onto the pillow, but Betsy shoved the chamber pot underneath her just in time, as her bowels loosened and liquid gushed down her thighs. But still Betsy wouldn't let her lie down—breathe slowly, breathe deeply, don't lie down, keep upright, crawl about on all fours—until she could thole the birthing showers no longer. Betsy sprinkled an odd tasting powder on her palm to lick and then propped her on a stool while she probed between her splayed legs. Tapsalteerie, she heard Betsy muttering before sinking into a stupor.

Waves of pain kept pummelling her, drawing her down further and deeper into the black, but when she tried to thrash upwards a heavy weight dragged her back down into the churning water. Pushing with all her might, she strained to rid herself of the burden until it burst from her womb, splitting her in two.

Slumped on the floor, she looked up to see Betsy dangling the gory bundle by the legs, its upside-down head, slick with blood and fluid, swaying back and forth. As Betsy gave it a good slap, mucous dribbled from its thrapple, splattering onto her cheek before the bairn opened up its toothless mouth to let out a piercing bawl. The Elisabeth fell into a deep sleep.

Days passed in a drowsy blur, broken only when Betsy raised her head to make her drink something. When at last she surfaced, she felt hollow, her womb scooped out and her belly shrunken. No pain now, only a dull throbbing lingered between her legs where a prickly dressing scratched the tender skin.

'If you'd stappit this up yourself as I told you at the time, you wouldn't be going through this now,' Betsy muttered as she changed the dressing. 'And neither would I. You had me worried for your life, Lisbeth.'

'Can I see my bairn now, Betsy?' she asked drowsily. 'Is it a laddie as you foretold?'

'Wheesht, my lass! There's time enough for that.' Betsy dabbed her brow with a cool cloth seeped in a soothing infusion of sweet-smelling herbs. As the bairn's head had torn its way through her tender flesh, she'd lost a lot of blood, but an infusion of lady's mantle helped to staunch the bleeding. Fretting she would contract the fever that often carried off newly delivered mothers, including Elisabeth's own, Betsy had added honey and birch fungus to the sphagnum moss dressing on her wound to stem any fever, and, since sleep was the best healer, had administered precisely measured doses of deadly nightshade to keep her slumbering.

When Elisabeth awoke and asked again to see her baby, Betsy wiped tears from her brimming eyes.

'Such a bonnie wee fighter,' she sobbed, 'but he wasn't sturdy enough to fight the fever that took him away. But don't fret, I baptised him—not with my ain spittle—but water fresh from the Tyne. Maybe not as grand as your godson's christening, but enough to send him safely into Meg's loving arms. Never vex, my thistledown, she'll look after him now.'

Elisabeth turned her head away, in silent acceptance of fate. 'So,' she said at last, sniffing back tears, 'when you christened my wee lad, Betsy, what did you cry him? Not Archie, I trow.' She managed a wan smile.

'Do you really want to ken?' Betsy frowned. In her experience, it was better not to dwell on it. Giving the child a name would only prolong her mourning, but the thrawn thistle nagged until she gave in.

'Well, I swithered about calling him Adam,' Betsy replied, 'for your ill-fated brother, and then David, being his father's son. But since he came into this world with such a blast I thought, this lad has his grandsire's lungs. Lungs fit for a preacher: at full throttle. So there you have it. John it was, for your uncle, Prior John Hepburn. Now think of your wee soul up there with Meg, among the heavenly host. One of God's divine trumpeters.'

St Mary's Abbey

On her return to the abbey, Sister Maryoth was waiting for Elisabeth, hardly able to contain her delight.

'I have joyous tidings for you, my dear.' The smug smirk tweaking at the corners of her mouth almost cracked into a smile. 'About your cousin Kate. You'll be pleased to ken that she's now married,' Sister Maryoth declared. '*Deo Gratias*. Does that not gladden your heart in this time of woe?'

Pity the man who's yoked to that hizzie, Elisabeth thought. He'll have a hard furrow to plough. He'll need all of God's grace. Let's pray that she's hitched to a Douglas, for then they would deserve each other.

'It's a good match, considering her lowly position,' Sister Maryoth babbled on. Our Blessed Lord has forgiven the woman taken in sin. She has been most fortunate to snare a man of the calibre of Sir David Lindsay.'

Elisabeth's ears pricked up. 'Sir David Lindsay? But he was slain at Flodden. His name was called out. I heard it myself.'

Sister Maryoth crossed herself. 'Aye, but that was another David, son of Lord Lindsay of the Byres. Kate, however, has wed the royal herald. She's now wife to Sir David Lindsay of the Mount and Garleton. Is that not a matter for great rejoicing?'

No, no! A howl of despair reverberated deep within Elisabeth's breast, unlocking the grief hidden in her heart. Alone in her cell she wept until there were no more tears to shed and dry, ragged sobs racked her bones and heaved along her spine. And then later another nightmare tormented her sleep.

She was standing outside, naked and shivering in the freezing snow, looking into a cosy room where a couple cuddling in front of a blazing fire were gently rocking a cradle. Misery and longing engulfed her. When a branch blown by the wind tapped at the window, their heads whirled round. She tried to withdraw into the shadows, but Kate began pointing and laughing at her. And then Lindsay held up a bundle to the window—but there was no infant in the shawl, only a hideously grinning skull.

8 September 1514

As usual, on the feast of the Virgin Mary's nativity, Prior Hepburn celebrated mass in honour of the abbey's patron saint. After blessing all the nuns in turn, he raised his hand over his niece's bowed head, saying, 'And blessed is the fruit of thy womb.'

The ironic words of the *Ave Maria* stabbed Elisabeth's empty belly. No longer, she thought.

Afterwards, in the vestry, the prior pulled her closer to the window, tilted her chin and studied her face closely. His finger traced the blue-black shadows under her eyes and across her sunken cheeks. As he encircled her wrist with his thumb and forefinger, his dark eyebrows puckered like two black kailworms.

'You haven't been eating, lass. You're like a skinned rabbit.'

Elisabeth hurriedly pulled down her sleeve so that he wouldn't notice the weals on her arms. Over the summer, the grief from losing her baby, her sister and her lover had numbed her to the marrow. When she'd chewed her fingernails to the quick until they were ragged and bleeding, she sought solace in biting deeply on her bottom lip. The tiny droplets of blood trickling onto her tongue had tasted sweet and wersh at the same time and helped to smoor her sorrow. Encouraged by the thought that physicians considered bloodletting as a cure for all sorts of ills, she had begun making little nicks in her arm with the sharp point of the silver crucifix on her rosary. Almost at once her heart lightened and her grief lessened. She'd continued until a filigree of purple cross-stitched scars now embroidered her arms.

Hepburn wasn't a man who felt ready sympathy for the pain of others, but seeing his niece so wretched moved him. 'You're too young to be losing your lustre, my precious pearl. You must regain your strength. It was God's will, lass. It wasn't meant to be.'

He took her scrawny hand and pulled her onto his knee. 'Grief is natural but you mustn't let it crush you to the point of despair, for that is a mortal sin. Take a lesson from Sister Maryoth. She lost her dear brother in the Flodden fray, but she doesn't mope.'

His plump, moist lips nuzzled her ear. ‘Perhaps a change of air will help. How does a spell in France suit you?’

France! Anywhere to leave the convent and bullying Sister Maryoth. In a flash, Elisabeth’s spirits rose. There was hope.

Chapter Twenty-Four
Knight of Love

What lord is yon (quoth she) have ye nae feill?
Has done to us so great humanity?
I loved him for his manly form.
—*The Testament of Cresseid*, Robert Henryson, 15th Century

Edinburgh Castle, Spring 1516

'Faster, Da Lindsay, Faster!'

Kate looked down on her husband crawling around on all fours with the child astride his back, digging in his heels and urging him to make haste. The thick clouded skies and the unceasing wind and rain had kept them indoors for days. Being cooped up in the gloomy quarters of a draughty castle all winter was becoming unbearable and the four-year-old child that Lindsay was doing his best to amuse was not their own. As keeper to the king's Grace, Lindsay was playing nursemaid to James V, king of Scots. Playing the fool more like, Kate sneered, as he cavorted about the floor. She, too, was not only bored but tired of playing second best to James who, however, high and mighty he might be, was only a bairn.

Where was the home she'd been promised as Lady Garleton? Instead, she had to endure constant flitting from castle to palace and back again, always on the move, like some common tinker's wife. And she wanted her own child, who would love her unconditionally, unlike this spoilt whelp. Not only did Lindsay spend his days attending to the needs of the child, at night he shared a room with the king, and often his bed too.

The child couldn't bear to sleep alone and would scream and scream, 'Sing me a song, Lindsay. Sing me Ginkerton' until Lindsay came to him. How could she—the invisible side of an eternal triangle—conceive a child in these circumstances?

'You're tiring him,' she snapped. 'Forbye, it's long past his bedtime.'

'Nay,' the boy king screeched and poked a little pink tongue out at her. Their jealous dislike was mutual. James resented this interloper and rival for the affections of Da Lindsay who had looked after him since his birth. 'Faster Da Lindsay,' he cried, digging his heels in more deeply and glaring at her.

Under her breath, Kate cursed the whining monarch. Snatching up her cushion, she flounced off to the solar to be amused by the court ladies indulging in their favourite game: gossip. With a quick glance over her shoulder to make sure Lindsay wasn't looking, she stuck her tongue out at the mewling infant.

In the sewing room, the ladies looked up greet her. 'Good day, Lady Katherine.'

No longer a spurned paramour, but the wife of the royal herald, Kate was welcome in their inner circle, though not for her sewing skills but her singing voice.

'Give us a song,' they chorused.

While Kate conferred with the lute player, the ladies pounced on the latest titbit of gossip. Now that the hasty marriage of Margaret Tudor and her 'Anguish', as she called her knavish consort, the earl of Angus, was unravelling, they had plenty to prattle about.

'I feel sorry that Margaret Hepburn died for nothing,' Lady Crawford said.

Kate's ears pricked up. 'Poor Meg,' she murmured, recalling their girlhood together. 'Is it true what they say about her untimely death?' she asked.

'Chancy for him: unchancy for her, poor lass.' Lady Crawford said. 'Uncanny you might say. 'Tongues wag that the queen herself had a hand in her last ailment.'

'Or his ain mother more like,' Lady Lennox snapped as she took the bait. 'Thon Elisabeth Drummond with her long neck is as ruthless as a swan when it comes to protecting her young. She'll do anything to advance her own.' She resented how the queen's new mother-in-law strutted about the court, puffed up with pride and challenging her position. Adding salt to her stew, she lowered her voice to whisper, 'Even stoop to sorcery. They say she gave her son a powder to fall in love with the queen.'

'Well, it's already worn off. And now he's found it's a puddock he's wed, not a princess,' Lady Crawford said. 'That will teach the lovebirds to marry in haste, for they'll repent at leisure.'

While Margaret had fled to her brother's court in London, stopping off in Northumberland to give birth to a daughter, her 'Anguish' was finding solace in the arms of another—Jane Stewart, the mysterious dark Lady of Traquair, rumoured to be carrying his bairn.

'While the queen's away, Bell the Cat's grandson will play,' Lady Crawford warbled. 'Were I the queen, I wouldn't have reeled in Cheeping Archie so soon,' she continued, 'I would have made the most of my freedom before buckling myself to another. Better to wait and see what other fish the sea may cast up. Such as the Duke of Albany,' she sighed. 'He's a brave looking man, is he not?'

Lady Lennox sniffed. 'With royal blood in his veins, John Stewart would have made a better mate for our queen. And she would not have lost the regency.'

Kate nodded her agreement; her husband shared that opinion. By the terms of James IV's will, Margaret Tudor was to have been appointed tutrix to her son during her widowhood, but the Scottish council argued that her marriage to Angus rendered that condition invalid. They then stripped her of her authority and appointed Albany, the French bred grandson of James II, as regent in her stead.

'Never mind the queen, I'd fain be tethered to the duke myself.' Lady Crawford said, 'and with his wife in France wasting away there may be a chance for me. Come Kate, give us a love song to lighten our hearts.'

'Not one with ribald refrains,' Lady Lennox added

While Kate and the lute player scratched their heads to think of a happy love song, Jinty Douglas came whizzing into the sewing room, arms whirling wildly, her wayward eyes rolling. 'I've just seen the beautiful knight. He bowed to me,' she squealed and then, just as quickly dashed out again.

'At least Jinty's not still mourning her sister-in-law and spreading doom and gloom with tales of her ghost haunting Tantallon,' Lady Lennox remarked.

'Lady Douglas will need all her arts to find a mate for squinty-eyed Jinty,' the dark-haired beauty Isobel Kennedy sneered.

'I wouldn't be too hasty in mocking the lass,' Lady Crawford said. 'She may be fey but her kind often attract men who think wandering eyes mean wanton wiles.'

'Well, she's taken a girlish fancy to *Mon Seigneur de la Beautie*.'

'The French knight is far too...' The ladies of the court sniggered, waiting for Lady Crawford to elucidate. Sophisticated? Handsome? '... well-endowed for a maiden like her,' she said at last.

Jinty's announcement made Kate's heart miss a beat. For she, too, was secretly smitten with the beautiful knight whom Lindsay had introduced. Unwilling to leave his sick wife and travel to that dreich land he'd never known, the Duke of Albany had sent an envoy in his stead. Renowned throughout Europe as a tournament champion, Antoine D'Arcie, Sieur de la Bastie, had set all hearts a-flutter, young and old. Strikingly handsome with blonde flowing locks, *Mon Seigneur de la Beautie* as they called him, stood out amongst the shorn, ruddy-haired Scots.

He'd learnt the secrets of love from a master in the orient, the ladies whispered excitedly, and kens how to pleasure a woman until she screams for mercy. Unlike their lords and masters who were only fit for a clumsy fumble in the dark, hurling between their thighs and huffing and puffing till it was all over. For them. Fingers fluttered to lips as the ladies gasped in feigned horror at this deliciously wicked rumour while shivers of barely containable excitement made their skin tingle. Compared to his father's splendid court, that of the toddler king was deadly dull and dreary, they bemoaned, but Antoine's arrival promised to add oriental spice to life.

While the court ladies vied with each other for the attention of the beautiful knight and darted jealous barbs at anyone he seemed to favour, D'Arcie cast his gaze randomly over them all, which, instead of seeming fair, caused even more friction. The ladies nit-picked his every move, his every glance. How long he had spoken to this one, how long he had looked at that one, whether or not he had bowed to one or kissed the hand of another and so on. No matter how much they squabbled over these details, each lady believed in her heart that she was the one he preferred: none more so than Kate. She could hardly wait for the Beltane festival when, as Queen of the May, she could choose him as her knight.

And so when Lindsay announced that being married disqualified her from the coveted rôle Kate was furious. 'It isn't fair. Forbye, Isobel Kennedy is no chaste maiden.'

'But she is unwed,' Lindsay replied. Despite her constant pestering, he refused to use his influence as master of revels to favour his own wife. *That,* he affirmed, wouldn't be fair. She must content herself with being a lady-in-waiting.

Kate, however, wasn't content to play second best yet again and was determined to outshine the forritsome Isobel. Flamboyant in scarlet, the colour that had first attracted royal attention, she smouldered alongside the virginal white of the icy May Queen. Snide comments and asides rippled among the ladies, but Kate was deaf to them all. When the procession of combatants passed, led by the French knight in his gleaming white armour, she deftly tossed her glove to Antoine who, with a mischievous wink, pinned it to his tunic. Now that he was her champion and she his paramour, she didn't care a jot for their criticism. Let them say what they like. Words are but wind, but dunts are the devil. How she was tempted to poke her tongue out at them all.

Later that evening, at the banquet in honour of the champions, Lindsay spent most of his time chasing the over-excited monarch round the hall, playing tig and hide-and-seek among the legs of the dancers and diners who dared not show their irritation. Not even when his squeals threatened to drown out Kate's song.

> Glad is my heart with you, sweet heart, to rest.
> For my heart is in thrall to your heart,
> Until I have no heart contrary to your heart's will.

The significant glances that Kate threw were not, however, in the direction of her husband. When at last the toddler king flung himself onto the floor, girning with exhaustion, Lindsay gathered him up and took his royal majesty off to bed. She'd be spending another night alone—or would she, Kate thought.

Alone in her bedchamber, she spent some time warming herself by the ingle. Goose flesh was never a pretty sight, and even less pleasurable to the touch. Throwing a cloak over her shoulders, she slipped out into the corridor. From behind some closed doors, drunken snores could be heard and, from others, the tell-tale rhythmical motion of creaking beds. Kate crept along the dimly lit passageways, as if pulled by an invisible thread.

Slumped across the doorway, the guard snuffled and snored, an empty flagon of ale by his side. Kate stepped over him, lifted the latch and quietly slipped into the chamber. It was pitch dark, no candles burned. The curtains of the four-poster bed were drawn. He must have retired for the night.

She was about to leave when something flashed past her ear and thudded into the heavy wooden door. She tried to move but her cloak was pinned firmly to the door by a dagger. One rough hand grabbed her arms, forcing them above her head while the other groped her all over. Antoine's blue eyes bored into hers.

'My lady Katherine?' He let out a deep breath as he released her. 'Forgive me, I have many enemies in this court and must be on my guard at all times. You have mistaken your chamber? Allow me to escort you back. One moment. A taper to help light your way.' As he pulled the dagger out of the door to free her cloak, she grabbed hold of his wrist.

'No, mistake, my lord,' Kate whispered, pressing her back against the door. 'It is indeed you I seek.'

'I am most flattered, my lady. How may I serve you?' As he bowed, his unbuttoned shirt fell open exposing his muscular torso, naked down to the top of his unlaced breeches She gave a little gasp and shrugged her shoulder, shedding her cloak to the floor. She licked her lips.

'May I congratulate my champion on his victory in the field today.'

He returned the compliment with a sweeping bow and then, taking her hand, he lightly brushed it with his lips. At this slight caress, a crimson flush passed over her creamy skin and her flesh craved to feel those lips searching out her every neuk and cranny.

'As my lord and champion, you may now claim your prize. I ...' She hesitated. 'I have come to offer you my favours.'

'I am honoured indeed, *ma dame*.'

Slowly she undid the drawstring of her nightgown and let it slip from her shoulders. Shaking back her golden hair, she drew the gown over her breasts down towards the curve of her hips, stopping just beneath her rounded belly to gather it modestly above the sensuous mount of Venus.

'It is more than a kiss on the hand that I offer.' Her voice had lowered to a hoarse whisper.

'My lady, you are too kind, but…' As Antoine put up a warning hand, Kate began to panic.

'You are my champion. You have won my favours. I am yours. Take me.' Then, more urgently, 'Please.'

Antoine hesitated. As tournament champion, he was forever being accosted by women willing to throw themselves at his feet and, being a perfect gentle knight, he had no desire to disappoint. Even other men looked upon his amorous conquests as just rewards for his courage and skill. Only the brave deserved the fair.

'*Ma dame*, you are most beautiful but I cannot deceive your husband. I am a chevalier sworn never to breach my code of honour.'

As he bent down to pick up the cloak to cover her nakedness, she lunged towards him, entwining her arms round his neck, her fingers gently stroking his skin.

'Do not trouble about my husband. He doesn't trouble about me. He has his own bedfellow. Don't worry. He'll never know. Nor care.' For he spends more time in his young master's bed than he does in mine, she wanted to add.

Clasping her arms firmly round his neck, she rubbed her breasts against his naked chest.

'But I cannot deceive him.' Prising her hands from his neck, he strove to be firm but gentle. 'I implore you, *ma dame*. It is not honourable.'

Fear again gripped her. If it were discovered she'd been spurned by the white knight, she'd be a laughing stock. Unseen eyes and ears were everywhere, spying. Someone would have spotted her coming to his room. And taken note of her leaving again almost immediately.

'Forgive me, my lord. I see you are indeed most honourable. It is all written here.'

With light fingertips she traced the weals and scars interlaced on his torso, evidence of the many injuries he'd been dealt in battle and combat, down towards the thick tuft of hair peeking out from beneath his breeches. As she caressed his navel, he stiffened and, seizing the opportunity, she knelt down quickly and nuzzled her face against his groin. He clutched at her hair and for a moment she thought he was about to pull her up, but no, he was drawing her head forward, encouraging her.

Smiling to herself, she ran her tongue over her lips, moistening them in readiness. The experienced King James had taught her many secrets of the bedchamber and this one never failed to please. With her skilful tongue flicking and squirming like the subtle serpent, she licked and sucked until she heard him gasp with surprise but mostly pleasure.

It was then she heard giggling from behind the curtains of the four-poster bed and then Isobel Kennedy's tousled-haired head poked out.

Chapter Twenty-Five
Auvergne

And saw this written upon a wall
Of what estate man that thou be
Obey and thank thy God of all.
—*The Abbey Walk*, Robert Henryson, 15th Century

Auvergne, France, 1515

What was Elisabeth expecting—the full-throated crooning of cooing doves in a dovecot? Instead, the refectory of the convent of *Nôtre Dame des Miracles* reverberated with the trilling and warbling of birds of paradise, mute by day but coming into full-throated song by night. Exotic in their winged headdresses, the sisters flitted around the convent, speaking only when necessary, a rule relaxed for the evening meal when they twittered and chirruped non-stop.

Her head dirling, Elisabeth turned to the novice sister who had taken her under her wing. Amidst all the squawking, Sister Agnes, calm and patient, never raised her voice as she strove to explain the elaborate pecking order to her. Thanks to the Auld Alliance, however, they had found words their languages shared, though the pronunciation differed. When Sister Agnes had proffered *une tasse du vin*, Elisabeth had beamed in recognition since a tassie in Scots was also a goblet for wine while an ashet, a large plate for serving food, *une assiette*. On feast days they also shared *gigot de mouton*, a joint of mutton.

Elisabeth brushed off some breadcrumbs that had fallen onto her lap. She didn't want to spoil her new habit nor stain her immaculately spotless linen. She stroked the creamy, fine-spun lambs-wool, marvelling at its softness. All the habits of this order seemed softer and cleaner, Elisabeth thought. One of her first requests after her long journey had been to bathe. While the maids filled an enormous tub, Sister Agnes had added handfuls of exotic smelling herbs to the steaming water. After Elisabeth had stripped off her coarse brown novice's habit and unwashed linen—grubby and stale after her journey—Sister Agnes handed her a cloth sprinkled with a strong-smelling oil—*lavande,* she explained—that dissolved the grime and softened her skin.

Wrapping Elisabeth in soft cotton *toile* to dry after her long soak in the tub, Sister Agnes couldn't help but notice the scars on her scrawny arms. With a knowing nod, she had smeared them with a soothing balm before shooing her out to the garden. The southern sun would bring some colour into her chalk-white Scottish complexion and a stroll among the fragrant beds of *lavande* would help to lift her mournful melancholy.

If dour Sister Maryoth had been sour vinegar, douce Sister Agnes was a heart-warming cordial, though she, too, rarely smiled. Her main responsibility was tending the convent physic garden where she had acquired a great knowledge of herbs and their various properties and uses, both culinary and medicinal. Healing was her vocation and, in order to restore this pale, melancholic Scots girl to health, she plied her with invigorating tonics and piled her plate with tempting morsels of meats, fruits and vegetables. As she went about her chores, Elisabeth trailed behind her like a feckless fledgling to be fed and watered at regular intervals.

When the bell rang to signal the end of the evening meal, the sisters filed out of the refectory for compline. The routine at the convent was more austere than at St Mary's, adhering more strictly to the daily order of offices, but Elisabeth and Sister Agnes were excused the evening service. Instead, they made their way to the scriptorium. At this time of the day, when the writing desks were empty after the day's work, they were assured peace and quiet. When Elisabeth had confessed that she couldn't read her precious *Book of Hours,* Sister Agnes had been surprised. Never mind that the French order believed in educating their nuns, surely it was essential for a future prioress to be literate?

'Sister Maryoth says I'm a wild child and incapable of learning. Forbye my aunt has been prioress many a year and she is unlettered.'

'How then can she attend to her affairs? How can the prioress know whether or not she is being deceived?'

'My aunt is too lazy to care. Forbye, Sister Maryoth does all the scrieving.'

Sister Agnes frowned. 'Then your aunt is not her own mistress but in thrall to this secretary. If you remain unlettered you, too, will be at the mercy of those who have these skills. Especially those men who use the powerful tool of learning to pursue their own ends and to hold sway over others.'

Sister Agnes took out the small book hidden in the pocket of her habit. They were studying *The City of Ladies,* not only because it was printed plainly in French—unlike the laborious Latin calligraphy of the *Book of Hours*—but because it contained more truth than many pronouncements from the pulpit. Also, the author was a woman. Christine de Pisan had been educated by her father, a Venetian lawyer, invited as astrologer to the French court. When her French husband died during an epidemic, leaving her with three young children, the young widow De Pisan took up her pen to earn her living.

Lamenting that so many men condemned the entire feminine sex as monstrosities of nature, De Pisan concluded that this must be true. Even learned scholars and clerics seemed to agree that God had formed a vile creature in creating woman, though she questioned how such a worthy artisan could have deigned to make such an evil and abominable work.

'Lady De Pisan takes comfort from the fact that, as creatures of suffering, we're able to overcome the trials and tribulations that life throws at us,' Sister Agnes explained. 'And she gives many examples of how much-maligned women have triumphed over these prejudices.'

Pondering these remarkable women, De Pisan concluded that God wasn't to blame, but men for fabricating false assumptions. Since women are weaker in body, they must be feeble in mind, too, and should be kept in childlike ignorance so as not to overtax their simpler minds. By these claims they sought to justify withholding education from women but there was a darker intention behind them: denying women the opportunity to read and discover all the lies written about them.

'Innocence might be a virtue, but ignorance certainly is not,' Sister Agnes said. 'Now you understand why men hold education in such high esteem. If you can't read, you can't form your own opinions and must only accept what you're told. So, now let us prove that women's minds are no weaker than those of men.'

Elisabeth watched enthralled as Sister Agnes formed letters of the alphabet into words. This double-edged process of reading and writing filled her with wonder. That marks on parchment could communicate in such a way was a powerful kind of magic. Reading more of this visionary book inspired Elisabeth to make a solemn vow.

'When I become prioress, I shall build my own City of Ladies where justice and reason and righteousness will prevail.'

For a fleeting moment, a ghost of a smile flitted over Sister Agnes's face, and just as quickly vanished.

Chapter Twenty-Six
The Papingo

Eagles flee alane, but sheep herd the gither.
—Proverb

Auvergne, Easter 1516

The gown was exquisite. Fashioned out of the palest pink satin, the overskirt trimmed with finest Flanders lace and the bodice encrusted with tiny seed pearls, it shimmered like fairy wings. Elisabeth gazed at it with longing and then said, 'Take it away. I will not wear it,'.

'Madame, you must. It is a gift from your uncle,' the seamstress said. 'The prior is coming to visit you today and wishes to see you in it,' she pleaded. This was one of her most fabulous creations. Was it not exquisite? Was it not the most expensive fabric? See the invisible stitching? But no matter how much she cajoled her, Elisabeth refused even to try it on.

As soon as the prior arrived the hapless seamstress flapped and flustered around him to explain that it wasn't her fault. That she'd done her best to dress the young mademoiselle. That the gown fitted perfectly and, with a frantic look at the prior's furrowed brow, that it would have to be paid for even if not worn.

'Stop skittering around and get out of here.' Hepburn swished her away like an irritating fly. Then he glared at his stubborn niece still in her habit and wimple.

‘If I were a bride about to be wed, I’d be proud to wear this,’ Elisabeth simpered innocently, ‘but am I not a bride of Christ? Have I not taken a vow of poverty?’

‘And one of obedience,’ Hepburn blurted, struggling to control his rising anger. Knowing how thrawn she could be, he drew breath to calm himself. ‘Perhaps it’s time to educate you in the ways of the world, my dear.’

Elisabeth raised her brow, unsure what kind of lesson to expect. He drew up a chair for her to sit down.

‘Tonight you are to meet a very important person,’ Hepburn began. ‘We’ve been invited to the Duke of Albany’s court. As you know, he was appointed Regent of Scotland following Margaret Tudor’s marriage to your erstwhile brother-in-law, Archie Douglas. This untimely and unwise union so infuriated the Scottish lairds that they appointed John Stewart regent in her place. With royal blood in his veins, the duke is more likely to keep some semblance of order among our quarrelsome lairds. That is all to the good. However, a strong hand is also needed to steer church affairs. As you ken, dearest Lisbeth, I’ve been managing the archbishopric of St Andrews, for James IV’s bastard son…’

‘But wasn’t Alexander killed at Flodden?’ Elisabeth interrupted.

Hepburn nodded. ‘Aye, and that means the position of archbishop is vacant. And, my dear niece, since I’ve already done so much for St Andrews—co-founding the college of St Leonards for poor clerks, where I’m building up an extensive library,’ he added proudly, ‘would you not agree that the post should be mine by rights?’

Elisabeth shrugged. ‘Since you’ve already been elected by the cathedral chapter, why of course, dear uncle. Is that why you’ve come to France? For the duke’s approval?’

Hepburn shook his head wearily. ‘Unfortunately, the post has attracted some competition. No doubt because of all the benefices it offers. Even the pope’s nephew has thrown his hat into the ring but since he has no intention of setting foot on Scottish soil, he's no real threat. Bishop Forman has little support and is therefore of little account. But Provost Gavin Douglas, who covets the position, has objected, arguing that my election is unlawful. And he has the combined clout of his nephew Angus and Queen Margaret.'

Archie Douglas again: what a thorn in the side he'd been to their family. Elisabeth sighed. But what had that to do with her putting on an elaborate gown?

Hepburn leant forward and took her hands in his. 'In order to compete with him, my dearest Lisbeth, I, too, need patronage. That's why I've come to France—to gain the duke's favour. Since his wife's younger sister is married to Lorenzo de Medici, Albany should also have some influence with the pope.'

While Elisabeth's head reeled with all the complicated relationships and political machinations, Hepburn became dewy eyed. Once he had secured the archbishopric, he dreamt of the day when a cardinal's hat would be placed on his head. Until now he'd had little success in petitioning the regent but, knowing that Albany nurtured a soft spot for chaste young virgins, Hepburn had designed this eye-catching gown for his niece's presentation to the influential duke.

'My dear lass, all I'm asking is that you wear this gown on this one occasion. If you're to press my case to the duke, you'll need to catch his bonny blue een. This is how the world works. You must wear it. Well, what do you say?'

Following the example of her heroines in *The City of Ladies* who would endure torture and death rather than betray their principles, Elisabeth had intended to stand her ground. After all, she was a nun, not a doll to be dressed up and dangled on display, but she feared that if she continued to refuse her furious uncle would force the gown on her himself—not a thought to relish. But if she could do something to spite the evil Archie and his Douglas clan, then...

Elisabeth nodded. 'If it's your desire for the duke to tak tent of me, uncle, then I shall make sure he will.'

'That's the way of it, lass. I knew you'd see sense,' Hepburn's heavy-jowled face relaxed into a smile and he chooked her under the chin. 'And mind and ask for the archbishop's mitre for me.'

Château de la Tour

Entering the elegantly turreted *Château de la Tour*, the Duke of Albany's palace, Elisabeth stopped to look more closely at an engraving on the lintel above the main door. The thistle and *fleur-de-lys* not only symbolised the Auld Alliance between nations but between the Scottish and French branches of the Stewart family. She had stopped in the stone-pillared entrance gallery to admire the life-sized paintings of Stewart knights and Stuart *chevaliers* at war when a herald thudded his ceremonial staff on the flagstones.

A grand procession was making its way along the gallery. The ladies in wide hooped gowns glided along swanlike; their magnificent bosoms, garnished with glittering gems, jutting before them as imposing as the prow of James IV's legendary ship, the *Great Michael.* Promenading behind them the gentlemen—in embroidered capes of every hue from azure to vermilion draped over vibrant satin shirts frilled and ruffled in snow-white lace—were no less dazzling.

Shrinking back into a neuk, Elisabeth was startled by a raucous shriek. She whirled round and bumped into a gilded cage, sending a multi-hued bird rocking back and forth wildly on its swing. She steadied the cage and put her nose to the bars. Was this a bird of paradise, like the one embroidered on Meg's cushion that she'd kept as a memento?

A liveried footman tottered over on his high heels and eased a titbit through the bars of the cage. The bird took the morsel in its beak and then passed it to its claw, to peck off tiny pieces, like a perjink lady nibbling at a dainty. Fixing its bead-like eye on its benefactor, the bird squawked, *Merci!* The courtiers clapped their kid-gloved hands and clucked their tongues in admiration at this wondrous creature.

At the tail of the procession Hepburn trudged puffing and panting in his heavy vestments, his high colour even ruddier than usual. His beetle brows furrowed as he looked daggers at Elisabeth.

'What did I ask of you?' he hissed, but before she could reply, the herald called them into the duke's presence chamber.

All eyes turned towards the odd couple traversing the grand reception hall. The prior's magnificent robes of heavy brocade, richly threaded through with gold and silver, were given nods of approval but short gasps of surprise greeted his niece. The courtiers rolled their eyes in disbelief at her garb. For this splendid occasion Elisabeth had retrieved her coarse brown novice's habit, simply adorned by a rosary dangling from her waist and a crude wooden crucifix. No one, not even a holy nun would dream of turning up at court in such humble attire.

Les Écossais! Ah! That would explain it. How quaint! How simple! How barbaric! A plain dunnock in the midst of all those exotic peacocks, Elisabeth certainly stood out.

'Isn't this what you wanted, uncle? For me to make my mark?' she whispered, as suppressed titters followed their progress up the hall.

'You're making a mockery of us,' Hepburn growled, struggling to restrain his anger. As they approached the ducal dais, he strove to smooth his twisted face into a smile.

Several attendants were standing behind the duke's throne but one particular popinjay flashed to Elisabeth's attention. Never mind the sumptuous royal blue velvet doublet slashed with silver, nor the immaculate white lace frothing at his throat and wrists—though that must be the bane of any washerwoman to keep clean—nor the exquisite sapphire brooch pinned to his velvet bonnet. No, what fascinated Elisabeth—and made her want to giggle—was the brightly coloured peacock feather curling upwards and outwards from the fop's bonnet and waving ridiculously in the air every time he moved his head.

As instructed, Elisabeth made a deep curtsey to the duke. Interested to see what had set his court chattering, Albany leant forward to study *les Ecossaises* and then, to everyone's surprise, he stood up. He shrugged off his velvet, ermine-trimmed cloak to free his arm, and then offered his manicured hand to Elisabeth, inviting her onto the dais. Albany scrutinised this plain specimen: her clear complexion unsullied by powder or paint, her high forehead—a feature much envied by those fashionable ladies who had to shave their brow—emphasised by the severe cut of the wimple. To this nobleman, jaded with the excesses of the French Renaissance court, Elisabeth's lack of affectation was refreshing.

'Eh bien, votre nièce! Elle est très charmante.'

Prior Hepburn's great barrel chest heaved with relief and then puffed up with pride. At the duke's signal, the plumed dandy stepped forward to hear his command. As the feather on his bonnet bobbed up and down, Elisabeth suppressed a giggle.

'Bonnie feathers make bonnie birds,' she quipped in an aside to her uncle.

'Aye, and gude claes open a' doors,' the dandy responded in her native Scots, 'though an exception has been made in your case, it would seem,' he added, scanning her dowdy garb with disapproval. 'His grace, the duke, would like to give you a gift. Anything you ask, as a token of his esteem and as a souvenir of your visit to France. Say but the word.'

The crowd of courtiers moved forward, straining to hear what she would ask for. Who, in her favoured position, wouldn't ask for a precious jewel? A ring or a brooch, perhaps? Confident that he knew the answer Hepburn looked around, smirking at those who'd so recently been mocking them. Elisabeth considered for a moment.

'Je désirais une... poulet,' she replied, unsure of the correct word.

It was now the dandy's turn to look surprised. '*Une poule? Un coq?*' he attempted to translate.

'Nay, not a cockerel. Not a hen either, but...' she said, searching for the word. 'A popinjay.'

'A popinjay? You have in mind a papingo? You ken that's a parrot, don't you?' The dandy was bewildered.

'Like the bird in the courtyard,' she explained. 'That can talk.'

That more than anything else, she'd decided, would be a fitting reminder of her visit to the French court. With the hint of a smile on his lips, but a definite gleam of amusement in his eyes, the dandy nodded, causing the peacock feather to twitch again.

Word immediately buzzed round the hall that the nun had desired *une paroquet! Quelle horreur! Quel dommage!* What a wasted opportunity! The nun was too *naïve* for words.

'*Mais, bien sûr.*' Her choice impressed the duke, especially since humility was not a quality he'd associated with the Scots: at least not in those he'd come across. Her wish would be granted, but she must also choose something of greater value.

'Go on. Ask him now,' Hepburn almost yelled in her ear.

No, that was it. 'I shall remain true to my vow of poverty,' she replied with a simpering smile that would put Sister Maryoth to shame.

At the banquet that evening, Elisabeth sat in place of honour at the high table beside the regent. He was interested to hear her views about the country and the people he'd inherited, both being quite foreign to him. The dandy constantly fluttered around the regent ready to swoop down to interpret for them. With Sister Agnes's tuition, Elisabeth's French had greatly improved, and his services were rarely required.

Further down the table, seated marginally above the salt, Hepburn was in no mood for polite conversation or even the exquisite food. His anger-induced bile was sticking in his craw and spoiling his appetite. How could she have missed her chance! A popinjay! What good was a talking bird? You couldn't even eat it. Was his niece trying to make a bauchle out of him?

The French courtiers watched in alarm and distaste as the stout, bearded Scotsman speared the tastiest morsels with his fearsome-looking dirk and quaffed copious tassies of blood red claret. No amount of drink could mellow Hepburn's temper, however. When the time came to take their leave, he watched expectantly as the duke kissed Elisabeth's hand and said, *'Adieu, ma chère papingo.'* Knowing his thrawn niece, Hepburn assumed she'd be waiting until the last minute before making her petition but Elisabeth only smiled her response.

'Why did you fail to grasp the thistle, lass,' her uncle hissed as they left the court. 'It was right there, in your hand, but you let it go. As well as a vow of poverty you've also taken one of obedience, mind. To me.'

'Nay, uncle, it was neither the time nor the place to petition the duke for your archbishop's mitre. He wouldn't have looked kindly on it. He wanted to give *me* a gift, not you. To flaunt his generosity to one of his ain folk in front of his courtiers.'

'Hmm,' Hepburn replied, dumbfounded for once. His pawkie-witted niece hadn't been wasting her time in France. She was turning out to be as cunning as any Vatican emissary.

She yawned, quite worn out with all the excitement. 'Never fash, uncle, when the time is ripe, I shall put in a good word for you,' she said with an innocent smile, leaving her uncle open-mouthed and flummoxed yet again.

Convent de Nôtre Dame des Miracles

Elaborately winged heads poked out of the windows on all sides of the cloister to watch the foppish French courtier mince across the courtyard, balancing a multi-hued parrot perched on one arm and swinging a cage in his other hand. Fascinated by the peacock plume in the dandy's bonnet, the bird strained at the chain round its leg in an attempt to attack it.

‘David Beaton at your service,’ he announced, holding the bird at arm’s length as he tried to bow.

‘She’s taken a scunner to your bonnet. Either because she sees it as a rival, or because she has simple tastes in fashion,’ Elisabeth quipped.

‘Like you,’ he laughed. ‘Not many would dare to grace duke's presence in a nun’s garb. I was surprised you weren't laughed out of court. Your conceit is to be admired. And how do you jalouse the bird is female? The male of the species has more colourful plumage, does it not?’

Elisabeth tilted her head to study the parrot. Its main body feathers were emerald green with flashes of iridescent red, while the wings were a deep sapphire blue. In contrast, its head was golden yellow and the soft breast down was speckled through with topaz and amber. Not one jewel but many embellished this exotic bird of paradise.

She put her nose to the cage. ‘What have you to say for yourself, my bonnie chookie? Which are you? Lad or lass?’

The parrot fluttered its wings and stretched its neck to screech loudly.

‘Wheesht! Wheesht!!’ Elisabeth cried, covering her ears. ‘I’d fain have a bird that can talk, not a wailing banshee.’

The parrot stopped and cocked one yellow gimlet eye at her intently. ‘Shee…’ it tried to whistle. ‘Whee… whee… sh…’

Elisabeth chortled. ‘Well, that’s a start, my pretty Papingo, for that shall be your name.’

‘She’s after a treat for her performance,’ Beaton explained as the little parrot pecked sharply at her sleeve.

‘Ah! So you admit it’s a she.’ Elisabeth laughed triumphantly.

‘Or an eunuch—only a larbar or a woman could be so shrill. But once she's been trained, she'll make a perfect pet. Like all of your sex, she needs a strong hand. Your uncle clearly needs to be firmer with you if you’re to become a great lady one day.’

Elisabeth shot him a challenging look. 'And if I do, I'll stand no cheek from a Frenchified page boy such as you.'

The corners of his mouth twitched, warping his wry, sarcastic smile to a peeved frown. 'You may jest, but as the fifth son of a humble Fife laird I have to make my own way in the world. Unlike you, my dear sister.'

Not so humble that his father couldn't afford to send him to the universities of Glasgow and St Andrews and then to Orleans to finish his education. A tongue fluent in French and an eye for fashion had endeared Beaton to the French *haute monde*, in particular the Duke of Albany, who had taken him into his service as interpreter and diplomat.

'I'd consider myself blessed to be given such an opportunity as yours,' he sighed.

Beaton had already sought information about Elisabeth, the future prioress of the richly endowed St Mary's Abbey, one of the wealthiest in Scotland. As prioress, she would have control, not only of the lands and tenancies but also of the great benefices they bestowed.

'Nevertheless,' he went on, 'To marry for silver may be one remedy for my sorry plight, but what highborn lady would wed a lad with no prospects? A career in the church would be another, but cold-hearted celibacy wouldn't suit my hot-blooded humour, I jalouse.' As he leaned towards her too closely to whisper, 'Nor you, I wager, my lusty prioress-in-waiting,' Elisabeth drew back.

Chapter Twenty-Seven
Rivals

Evil words cut more than swords.
—Proverb

Auvergne, 1518

'What's this I hear?' Bishop Hepburn wheezed, breaking off his flow of speech to catch his breath. 'I trust these rumours about you and that pompous peacock are unfounded.'

He'd just returned from a short visit to Scotland where he'd had important matters to settle: matters that had clearly affected his digestion.

'All this rich French food is spoiling my stomach,' he complained, squirming in his chair and cradling his paunch, 'and now I hear this bruit about you and Beaton. As if I didn't have enough to worry about. Thon treacherous scoundrel, Home, has been plotting behind everyone's back. He's tricked me out of the archiepiscopal title.' He let out a bilious belch.

Elisabeth listened sympathetically to her uncle's gripes. While Hepburn had been petitioning the duke to sanction his election by the cathedral chapter, Home, the wily lord chamberlain, had proclaimed the Papal Bull in favour of Andrew Forman at the cross of Edinburgh.

'If you've been elected fairly and squarely, uncle, then surely you can appeal to the pope?' Elisabeth said.

Hepburn shook his head. 'Though it sticks in my craw that Home has trounced me, I dare not oppose Pope Leo's decision and risk excommunication. By way of a sop they have offered me Forman's former post, the bishopric of Moray. Hardly adequate compensation for losing the biggest prize,' he grumbled. 'They will live to regret insulting me thus.'

While in Scotland he'd already begun his revenge campaign by bullying the weak, frail Forman into giving up the revenues of the see in his favour. He was now planning his next move. On Forman's death—in the not-too-distant future given his poor health—Hepburn intended to make sure that he would be appointed Archbishop of St Andrews.

While his French physician had told him to eat less and only plain fare, it was difficult for Hepburn to curb the voracious appetite of a lifetime. Besides, no amount of food could satisfy the gnawing emptiness in his belly. Now he took out his frustration on his niece.

'While I've been suffering in my sickbed, you've been billing and cooing with thon fancy-feathered young fop. A nobody who has to live by his wits. I might have known he was up to something. The whole court is buzzing with clash of you two.'

He'd been ordered to rest but how could he with this scandal going on? No wonder his heart was galumphing wildly.

'Calm yourself, uncle,' Elisabeth now said. 'You mustn't get upset. Shall I ask them to bring you a soothing tisane? With mint for your stomach's sake?'

'Tisane! The devil take your tisanes. A strong cognac is what I need.'

Well-accustomed to her uncle's fickle humour—full of blame and bombast one minute and apologising the next—Elisabeth waited for the storm to subside.

'Believe me, my dear lass, his intentions are in no way honourable. Davie Beaton has a reputation as a gallant. Thinks he's cock of the walk crowing over his dunghill. Even nuns are fair game to him. Plucking your maidenhood would be a triumph. Another feather in his foppish cap.'

It was nothing but idle gossip, she assured him. Why shouldn't compatriots abroad meet to converse in their own language? And Beaton had an endless fund of amusing stories about the personalities and conspiracies at the French court that he dared not share with anyone else.

Dismissing her explanation, Hepburn replied, 'Not only is he out to sully your good name, he wants to discredit me with the duke. Don't be fooled by his glib-tongue and swankie clothes. Davie Beaton is a sleekit tod.'

Since his mastery of the French language was negligible, Hepburn had to rely on him as interpreter in his dealings with the duke. Behind his back, however, the miniature Machiavelli had been using his privileged relationship to petition on behalf of his uncle, chancellor of Scotland and archbishop of Glasgow, James Beaton.

'Aye poking his meddlesome nose into affairs that don't concern him. How dare his uncle try to compete against me! As for that young fop, strutting like a crow in the gutter! How dare he have the barefaced cheek to seduce my niece! I swear I'll thrash all that flumgummery out of him.' Hepburn's face, livid with rage, suddenly drained, taking on an unhealthy pallor.

He fell back into his chair. 'Oh, this isn't good for my heart,' he gasped, thumping his chest with one hand. 'Laughing while you draw the blear over my eyes and scheme behind my back. I forbid you to see him, do you hear? Mark my words: yon Davie Beaton will come to a bad end. The likes of him always do.'

While it was true that a *frisson* had developed between Elisabeth and Davie Beaton, it stemmed from a contest of wills rather than physical attraction, at least on her part. In their flyting, with each striving to triumph over the other and neither yielding, they had become rivals more than friends. Their first serious clash had occurred when Beaton had scoffed at her lessons with Sister Agnes.

‘Lasses who take to learning lose what the French cry their *naïveté,* their charming *simplicité,* and soon become tiresome.’

Elisabeth had bristled. ‘You mean they learn not to be taken in by your wiles and become bold enough to answer back. Or do you consider my feminine mind too feeble for such study?’

‘Ladies of your standing don’t need to bother themselves with such lowly occupations as scrieving.’ Beaton retorted. And, as future prioress, you’ll have no need to concern yourself with letters and suchlike. Other people can do that for you.’

‘Such as a man, you mean? Then your reasoning only serves to strengthen my resolve.’

They’d crossed swords again on discovering that their ambitious uncles were competing for the post of primate of all Scotland.

‘My uncle has been dealt with unjustly. He sought his election by peaceful means. Unlike Angus, he wouldn’t use a force of men to elect a man of God,’ Elisabeth stated.

'Unjustly! By peaceful means! You’re not as worldly-wise as you think, Elisabeth,’ Beaton sneered. ‘See how your own uncle has managed to deceive you with his artful tongue! But you cannot be blamed for that. Hepburn is well-kent as a man of subtle mind who hides his malicious intent behind crafty eloquence. Let me enlighten your gullible feminine mind. Your sainted uncle is as conniving as his consecrated colleagues when it comes to achieving a position of power. And there are always two sides to any story. Clearly he has omitted to tell you how he laid siege to St Andrews Castle to oust the Douglas faction?’

How she would love to wipe that smug sneer from his thick lips.

‘Oh, aye,’ Beaton waggled his head. ‘Weary of waiting for parliament or the pope to make up their minds, Angus occupied the castle and installed his uncle, Provost Gavin Douglas, poet and translator of Virgil’s *Aeneid* into Scots. But, as an educated lady, I'm sure you already knew that, and no doubt, may even have read it.' He smirked.

Without giving her a chance to answer—that she did know about the famous the makar from Lindsay but that she hadn't read the poem—Beaton rattled on:

'Prior Hepburn, however, wasn't one to see his prize being snatched from under his very nose. And what do you think he did? Use his glib tongue to coax Archie Douglas into handing the castle back to him?'

Elisabeth recoiled as Beaton thrust his face into hers.

'Nay, he used it to call up an even greater force and attacked not only the castle but the town of St Andrews itself, slaughtering and sparing no mercy for the townsfolk—not only men but women and children. He then cast his fere and foe, Provost Douglas, into the sea tower.'

Elisabeth folded her arms defensively. 'We Hepburns are a noble family, one of the foremost in our land,' she maintained, irritated at Beaton for this version of events. Though aware of her uncle's self-seeking ambitions and herself a victim of his despotic rule, she wouldn't allow anyone else to criticise him. It had been drummed into her to defend any family member, no matter their faults: *Keep Tryst.*

'Of that I have no doubt. I admire your loyalty and I trow you will respect mine. Let's declare *touché.*' Beaton had then taken his leave, with an exaggerated bow and sweeping flourish of his feather bonnet.

A few days later Elisabeth was returning to her cell after the midday meal when she heard Papingo squawking in alarm. 'Wheesht! Wheesht! Haud yer wheesht!'.

What was all the bruit about? And where was her elderly chaperone? She was trying to soothe the bird when a noise made her turn round. Sleekit Beaton had slipped past the old nun and hidden himself in her cell. He closed the door behind him and then tiptoed over to deal with Papingo.

‘Let's silence yon clapper-din before she rouses the whole convent,’ he said and wrapped the coverlet round the birdcage. Taking the darkness for night, the parrot tucked her little head under her wing and fell asleep.

‘I’d have thought with all your learning, you’d have taught her to say something more challenging. But then your wee Papingo is a lassie after all,’ he added with his infuriating, sardonic grin.

‘How did you get in? My uncle has forbidden you to see me.’

‘Unlike you, Elisabeth, who fails to be moved by this humble and contrite heart, your sisters are more merciful,’ he whimpered. He placed his hand on his chest and pulled a ridiculously pitiful face. ‘This may be our last meeting,’ he whined, ‘Ever. I'm being sent back to Scotland and I cannot leave with this ill-feeling between us. Forgive me if I've angered you but I'm here to make my peace afore I go.’

‘Had you donned sackcloth and sprinkled your curly hair with ashes I might have been gulled. For a vain peacock like you, that would indeed be a sacrifice.’ In vain, she tried to smother a smirk, for his withering look suggested she’d touched a sore spot. She’d never known a man who fussed so much with his appearance and never missed a chance to tease him about his wardrobe as extensive and elaborate as that of any fine lady.

Indeed, his figure and bearing were more feminine than masculine. Though his features were pleasant enough, they were not what she considered handsome, being too rounded, too feminine for her taste, with soft, chubby cheeks, full lips like a lassie and plump fingers. His thickset thighs and calves may signify virility but were not, in her view, enhanced by obscenely tight hose.

And there was a whiff about him, a sweet, cloying odour, unpleasant to her nose. In a state of arousal or excitement, his skin oozed an oily film which, when mingled with the potent scents he lavished on his flesh, produced a stale, slightly putrid tang. By his reek shall you know him, and Beaton reeked of smugness and self-satisfaction and an appetite for the good life. He would grow into a fat, pompous libertine if he weren't careful.

'Please, I beseech you, cruel damsel, punish me no more.' He knelt down on one knee and placed his palms together in a gesture of appeal.

'Must I leave, starved of your affection, without tasting one tiny morsel of tenderness from your lips?'

When he lowered his eyelids to peek coquettishly from under his long eyelashes, Elisabeth gave a startled gasp. Kate! That's who his mannerisms reminded her of. That's why she was taking such a scunner against him. Gazing with rounded, imploring eyes, he reached out for her hands which she thrust into the folds of her habit to avoid his greasy grip. To a man like Beaton, brought up in a French court, conducting affairs of the heart was as natural as political intrigue, but Elisabeth was ill at ease with the sophisticated rituals of courtly love.

She cleared her throat before asking, 'Why are you going back to Scotland?'

'I'll tell you, cold-hearted maiden. After a kiss.' He puckered his rosy-red chubby lips in readiness as he moved in close.

Instinctively Elisabeth shrank back from that smell, that cloying, oily scent that would quench any passion he might try to arouse.

'Will you never take no for an answer, Davie Beaton? I'm a nun, mind.'

'But against your will,' he purred. 'Have you not confessed as much? A spirited lass like you should not be locked away denying men's eyes the pleasures of your youth and beauty. Why should we not succumb to our true natures?'

'Mine does not include a desire to yield to you, Davie Beaton. For you're the devil's man: in thrall to Auld Hornie himself. Even Satan would give up if he found the door steekit against him. Now behave yourself.' As she shoved him firmly in the chest, he took the opportunity to grab hold of her hands.

'Aye, but the devil also bides his day. Which I trow will be now. Come on, let's have no more tittle-tattle when I am ready for a tussle,' he chided.

Elisabeth wrenched free and tucked her hands firmly under her oxters. '*Et ne nos inducas in tentationem,*' she pronounced, her mouth set tight.

'You realise, cruel lady, that I may be going to my death,' Beaton moaned as he wiped his slimy brow with an embroidered linen handkerchief.

Beaton was not jesting. He truly feared for his life. When, after a short sojourn in Scotland, the Duke of Albany had returned to France, leaving Antoine D'Arcie, his first lieutenant, in his stead, trouble had immediately broken out among the rival factions. Then, when D'Arcie was ambushed and brutally murdered, the regency council implored the duke to return to impose order. Wary of the wayward Scots, the cautious regent was sending Beaton ahead as his scout to ascertain the seriousness of the problem and whether or not his presence was essential.

'Are you unmoved that we may never see each other again? For you, that may not be important but for me... This may be our last ever meeting,' he pleaded. There was every possibility that, as the duke's ambassador, he would share D'Arcie's fate. The prospect of cold steel on his neck may have chilled his belly but unexpectedly warmed his loins. 'Is there really no chance of kindling a spark?'

'You're being too hasty Davie,' Elisabeth replied, irritated and impatient with this performance. 'As we Scots say: slow fires make sweet meat.'

'Ah! So there is hope!' he cried, pouncing on her. A firm thrust from Elisabeth upset his balance and he toppled against the birdcage, dislodging the cover and waking the parrot.

'Wheesht! Wheesht! Haud yer wheesht!' Papingo shrieked in alarm.

Steps could be heard running along the corridor and the cell door flew open.

Beaton cringed. ‘Good heavens. It’s the Lamb of God: *Agnus Dei. Miserere nobis.*’

The usually benign Sister Agnes was shaking with anger. Behind her, the elderly nun assigned as Elisabeth's chaperone, hung her head sheepishly and tried to hide the bonbon bulging in her cheek. As penance for her lapse, she’d now have to surrender the rest of the confits Beaton had given her to sweeten his way into Elisabeth’s cell.

‘Don’t be alarmed, Sister,’ Beaton said, switching on the charm. ‘I’m here to seek advice from our dear sister for my dearest sister.’ His younger sister Katherine yearned to take the veil, just as well since she’d have no dowry, and he was making enquiries about the regime at St Mary’s Abbey. ‘As long as her delicate mind was not overtaxed with learning,’ he said, with a sidelong glance at Elisabeth, ‘it should suit her very well.’ Then, raising his hand in benediction he took his leave. ‘*Pax vobiscum*.... And to you, Sister Agnus Dei.’

‘Et cum spiritu tuo,' the elderly nun responded from force of habit, before swiftly swallowing the sinfully sweet bonbon. Sister Agnes glared at Beaton, her suspicious eyes following him to the end of the corridor where he turned to give them all a cheeky, cheery wave.

Chapter Twenty-Eight
Prioress Elect

Veni, Sancte Spiritus,
Et tui amoris in eis ignem accende.
—Prayer

St Mary's Abbey, 1521

Sister Maryoth placed a coin on each sightless eye and covered the bloated, brosie face of the prioress with a linen cloth. Prioress Janet Hepburn's final agony was over. Sister Maryoth had watched with blank impassive eyes as the prioress grappled for every breath, her grossly overweight body swelling up until fit to burst. There was little Sister Maryoth could do to relieve her suffering, she convinced herself. After all, who was she to meddle in divine punishment for all those years of self-indulgence? When the prioress gasped her last breath and gave up her soul for judgment, Maryoth followed St Paul's instructions and did not lament. She said a prayer for the dead and gave thanks to God.

To the sisters who twittered about the unseemly haste Sister Maryoth explained that the funeral had to be conducted swiftly for fear of rapid decomposition, adding under her breath, proof —if any were needed—that Prioress Janet was no saint. Now as she shepherded the twenty-one sisters into the chapter house to organise the election of a new prioress, Sister Katherine Beaton objected.

‘We must wait until Bishop Hepburn arrives, for he’ll advise us what to do.’

Sister Maryoth’s lips tightened. She mistrusted this recently ordained nun, whose enthusiasm, coming perilously close to zealotry, she’d tried to curb.

‘*Bishop* Hepburn,’ she said through clenched teeth, ‘won’t be giving us advice, but orders. He’ll not be asking us whom we favour: neither will he call on the Holy Spirit to guide us. He'll appoint whom *he* wishes. And we all ken who that will be. We don’t need him to tell us what to do. We can decide for ourselves.’

‘Then we should wait for the instructions from the archbishop of St Andrews,’ Sister Katherine replied.

‘We have no need of the archbishop's authority, either. We can elect our own prioress,' Sister Maryoth affirmed. ‘It is our prerogative, our right.’

Uneasy and uncomprehending, the sisters whispered and muttered amongst themselves.

‘It’s all inscribed here.’ Sister Maryoth tapped her forefinger on a large leather-bound tome. She’d read all the documents pertaining to the nomination and been apprised of the election procedures, a claim which none of them could either make or refute.

‘Our new prioress shall be elected *Per viam Spiritus Sancti,*’ she explained. ‘As the Holy Spirit, in the guise of a dove descended on the apostles, filling their souls with grace and knowledge, so shall we pray for him to come down among us to kindle our hearts. Then, with one voice, we shall name the successor to our dearly departed sister. Our decision, sanctified by the Holy Ghost, will then be sanctioned by Archbishop Forman.’

Could they? Would he? Although the illiterate nuns could not dispute the rules as stated by Sister Maryoth, there was no memory of a prioress ever having been elected. Since the inauguration of the abbey, the prioress had always been appointed—and she had always been a Hepburn. It was no easy matter to persuade these subservient women to take matters into their own hands and act without male authorisation. Fearing to frighten them off, she appealed to an even higher authority.

'Sisters! Mind whom we serve! We are brides of Christ, chosen to love and serve him in this world. Do we not strive to be worthy of his love? Almighty God himself is showing us the way forward by giving us the chance to choose our spiritual leader. One who can guide us back to the path of righteousness. Have we not pledged vows of chastity, obedience and poverty? Would you not sooner elect your own prioress? One who has served and prayed with you for many years? One who follows faithfully the teachings of Christ Our Lord? Do not let this chalice pass us by.'

Wimpled heads nodded. It was true. Dame Janet had not led what could be called a holy life, whereas Sister Maryoth had all the right credentials. Well-bred—she was the daughter of William Hay, the Baron of Yester—and well-educated—she knew her letters, unlike the late illiterate prioress. Her night long vigils, prostrate on the stone-cold chapel floor testified to her piety and her capacity for suffering. Severe and unsmiling, her emotions veiled beneath a solemn mask, she personified sanctimony.

And there was one more argument in her favour: her age. Mindful that the position should go to someone older, wiser and in their middle years, the Cistercian Statutes stated that no-one under the age of thirty could be appointed prioress. Sister Maryoth was forty-two-years-old, she reminded them, while Elisabeth was not yet four and twenty. Would they dare to disobey canon law? she challenged Sister Katherine.

To settle matters once and for all, Sister Maryoth took the irksome novice aside to mention the unmentionable: the rumours about Elisabeth's legitimacy, which if proved to be true, would mean that she could not possibly be elected.

'*If* proved to be true,' Sister Katherine retorted, instinctively taking Elisabeth's side for, although she'd never met her, her brother David spoke well of her. 'Besides,' she went on, 'there's no denying the fact that Dame Janet and, more importantly, Bishop John had intended their niece, Elisabeth, to succeed her. By defying them, the sisters fear severe reprisals: facing the infernal wrath of Bishop Hepburn in the here and now and being cursed to hell by the ghost of the dearly departed prioress from the hereafter.'

Superstitious nonsense, Sister Maryoth hissed under her breath. To allay their anxiety, however, she served up some strong cordials usually reserved to reinvigorate those who'd been fasting but now needed to lubricate the mysterious workings of the Holy Spirit.

Once fortified, the nuns knelt in front of the Black Madonna, where Sister Maryoth led a recitation of the rosary. The Glorious Mysteries which appealed to the Holy Ghost for inspiration would be right and fitting, she decided. After the *Gloria* in the third decade, Sister Philomena sprang up to announce that, Glory be to God indeed, a tongue of flame was blazing through her breast. Her cheeks flushed with ecstasy, she raised her arms to heaven to rejoice that the Paraclete had chosen her among many to convey his message.

These pearls of divine wisdom, however, were lost among the cries from those who, not to be outdone, claimed that they, too, had been filled with the Holy Spirit. Elbowing each other out of the way, they scrambled to prostrate themselves in front of the Black Madonna.

Sister Maryoth hadn't planned for this mass frenzy. Only her accomplice, selected for her loyalty to Maryoth and her strident singing voice, was to deliver the divine message. Bellowing above the clamour, Sister Philomena proclaimed that the Holy Spirit had consecrated Sister Maryoth as their sister superior and mother of their flock. Subdued, the nuns meekly agreed, bleating with one voice.

Amid traditional protestations of humility and mild resistance, the newly elected prioress was seated on the elaborately carved ceremonial chair. To the accompaniment of the thanksgiving hymn, *Te Deum*, the nuns bore Prioress Maryoth up the aisle. Stopping in front of the Black Madonna, she draped her rosary beads round the Virgin's hand as a token of her gratitude. Now that she'd been elected *Per viam Spiritus Sancti*, no-one could gainsay her victory. While the other nuns knelt before Prioress Maryoth to pledge their allegiance, Sister Katherine, who'd kept a clear head by refusing the cordials, slipped out of the chapel.

Chapter Twenty-Nine
Prioress Appointed

Te Deum laudamus
—Hymn

Convent de Nôtre Dame des Miracles

Sister Agnes watched in silent misery as Elisabeth bustled about her cell preparing to leave the convent. When word reached Hepburn that, not only had Dame Janet's funeral already taken place but, more significantly, the election for the new prioress, he was incandescent that yet another post had been snatched from the noble Hepburn family.

'How dare they take matters into their own hands! How dare they elect someone without my permission,' he fumed and made arrangements to set sail forthwith for St Andrews: he wanted words with the archbishop.

Though she loved France, Elisabeth was eager to return home. 'Have I really been here for seven years? My goodness. *Seven long years were gone and past,*' she recited. 'True Thomas was spirited away by the Fairy Queen to Elfland, and when he returned home no-one recognised him.' She broke off abruptly, becoming wistful. 'But then he recognised no-one, either.'

'That will not happen to you,' Sister Agnes comforted her.

'Why not? I'm not the same as when I arrived here. I've changed. I've grown up. And thanks to you, *ma chère* Agnes, I have learnt so much. Why, I can read, write and count. Without your help, I'd never have felt able to take on such a responsible position as prioress.'

While she prattled on, busy with her packing, an odd sound made her look round. Sister Agnes was quaking from head to toe, large teardrops distorting her placid face.

'I… I'll never ever see you again,' she blurted, through trembling lips. 'There is nobody else in the whole world I care for. May God forgive me for my selfishness.'

The serene, self-possessed Sister Agnes was crumpling under the weight of her grief, which, despite all her prayers, wouldn't lift. She'd never intended to reveal her feelings –sinful in the eyes of their order—and had prayed for guidance, but watching Elisabeth gather up her belongings was more than she could bear. Startled by the intensity of her emotion, Elisabeth put her arms around her to calm her. Agnes clung to her tightly, her whole body heaving in distress while the parrot shrieked her commiserations.

'Wheesht! Wheesht! Haud yer wheesht!'

St Andrews, 1523

High up in the crow's nest, the lookout yelled that St Andrews was in sight. Impatient to see her homeland again, Elisabeth stretched out over the prow of the galley as it ploughed the chilly grey waters, while Sister Agnes clung, white knuckled, to the side-rail, hoping that the tingling salt spray would whip some healthy colour into her greenish-white complexion. The ginger root she was struggling to suck was doing little to quell her sickness.

Though the coastline was a faint smudge, barely visible through the damp, swirling fog, Agnes could hear a bell ringing to guide them in towards the shore. Gradually tall spires, towers and pinnacles emerged out of the ghostly mist and then the huge walls of the castle of St Andrews appeared. Elisabeth sniffed the air hungrily for familiar smells, blown by the offshore wind.

'You don't regret coming, do you?' Elisabeth asked. 'How could I leave my dear *Agnus Dei* behind?' she said.

A wan smile passed over Sister Agnes's pasty face. However seasick or homesick she was feeling now, it was as nothing compared to the desolation she would have felt at being left behind.

While Haddington had its fair share of religious establishments, the *raison d'être* of St Andrews, the seat of the Roman Catholic Church in Scotland, was clearly ecclesiastical administration. Nearly everyone they passed along the noisy, bustling streets was dressed in some form of clerical garb: friars, monks, nuns and guards in arch-episcopal uniform, all rushing about in the service of the Lord.

'At least we're not as out of place here, as I was at the French Court.'

Pleased to be anywhere with her soulmate, Sister Agnes managed a smile at Elisabeth's remark. Never in her most fervent prayers did she imagine that the French convent would let her go, but Elisabeth's wish was her uncle's command. If his beloved niece needed to have Sister Agnes by her side, then he would arrange it. In compensation for the loss of their dear sister the French abbess gratefully accepted a suitable *dot*, or dowry.

'Make haste, won't you?' Bishop Hepburn scurried along in front, impatient to confront the archbishop of St Andrews. However powerless the mild-mannered Forman professed to be, a pawn manipulated by the bishops and knights on the ecclesiastical chessboard, what he'd done was unforgivable and Hepburn was unforgiving. The archbishop owed him a favour and he would see to it that Elisabeth received her rightful inheritance

Archbishop Forman, whose health had never been robust, had been ailing for some time. Enshrouded in a thick woollen blanket, a scarf wound round his head and neck, the ascetic archbishop shrank at the prospect of confrontation with the burly Hepburn.

'I'm here to ensure that my niece is appointed prioress of St Mary's,' Hepburn demanded brusquely, unable to bring himself to address Forman with due deference.

'The post is already filled,' the archbishop answered, his weak voice muffled by the scarf. 'The sisters of the abbey are quite within their right to elect their own prioress and have already elected their successor.'

'Then you'll have to overrule it,' Hepburn demanded

'But I've already given them my blessing,' Forman squeaked in alarm. His head poked out of his scarf like a tortoise emerging from its shell.

'Has the Papal Bull been sent to the Vatican yet?'

Forman's head waggled clumsily from side to side. Thank goodness, Hepburn thought. For then it would have been more difficult to have the decision retracted: difficult, but not impossible.

'But your niece is too young to take on such a responsible position' Forman mumbled.

'Too young! Why, I was appointed prior when I was but sixteen. My niece will soon have completed her twenty-fourth year.'

Forman stood his ground. 'That is still six years below the canonical age for such a promotion.'

'Such rules, as you well know, are not canon law and can be altered to take account of the circumstances,' Hepburn retorted. 'My niece is a Hepburn and is perfectly capable of discharging the duties required of her station. I myself have overseen her schooling.'

'Indeed.' Forman shrank into himself, drawing in his scrawny neck before mumbling, 'but another question has been raised, that she was not born of lawful bed ... '

Hepburn leaned over him. 'By Maryoth Hay, perchance, and her brother John Hay, the notorious Wizard of Yester?' he growled, breathing heavily into Forman's face. 'You would believe thon witch and warlock? If you refuse, I shall petition Rome who will grant a dispensation for her defect of age and, if required, will clear up the matter of my niece's legitimacy.' The large sum he was willing to donate to the papal coffers should take care of both.

Forman slumped even further down in his chair. The wasting disease he'd been suffering from for many years had worsened and he sensed that his end was near. Soon he would depart this vale of tears, this land of scheming scoundrels where he, a dutiful cleric, had striven all his life to uphold canon law. In a country of near pagans, that was often a thankless task. Why had Christ promised that the meek would inherit the earth? He, for one, didn't want it and spent his final days in prayer, preparing his soul to meet his Maker. He glanced down at his liver-spotted hands. May God forgive me this one last act, he muttered, for he had no strength left to stand up to a bully like John Hepburn.

St Mary's Abbey

Bishop Hepburn was poring over the abbey's accounts when the air in the scriptorium turned chilly. Sister Maryoth with her power to slip into a room like a spectre had materialised at his side.

'I have come to inform you that I intend to appeal to the highest authority,' she said. Her manner was no longer submissive but challenging, her gaze no longer lowered but forthright. 'Your niece has no right to be appointed prioress. Apart from the issues of her age and dubious birth, I ken for a fact that she's no virgin,' Maryoth stated, her voice shrill.

'Indeed.' Hepburn narrowed his intense blue eyes and glowered at her. 'Let's take that last point first. Did you not swear to silence? Do you now intend to break that oath?'

'If necessary.' Sister Maryoth's thin lips clamped together.

'I see.' Hepburn lowered his head and began sifting through the documents. 'Of course, I have no power to prevent you, sister, but before you do...' he paused before picking up a ledger, 'would you mind clearing up a few discrepancies that appear to have crept into the financial records?'

Sister Maryoth's face paled and she began trembling.

Hepburn jabbed at the ledger with his finger. 'Had you been elected prioress this may never have come to light. Is that what you were hoping? A reliable and trustworthy witness—I am not at liberty to say who—has alerted me to certain malpractices. For example, cartloads of grain and other produce have been seen to leave the abbey every week, bound for the estate of Yester, but no payment seems to have been recorded. Not only that, but the figures in the accounts do not seem to add up. I suspect that substantial sums of missing funds have been finding their way into the coffers of your nephew. What do you say to that, Maryoth?'

Nothing. She cast down her eyes in her customary attitude of humility.

Hepburn's eyes narrowed. 'Did you know that the late king James—may God rest his soul—denounced Lord John Hay of Yester, the Wizard of Goblin Ha', for practising the black arts? And that this worshipper of Satan has been using his share of the abbey finances to squander and indulge his wicked ways. Tsk. Tsk. Not a good family connection for a holy nun, never mind a prioress.'

Sister Maryoth crossed herself continuously and kissed the crucifix on her rosary as Hepburn spat out these allegations.

'May the Virgin protect me! It was not my idea! I mean, I had no idea... It was my nephew who...' she trailed off.

'Whether you had any idea or not, sister, the fact still remains that serious misconduct has taken place. Let's say that your nephew bewitched you, that you fell under his evil influence, but that does not expiate your guilt. God did not excuse Adam when he exiled him with Eve from the Garden of

Eden. Now I think about it, banishment seems to be the most appropriate punishment for you. That's it. To a closed order where you shall take a vow of silence to gag your clacking tongue.'

Bishop Hepburn ordered the sisterhood to gather in the chapel where he addressed them with stern words.

'Sisters of St Mary's, be sure your sins will find you out. In the past few weeks you've been sheltering the arch-demon Satan in your midst. The Prince of Darkness has been warping your minds and twisting your reason.'

The bishop's accusation sent shudders up and down the spines of the susceptible sisters and the fear of hell into their ignorant souls. Auld Nick, Auld Hornie was real to them, a figure forever omnipresent, ready to jump out on the unwary, grab them with his horny claws and haul them down to the fiery depths of hell.

'On the day you elected Sister Maryoth as prioress, you all believed the Holy Ghost descended into your souls but you were grossly deceived. In the same way he tempted Eve in the Garden of Eden, the arch-demon whispered into Sister Maryoth's ear and lured her into giving you a potion that would cloud your reason. While she has been tainted by the serpent's subtle tongue, you, my dear sisters in Christ, are likewise guilty of sin: for choosing as your prioress one who will lead you down the fiery path to hell. And you all know the punishment for serving Satan: Thou shalt not suffer a witch to live. Burning at the stake is the only way to purge this accursed coven.'

The bishop leaned out across the pulpit to point an accusing finger at them all in turn. Gasps and sobs broke out among the nuns who threw themselves onto their knees, beating their breasts and begging for mercy. Terror rather than divine revelation, was now striking the soul of Sister Maryoth's chosen messenger. When Sister Philomena fainted, falling forwards and hitting her skull against the flagstones with a crack, Elisabeth dashed up to the pulpit.

‘Uncle!’ she hissed, flashing those ferny green eyes. ‘You cannot do this! You cannot punish all of them. Punish Sister Maryoth if you care but leave the rest in peace.’

Softening his angry scowl he beckoned her up into the pulpit. He put both hands on her shoulders and turned her to face the cowering sisterhood.

‘Behold, how your rightful prioress harbours no resentment but pleads for mercy to be shown to you sinners. Be mindful that Our Holy Father, Pope Leo X himself has confirmed her appointment by papal decree and will brook no defiance. It is now your obligation to accept her with the humility and obedience that befit your vocation.’

Then, his lips grazing her ear, he whispered, ‘Your shrewdness does you credit, my precious jewel. The nuns will now be forever grateful to you for saving their lives. And aye keep this in mind; the best tool for keeping order is the rule of fear.’

Chapter Thirty
Consecration

'Ah sweet, are ye a worldly creature.
Or heavenly thing in likeness of nature?'
—'The King's Quair', James I, 15th Century

St Mary's Abbey, 1521

'I'm the earl of Bothwell and you are my lieges. You will do my bidding.'

The assembled group of choirboys glowered suspiciously at the lad in the plush blue velvet breeches and feathered cap, who stood on the carved stone outside the abbey chapel to lord it over them. They'd been warned to be in best voice for a very important visitor but it was not, they grumbled, this cocky little fop.

'No, we'll no. No, we'll no,' they yelled back in unison.

As he waved his miniature bejewelled sword in his right hand, Patrick the young earl of Bothwell, wiped away a snotter from his perpetually running nose on his left sleeve. 'My uncle, the bishop, will have your bellies slit and your guts torn out if you disobey,' he whinged, before his bottom lip began to tremble.

Sniffing out weakness, one of the choirboys dashed forward to yank off his lordship's cap and ran off with it. Stamping his foot in a fit of pique, Earl Patrick pointed his sword at another boy and ordered him to retrieve it.

'You're the lord with the sword. Fetch it yourself,' he retorted.

While the bonnet was pitched from one lad to another, the earl joined in, leaping up and down like a flea trying to catch it. On the sidelines, a stocky dark-haired choir boy in a black soutane watched and waited till the lad waving the trophy scampered past him. Swiftly extending his foot, he tripped up the lad, snatched the cap and held it aloft, challenging all comers. Meanwhile, the peevish earl of Bothwell had slumped to the ground, sniffling and snivelling that he had a stitch in his side. The stocky choir boy knelt beside him and crammed the hat on his head, but he couldn't stick the fallen feather back on.

'Well done, my lad,' a woman's voice said.

The choir boy scrambled from his knees to behold a magnificent creature in a cream-coloured robe and immaculate white winged headdress. He stood transfixed. None other than the Queen of Heaven. The Mother of God, every inch a queen and nothing at all like the crude Black Madonna in the chapel, was gazing down on him. Chained to her wrist, an exotic multi-coloured bird of paradise fluttered its wings and pecked at her sleeve. Overcome by awe and wonder, he was torn between kneeling down to worship at her feet or running off to hide behind Betsy's voluminous skirts. Instead he blurted, '*All hail thou mighty Queen of Heaven*! *For thy peer on earth I never did see*!'

A beatific beam lit up her face as she took up the refrain:

'*Oh no, no, no, Thomas*', she said, '*That name does not belong to me*.'

'Lisbeth! My Lisbeth has come at last!' Betsy Learmont was hirpling across the courtyard as fast as her rickety legs could carry her. She hurled herself at the Fairy Queen and hugged her tightly, laughing and crying at the same time. Peeved at not being shown due deference, Earl Patrick, tugged at Betsy's skirt, demanding to be presented to the lady.

Through jaundiced eyes Prioress Janet had doted on her golden-haired angel, Earl Patrick, ruining his appetite with sweetmeats and spoiling his temper by filling him with a high conceit of himself. Earl of Bothwell he may be, but he was a thin, ingle-backit child, with stooped shoulders and an unhealthy pallor, his weak lungs aye wheezing and coughing. Try as she might, Betsy could not muster up any fondness for this orphan bairn, abandoned by a mother who, as Dame Janet herself had predicted, lowped the dyke, adding two more husbands to her tally.

'What's that bird?' he bawled, pointing his sword at the bird.

'This is a parakeet. I call her my Papingo.'

Patrick drew back as the parakeet tapped her beak irritably against the sharp weapon.

So he was right, the stocky lad marvelled. She must indeed be the Queen of Heaven, for wasn't the Paraclete another name for the Holy Ghost? Unsure how to behave in the company of such divine dignitaries, he hung back until Betsy pushed him forward.

'And do you mind your godson? John, greet your godmother.'

Knox was spellbound. The Queen of Heaven was his godmother? The Mother of God was his godmother?

Clamping his gawping mouth shut, Knox began to fidget nervously, wishing he had some kind of offering to give her. When he thrust out the bedraggled feather, she took it from him with a twinkling smile and squeezed his hand gently. He gave a little start. Her soft, smooth hands were a world away from Betsy's, rough and calloused from endless daily chores.

And she smelt heavenly. Not the camphoric stink of unclean clothes or the stale sweat of unwashed bodies, but fresh and fragrant. Betsy didn't believe in bathing too frequently—once a year in spring after wintering in smoky rooms was often enough—otherwise precious oils were washed from the skin, leaving you prey to any number of dreaded diseases. The celestial vision crouched down, still holding his hand.

'I'll wager that it was Betsy who taught you the *Ballad of True Thomas*.'

He nodded. To his surprise she leant over and skimmed his cheek lightly with her lips. His hand flew up, as if scalded. Betsy was generous with hugs but, as far as he could recall, she'd never kissed him. He blushed from the tips of his toes to the top of his scalp. Like the Queen of Fairy in the ballad, his godmother had gained his eternal loyalty with a kiss. At that moment he vowed to be her faithful servant, forever and ever. *Amen.*

Knox's first task for the prioress was to serve as altar boy at her inauguration Mass, celebrated by Bishop Hepburn. Now dottered and dithering, he kept losing concentration and stumbled his way through the service, but Knox kept a keen eye on the frail bishop's every move in case he spilt the sacred communion wine or wafers. He was ringing the *Sanctus* bell to signal silence when a commotion broke out at the back of the chapel. Some of the nuns were leaping up and down and hooching as if in a reel. Only Sister Agnes remained on her knees gazing steadfastly heavenwards.

Alarmed by the sea of waving hands, a multi-coloured bird was swooping and wheeling and, in its distress, dropping little white plops of gloop everywhere. The nuns ducked and dived to keep it from splattering their immaculate white wimples and cream habits.

'Someone shoo thon devil's bird out of here,' Bishop Hepburn croaked.

Reluctant to descend into the turmoil below, the parrot landed on a rafter to roost. Knox rushed down from the altar and tried to calm the nuns.

'Wheesht! Will you all haud your wheesht! You're only scaring it.'

On hearing the one phrase comprehensible to her, Papingo cocked her ear and gracefully descended to land on his head. Even though its sharp talons scraped his scalp Knox dared not move and waited for Elisabeth to inch forward, slowly so as not to startle the bird. As she grasped the parrot's claw and tied it to her wrist with her rosary beads, it stretched out to peck at something. A shiny trinket on the Black Madonna's finger had caught its gimlet eye.

'No treats for you, naughty Papingo,' Elisabeth chided, tapping it on the beak.

'I found that in the vestry,' John said, 'I thought I'd put it there in case the owner came back.'

Peering at it more closely, the prioress gave a little start. 'And so she has, John,' she said thoughtfully, slipping it into her pocket. 'So she has.'

Sniggering behind his hand, earl Patrick observed the mayhem from the back of the chapel. His practical joke had turned out even better than he'd planned. The nuns' habits beshitten with bird's droppings was a bonus. It was even more amusing than the time he'd released mice into the chapel to scuttle about and become entangled in their long skirts. Because he was the earl of Bothwell, the nuns dared not complain but had to tolerate and even forgive the silly pranks he played on them. That would show them, for Patrick had been deeply offended by Bishop John's remarks.

'What mealy-mouthed milksop have we here? Never mind Hepburn blood, is there any blood running in him at all?'

Patrick had winced as Bishop John pinched his pallid cheeks to redden them and pushed back his shoulders to straighten his back.

'God forbid that his mother was carrying a spineless Stewart when she married Adam. Let's see if he kens his scripture.'

Patrick also attended St Mary's Church choir school but, whenever the dominie asked him a question, he turned with glaikit eyes and slack jaw to Knox who answered promptly and correctly for him. Far from feeling ashamed, dull-witted Patrick considered book learning beneath his lordly dignity. That was for the likes of common lads such as Knox.

'So, John not only protects you from bullying by the other lads, but he speaks for you too? Hepburns are doughty fighters. You'll have to learn to wag your own tongue and bare your own knuckles, my lad,' Bishop Hepburn reprimanded.

Being in the company of indulgent women was clearly spoiling his nephew's nature and so, to strengthen and straighten his backbone, Hepburn resolved to send him to St Andrews Priory. There, his uncle and namesake, Prior Patrick, who had taken over his former post, would supervise his studies. While ridiculing his noble-born nephew, Hepburn had praised the orphan Knox who could recite the whole of the Mass in Latin, both the antiphons and responses, useful when the parish priest forgot his words, or was too befuddled by communion wine to dredge them up. Or both.

'Forbye, I John Knox is our godson, uncle. I breathed life into his lungs and you christened him,' Elisabeth reminded him.

'Aye, I mind fine. Baptised in the name of the Holy Trinity he's a thrice blessed lad indeed,' the bishop wheezed.

When their mother died a few years ago, John's older brother, William, had been apprenticed to a sea merchant in Prestonpans. Betsy had laid claim to John as Elisabeth's godson, taking him to Hailes as a playmate for the abandoned Earl Patrick. His future, however, was uncertain. When the bishop proposed a position in his episcopal guard, Elisabeth wasn't keen. Such intelligence should not be wasted in soldiery.

'You're right, my jewel. We need lads like him. He has the makings of a churchman. A parish priest perhaps.'

Elisabeth, however, had higher ambitions for her godson. With Bishop Hepburn's patronage, Knox would be assured not only a place at the local grammar school, but at St Leonards the college he'd co-founded at St Andrews University. And as his godmother, she would do all in her power to ensure that he rose to become at least a bishop, if not an archbishop, and even the cardinal's hat that Hepburn coveted.

Chapter Thirty-One
Last Rites

The state of man does change and vary,
Now sound, now sick, now blyth, now sary
Now dansand merry, now like to dee:
Timor mortis conturbat me.
—*Lament for the Makars*,
William Dunbar, 15th–16th Century

St Andrews, 1522

Bishop Hepburn eased himself onto his bony elbows and, though his sight was failing, his faded blue eyes gleamed with anticipation.

'Has the envoy arrived yet?' he croaked.

This same question he'd been asking endlessly, day after day. His nephew, Prior Patrick, shook his head. Bishop John had suffered another seizure and his condition was rapidly deteriorating. Like the drapes and folds of his elaborate vestments, his skin now hung loosely on him. Most of his teeth had fallen out causing his jowls, tinged with episcopal purple, to collapse. The fleshy, lascivious lips had withered and were now puckered with the permanent indignation of slighted worth. Wisps of silvery hair straggled from beneath his biretta. His body was covered in stinking bedsores that refused to heal.

Even as he lay on his deathbed, Hepburn had not lost hope of securing the long-coveted title. Now that Andrew Forman had died, he eagerly awaited the papal emissary with the Bull declaring him primate of Scotland.

The bishop cast an undisguised look of contempt at his nephew and barely deigned to speak to him. A stout young man with the same heavy, Hepburn jowls, but with a slackness about the mouth which bore the marks of a life well-lived, Prior Patrick was altogether a weaker character who lacked the Hepburn drive and ambition. Had it been a mistake to send the young earl to be educated by this wastrel?

'Where is Lisbeth? Bring me my precious pearl and get out of my sight!'

'Don't fret, uncle, I'm here,' Elisabeth said. Seeing her proud uncle so decrepit and infirm, with only the hope of the primacy keeping him alive, tore at her heart.

His gnarled hands groped for her, pulling her down towards him. The voice that had boomed throughout chapels, churches and cathedrals had become hoarse and faint. His foul breath stank and, as tactfully as she could, Elisabeth covered her nose and mouth with a fine cambric handkerchief.

Bishop Hepburn—whose personal motto *Ad vitam* adorned the walls of his college St Leonards—was scared stiff of death, or more truthfully, of hell and eternal damnation. As insurance against such a fate, he'd undergone the last rites several times to guarantee absolution for every sinful act knowingly or unknowingly committed, confessed and unconfessed.

'Father. Let me hear you say it. Father,' he whispered gruffly into her ear as she leant over him.

'As you wish. Father.' Elisabeth complied, assuming that, in his delirium, he was confusing her with his confessor.

'May God in his infinite mercy forgive me, a poor sinner. I wasn't strong enough to resist the temptations of the flesh. Afflicted by the same weaknesses as other men. Och, women are indeed the very devil,' he rasped. The more his breathing became laboured, the tighter his knobbly fingers grasped her hand. He pulled her in closer.

'I can't take this lie to the grave with me,' he wheezed. 'When I said you were ill-begotten, that you were the fruit of your mother's adultery, that was true. But what I said about your father, that wasn't true—apart being a buttery-lippit blackguard.' Hepburn attempted a smile. 'But he didn't die in a border foray.' When he paused to inhale deeply a rattle sounded deep in his throat. 'He lives still. For you see, your father... is me.'

Despite his foul breath, Elisabeth leant in more closely. Had she heard him aright?

'I don't understand, uncle. What are you saying?'

'My dearest Lisbeth, *I* am your father.' His rheumy eyes sought hers, beseeching her forgiveness.

'My father?' She stared at him in disbelief. 'But if you are my father—then who is my mother?'

'Oh, never fear, you are your mother's daughter. How I worshipped her! To my dying day, I'll never forgive my brother. When his first wife died, he was given the choice of the earl of Huntly's two daughters; whichever would best please him. Everyone assumed he'd take the elder sister, Katherine Gordon. That would have been the right and proper thing to do. But... but...' he choked back tears, 'he chose Margaret. He stole her from under my nose. Out of sheer spite.'

His knotted hands began to knead the blanket as he became more and more agitated. 'Since you can never wed, said he, I'll have Margaret, for she's bonnier and daintier than her sister. Though she was forced to marry Patrick, it was me she truly loved. And you weren't ill-begotten, my precious pearl, but love-begotten.'

Elisabeth dabbed at the tears flowing down the deep furrowed lines of his face. Sniffling he went on. 'For Patrick paid her scant attention. Too busy with the conspiracies and intrigues that may have gained him an earldom but lost her douce, warm heart. While he was swaggering about France and Spain and all the airts, I did my best to comfort Margaret, my most precious pearl. However profane our love may have been in the eyes of the church for us it was sacred.'

His watery eyes narrowed and, for a second, flashed intensely blue. 'Then when your birth ripped my beloved Margaret from me, I blamed you. I couldn't bear to set eyes on you, but when I did, I was stunned. You are indeed your mother's daughter. You have her ferny green eyes, with hazel tints that flicker and glint in the sunlight, and yon bonnie russet hair. I may have lost my dearest love, but I've gained you, my precious jewel.' He squeezed her hand. 'And you are mine. You are,' he rasped, 'you are my daughter. In whom I am well pleased,' he finally managed to declare, a faint smile flitting across his ravished features.

Elisabeth frowned. A band of pain clamped her forehead as she struggled to grasp the significance of this revelation. Her uncle was her father. The prioress was a bishop's daughter. Her head began to dirl with it all.

'My own daughter! Prioress of St Mary's! And when I am archbishop—nay, cardinal—you and I shall have all of Fife and the Lothians under our control. What a formidable pair we shall be! We shall show those conniving Beatons!'

Gripped by a searing pain in his chest, he collapsed back onto his pillows.

The men in full regalia who arrived at St Andrews Priory were not the escort of the long-awaited Papal Nuncio bringing news of Hepburn's appointment, but the arch-episcopal guard—headed by David Beaton whose drab clerical garb was enlivened by a conical-shaped hat with green tassels. Elisabeth greeted him at the main door of the priory—before he had the chance to force his way into the bishop's bedchamber. Quashing a mischievous urge to flick his silly tassels she invited him into the bishop's antechamber and offered him some wine.

'So you survived certain death at the hands of the Scottish lairds?' she asked.

'As you see,' Beaton replied and raised his goblet. 'And now, my lady prioress, let's congratulate each other on our new appointments.'

'*You* have a new appointment?'

'Aye. I've left the Duke of Albany's service and now act as private secretary to my uncle, James Beaton.'

This surprised Elisabeth. 'But why give up such an important position?'

Beaton tapped the side of his nose. Albany's intermittent government was a disaster. Whenever he visited Scotland, stability reigned, only to be followed by chaos and anarchy whenever he departed. Beaton could see great changes ahead: time was fast approaching when the duke may be forced to give up the regency.

'And, since he has resisted Margaret Tudor's charms...'

'What? Elisabeth snorted. 'The puddock princess tried to seduce him?'

'Oh aye, on his visits here they spent many hours closeted together and not only to discuss politics. As his secretary, I should ken. I suspect she may have been seeking his support to divorce Angus and may even have made him a proposal of marriage. But the duke is not so daft. He has no intention of staying in Scotland and as soon as he goes there will be a right old tug-o'-war between her and Angus for control of the young king. For, when he reaches his twelfth birthday in April 1524, James can be declared of age to rule.

'Since Albany's heart is not here in Scotland, I've decided it would be best to leave his service now. I intend to assist my uncle who, like me, does have our country's best interests at heart,' Davie Beaton added.

'Indeed,' Elisabeth replied while thinking that Beaton's own ambitious interests would be nearer his heart.

'And, to that end, I come with a message for your uncle.'

‘Good news, I hope. My… my uncle…’ Elisabeth hesitated as she considered her newly informed relationship, ‘is very ill. May I ken what that may be so as to forewarn him?’

‘My commission is to deliver the message to Bishop Hepburn himself,’ Beaton replied. The rivalry between them was still as strong as ever and he was clearly set on winning this round. Taken aback by his high-handed manner, Elisabeth searched Beaton's eyes for the twinkle that would indicate he was only teasing, but she was met by a stern, humourless glare.

Beaton drained his goblet and slammed it down on the table. When he tried to push past her, she stood firm.

‘From the smug look on your face I jalouse that you’re not going to tell him what he desperately wants to hear. My ...’ again she had to stop and think, ‘My uncle is dying. For pity’s sake, let him die in peace. Let him die in hope. Be merciful, Davie.’

‘He who lives on hope dies fasting. Your family loyalty is praiseworthy, Lisbeth, but I, too, must fulfil my office. As the arch-episcopal emissary, I have full authority to command you to stand aside,’ he said with his self-important sneer.

Elisabeth stared back, grim-faced and unsmiling. How tempted she was to slap the birkie’s flabby, well-fed face. Or knock that jaunty hat off his swollen head. He ordered her to wait outside while he informed Hepburn that the post of Archbishop of St Andrews had been given to James Beaton.

Only once the deed was done did Beaton crinkle up his eyes and give her an insolent wink.

‘It would seem that my uncle has won this particular race.’

Beaton’s brusque communication crushed John Hepburn, squeezing the last vestiges of vibrancy out of him: his violet eyes dimmed and sank into their sockets. As she mopped the beads of sweat from his brow Elisabeth tried to console him.

‘There is some hope,’ she said softly. ‘Your nephew, Prior Patrick, may one day gain the position you coveted.’

'Patrick? Nay, never that one,' he snarled in a moment of stark lucidity. 'That ill-begotten, fushionless nephew of mine has only risen because of me. He lacks ambition. There is no fire in his blood, no hunger for power. He craves only a full belly and a filled bed.' Spittle drooled from the corners of his mouth.

'If only you'd been born a man, Elisabeth, you'd have had the smeddum to fulfil my ambition.' Seeking her hand again, he lay still to catch his breath. His eyes moistened with tears as he whispered, 'It's a pity about your bairn. That he...' Hepburn broke off. 'That he failed to thrive. The Lord only kens but my grandson might have been a worthy successor to me.'

Sitting by his bedside, listening to Hepburn's rasping breath as he slowly ebbed away, Elisabeth fought back tears. That he might, she thought, and then said, 'Aye, but our godson has the makings of becoming a great bishop one day.'

Hepburn's blue eyes flickered for a moment. 'I mind the day I baptised the lad,' he gasped, 'John Knox. Make sure to enrol your godson in my college at St Leonards. Tell them he has my patronage. May my blessing be upon him.'

'I shall make sure John follows in your footsteps,' she gulped before adding, 'father.'

Hepburn had held fast on to Elisabeth's hand until he breathed his last. No sooner had she wiped his damp, chilling brow than Prior Patrick pushed her aside. She must go to her chamber now and stay there until after the funeral: she would have no say in the arrangements. Since it was not the custom for women to attend funerals—even a queen was excluded from her royal husband's requiem—Elisabeth had no choice. Birth was women's labour: death, it seemed, was man's domain.

On the eve of the funeral, while Prior Patrick entertained the invited dignitaries, Elisabeth defied his orders and sneaked into St Andrews Cathedral to pay her last respects. Hepburn's open coffin lay on a bier surrounded by lit candles. His corpse was dressed in lavish vestments of episcopal purple and a crucifix placed between his hands, but his bishop's ring was missing from his finger. Certain that his clerical cronies—after feasting on the elaborate funeral meats—would appoint him Bishop of Moray in his uncle's place, Prior Patrick had already taken possession of this symbol of office.

Elisabeth pulled up a stool next to the coffin and massaged her bruised hand. Hepburn, she reflected, had been a difficult, exasperating man: like God the Father himself, he was often unfair and unjust. Domineering and dictatorial, he had demanded obedience and subservience and few dared to oppose him. But then, being disappointed in love had determined his life. Although it had not been his choice, he had funnelled all his frustrated desire, all his thwarted passion into a career in the Church.

No doubt Hepburn's life had shaped his character: she was beginning to understand and even appreciate his rage and resentment. Besides, was her life not following a similar path? Forsaken in love, forced into a priory—she truly was her father's daughter, she thought ruefully. So, if Hepburn had been able to forgive her—not only for her mother's death but for her youthful rebellion and misdemeanours—then she, too, would find it in her heart to forgive him his trespasses.

Hearing footsteps on the flagstones, Elisabeth whirled round to see Betsy trailing Earl Patrick behind her and John Knox tugging her eagerly forward. Catching sight of his godmother, John broke free and dashed up to tell her all about his first sea crossing: how his brave brother, William had sailed them across from Aberlady and how he hadn't been sick once. Not like Earl Patrick who had puked all the way.

'Tsk. Tsk,' Betsy scolded. 'No telling tales, Johnnie, and certainly not in a holy place.'

Abashed, John hung his head and said sorry to Patrick who had slumped down onto the flagstones. Betsy propped him up against a pillar and wiped his ghostly white face.

'Oh Betsy! Thank goodness you're here.' Elisabeth collapsed into the comforting arms of her nurse and sobbed her heart out.

'Wheesht, now,' Betsy said as she gathered her orphans round her. 'A good night's sleep will do us all some good.'

Later, when the lads were tucked up together in a truckle bed and Betsy had mulled some spiced wine, she explained how Prior Patrick had ordered her to bring the young earl as head of the clan to attend their uncle's funeral. On her own initiative, she had also brought John. After all, as Bishop Hepburn's godson he should be entitled to serve at the requiem Mass. Elisabeth agreed. Surely Prior Patrick could not object to that.

She cradled the tassie of spiced wine, still too hot to drink, and said, 'To think how often I taunted Kate for being a gowk and all the time it was me that was the cuckoo in the nest.' She glanced sideways at her nurse. 'You knew, Betsy, didn't you? Why did you never tell me?'

Betsy added a few drops of aquavitae to fortify her wine. 'Aye, I did ken but I said nothing. For one thing, it wasn't my place to do so and, for another, why should I bother? It might only have caused you grief. Families are never simple. They're all taigled up and tapsalteerie. After all, your sister Joanna was your father's daughter by his first wife, Joanna Douglas, and your ill-begotten sister-in-law Nancy had the king's bairn. One way or another you're all gowks.'

Elisabeth laughed. She hardly knew Joanna who was more than fifteen years older and had married Lord Seton in 1506. Widowed by Flodden, Joanna had vowed to set up a Dominican convent in Edinburgh, which she intended to enter when her son came of age. Another abbess in the family might be a blessing, Elisabeth considered.

'Aye, it's true what they say,' Betsy was chuckling. 'In the great scheme of things, what does it matter who your parents are? Forbye, some things are better left unsaid.' She took a long draft of fortified wine and then added, 'Till the time is ripe.'

Chapter Thirty-Two
The Miraculous Cure

The vices of the evil will fall on their heads.
—*The City of Ladies*, Christine de Pisan, 14th–15th Century

St Mary's Abbey, 1523

David Beaton's hooded eyes surveyed her chamber, noting the books on her shelves before alighting on the pomanders filled with sweet-smelling herbs that perfumed the air.

'True to his name, Father Dudgeon is in high dudgeon.' While his lips attempted a wry smile his eyes remained wary. 'He has made several complaints to the archbishop about the changes you're making at the abbey. I warn you, Lisbeth, he will stab you in the back if you continue to pay him no heed.'

Her aunt had always deferred to him, the parish priest had whined, but then Dame Janet had known her place. This niece of hers with her learning and that nun from France with her foreign ways did not bestow on him the respect that was his due.

Before Elisabeth could stop him, Beaton had picked a small book from the shelf and was flicking through it.

'The fact that you're teaching your sisters their letters... '

'Let Father Dudgeon not suffer the sin of envy. Tell him he would be most welcome to attend my lessons,' Elisabeth said.

'When they should be spending time in more spiritual pursuits of prayer and contemplation,' Beaton retorted.

The exasperating way that Beaton smacked his plump lips in an indulgent smile infuriated her. She snatched *The City of Ladies* from him, hoping that he hadn't had time to read any of it. She didn't want him to have further grounds for complaint.

'So, he agrees with you, Davie Beaton? That schooling women is about as useful as polishing the inside of a chamber pot?'

Beaton smirked. 'I wouldn't put it quite so crudely. In some cases, I admit, it may be beneficial. In your position as prioress, I concede it may be to your advantage to be literate.'

And the way Davie Beaton looked down his nose to examine his meticulously manicured fingernails grated on her nerves.

'Forbye your own sister, Katherine, is one of our more eager and able pupils, you'll be pleased to know,' Elisabeth informed him.

'Venerable virtues, I'm sure, but too much learning may blight her spiritual vocation.'

'You have a gey low opinion of women's abilities, Davie Beaton,' she retorted, 'yet you gladly lend an ear to the haverings of Father Dudgeon who can hardly spell his own name. Just because he's an ordained priest, I have to respect him and let him stand in judgement over me.' She struggled to keep her seething resentment at this unlearned cleric's superiority from boiling over.

Tapping his chin he said, 'That's another of his complaints. He's taken a tirrivee because you've dismissed him as your confessor.'

'You ken fine the reason. Our reverend father is a drunkard and a sot who would sell his soul for a drink,' Elisabeth retaliated. 'By inventing sins to blab about to his drinking cronies, he's betraying the sanctity of the confessional. Why, you should be persecuting him, not me. What stories he spins about us, I can jalouse. Doubtless he also tells you that we're running a whorehouse?'

‘Now you come to mention it,’ Beaton said with a smirk, before proceeding to polish his immaculately filed fingernails on his sleeve. ‘But he has a more serious charge. Since a miraculous cure has taken place here without his knowledge or approval, you nuns must be witches, consorting with Auld Nick.’

The whorehouse at the Abbey of St Mary’s was steadily earning a reputation as a refuge for women. In Dame Janet’s time wealthy patronesses had been welcomed, providing a substantial source of income for the abbey: devout virgins and widows seeking a spiritual retreat from the world, worthy matrons, worn-out and weary after years of childbearing, craving rest and recuperation. The poor, meanwhile, had been given alms and sent on their way and the sick directed to the infirmary run by the Friars of St Laurence. Neither Dame Janet nor Sister Maryoth had suffered scrofulous scavengers and scroungers cluttering up her priory.

Now that Sister Maryoth had been exiled to the cloistered Abbey of Coldingham, the new prioress and her sisters were free to dole out more Christian charity. Mindful of their dream to establish a City of Ladies, they turned away no-one and every day more and more women came to the abbey seeking sanctuary. Not only beggars, but abused, downtrodden women; whores, diseased and sodden with drink, wives maltreated by their husbands, despoiled daughters thrown out by their families, shrunken old crones and destitute widows, poor witless souls cried after in the street as witches. The list, it seemed, was endless.

It had begun in a small way with Sister Agnes dispensing medications and ointments made from the herbs and plants she grew in the kitchen garden. She’d set up an apothecary in one of the outhouses where she worked alongside Betsy who not only had a wide knowledge of native herb-lore, but an uncanny talent for diagnosis. She would peer into the sufferer’s eyes, examining the whites and the pupils for tell-tale signs, inspect the pallor of the skin and sniff the breath to determine their ailment. How they could attend patiently to those ragged scraps of humanity when the sight and stench of their suppurating sores and scabs made her stomach heave, was a miracle in itself to Elisabeth.

When a woman with deformed growths on her neck had come begging for a cure, Betsy's remedy had been to hang the leaves of the noble figwort round her neck as a charm to ward off the scrofula. Mindful that there was often an element of truth in these old cantrips, Sister Agnes had crushed the tubers of the plant to make a poultice and applied it to the woman's neck. Gradually her skin began to knit together until it was healed.

'A miracle! A miracle!' the ecstatic patient declared.

With Sister Agnes being hailed as a saint, queues of lepers and sufferers of scrofula were soon queuing outside the apothecary to kiss the hem of her robe. Tortured with embarrassment, Agnes implored them to seek help at St Laurence, but they howled their refusal.

'For we are sure to die in the infirmary, if not of the sickness we have, then of the wasting disease, or the pox. The friars there skirp at us women. To them we are the damned. They wouldn't even pray for our wicked souls.'

While most of the women had sat down in the courtyard, refusing to move, a few had slipped into the chapel to demand the sanctuary of a holy place. Sister Agnes gazed with pity on the swarm of wretched women.

'We must do something for them. We must build our own hospice.'

'Who will look after them all?' Certainly not those nuns who had entered the convent for a life free from such worldly and womanly cares as nursing the sick. Neither their vows nor their vocation demanded such sacrifice. The idea unsettled Elisabeth. 'And how will it be paid for?' The sick and destitute were already a constant drain on their resources, a seeping sore of human decomposition.

'God shall provide,' Sister Katherine affirmed with the confidence of the righteous. 'Does He not help those who help themselves? And that is what the women shall do. In return for their bed and board, we shall teach them to look after each other.'

'And show them that clean water works better than holy water to cure many ills,' Agnes added.

Elisabeth had laughed. 'Such faith: such hope: such charity. How could I be such a scatter-wit? Now that you're a saint, Agnes, you're the one to work miracles.'

Elisabeth finished summarising their story to David Beaton and said 'So that's what's set Father Dudgeon's teeth on edge. He seems to think this is a coven, not a convent. Come and see for yourself what magic spells and potions our carlin is cooking up.'

Swirling mists of pungent-smelling steam from simmering pots and pans made Beaton's eyes smart as he examined the rows of meticulously labelled jars and flasks and phials. Selecting a small pot Beaton lifted the lid and sniffed.

'Ugh! What on God's earth is this?' His nose wrinkled in disgust. 'I know! Such a foul-smelling ointment can only be the elixir of eternal youth! Many a lady would sell her soul for this! Or do you already?' he said wining at Elisabeth.

While he chortled gaily at his little jest, Sister Agnes earnestly explained that the unguent, prepared from burdock, goose grass, red dock and garlic, was to treat the lepers at the hospice of the friars of St Laurence.

'Thon disgusting stench would be enough to drive out the disease,' he joked.

'Sadly, nothing can cure that dreadful ailment,' Sister Agnes continued gravely, 'but it helps to relieve the pain. Besides, the poor souls believe that it keeps away the evil eye.'

Beaton's eyes gleamed on hearing this snippet. 'Ah, not only lepers believe in the evil eye, I've been told. Is it true that you place herbs in your undergarments to fend off evil spirits?'

'A posy of cinquefoil helps to stifle foul smells in the same way that we sprinkle lavender oil on these.' Agnes pointed to a row of dried herbs and heather tied in bunches. 'As for evil spirits...' She shrugged. 'For some people, the belief that their illness has been caused by a malevolent spirit is very strong.'

'But that is just superstitious nonsense,' Beaton scoffed.

'Who is to say they are wrong? Do we not believe in the power of Satan who is evil incarnate? And do you, as custodian of the relics of St Andrew, not urge your flock to venerate them and pray to the saint for help?

'Yes, but...' Beaton seemed stumped for a moment before replying. 'We must distinguish between spells which stem from sorcery and miracles which occur through divine intervention.'

Sister Agnes stiffened as she guessed at his intention.

'No miracle has taken place here.'

'Though many would beg to disagree,' Beaton replied. 'Including Father Dudgeon. Tell me, Sister Agnes, is it true that, you as well as doling out charity you profit from vanity? That you concoct—if not the elixir of youth—then creams and lotions which preserve and prolong beauty? For which grateful ladies of worth generously reward the abbey? Just how generously Father Dudgeon is eager to know.'

'So *that* explains why Dudgeon is in high dudgeon,' Elisabeth exclaimed. 'Not because he isn't receiving due respect: but because he isn't receiving any financial due. Is that what's required to keep his mouth shut?'

Beaton shot her a look of shocked disapproval.

'Tut, tut! How can you suspect your parish priest of avarice? We servants of the church should share and share alike in our dealings with Mammon, should we not? I, for one, am more than willing to turn a blind eye to your activities here in return for a small recompense.' The devilish glint in his eyes betrayed his innocent expression.

'I'm sure Sister Agnes will be able to concoct something appropriate for you. A bitter purgative for your swollen pride, perhaps, or a salve for your conscience,' she retorted. Either of which she'd be more than happy to administer.

'Your new confessor will require more than some balm to grease his palm,' Beaton smirked, 'for I am honoured to be given that rôle.'

'What? You? Our confessor?' Elisabeth was beginning to regret her hasty dismissal of Father Dudgeon. The devil they knew was preferable to Beaton.

'That's impossible, Davie Beaton. You haven't taken Major Orders.'

He scowled at her. 'But I am to be appointed Abbot of Arbroath. And I will be ordained.' He drummed his chin with his fingers and waggled his head. 'In due course, in due course. Until then I would like you to look upon me as your guardian. Without the guidance and support of your late uncle, you and your sisters need a spiritual and temporal adviser to champion your cause. Gratis, of course. And don't be losing sleep over the secrets of your confessions,' he waggled his forefinger cheekily, 'I'm sure there will be no mortal sin worthy of hellfire. Not a sin worth a damn.'

Chapter Thirty-Three
A Case of Courtly Love

Open rebuke is better than secret love.
—Proverbs 27:5

St Mary's Abbey, Autumn 1525

The Edinburgh lawyers were dragging their heels dealing with the claims that Lord John Hay of Yester was pursuing against the abbey. How long had it been now? How many months, if not years? Of the two actions he had brought, the first—to prohibit the cutting of peats on his land—was unjust, since it violated a right bestowed on the abbey centuries ago by their founder, Countess Ada, and the second—to prohibit the passing of any carts or animals within a mile of his land—was malicious, since it would curtail access to their sheep granges and also mean a longer and therefore more expensive journey to deliver goods to the abbey.

'He's doing it out of revenge,' Sister Katherine maintained. 'Ever since that business with his aunt, Sister Maryoth, he's been harassing us.'

Elisabeth nodded. With a mind as astute as her brother's, Katherine had quickly learnt to read and write and was proving to be invaluable in helping her to manage the abbey's affairs. Now, as they sat side-by-side in the scriptorium, the prioress placed her hand on Katherine's sleeve. 'It was thanks to you that their cheating was uncovered.'

Sister Katherine moved her arm away. 'When I saw what they were up to, I couldn't simply close my eyes. I only did what was right. And now I'm beginning to think that either our lawyers are in the pockets of Hay or they are too frightened to contest such a fiercesome opponent.'

It was rumoured that Lord Hay, like his notorious ancestor Hugo de Gifford, the original Wizard of Goblin Ha', could summon dark forces. There was indeed the mark of Satan about him, with his full black beard and eyes that blazed like diabolic beacons whenever his will was challenged—which Elisabeth had dared to do.

Moreover, Hay was married to Elizabeth Douglas, sister of Angus who, as Beaton had predicted, was winning the struggle for the regency. A rotating council for control of the king had been set up but, now that it was time for Angus to hand James over, he was refusing to do so. A demon in his own right, many might consider, Angus would doubtless side with his brother-in-law against his ex-wife Meg's sister.

'If Bishop Hepburn were still alive, Hay wouldn't be pursuing us so forcefully for such petty causes,' Katherine said. 'He assumes we're weak women. Since the lackadaisical Edinburgh lawyers seem afraid to raise the hackles of the Wizard and Angus, perhaps now is time to call on our self-appointed champion and test his mettle.'

Elisabeth agreed. While Davie Beaton was attending the court in Edinburgh to defend a case brought against his patron, Lord Ogilvie, they would ask him to look into the affair.

When Abbot Beaton returned from the city he was a man transfigured. His robes tailored in the French style hung loosely from his leaner body, his hawkish eyes had lost their predatory look and his whole being radiated happiness and joy..

Curious, Elisabeth asked, 'Have we beaten Sister Maryoth's curse? Or has the Wizard of Goblin Ha' put a spell on you?'

To her surprise Beaton threw up his arms and twirled round her chamber on tiptoe like a giddy girl. 'A lesser man I may be in body but a greater one in heart! What I have lost in flesh I have gained in spirit! The most wonderful thing has happened to me! You are the first to know. I am in love!'

Again? She knew Beaton of old and his weakness for a pretty face.

'You've been beglamoured,' Elisabeth taunted. 'Or else you've secretly been taking one of Agnes's love philtres.'

'Really in love this time,' he sighed. 'Truly. Madly. Deeply. However,' he lowered his voice to a conspiratorial whisper, 'not a word of this to Katherine. She won't approve.'

Lady Marion Ogilvie had stood in court with her head held high, refusing to be intimidated by her great-nephew's lawyers. She knew their opinion of this maiden aunt, this thorn in their side. A child of her father's marriage left dowerless on his death, she should be grateful to Lord Ogilvie for deigning to grant her a place in his household.

Lady Marion, however, was no compliant spinster aunt, grateful for any crumb left over from her master's table. She was a mature woman, nearing thirty, brought up by her mother to manage her own affairs and now she was defending her right to recover the value of her father's livestock requisitioned by her great-nephew. When his lawyers argued that he needed to recoup the costs of her bed and board, she reminded them that she was a lord's daughter, not a common lodger, and being granted grace and favour should mean just that. Would any of them divest a distressed gentlewoman of their own kin of her lawful legacy or ask her to pay for her keep?

A bonnie fighter, David Beaton had thought, as she stood opposite him in court, her face flushed, her intelligent eyes flashing to defend her rights. His heart swooped and soared at identifying a kindred spirit who, like him, was striving against the odds to make her own way in the world. The doughty aunt so bedazzled Beaton that he was willing to flout her great-nephew's wishes and find in her favour. His patron, Lord Ogilvie, would not be pleased but Beaton cared not a jot.

Before leaving Edinburgh, he was thrilled to find that he'd not only met his soulmate but his bedfellow, a woman whose passion could match his. For, though her nephew's lawyers poked fun at her by saying her tinderbox must be dry, once lit, Lady Marion instantly burst into flame. At her age there was little time for virginal coyness. Her feistiness, her age and lack of a dowry had doubtless put many a suitor off, but not Beaton.

Davie Beaton was clearly smitten. 'She's a fine woman of noble birth whom I love and respect with all my heart,' he sighed in admiration.

'And from what you say, she is learned too,' Elisabeth couldn't resist pointing out.

Beaton shrugged. '*Touché*. Her mother made sure of that, for she knew she'd have to struggle in life. Hard-headed highlander that she is, Marion isn't vexed by the opinion of others and, since she doesn't trouble with ceremony, we've already pledged our troth to each other. For the present, our handfasting is sufficient.'

At this mention of handfasting, Elisabeth felt her heart wrenching and her womb clenching. She turned away to hide her discomfort and regain her self-control.

'But what will the archbishop say? And your sister? What will Katherine say?'

'As long as I'm discreet, my uncle will turn a blind eye,' Beaton replied. 'My beloved Marion will become mistress of Ethie Castle in Angus. No more grace and favour for her. And she's even agreed to take on my two bairns! On condition there will be no more. At least from any other mistress.' His eyes twinkled mischievously. 'As for Katherine, well, I am sure that once she meets Marion, she, too, will be smitten.'

If she consented to meet her, for Katherine was as rigid in her morals as her brother was flexible in his.

'And what of our little crusade against Lord Hay? Has that come to naught?' she enquired. 'Or did you lose your head as well as your heart in the Edinburgh court?'

'The Wizard of Goblin Ha' won't be casting his evil eye on you again. The case has been dropped. At the behest of Angus himself.'

Elisabeth bridled at the mention of his name but Beaton raised a cautionary hand. Despite being in the throes of an acrimonious divorce from Margaret Tudor, Archie Douglas had shown some sympathy for Elisabeth's plight. He seemed to be most contrite, Beaton said as he described their meeting.

'To think I traded white spun gold for brazen brass,' the morose Angus had moaned. 'A delicate Scots harebell for a coarse English drab. What a fool I was! Thon Tudor witch must have charmed me with one of her love philtres. How could I have mistaken thon puddock for a princess?' he muttered. 'So now Hay is lording it over St Mary's, is he? He may be my brother-in-law but John Hay is a conniving rogue, as curly and crooked as Auld Clootie's horns. Let him dare meddle with the Hepburns and he meddles with me,' he growled and ordered Hay to desist from pursuing his case forthwith.

When Beaton thanked him, Angus had replied, 'Small recompense, small recompense.'

'What do you think he meant by that?'

Elisabeth sighed and shook her head. Was it conceivable that the treacherous Archie might be feeling remorse for Meg's untimely death?

'Ah, well. *Requiescat in pace* to that case,' Beaton said, giving her a mock blessing.

'Aye,' she murmured, 'and *Requiescat in pace*, my dearest sister Meg.'

PART THREE

Chapter Thirty-Four
The Complaint

After that I the lang winters nicht
Had lyne waking, in to my bed, alone,
Through heavy thocht, that no way sleep I micht
Remembering of divers things gone.
—*The Complaint*, Sir David Lindsay, 16th Century

Garleton Castle, December 1527

The goose feather quill kept slipping from his chilled fingers and the ink, crushed and pounded from oak gallnuts, had frozen in its pot. Galling indeed, and while these bile blisters might reflect his bitter mood, where was the use in registering his resentment in rhyme? Lindsay threw down his quill and pulled his Yuletide gift from Margaret Tudor more tightly round him. The expensive cloak of dark red velvet, trimmed with fox fur, was a peace offering to show that the queen mother bore him no ill feeling.

He waddled across the oratory and peeked out of the casement window. The dark clouds louring in the moonless January sky threatened snow. With a shiver he turned towards the ingle to rake together the last dying embers. The wind howled in the chimneybreast. Another sleepless night.

The wine he'd drunk at supper had put him to sleep at first but then he'd woken up, wakerife and unrested, in the early hours of the morning. A feeling of deep unease crushed him. Where was he going? What was the point of his life? He'd soon be approaching his fortieth year. Two score already: one score and ten left of his earthly span. Why did the pace of life speed up as he grew older? Like climbing a hill—a long, trauchlesome scramble to the top, followed by a decline as swift as Lisbeth's high-spirited tumble down the brae.

Since James's birth, on the twelfth of April 1512, he'd never left the monarch's side. Ever the faithful servant, Lindsay had carried the infant to his coronation at Stirling, had soothed him through nights of painful teething, had bathed and dressed his skinned knees. But worried that he had become too close to her son, the queen mother had dismissed Lindsay from royal service. She had given his position of master usher to Andrew Stewart, a distant cousin of her late husband, James IV, and whose brother, Henry, so gossipmongers whispered, had replaced Angus in her bedchamber. What would become of young King James now? he fretted.

It had saddened Lindsay to leave the palace that James IV had built for his Tudor bride. With a lump in his throat, Lindsay had been packing up his books and manuscripts, pens and parchments, when the young James had lumbered in, armed to the hilt with the various hunting gifts his English uncle, Henry VIII, had sent him. One of them was not to the twelve-year-old King of Scots satisfaction, however.

'And I've requested an English buckler,' he declared, screwing up his nose at the miniature sword dangling from one finger. 'One fit for a man and not a toy for a boy.'

Disappointed, Lindsay shook his head. What of his singing and dancing? Had he forgotten those skills, so delighting the visiting English ambassador that he'd given good report to his uncle Henry? Lindsay's remarks fell on deaf ears. As his personal wappinschaw clearly demonstrated, weapons of war were more to the young monarch's taste than the arts, a taste being encouraged by his new guardians. Had they all forgotten that it was his father's zealous devotion to the cult of chivalry that had been his undoing?

‘And poetry? What about the songs and verses I sang to you?’

‘The earl of Angus’s brother is to take charge of my schooling now and he says that poetry is for lovelorn milksops.’

‘Indeed. And by learning the honourable George Douglas of Pittendreich doesn’t mean Latin, Greek and Grammar, but wine, women and wastreling.’

For protesting too much, Lindsay had been banished to his lands at Garleton, leaving the Douglas faction free to abuse power for their own profit and advancement. Now there would be no-one to give the young monarch good advice.

Imprudently, like witless fools,
They took that young Prince from the schools.

But what was the use of penning a *Complaint* if it was never read?

Stamping his feet in cold and frustration, Lindsay trampled on his fallen quill and groaned. Was it a sign that he should give up his task? As he examined his broken quill, a loud banging from below disturbed him: the metal knocker was clanging insistently against the oak door. Opening the shutter slightly, he peeked out to see someone at the main door, clapping his arms vigorously against his chest. One of Angus’s men, Lindsay assumed, and was about to warn the doorkeeper not to open up at such a late hour. But then, he reconsidered, if the regent had wanted rid of him, he wouldn’t have sent one solitary brigand with his sword sheathed.

The visitor cupped his hands to call up to the window. ‘John Hepburn, master of Hailes has sent me.’ Melting snow dripped from the messenger’s boots as he delivered his warning. Angus was on the rampage. Constant challenges to his authority were trying the regent’s patience and he was now marauding his way through the land, dinging down anyone who opposed him. Already the earl of Lennox had been slain for attempting to abduct the king and David Beaton flung in prison for his part in the conspiracy. Closer to home, Bolton Castle had been burnt to the ground, on suspicion that the master of Hailes was harbouring rebels.

Now Angus was setting his sights on Lindsay. In her divorce petition, Margaret Tudor, was claiming that James IV was still alive and had not been slain at Flodden. The tale at the time about four mysterious horsemen carrying the king off the field was true, she insisted, and James was on pilgrimage to the Holy Land, doing penance for his sins. However fanciful her grounds might be, Angus feared that if they were divorced, he would lose the regency and guardianship of the young king would be entrusted to someone else.

'And so Angus thinks I might be a possible candidate? I should be flattered but I'd rather not cross swords with such a formidable foe as Archie Douglas,' Lindsay said. 'And what about you, Harry Cockburn? Are you a rebel?'

Though now broad shouldered and bearded, Harry's distinctive red hair, long and tousled and tied untidily at the neck with a piece of hempen string, betrayed him. After fleeing the clutches of the drunken abbey watchmen, he'd joined a band of border reivers, charged with keeping order in Liddesdale, though changing sides depending on whoever paid them. Now he was in the pay of John Hepburn, master of Hailes.

'A rebel?' Harry frowned as he thought about this. Then he broke into a wide grin displaying broken, blackened teeth. 'That I am, Sir David, for I'm aye the king's loyal subject. And Angus is intent on redding out his enemies. That's why ...' He broke off at the sound of drumming hooves in the courtyard. When they heard raised voices and doors being kicked open, Harry drew his sword and melted into the shadows.

Lindsay sped downstairs, only for his way to be barred by a scruffy looking soldier who bawled by way of greeting, 'I'm captain of the royal guard.'

Indeed? Noting the shabby canvas jerkin and lack of any insignia, Lindsay doubted it—or standards were slipping at the royal palace.

'Make yourself ready, Sir David,' he commanded. 'His grace has called for you.'

'His grace?' Lindsay queried.

'Aye. At the request of King James himself you're to come at once.'

The slight movement of the captain's hand towards the hilt of his sword alerted Lindsay. There should be no need for coercion if his request were true.

Happit in his royal velvet cloak, he was bundled out into the murky, mucky January night. The biting wind tore at his face as they rode down the hill towards Aberlady, but when they turned right instead of left, his fears were confirmed. So, they were travelling eastwards along the coast and not westwards towards Edinburgh and the king. Above the gale, he could hear waves pounding against the cliffs—Tantallon crags, no doubt. With a sudden whack, the masked rider next to him slapped the flank of his horse.

'His horse is affrighted. I'll go after him,' the masked rider yelled.

Lindsay galloped towards the cliff edge, pursued by the rider who now grabbed hold of the spooked horse's bridle to slow it down. Pulling down his kerchief Harry Cockburn said, 'Lowp off when I tell you.' A few seconds later he shouted, 'Now!' and spanked the horse's flanks.

The horse reared up, throwing Lindsay off. His knees buckled under as he hit the ground and he tumbled over, rolling dangerously close to the rocky escarpment.

'He's fallen over the cliff,' he heard Harry's voice shouting above the gale. 'Shall I go after him?'

'Nay, leave him to the crags and gulls,' the captain called out. 'Saves us the trouble. But go after his mount; that's of mair worth.'

Lindsay crawled on his hands and knees, groping his way along the cliff. The driving rain had turned to sleet and, with his head and face wrapped in the hood of his cloak, he could only see a few inches in front of him. Divots had softened his fall and stopped him from plunging over the edge but if he lost his footing he'd fall to his death. Finding a narrow ledge, he contorted himself into the cramped space to wait.

Out of the mist she drifted slowly towards him, her face a hazy blur until she came near. Kate? Her smile changed to bewildered sadness before gradually fading. Lisbeth! He jolted himself awake.

He strained to raise himself up, but the dampness that had seeped through every bone and sinew drew him down. To ease the cramps in his creaking joints, he rubbed his arms and legs vigorously and then cocooned himself tightly in his cloak. After a while he began to feel pleasantly drowsy. To sleep was all he desired and to dream of his beloved Lisbeth, but from the fog of his memory he couldn't conjure up her face, just a line from his poem. *What was her name? She answered courteously, 'I am Dame Remembrance.'*

Chapter Thirty-Five
The Clerk's Play

John come kiss me noo,
John come kiss me by and by
And make no more ado.
— Traditional song

Haddington, Yuletide 1528

'Cross my palm with silver, young master, and I'll tell your fate.'

The young gypsy lass stood, legs astride, blocking his path, her dark eyes fixing him with a bold stare. She held out a grimy hand from under a garishly coloured shawl. When Knox tried to push past her, she grabbed hold of his elbow.

'Cross my palm, young master,' she wheedled.

'Begone, wretched carlin. I'll have no dealings with spaewives and witches,' the indignant cleric replied, trying to shake her off. 'How can you see what the future holds for me in the palm of my hand? Only the Lord God Almighty kens our destiny.'

'The devil swarbit on you, for it is bad luck to spurn one of our ain folk.' Her black eyes flashed with anger. 'There's no fleeing from fate.' As he moved to brush her aside, she slipped the shawl down to bare a nut-brown shoulder and winked at him. 'And mark this, young sir, our paths will cross again afore the day is out.'

Knox was staring after her, bemused, when a guildsman ran up to him, shouting, 'Master Knox! Master Knox! Come at once.'

Outside the abbey a protracted argument about the order of precedence was delaying the Christ's Mass procession. By long-standing tradition and a regular payment, the bakers had always marched immediately behind the clerics carrying the Black Madonna. While the masons and the wrights were arguing for a change, the bakers were digging in their heels.

The baillie was beyond making a sensible judgement. Befuddled from too much mulled ale, he swayed back and forth trying to gather his wits and recall which side had given him the biggest bribe. The whole procession had now come to a standstill and the guildsmen were looking to Master Knox for the way forward.

A Franciscan friar who'd been following the wranglings with interest, hobbled over on a crutch. He took the flummoxed cleric aside and whispered in his ear. Knox listened attentively, nodded and then turned to address the thrawn guildsmen.

'Here's what must be done, brothers. This is a religious procession, is it no?'

There was no disputing that.

'In which you must all take part as brethren?'

Again, heads nodded.

'No one guild being above any other?'

That was more controversial, especially to the bakers.

'Then you shall process together in oxters, as brothers.'

Knox then linked up a member of each guild so that a mason, a wright, a smith and a hammerman walked in line, arm in arm. All except the disgruntled bakers, who stood their ground, threatening to withdraw altogether if they weren't given precedence. The friar again hobbled forward, to address them himself this time. Recognising the habit of the Observantine Friars of St Francis, a holy order with the reputation of being highly trained in canon law, the guildsmen listened to him.

'Hark at my words!' the friar said, commanding his audience with his authoritative voice. 'For the offence of refusing to take part in a holy procession the parish priest will impose a penalty of forty shillings sterling.'

A blow at their pockets changed the minds of the bakers who agreed to process—on condition that they linked up only with their own. In that case, the friar insisted, they'd have to march at the back behind the others. Finally setting out, the procession trudged towards the marketplace where a convoy of carts was forming a circle.

'Make way for the Clerk's Play! Make way for the Clerk's Play!' he called out.

The crowd surged forward, jostling each other for a better view. To resurrect some Christian significance from the pagan Yule festivities, the Roman Church encouraged the local trade guilds to put on Biblical tableaux under the direction of the clergy. These clerk's plays were performed as early as possible in the day—before too much drink paralysed the masqueraders and stupefied the audience.

This year, instead of the usual dumb shows—silent, unmoving tableaux—Knox had written scripts for the players to perform. He'd spent hours translating Gospel texts into the vernacular for the common folk to understand more easily. Rehearsals had been shambolic since few of the guildsmen could read and could only memorise their lines by constant repetition.

A blast of a trumpet signalled the start of the Guild of Wheelwrights' contribution: The Annunciation. Toiling to flap his makeshift wings, the Archangel Gabriel lumbered gracelessly in front of the kneeling Virgin who clasped her hands to her heart in wonder.

'Hail Mary! Do not be afeart,' Gabriel boomed.

'Is it any wonder she's afeart? What lass wouldn't take fright at a muckle hooded craw such as thon?'

Paying the heckler no heed Gabriel went on, 'Behold, the Lord is with thee. Blessed art thou among women for thou art chosen to bear the Son of God.'

'How can this be?' Mary piped up. Well past the first flush of youth, the wheelwright's wife squeaked her lines in a high-pitched voice to suggest *virgo intacta*.

'Surely you ken by now, mistress? If your guid man cannot kittle you up, there's one here that will!' the heckler jeered.

Undaunted, Gabriel continued with his speech in the singsong intonation he considered appropriate to the script: 'The Holy Ghost will come down to bless your womb with his holy rod.'

'The Holy Ghost's holy rod!' the heckler hollered. 'Shouldn't Joseph the wood-wright be the one to bore his shaft into her dook-hole?' The rabble hooted and waggled their fingers in obscene gestures.

Knox leapt onto the makeshift stage and yelled, 'Enough of this mockery! Bedone with this blasphemy! You're making a bauchle of the Holy Scripture. I warn you. Take heed of the Word of the Lord, lest your immortal souls be damned to the flames of hell.'

'Master Knox seems fair put out, poor lad. Look at him lowping up and down like a freshly caught finnock. Johnnie, my lad, don't be such a marfeast,' the heckler shouted back. 'Spare the preaching for Sunday Mass. For at yuletide, the Abbot of Unreason and the Monk of Misrule hold court! Let the devil take us till the auld year's wede awa'!'

Then, casting off their rôles and ditching their badly rehearsed lines, the players began improvising, responding to hecklers and scoffers with increasingly lewd wisecracks.

Despairing of the mob's profanity, Knox abandoned the Annunciation to attend the Nativity. A more respectful audience—mostly women—were cooing and clucking over the chubby little infant in the crib. But the boisterous rabble was running amok and no mercy was spared for the newly delivered mother of Christ.

'Hark at her: mild as mead. And whose wean is she nursing in her arms? The father could be one of any number. Mark my words, it's no the angel Gabriel's.'

Meanwhile, the despot Herod's cruel order to slaughter all babes under two years old had infuriated his audience who were bombarding him with food scraps. Herod's rage at being duped by the Three Wise Men was as nothing compared to Knox's wrath. In a voice hoarse with fury, he railed at them until something slimy and wet smacking the side of his face silenced him. He jumped off the cart, his blue eyes blazing and fists flailing ready to take on whoever had thrown the haddock. The jeering revellers grabbed his arms and spun him round till his head was birling.

'Jocky Knox, high on the cnocks,
Maun take the knocks.
Jocky Knox—you're unco sma',
Are you going awa' to tell your ma?
Jocky Knox—who's your ma?
Nay, whore's your ma!
Your ma's your holy sister!
Where's your ma, your holy ma?
In behind the priory wa',
In the whorehoose,
Of the lemand Lamp o' Lothian!

They pushed and pulled him, hither and thither, towting and taunting until he tripped and fell on the greasy cobbles. He was in danger of being trampled underfoot when he was grabbed by the collar and pulled clear of the mockrife mob. The friar set him on his feet and then turned back to tackle his tormentors, letting fly with his crutch and whacking whoever got in his way.

Knox took refuge in the vennel where he leant against the wall to catch his breath. Out of the shadows staggered the gypsy girl who'd clearly been spending her earnings in the tavern. Her shawl had slipped even further down from her shoulders and was now tied loosely round her waist. The lace on her thin cotton blouse had come undone, revealing one pink nipple that poked out provocatively, with the other threatening to do so. Just a touch and it, too, would pop out.

'Did I no tell you we'd meet again? Come on, Johnnie lad,' she slurred. 'Let's see what the future holds. It can do you no harm. What's for you will no go by you.'

A slattern, he told himself in an effort to control the feelings she stirred, slovenly and unclean. These 'light' women, hussies of easy virtue and loose morals were the butt of smutty jokes by the grammar school lads curious about tail-toddle, though he tried not to listen to their smickering for he was to be a priest. He had to keep his mind and body clean and dared not be tempted by sins of the flesh. Forbye, his godmother had drummed it into him to respect women.

But sluts such as this gypsy spaewife were of a different order. Heathens, unbelievers who traded in superstitions and sold their bodies for drink were beneath contempt. Yet he couldn't take his eyes off her naked breasts. What harm would it do to hear her prophecy? No more dangerous than listening to Betsy. And wasn't unreason the rule at Yule? Stricken numb he couldn't push her away when she took hold of his elbow.

With a furtive glance to check that no-one was watching, he let himself be led further into the vennel. The hand that stroked his palm was ingrained with dirt, the fingernails embedded with filth. Her unkempt, oily hair stank of wood smoke. Her skirt, high-kiltit to the knee, revealed bare legs streaked with the ordure of the street. She was wild and wanton. A pagan. A heathen. But she had lustrous cherry lips, licked moist by her tongue and deep, dark, lustful eyes. As if bewitched, he let his right hand be caressed by the seductress.

'This palm tells who you are, but yours is gey difficult to read. I see you can be a bit trauchlesome and quick to take offence. You can be standfray and thrawn when it suits. Aye, you are indeed a true Taurus. The horned bull.'

'Ha!' he scoffed. 'There you are mistaken. The ale has bleared your second sight. I was born on St Andrew's feast day. Under the sign of Sagittarius.'

Scraping her greasy hair out of her eyes, she squinted at him sceptically. 'Nay,' she insisted, 'the palm never lies. Those born neath the Archer are flichty and fickle but a Taurus is stockit and steady, bull-horned and thrawn. Like you are. And it's all here, scrievit on your palm. Are you sure you're your mother's bairn?'

Knox had always shrugged off the mob's ignorant jeers, questioning his maternity, as a common enough insult, but her chuckling insinuation struck a nerve. He snatched his hand away.

'Well then, let's see what lies afore you.' Quick as lightning she'd grasped his left hand and was tracing the lines on his palm. 'I see a long life, but not without its troubles. You will thole great pain which will skaith your health.'

The soft tickling of her hand was sending exquisite shivers up his spine: he could hardly take in what she was saying.

'Ach, but this is of more note. Look, see where this line splits in twa.'

Unwillingly, Knox tore his eyes away from the fleshy mounds of her breasts and glanced at the line she was etching on his palm.

'I foresee two great loves in your life but you'll have to choose between them. It will be a great wrench from one to another. Whatere you decide, once you've chosen, there will be no going back. You're a man of strong character. That I can see clearly.'

As she stared at him, her dark, knowing eyes seemed to penetrate his soul.

Breaking her spell he exclaimed, ‘Ha! You claim to see the future but you cannae see that I'm a prelate! I can never marry, and I'll have no doings with women.’

‘Women? Did I speak of women? There can be other loves in a man's life, apart from quines.’ The gypsy smiled enigmatically, squeezing his hand. ‘But if you cross my hand with mair silver, I’ll show you how a wench can lead you to paradise. Here. On earth. In this very vennel,’ she murmured, slipping her blouse down to expose the other brown-ringed nipple.

As she tweaked and twiddled her teat, making it ripe for the sucking, Knox gawped, painfully aware of a throbbing in his loins. Then, when she threw her head back and flicked out her tongue, his body moved forward of its own volition.

‘Master Knox! What are you doing up Strumpet’s Close? Unyoke thon cow-clink and come quick. While you’ve been fyking, your friar friend’s been flayed alive.’

A crowd had gathered round the friar lying face down, kissing the causey indeed. As Knox pulled back his cowl, the blood from his matted hair dribbled onto the icy cobbles, freezing into tiny red rubies.

‘Fetch a cart,’ he shouted to the contrite-looking guildsmen, ‘and take him to the abbey infirmary. At once.’

Chapter Thirty-Six
Resurrection

> Because I see thy spirit, without measure,
> So sore perturbit by melancholy,
> Causing thy corps to wax cauld and dry
> Therefore get up, and gang anone with me.
> —*The Dream*, Sir David Lindsay, 16th Century

St Mary's Abbey, January 1528

'No men are to be admitted here: dead or alive. You, more than anyone, should ken the rules, John. Take him away to the friars at St Laurence. They take in all and sundry. Let them bring him back to life, if they will, or bury him if necessary.'

As Knox opened his mouth to protest, Sister Katherine turned on her heels and clattered off to the cloister. Whenever the prioress had business in Edinburgh, the stern Sister Katherine was in charge and there was no gainsaying her. The prioress was visiting her sister at the convent of St Catherine of Siena, where now that her eldest son had come of age, Lady Joanna Seton was free to enter. Impressed by the City of Ladies at St Mary's she, too, wished to establish a hospice and sought Elisabeth's advice.

Catching sight of Sister Agnes outside infirmary Knox grabbed her arm. 'The friar saved me from the rabble and now he needs help. He's bleeding badly. I cannot take him to the leper colony where the friars will leave him to die.'

Sister Agnes loosened the top of the friar's habit to ease his breathing and put her ear to his chest to listen for a heartbeat.

As she fumbled with the lacing, her fingers got tangled up in a cord round his neck. A holy scapular she assumed, with its intricate knot symbolising some Celtic saint, perhaps.

'Take him in,' Sister Agnes said, 'and don't worry about Sister Katherine. I'll speak to her.'

The friar looked out of place in the women's infirmary. The bed was too small for him and his feet dangled over the edge. Sister Agnes was fearful of bending his legs, one of which must be lame since he'd been using a crutch. Running her fingers over his chest, she detected a few broken ribs. His face was badly bruised, his eyes swollen and cheekbone probably cracked. Agnes was more worried about the head injuries that might affect his sight, or worse still, the delicate workings of the brain.

It was strange, she thought parting his hair, that it hadn't been tonsured, but perhaps Scottish Franciscans had their own rule. Gently she applied poultices of knitbone to reduce the swelling and comfrey leaves to ease the bruising, and then swathed his head in a bandage.

'How is he?' Knox's anxiety was mixed with feelings of guilt and shame for being the cause of the friar's injuries. If he hadn't loitered with the gypsy girl, he might have been able to come to his aid earlier.

'He hasn't opened his eyes yet. I fear that if he doesn't come round soon then...'

'Then what?' Knox yelped.

'Then it could be that he never will. It's hard to say how badly he's been injured.'

'When will we ken?'

'The next four and twenty are the reckoning hours. Watch over him with care. And pray,' Sister Agnes added as she went off to rest, leaving Knox to keep vigil.

He crouched on a stool by the bedside, sponging the friar's parched lips with weak ale, all the while keeping alert for the slightest change: the flickering of an eyelid, the movement of a finger, a change in his breathing. Under his breath he kept reciting a simple prayer: Please God, let him live—and I vow never again to tangle with a lass. In the early hours, before matins, Sister Katherine passed on her rounds. After one look at the lolling head and grey face, she sent John to fetch the priest.

'We've done what we can for his body,' she said. 'He's in God's hands now. For the sake of his immortal soul, he should be given the last rites.'

Father Dudgeon lay like a streekit corpse on his cot where he'd collapsed, fully clothed, to sleep off the excesses of his yuletide spree. A few drops of icy water splashed onto his face weren't enough to revive him. 'Extreme measures for Extreme Unction,' Knox muttered as he emptied the whole bucket to resurrect him.

At the infirmary, Sister Katherine's nose twitched as she caught the whiff of drink on the priest's boozy breath. Since he could hardly say his own name, never mind administer the last sacrament, Knox had to guide his shaking hand to anoint the friar's eyes, ears, nostrils, mouth and hands—the five portals through which sin could pass. Sister Katherine scowled as the dithering priest dribbled the holy oils all over the bedsheets and clumsily tried to cram the sacred host between the dying man's lips.

As Father Dudgeon slurred the sacred words of the prayer of consolation for the dying, she fretted that they wouldn't be valid. Would his garbled rendition guarantee three years' indulgence from the torments of purgatory or would the scribes' demon, Titivillus, register it as a sin in hell? Just in case, she nudged John and asked him to recite the *De Profundis,* the powerful prayer that struck fear and awe into the soul but also made the flesh creep.

'*Out of the depths I have cried to thee, O Lord. Lord, hear my voice...*'

‘So, my time has come,’ a feeble voice grumbled from the depths of the pillows. His eyelids fluttered before slowly opening. In the pearly light of dawn, the candles were guttering, the smell of incense and oils pervaded the chamber and in the dim light, a winged angel hovered before him.

‘Gabriel,’ he managed to say and sank back again.

‘He speaks.’ Sister Katherine blessed herself. *‘Deo Gratias.’*

Knox gave a nervous chuckle. ‘He thinks he’s already in heaven.’

Father Dudgeon swayed over him. ‘He’ll need to make a contrite confession first.’

The patient again stirred and mumbled, ‘As long as I’m not in purgatory: that's the last place I’d wish to be. Hell would be preferable to an eternity of uncertainty.’

Knox suppressed a snigger. ‘Have no fear. You’re still among the quick, not the dead.’

The patient nodded and smiled weakly. Sister Agnes’s fears that his mental faculties might be impaired were proving to be unfounded. In spite of his frailty, the friar was revealing a dark sense of humour, a good sign that his spark of life would not be easily extinguished.

Sticking out his tongue, the friar followed the blessed wafer, wavering in the priest’s trembling hand until it landed between his teeth. Sister Katherine shook her head. This drunken cleric was unworthy to handle the sacred Body of Christ, but if the friar could keep down the Eucharist without heaving it up, then he would survive.

Knox tilted the patient’s bandaged head for him to take a sip of the consecrated wine.

‘Ah that's good. I can feel the blood of life seeping back into me.’

‘Like Lazarus raised back to life,’ Father Dudgeon said and drained the chalice to the dregs. ‘No drop of Christ’s blood must be left to be defiled by the unsanctified,’ he explained to the disapproving onlookers.

Chapter Thirty-Seven
Purification

Take manly courage and leave thine insolence,
And use counsel of noble dame Prudence
Found thee firmly on faith and fortitude.
—*The Dream,* Sir David Lindsay, 16th Century

St Mary's Abbey, Candlemas 1528

'Why is John not at St Andrews?' Sister Agnes asked, as they left the chapel after early Mass. 'Has there been an outbreak of some disease?'

'My brother would say so,' Sister Katherine replied, pursing her lips. 'A serious rash of heresy which, on this feast of Our Blessed Virgin's Purification, he plans to clear up.'

Beaton had indeed dispersed the students to all the airts, sending them home until he'd eradicated the perfidious ideas circulating at the university.

'At least he can continue his studies with Friar Lazarus,' Sister Agnes said. 'He seems a knowledgeable and skilful tutor.'

Sister Katherine bit her tongue. Though she'd given in to her cajoling and allowed him to stay until he recovered, she was leery of the time John spent with the convalescing friar. Her eyes narrowed as she watched them set out on their daily walk prescribed by Sister Agnes.

While Friar Lazarus stumped along on his crutch, Knox shuffled wearily behind. He was cold, tired and out of temper. The freezing hail whipped his cheeks and then melted down his neck. He pulled his felt scholar's cap down round his ears and blew on his chilblained fingers before tucking them under his oxters. He'd been up long before daybreak to serve at Mass for the nuns in the chapel, afterwards crossing the bridge to join the congregation at St Mary's Parish Church. As a chorister at St Andrews Cathedral, sitting in the choir stalls in front of the rood screen, Knox was separated from the riffraff but standing with the lay folk in the body of the kirk, he'd been taken aback by their constant yatter. Only when the *Sanctus* bell rang to signal the raising of the Holy Eucharist did they fall silent.

Friar Lazarus cast a sideways glance at the lad who kept rubbing his eyes, bleary from lack of sleep and yawning. 'Come, that's enough exercise in the chilly wind for today.'

In the guest's chamber, while Knox glaised his hands by the fire—a comfort not allowed in his own tiny cell—the friar poured some wine into a skillet, stirred in cinnamon and cloves and set it to heat gently on the embers. Even the rich, spicy smell was warming enough.

'You could try pissing on your mouls, John,' the friar said. 'They say that cures the itch.'

Knox quickly drew his hands away and cupped them round the tassie that the friar held out. Chilblains were the scholar's scourge. Too cold and the fingers couldn't hold a quill, too hot and the fiery mouls throbbed beyond forbearance.

'Why do we have services in Latin that the lay folk cannot understand?' Knox asked. 'Who can blame them for blethering behind the back of a drunken, unlearned priest who barely understands it himself, since he's learned it all by rote, parrot fashion? The prioress's parakeet has more understanding of the Bible than Father Dudgeon. His sermons are all: Thou shalt not do this; Thou shalt not do that, with no explanation of Holy Scripture. Is it any wonder that the folk have contempt for the clergy? They drag themselves to Mass, not from any sense of devotion, but for fear of hell and eternal damnation.'

The friar smiled sympathetically at this fourteen-year-old scholar, full of youthful enthusiasm and proselytising zeal. Those ever-vigilant dark blue een, the far-seeing eyes of a prophet, smouldered when his dander was up. No wonder he was tired; kept awake at night by his righteous indignation.

'Then it is the clergy who are in need of reform,' Friar Lazarus suggested. 'Teach them first and then we can teach the faithful.'

'My tutor John Mair would agree with you. But he says that the church fathers have no interest in doing so but strive to keep the mystery to themselves.'

Too late Knox's hand flew to his lips. He shouldn't have mentioned Mair who was one of those being persecuted by Beaton for his sacrilegious teachings, but to his astonishment, the friar agreed.

'Aye, he's right and not only that. Priests pilfering from the poor and friars living off the fat of the land cloistered behind high walls have become too grasping and greedy.'

'Contrary to their vow of poverty, but you aren't one of them, friar. Tell me, why did you become a Franciscan?' Knox asked.

Friar Lazarus mulled over the question before replying. 'Because I believe in the principles of St Francis of Assisi. He established the order so as to preach the true word to the common folk. Our order has strict rules.'

'Unlike the Franciscan Friary here that they cry the lemand Lamp of Lothian.' Knox's face reddened, ashamed that he may have offended him.

'Sadly, you're right,' the friar surprisingly agreed. 'For ribaldry and debauchery are mockrife in monasteries where they are in thrall to Dame Sensual and throw out Dame Chastity. In the words of one of our makars:

Soon they forget to study, pray and preach,
And think it a pain poor people for to teach.

Knox laughed and then quickly stanched it. Bashfully he lowered his eyes to ask, 'Forgive me for asking, but do you find it hard to keep this vow?'

The friar hesitated. 'Aye, we all do, lad.'

'For I have a confession to make,' Knox mumbled, still refusing to look up.

Again the friar paused. 'Confession? You may tell me what is on your mind, John, though I may not be able to give you absolution. Only your confessor can do that.'

Heaven forfend that his sin could not be absolved. Knox winced as he scratched at his chilblains. 'At the yuletide fair I was accosted by a lass,' he blurted.

'What lad has not been given the glad eye by a lass at a fair?' Friar Lazarus winked.

'But she was a gypsy and offered to read my palm.'

'And did she tell you anything of interest? Don't fret, John. The church, like Fortune herself, turns a blind eye when the ignorant rabble seek carnival and revelry to thole their drearisome existence.'

Knox's brow furrowed as he tried to follow the friar's reasoning. 'Surely the future cannot already be set down? If we have free will, then we must work out our own fate.'

'Ah, the age-old dilemma that so unsettled St Augustine has been bothering the church for centuries,' the friar nodded. 'And since they cannot solve it, they decry it as heresy.'

When blood oozed from Knox's itchy chilblains, the friar leaned forward and tapped him on the fingers. Grimacing, Knox shoved his hands under his oxters.

'But I jalouse that it is neither the Augustinian heresy nor the church's stance on fortune-telling that is troubling you, John.' The friar's eyes twinkled. 'Did the gypsy lass offer to stroke more than your palm?'

The discomfited lad blushed to the roots of his hair. How could he confess to the unchaste thoughts about the half-naked gypsy girl with her black flirting eyes and flaunting ruby lips that buzzed in his brain? Even now he twitched uncomfortably as he felt his pistle harden at the thought of her provocative breasts and the brown buds of her nipples. A sheen of sweat glistened on his forehead. Until recently, chastity had just been a word for one of the vows he'd have to take as a cleric. He'd foreseen no difficulties being forbidden to marry for he had no desire to procreate. His destiny was to live by the spirit. Yet now that his body was betraying him he was powerless to control these perturbing, physical sensations aroused by the gypsy girl. These were the first inklings of lust, he suspected, and therefore sinful.

Friar Lazarus leant closer and whispered confidentially. 'You've been taught, I'm sure, that chastity symbolises purity and that celibacy enables the clergy to devote all their time and energy to Christ's ministry. But Luther believes there is no need for clerics to remain chaste.'

Knox leapt from his seat as if scalded. Even to utter the heretic's name was blasphemous. He glanced nervously around, in panic that they might have been overheard.

'Nowhere in his teaching does Christ mention celibacy and Luther has exposed the church's reason behind it. Realising that its wealth was being dispersed whenever the children of clergy inherited, the Vatican forbade them to marry. Celibacy then became a convenient piece of dogma, enshrined in canon law for the enrichment of Rome.'

Knox gawped at Friar Lazarus. That a cleric should suggest that the rules of the church were not set in stone and that the church fathers could invent articles of faith to their own advantage, was not only shocking but teetered on heresy.

'In all earnest, John, until the Vatican changes its mind again, now is the time to decide whether or not you want to follow a religious path. Such feelings won't melt away. Not unless you are libbed like a bull-segg. Only you can decide whether you are strong enough to conquer them. But bear in mind, yon gypsy girl with her flashing eyes doesn't promise love but raw, naked lust.'

Knox looked away. Whatever else might have diverted him from his spiritual path, he hadn't reckoned on this sexual power of the female to lead him astray.

'Though it may feel as if you are spitting into the wind, John, you must not give up your vocation.'

Chapter Thirty-Eight
Inquisition

Anger punishes itself.
—Proverb

St Mary's Abbey, 14 February 1528

Abbot Beaton paced up and down the aisle of St Mary's chapel, brandishing a heavy cane aimlessly in the air with his right hand, while his left hand kept rubbing the side of his face. Damned toothache. He prided himself on being able to thole any measure of pain, but not this constant nag. His right cheek was beginning to swell and his whole head was throbbing from not enough sleep and too much cognac, though no amount of the precious French brandy seemed to quell the maddening torture.

He took another swig from the silver flask hidden within his robes and ordered Knox to kneel, hands clasped in front, head bowed. He then grabbed at the short tuft of hair encircling the postulant's tonsure and jerked his head back, forcing him to look upon the statue of the Black Madonna.

'Before you answer my questions, you will swear to Almighty God and his Holy Mother to tell the truth.'

With his thrapple constricted, Knox could only mumble the oath.

'Louder,' Beaton bellowed, as much to drown out the throbbing in his cheek as to intimidate the penitent.

From under his dark eyebrows Knox scowled. He neither liked nor trusted this extravagantly dressed priest who, since his uncle's promotion to archbishop, was ruling the roost at St Andrews. The abbot of Arbroath's overweening behaviour had angered many of the students: the more so for discontinuing their studies and sending them all home.

'Look at me when you answer,' Beaton now commanded and twisted his head round. 'The light of the soul shines through the eyes. Let's see whether or not you are consumed with the darkness of evil and deceit.'

He let go of his hair and stood before him, his legs apart, languorously stroking the large cane. He circled his victim slowly before asking.

'Do you believe in the one true catholic and apostolic church?' The words stumbled from his tongue thick and swollen with pain.

Knox replied with a cursory nod.

'Did you not hear me? You will respond as a Christian and not as a heathen donkey.'

'Credo in unam sanctam catholicam et apostolicam ecclesiam,' Knox recited the words of the Creed.

'And do you believe that the teachings of Jesus Christ—as written in the Gospels—are the word of Our Lord Our God?'

'I do believe,' Knox mumbled back.

'And do you believe that the doctrines of this one, true, catholic and apostolic church founded by Christ Himself should be meddled with, by those who call themselves servants of the Lord?'

Flummoxed by the question, Knox was about to nod his head, but swiftly shook it instead. The abbot was well-kent as a wily tactician and practised inquisitor.

'You have heard of the heretic Martin Luther and his satanic Theses?'

Beaton had moved closer and was lifting his chin with the cane.

'Aye.' Knox shrank back from the strong brandy fumes. 'But he has been condemned as an enemy of the one true church.'

'And excommunicated. And his soul will be condemned to the eternal fires of hell. Along with those of his infernal legion,' Beaton roared. 'Amongst them the treacherous heretic, Patrick Hamilton.'

Knox stiffened. It was one thing to condemn the German reformer, Martin Luther, as a devil's disciple. His face was unknown to him, whereas Patrick Hamilton was a popular preacher, a natural leader and inspirational teacher who cared deeply about his religion, unlike many of their jaded ecclesiastical tutors. Illicit copies of his work, *Patrick's Places*, had been circulating secretly among the students at St Andrews. A fellow student, George Buchanan, had passed it on for him to read, but so far Knox had never dared.

'It's my responsibility to save you from falling under the evil spell of these reformist ideas. Heresy is like the Black Death which comes like a thief in the night, creeping stealthily under cover of darkness. Sleekit and sly, it spares no-one who is smitten.'

Troubled and confused, Knox listened to Beaton with one ear while the other rang with Friar Lazarus's harangue of the clergy who were bringing the church into disrepute. It was they who were in need of reform, not the organisation itself. Other faithful church servants agreed and were calling for amputation of the infected, decaying parts to save the health of the whole. That would be fatal in Beaton's view.

The Roman Catholic Church was an indivisible body, with Christ as its head, and the clergy and congregation its various limbs: one, holy and whole. As limbs cannot be severed without damage to the body, the church couldn't sustain the dismemberment of its hierarchy. Such a slow death, blow by blow by a few feckless priests must not be allowed to happen.

'The heretic Hamilton isn't worth your loyalty,' the abbot lowered his voice to an insidious whisper, the hiss of the serpent seducing Eve. 'Confess that he has poisoned your mind and corrupted your soul and you shall be forgiven and absolved. Your conscience will then be clear.'

But would it? If Hamilton were found guilty, he would be burnt at the stake, cleansing by fire being the only punishment for a heretic. Knox couldn't bring himself to testify against such a gentle man who had shown nothing but Christian charity to all those he encountered.

A stabbing pain through his jaw made Beaton flinch. This interrogation was taking too long. Why was the lad being so stubborn and thrawn? He desperately needed another numbing shot of cognac. Now. Losing patience, he ordered him to bare his buttocks and bend over. By God, he would thrash a confession out of him. He drew the cane up over his shoulder and struck him several times. Knox bit his lip, drawing blood, but yet he did not cry out. A beating from Beaton would be over soon. The death of an innocent man would be branded on his soul for the rest of his days.

'See how Satan has entered your soul and struck you dumb. We must unleash his power, and loosen your tongue,' Beaton ranted as he drew back the cane and brought it down again and again. 'And beat the disobedience out of your damned soul.'

As the blood rushed to his head, Knox gazed up at the Black Madonna swimming before his eyes. *Salve Regina*, Hail, Queen of Heaven! Give me strength... For what I am about to receive...

'Stay your stick, David Beaton,' a voice boomed from the rafters—powerful and authoritative. Startled, the abbot glanced upwards but could see no-one. Was it the voice of God rebuking him? Or that of Satan? This accursed toothache was surely unhinging him. He was about to strike the lad again when the cane was knocked from his hand.

No sooner had she returned from Edinburgh than Elisabeth was confronted with the most bewildering circumstances. Sister Katherine was protesting about a brother who'd been admitted to the infirmary against her better judgement while Betsy moaned that John was in the infirmary, put there by Sister Katherine's brother. With Betsy trailing after her, Elisabeth hurried to her chamber to find Beaton helping himself from her stock of rare French cognac.

'Our lad's been battered black and blue,' Betsy grumbled. 'This one here has given him a fair sackful of sair bones.'

Absorbed in rolling the brandy round his tongue and coating the inside of his cheek, Beaton glowered at her. 'I was acting on the orders of my uncle, the archbishop,' he began. Then, fixing his eyes on the insolent old nurse her, he added, 'I, for one, defer to my superiors.'

Patrick Hamilton, the abbot of Fearn, had already been brought to his attention two years ago. Because Beaton suspected him of fostering Lutheran sympathies, he'd urged his uncle to accuse him of heresy, but the archbishop was reluctant. As the son of Sir Patrick Hamilton and Catherine Stewart, the Duke of Albany's natural daughter, Hamilton had connections with clout.

Yet that shouldn't shield him from the Vatican's investigation, Beaton berated his uncle. No matter from whose tongue it fell, heresy was heresy and should be ripped out, before it infected the one, true church. Being too weak and sick to argue, the archbishop washed his hands of the whole business and let his nephew deal with it.

Forewarned of Beaton's suspicions, Hamilton had fled to the continent, but his series of theological propositions setting out Luther's doctrines was being secretly circulated as *Patrick's Places*. Hamilton may have evaded Beaton's net once, but on his return to Scotland, Beaton made sure he wouldn't escape a second time. He set the Dominican Prior, Alexander Campbell, to spy on him and was, himself, gathering evidence to support the charge of heresy. He intended to make an example of him.

'Surely the testimony of your sanctimonious clype, Campbell, will suffice?' Elisabeth declared. 'The word of a respected Dominican against a reviled heretic? You don't need a confession thrashed out of a fourteen-year-old lad.'

Beaton patted the side of his head several times to stop his ears ringing. Had he heard correctly? Was she defying him? Her impudence was staggering.

'My godson, John, is a devout lad, who intends to dedicate himself to the Church,' Elisabeth was saying.

'In which case, his first lesson will be to learn obedience,' Beaton shot back. 'I'm disappointed that his godmother is not setting a good example.'

Elisabeth arched her fine eyebrows. 'I've always taught him to listen to his conscience and never be led by falsehood.'

'Which is why he needs to be saved from this plague spreading like wildfire across continent. We cannot permit one pestersome priest to corrupt the minds of the young,' Beaton ranted. 'Our future is at stake. Before heresy becomes rife, it must be stamped out.

'Or beaten out.' She smirked.

'Better still—burnt out,' Beaton threatened.

A chill ran through her. 'You mean to burn Hamilton? And you want John to give evidence in such a trial? I won't allow his testimony to add fuel to your fire. Have the courage to be your own judge, jury and executioner, Abbot Beaton, if you're determined to be rid of Hamilton.'

Beaton's eyes narrowed to slits in his puffy face.

'No one else would dare to question me thus,' he said gruffly. 'And who is this meddlesome monk who ca'ed the cane from my hand with his crutch? Why is he here?'

'The friar was set upon by a drunken mob,' Betsy butted in, 'and is here to recover from his wounds.'

'Indeed.' Beaton turned to scowl at the nurse for her cheek in answering.

'It seems our coven has raised Friar Lazarus from the dead. With spells and cantrips, no doubt,' Elisabeth added with a wry smile. But the ill-humoured Beaton failed to respond to her witty banter. His face darkened.

'Let me speak with him.'

'That's not possible. He's taken a vow of silence,' Betsy butted in again.

'Not when he bellowed at me, he hadn't.' Beaton was rubbing his cheek furiously. 'He has no right to be here. I'll send him on his way. Now, this minute.'

'He's not fit to leave yet,' the nurse had the cheek to say.

The abbot was about to explode at her impudence when she hirpled up to him, and without begging his leave, jammed his head hard against the wall and yanked his mouth open.

'Toothache, they say, is the devil's own punishment. What have you done to deserve this?'

There was no mistaking the wicked glint in her eye but, before Beaton could reply, the old carlin had produced a tool, the like of which he'd only ever seen in the hands of a blacksmith or an inquisitor.

'It doesn't take the second sight to see yon troublesome tooth will have to come out,' she predicted. As she poked around his jaws, sending shards of pain shrieking through his skull, Beaton's head jerked backwards. 'If you leave it to rot, then you'll soon ken what suffering is.'

A few more measures of brandy were administered before he would agree to endure her primitive surgery. Sister Agnes and his own sister, Katherine, summoned to hold him down, did so with obvious pleasure. Pushing against his chest with one hand and brandishing the instrument of torture with the other, Betsy wrenched with all her might.

'I'd rather my limbs were stretched on the rack and my bones splintered than suffer this,' he screamed out.

'What better way to commemorate the martyr St Valentine than to emulate his suffering?' Elisabeth said sweetly.

Triumphantly Betsy held up the twisted, blackened tooth for him to see.

'That is also my business,' he mumbled, his mouth filling up with blood. 'To pull out the rotten tooth that infects the body of the Church.'

Chapter Thirty-Nine
Pride and Grace

Pride and grace ne'er dwelt in the one place.
—Proverb

St Mary's Abbey, 14 February 1528

'But you must join us for dinner,' Elisabeth said. 'The fatted calf has been prepared.'

Beaton's swollen face contorted into a grimace, whether a smile or scowl was unclear, Betsy had stapped the cavity with some putrid smelling substance which she assured him, would eventually dull the pain. Groaning he tried to pour cognac into the other side of his mouth.

'Forgive me but I must decline. All I want to do is crawl away like a wounded animal and lie down in a darkened room—in peace.'

Elisabeth had no sooner closed the door than it opened again. 'This is where you've gone to ground.' He opened his eyes: his sister Katherine had found out his bed.

'You'll be renouncing your concubine now that you are about to take Holy Orders,' his merciless sister stated rather than asked. While his own tongue niggled away at the bloody cavity, hers nagged at his conscience.

Beaton closed his eyes wearily. It irked him sorely that he hadn't been born with the advantages that others took for granted. It stuck in his craw to think that he had more sense in his pinkie than all those gormless gowks who, by sheer accident of birth, wielded power. With no lands or title, he had to live by his wits and grasp the opportunities that came his way.

As his uncle's secretary, his rôle had been limited, but now that the archbishop was ailing, Beaton had ambitions to take over his post and become lord chancellor of the regency council. To do so, however, he would need to take Major Orders. As a lay abbot he could marry, but he wouldn't be considered for promotion. It galled him that whereas a king's bastard son might be legitimately appointed to the post of archbishop, Beaton had no such pedigree. He knew that there would be a price to pay for a bishop's mitre, or better still, a cardinal's hat. After all, high office demanded high sacrifices. Though he would willingly renounce matrimony for Holy Orders, he was not prepared to abandon his Lady Marion.

'My dear sister, while you're fretting over my domestic arrangements, the enemies of the church are battering at her door at this very moment. The forces of evil are not only gathering on the continent but right here on our own doorstep, Henry's Chancellor Wolsey is seeking to swallow us up into the episcopacy of York. But the Scottish church, the pope's special daughter, is subject only to Rome and we must keep our independence. With such formidable foes louring on the horizon, my home affairs are small salt.'

Katherine listened, tight-lipped and scowling, to this tirade.

'None of what you say pardons you from living in sin and bringing bastard bairns into the world: *What doth it profit a man if he gain the whole world ...*'

'My bastard bairns, as you call them, will hold important positions in the church one day. That way, at least, I may be assured of some family loyalty. Now, if you've come only to castigate me, I've endured enough torture for one day.'

'So that's your purpose!' she spat out. 'To swell episcopal sees with your own spawn!'

'I have to admit the notion of founding my own dynasty is not unappealing. Forbye, both Marion and I made our promises to each other in good faith and neither is prepared to give up the other. Since she has shown willingness to be the mother of my children and endure society's scorn for me, in return, I swear to be faithful to her and give her children my name. I have crossed my heart and promised never to let her down.'

'Promises, promises, what use are your promises when you are sinning against the law of God?' Katherine thundered. 'You mean to keep Lady Marion as your mistress and bear your children while you pursue a priestly path?'

'Let me remind you that I am, as yet, a lay abbot, mind, unlike thon fornicator, the abbot of Fearn who, since he cannot abstain from fyking, challenges the celibacy rule. Hamilton seeks not to spread God's word but his own seed.'

'I hear he has now wed,' Katherine retorted.

'And has therefore broken his sacred vows. Is that not a graver sin? Whereas I've taken no vow of chastity. And since neither of us is married, neither can we be guilty of adultery. The church my dear sister, makes rules ...' he broke off, his face contorting in pain.

'For you to break.' Katherine snorted in disgust. Trust her brother to bend the rules to suit his own selfish purposes. From the way his puffy face was turning purple and beads of perspiration were breaking out on his forehead, she had clearly poked a festering sore.

Unlike her profligate brother, Sister Katherine had a true vocation. Of that she had no doubt. Being called by God had given her a strong sense of moral purpose and the courage to hold true to the principles and rules of the one, true Roman Catholic Church. Entering as a novice at St Mary's, she had been eagerly looking forward to a rigid regime of discipline and self-denial in a community of like-minded and like-hearted women. Instead, Prioress Janet had languished in luxurious indolence, rarely leaving her overheated chamber while the nuns cowered in fear of Sister Maryoth.

For the good of the priory, she had agreed to spy for her brother during Maryoth's reign but on the arrival of Elisabeth and Agnes with their new vision for St Mary's, Katherine had changed sides. Now that she could read and write and, more importantly, think for herself she was less willing to be browbeaten by her brother.

'I was about to say that, when making rules, canon law takes account of the facts of life. I am a realist. You, however, are an idealist, my dear sister. The church has need of us both. Speak not of what you don't understand. Go back to your beads, wee sister.'

'I am no naïve nun. Well I ken about the wantonness and vice rife among the whoremongers and fornicators of the clergy, but I had thought my own brother would smite them down. Instead of setting an example to your weaker brethren, you are wallowing in the stinking mire yourself. I am ashamed to call you brother.'

Flabbergasted by her outburst, Beaton's eyes bulged. The women of this abbey were becoming too brazen, the fault of too much learning, as he'd predicted.

'Would you rather have hedonistic heretics and rampant reformists overrun your beloved church?' he snarled, his lips drooling flecks of bloody spittle. 'Mind this. In the eyes of Rome, your despicable brother is a champion. The only man in Scotland who can slay the two-headed dragon of schism and reform and redd the country of loathsome snakes.'

'How grand you've become, brother,' Katherine sneered. 'Not only do you compare yourself to St George but St Patrick as well? It's a pity that Wales already has a David as its patron, otherwise... Nay, only Lucifer who dared to exalt himself above the law of God showed such presumption. Beware, Davie, that you are not cast down to the uttermost recesses of the fiery pit.'

Chapter Forty
Revelation

'O where hae ye been, my long, long love,
These seven long years and more?'
'O I'm come to seek my former vows,
That ye promised me before.'
—*The Ballad of the Demon Lover*, Traditional

St Mary's Abbey, March 1528

Elisabeth dropped her fist. She had been about to knock, but the door was slightly ajar and the lowered voices from inside made her pause. The door swung open at her touch, but the two heads bent over the writing table were too engrossed to notice.

'Forgive me for disturbing you, but I have come to offer my thanks.'

The two heads sprang apart. John, looking bashful, avoided her eyes, while the friar quickly slipped something up the wide sleeve of his habit. He struggled to his feet and leant against the desk. His mouth gawped open like a landed haddock and he clutched at his chest. Alarmed, John put out a hand to steady him.

'*Me thought ane lady, of portraiture perfect*,' he mumbled, '*Did salute me with benign countenance. What was her name? Dame Remembrance.*'

'Nay, I am Dame Elisabeth, prioress of this abbey.'

'Dame Elisabeth? Prioress? It cannot be...' the friar tottered back against the table. The crease etched between his thick, dark eyebrows deepened. 'Lisbeth? Or her ghost come to haunt me?'

His jaw had slackened leaving his mouth drooping like a drooling fool. A scraggly beard sprouted from his chin and his scrawny neck poked out from the ill-fitting habit hanging loosely on him. His hair, inexpertly hacked by Sister Agnes before bandaging his head, stood up in ridiculous tufts like Papingo's mottled crest. The lines on his face, still healing from the bruises, were testimony to the years. Years they had spent apart. For the voice, sounding so familiar, was despite its hoarseness, undeniably that of Davie Lindsay.

Elisabeth's heart skipped several beats. 'I'm not the only one to have risen from the dead, Friar Lazarus.' She gave a short, nervous laugh before turning to Knox whose head was swivelling from one to the other. 'I fear the friar is about to swelt, John. Run along to the apothecary and ask Sister Agnes for a tonic to revive him.'

To steady his trembling knees, Lindsay leant heavily against the writing table. Elisabeth had pulled out the stool and was helping him to sit down when the manuscript hidden up his sleeve slipped onto the floor. They both lunged forward to pick it up, banging their foreheads together with a stomach-churning crunch. Sprites flashed in front of her eyes.

'Our first meeting and we've locked horns already,' Lindsay quipped as he nursed the bruise on his brow. 'Here you are, Lisbeth, hale and hearty: spiky as ever and as speedy to crack my neb. Even your vow to chop off my shanks has come true.' He glanced at his crutch leaning against the wall.

'Do you mind the other hex I put on you?' Her brusque tone was belied by a laugh catching in her throat. 'That if you ever kissed another lass, you'd turn into a puddock? Is that why you're in a monk's guise?'

Lindsay beamed his crinkly, lop-sided, grin. 'Frog or friar! Not so different perhaps. I should be wary of dealing with a carlin such as you.'

'It serves you right. For marrying Kate.'

Though her lips were dry and her tongue stuck to the roof of her mouth, she couldn't contain the accusation. She inhaled deeply to quell the spasm of grief that cramped her heart. Whenever that agonising nightmare—with Kate and Lindsay rocking her baby in a cradle—had threatened to rip her grief-stricken heart to shreds, she had resisted it with all her might. With neat, precise stitches, she had darned the frayed ends of the torn wound and then, after the last double stitch, had bitten off the end of the thread. Cleanly, with sharp teeth—the way Betsy had bitten off her bairn's umbilical cord. And, whenever a tiny pinprick of pity had threatened to undo her hidden pocket of grief, Elisabeth had quickly stitched it back again. The darn was almost invisible and so skilfully sewn that it could never be unravelled. Never, she had assured herself, until now. Though nearing thirty, she wanted to pummel his chest like her feisty thirteen-year-old self.

'Only because I believed you were dead, Lisbeth. May God forgive me! Had I known, I would never have... Please don't blame me,' he stuttered plaintively.

'Who told you I was dead?' Elisabeth asked.

Remorse and regret contorted his face. 'She did. Thon nun. I did come back for you, Lisbeth. I did keep my word, but she said you'd passed on.'

After Flodden, when it was feared that the infant heir to the throne would be kidnapped, or even murdered, if not by the English then by ruthless pretenders to the Scottish Crown, Lindsay had taken his young charge into hiding. Not until the late summer of 1514 had Lindsay been able to return to the abbey. On the fifteenth of August to be exact, the first anniversary of their handfasting.

‘Sister Elisabeth is no longer with us,’ a pious looking nun had told him. She then reverentially raised her eyes to heaven before crossing herself with her rosary and kissing the tiny figure of the crucified Christ.

‘Pray for her,’ she implored, and then, eyes blazing with fervent zeal, she went on, ‘Lest her soul roast forever in the fires of eternal damnation. And may we all rest in peace.’

And then she had clanged the gate shut in his face, leaving him forsaken and forlorn.

Chapter Forty-One
Wandering Willie's Tale

I will sing to you a woeful song
Will grieve your heart full sair.
—*The Ballad of the Clerks of Oxenford,* Traditional

Tibbie's Tavern, Nungate, Haddington

'Twas on the last day of February when the reformist, Patrick Hamilton, was tried for heresy,' Wandering Willie began his tale. 'A snell east wind was howling around the cathedral in the city of St Andrews that dreich and dreadful day. The Dominican Prior, Alexander Campbell, got up to present his case, crying forth as his chief witness, James Hamilton of Finnart, known as the Bastard, bribed no doubt by Abbot Beaton to denounce his ain cousin. The Bastard Finnart has sold his ain soul often enough so it's no wonder that he was ready to sell that of his kinsman and all.'

Knox jostled with the rowdy crowd for a standing space at the back of the alehouse. Regular drinkers were sitting round the ingle where Wandering Willie had pride of place. For a jug of porter to wet his whistle, he was willing to tell the tale of the reformist's brutal end. The seasoned old storyteller waited till the mob had settled down before continuing.

'The Archbishop of St Andrews, James Beaton, and his nephew, Abbot Beaton, sat surrounded by bishops, abbots and...'

‘And their whores and limmers, no doubt,’ a heckler shouted.

‘Foutering away while the holy martyr burns,’ another added.

‘Aye, the Beatons are namely for their whore-mongering.’

‘Not only the Beatons—all the high heid yins of the Church,’ the heckler mocked and then began chanting:

The Monks o’ Melrose supped good kail
On Fridays when they fasted
They never wanted beef or ale
As long as their neighbours lasted.

As the crowd took up the chorus, Willie thumped down his empty tankard, spat onto the sawdust and turned his back on them all to glare curmudgeonly into the flames.

‘Wheesht, wheesht!’ Tibbie the alewife bawled. ‘Steek your gabs! Let Willie tell his story. There’ll be nae mair ale for any of you until he’s finished.’

She slapped another foaming tankard down in front of Willie to slake his drouth and chivvy him out of his glunders. There was silence in the tavern while he took his time slurping it. Only after wiping his lips, was he ready to go on.

‘The doomster passed sentence. Patrick Hamilton was to be burned at the stake. Unmovit, the reformist bowed his head and accepted his fate for he wouldn’t recant of his sins for awe of the fire. Nay, he'd rather burn speedily in their fire for heeding his conscience than burn forever in the fires of hell for no heeding it.’

The tavern chorus hummed in assent.

‘They were no slouches when it came to the bigging up of the stake. All kinds of kindling—bundles of faggots, sticks—had been gathered at the gates of St Salvator's College. When they led Hamilton out, he took off his coat and gave it to his servant. It was just like his master, he wept, to have such forethought for others and no think of himself. He was aye giving to the poor and needy.’

His audience, too, became tearful, snivelling and slavering into their tankards.

'Thereupon he was thirled firmly to the stob with ropes and bindings. If you've ever seen a burning, you'll ken that oftimes the merciful smoke chokes its victim long afore the body goes up like a blazing torch. But in the gale howling from the sea the fire wouldn't spark and neither would the damp powder strike. When at last the flames did take hold, they only skrimpled the martyr's left hand and the side of his face, for the rain kept smooring the fire. Hamilton had to thole his agony for six hours.'

Willie paused for dramatic effect and to take a swig of ale. 'Six... long... hours he was tormented, as many hours as Christ Our Lord did dree on the cross. All the while Prior Campbell taunted him with cries of: Convert heretic! And goaded him to recite the *Salve Regina*. But the raging heat had melted Hamilton's tongue to the roof of his mouth making him dumb. He lifted up three blackened fingers. Whether in blessing or cursing, who can say.'

In a corner of the tavern, Knox had hunkered down on the floor, hugging his knees tightly to stop himself from fainting. He dug his nails into his arms and forced himself to listen to Wandering Willie's grisly description.

'Mercifully, at long last, the fire became fierce enough to end this burning of flesh and bone, the like of which has never before been seen within the realm of Scotland and, God willing, never again.'

While the superstitious listeners touched the wood of the trestles or settles, the more religious ones signed themselves with the cross.

'As the flames scorched the young martyr, Davie Beaton's eyes glowed like the coals of hell,' Wandering Willie went on, 'and no wonder. He's becoming namely as a butcher of heretics. The University of Louvain, no less, has praised his uncle, the archbishop, for his zeal in defending the one, true faith and thanked him for purging the church of an infidel. Yet, for Friar Campbell who taunted him in his last agony, there would be no such thanks. He died a few days later. Of a stroke, some say. Of despair say others. Whether by the hand of God or Auld Nick—who rightly kens?'

St Mary's Abbey

Knox patted the murky black inkblot seeping across the creamy parchment with a rag. Too much ink on the quill had dripped onto the page, and when he tried to dab at it, the stain spread even more. As a rule his work was scrupulous but fearsome images of Patrick Hamilton's martyrdom and his own guilt-stricken conscience had kept him awake till dawn. A sleepless night had left him too woolly-headed and clumsy to concentrate on the document he had to copy.

Was the mild-mannered Hamilton a heretic or a martyr? A fool or a saint? A foolish saint or a heretical martyr? This dilemma raised a more profound question: that of his own bravery. Would he be willing to die for his convictions? And, if so, would he have the courage to go so heroically to the stake?

Thought-stricken, he didn't hear the prioress come into the scriptorium. As she glanced over his shoulder, he hunched over his desk and curled his arm protectively round the smudged document.

'It's only a blot, John. I'll get you another parchment.'

'Oh, that it were as easy to restore a man to life,' he mumbled, his dark blue eyes glistening with unwept tears.

'So that's what's upsetting you, John.' Elisabeth said. 'Don't fret. Patrick Hamilton died because he was mistaken in his beliefs. Satan had so possessed the heretic's soul that he'd never have recanted.'

'Would a man give up his life for a falsehood?' he growled.

She patted a comforting hand on his shoulder but he shrugged her off. As a woman she'd have little understanding of theological issues.

'Friar Lazarus says there are many who share Hamilton's views,' he went on. 'Friar Lazarus says they are not heretics but seekers after truth.' His expression hardened; his blue eyes resolute.

Elisabeth frowned. 'Friar Lazarus says all this? Has he been filling your head with heresy? Then you'd be better to speak to Abbot Beaton.'

Knox sneered. 'Abbot Beaton. Thon champion of the church is doing more harm than good. Do you ken what they're saying about him? That if he burns any more martyrs, then he'd better burn them in deep cellars. For the reek of Master Patrick Hamilton has infected as many as it blew upon.'

Alarmed at the vehemence in his voice, Elisabeth crouched down beside him and placed her hand on his. Unable to resist her soft touch, Knox let her uncurl his tightly clenched fist. As her cool fingertips stroked his tingling chilblains, he flinched in exquisite pain.

'No wonder you're crabbit, John. These mouls are so red and inflamed they'd try the patience of a saint—or even a martyr,' she teased, giving his hand an affectionate squeeze. 'I'll ask Sister Agnes to make up a soothing ointment—and how about a sweet cordial to ease the itch?'

Unable to meet her eyes full of tender concern, he kept his head bowed. Gently she brushed a stray lock of hair from his clammy brow and then murmured, her sweet breath caressing his cheek, 'I'm only doing what's best for you, John. I have no wish to see you consumed by the fiery flames of heresy.'

Chapter Forty-Two
Birdsong

Of her courage, she would, without my lore,
Sing like the merle, and craw like to the cock,
Pew like the glad and chant like the laverock.
—*The Testament of the Papingo*,
Sir David Lindsay, 16th Century

St Mary's Abbey, May 1528

Singing to her Papingo whenever she was troubled was Elisabeth's remedy against a heavy heart. The way the bird would cock its head in rapt attention and then try to mimic her made her laugh. And she'd had plenty to concern her recently, not least her godson's youthful rebellion. As a lad, John had shown such promise, such enthusiasm, but since he'd been attending St Leonards's College he'd become thrawn and secretive.

It wasn't the rigorous regime that worried her but the reformist teachings of some of his tutors, leading him astray. Elisabeth had no wish to clype on him, for that would only inflame Beaton's persecuting zeal. Once John left university she might be able to dissuade him from this dangerous path, but then Friar Lazarus had entered the scene to sabotage her plan. When the disgruntled Papingo squawked to gain her attention, began to sing a verse from the *Ballad of True Thomas:*

'The fig and also the wine-berry,
The nightingales lying on their nest...'

Before she could finish the lines, another voice chirped up:

> 'The popinjays fast about gang fly,
> And thrushes sing would have no rest.'

Startled, she whirled round to see Lindsay leaning on his crutch in the doorway. He had knocked, he maintained, but the songbird's voice had drowned out all other sound, he said, a wide grin splitting his face.

'Which songbird?' Elisabeth queried, sensing a jest, for she would be the first to admit she couldn't hold a tune. 'The linnet? The mavis? Or the song thrush perhaps?'

'I was thinking more the storm cock, or the rawky crow. Or even your squawking Papingo,' Lindsay teased

'Wheesht, wheesht! Haud yer wheesht!' the bird screeched at her name being taken in vain.

He deserved having the door slammed in his face for such a jibe, but before she could, Lindsay deftly manoeuvred his crutches to sidle in and close it firmly behind him.

'At least my pretty popinjay brightens up my dull life and cheers my spirits too,' Elisabeth retorted. 'Which is more than can be said for you, Davie Lindsay.'

'Still throwing out barbs, my prickly thistle.'

'And *your* tongue is still as sharp and spiky. The years have not lent it sweetness. Nor has your service at court taught you the art of fulsome praise.' There was so much more to say but she tightened her lips so as not to spit out the bitter resentment she was feeling.

'I was never one for the lickspittle, as you well ken. I only give praise where it is due. If it pleases you, I shall earn my bed and board, and pen a fitting eulogy for a lady fair.'

With difficulty Lindsay manipulated his right hand to pull out a scroll lodged between the crutch and the oxter of his left arm. Elisabeth watched him struggle lending a hand. Let him wriggle. He placed the scroll on her desk, unrolling the parchment clumsily with one hand before borrowing a quill from her desk which he waved with a dramatic flourish.

'Or perhaps a hymn or a psalm would be more fitting for my lady prioress?' he asked in the obsequious tones of a crawling clerk.

Elisabeth tucked her hands into the sleeves of her habit and tried not to laugh. His glib tongue would not win her round.

'God forbid!' she exclaimed, 'I've never been one for praying and chanting. Forbye, my head is too full of taxes and teinds, and rents and dues nowadays.'

'Taxes and teinds! What a woman of affairs you have become, Lisbeth.'

'I had no option. And see what a good wife I would have made, if you hadn't deserted me.' There, she had said it.

Seeing the reproach in her eyes, he beat his breast contritely. '*Mea culpa*.'

'As good a wife as Kate, even though I cannot sing so sweet,' she added.

Lindsay's shoulders sagged. 'The years haven't softened your spiky tongue, my jaggy thistle.'

'Nay, on the contrary, they have taught me to harden my heart. And it's high time you left here.' She gripped her elbows more tightly and glared at him. 'Our cosy wee hencoop needs no cockerel to ruffle our feathers. Nor does my godson need to listen to any more from your forked tongue.'

The crinkly corners of his mouth drooped. 'Have mercy, Lisbeth. I am not long snatched from the jowls of death. You surely don't want to cast me back. I wouldn't like to face Sister Agnes's wrath if that were to happen.'

Painstakingly over the years, Elisabeth had polished her heart to a kernel as smooth and hardened as that of the St John's nut so that now his pleas failed to crack its surface but slid off painlessly.

'But Lisbeth, you must let me explain.' His voice dropped to barely audible whisper. 'You're the only one I have ever loved. Will you believe me?'

Lindsay leant his crutches against the wall and limped towards her. He was about to place his hands on her shoulders when the latch rattled and the door opened. Armed with a bucket of water and some rags for the weekly cleaning of the parrot's cage, Sister Agnes stood in the doorway and narrowed her eyes suspiciously. The way the two of them were standing stockstill, their arms straight down by their sides, like stooks in a cornfield, unsettled her.

Chapter Forty-Three
Extreme Unction

The ladies of France may wail and mourn,
May wail and mourn full sair,
For the bonny Beaut's long fair locks
They'll ne'er see waving mair.
—*Ballad of the Death of la Beauté,* Traditional

St Mary's Abbey, May 1528

Chased out of the prioress's chamber by Sister Agnes for the weekly cage cleaning, Elisabeth and Lindsay took refuge in the walled garden. She led Lindsay round Sister Agnes's potagerie with its neatly trimmed lavender bushes and regular lines of planted seedlings before sitting down on a sheltered bench strewn with wild cherry blossom. Chilled by the light spring breeze, Elisabeth shivered, but Lindsay resisted the temptation to wrap his cloak around her and pull her in. That would not be welcome, he decided. Not until he had given her an explanation of his marriage to Kate.

Craigmillar Castle, 1517

The plague was filling the kirkyards of Edinburgh. While the townsfolk were confined within the city walls to prevent the disease spreading, the court had moved from Edinburgh castle to Craigmillar, situated on higher ground in the south-east of the city, beyond the filth and stench of the narrow streets and wynds. The young king had to be protected from the botch at all costs, especially since the sudden death of his younger brother. Rumours that the Duke of Albany had poisoned the infant Alexander to secure his place as next in line to the throne were as rife as the plague. As the one and only legitimate heir, James V was all the more precious for that, and Lindsay ordered new locks made for his chamber and two iron gates to be erected.

Preoccupied with looking after the monarch, Lindsay knew that he neglected Kate and had turned a blind eye to her indiscretions but he'd never imagined the extent of her betrayal.

Returning from parliament with dreadful news, he sank heavily into a chair and leant forward, head in hands, to keep from lashing out.

'What ails thee?' Kate hopped from one foot to the other, her hands fluttering helplessly in alarm. Had he come down with the botch that had broken out in the city? She was wary of touching him lest she herself became infected. 'Shall I send for the apothecary? Some wine perhaps or something stronger? Aquavitae?' she said holding up a flagon.

'The court ladies believe a small daily dose aquavitae to be beneficial to the health and a safeguard against disease. It not only strengthens the blood but lightens the melancholia brought on by unpleasant thoughts of pestilence and death,' she prattled on.

He shook his head violently. 'Of all people! I can't believe it! The most valiant knight in Christendom, the knight of beauty and truth…' he stammered, choking on his words.

His tear-drenched eyes flashed with fury. Kate had never seen Lindsay so angry and upset before. As the court jester, the clown, it was his business to amuse people, make them laugh. Had he found out about her liaison with the beautiful knight, Antoine D'Arcie? Castle walls had ears. No secrets could be kept in the close confines of the court. Who had told him? The jealous and spiteful Isobel Kennedy, no doubt. Or the fickle, faithless Nancy Stewart, perhaps?

‘Who... who dealt the fatal blow?’ Kate asked, trying to keep her voice calm but, as she poured some aquavitae, her hand was trembling.

Lindsay got to his feet. ‘I thought you could tell me that,’ he hissed and whacked the pewter goblet flying out of her hand.

His dear friend and honourable knight had been brutally murdered—in cold blood by thon coward, Home of Wedderburn, and his tribe of ruthless reivers. Hell-raising outlaws who, it was said, never even flinched when slaying their king at Flodden.

Kate cowered as he came towards her with flailing arms, but he only grabbed her by the shoulders. Had she told anyone of Antoine’s plans? His voice was low and menacing. She shook her head and looked longingly at the pitcher on the table. Even a sip would steady her quivering hands.

‘Nay,’ he yelled, so forcefully that she jolted. His fingers dug into her flesh as he forced her to listen.

No sooner had the Duke of Albany returned to France, leaving Antoine D’Arcie as lieutenant governor of Scotland in his absence, than trouble had broken out in the Debatable Lands. After rounding up the treacherous Homes of Wedderburn, D’Arcie sentenced them to hang and then ordered their heads to be impaled on spikes outside the Tolbooth prison for all to see and take heed.

‘It was only what those brigands deserved, but do you know what their henchmen did then? Look at me,’ he growled, holding her fast by the arm. She flinched. ‘Look at me and listen to the full horror of your deed.’ Lindsay’s ashen face, contorted into an ugly grimace, was unbearable to behold.

Antoine had been billeting secretly at Dunbar Castle when he’d been alerted to a skirmish, only to find it was all over when he got there. On the way to another alleged incident, he and his men were ambushed by a gang led by one of Home’s sons seeking vengeance against the interfering Frenchman. The so-called skirmish was a decoy, a cowardly trick to lure him from hiding. How did they know he was at the castle?

'Who told them?' Lindsay glared at her. 'Only a handful of people knew and you, being his lady fair, were one of them.'

Knowing that the day must come when he'd find out, Kate had thoroughly rehearsed her excuses to justify her infidelity but now, being confronted, she could only blurt them out. That she was not to blame, that he didn't care about her, that his neglect had forced her to find comfort in the arms of another. And it wasn't her fault that Antoine had been ambushed. She'd been tricked. By that whore, Nancy Stewart, who'd betrayed Adam's memory by marrying that rogue, Alexander Home, in unseemly haste.

At first Nancy had feigned innocent curiosity about Kate's trysts with Antoine, flattering her vanity, saying how lucky she was to have ensnared the heart of such a champion before asking seemingly innocent questions: Where was he? When would she be seeing him again? Puffed up with smug superiority, Kate had taken pleasure in making Nancy jealous: sweet revenge on the dudron who had stolen Adam from under her nose.

'He that speaks the things he shouldn't, will hear the things he wouldn't,' Lindsay growled his voice loaded with contempt. 'Shall I tell you the story of his untimely murder? The tragedy of your brave knight?'

He pushed her roughly onto a chair and knelt before her. 'Thrown into disarray, D'Arcie's company scattered, leaving him to be chased by the horde through the bogs and marshes of the Merse. Well acquainted with their own border country, the reivers hounded Antoine and his beautiful white charger into a swamp.'

'Oh no!' Kate cried out. 'Did he drown in the mire?'

'Nay, that would have been a merciful ending compared to what he had to thole.' Lindsay inhaled deeply before continuing. 'D'Arcie put up a brave fight. But one single man against many—even such a valiant knight against a gang of cowardly blackguards—was hopeless. They overpowered him, taking turns to pierce him through and through. They tore out his noble heart and hacked through his entrails. And then…' his voice began to break as he strove to fight back tears, 'as if those tortures were not enough, what did those fiends do? They hacked off his head with a sword. While he was still alive.'

'Oh, may the Lord have mercy on his soul!' Kate crossed herself. Imagining the flesh she had so lovingly caressed being ripped apart, his blood gushing from mortal wounds, was more than she could bear. Her hands flew up to her face but Lindsay wrenched them away. Then, when she tried to cover her ears to drown out his pitiless tale, he slapped them down, for she must hear the final insult.

'After his fiendish henchmen had plaited your beautiful knight's long hair into a golden wreath, thon wolf in wedderskins, Home of Wedderburn, rode off with Antoine's head tied to his saddle. Bumping and jolting it all through the borderlands, to the town of Duns, he then stuck it on a spear for all to see. That's the justice of your border reivers,' he snarled angrily into her face. 'And all because you couldn't keep your wanton tongue between your teeth.'

Kate put a hand to her throat. She feared she would faint if she didn't get some air —or, better still, a reviving drink—but Lindsay was prolonging the torture.

'Thon rogues had been tried in the highest court of the land and found guilty of treason, the punishment being their life. Whereas Antoine had no trial and was hunted down like a beast and torn apart, limb from limb.'

Dumbstruck, Kate could only shake her head. With a look of utmost disgust, Lindsay got to his feet and shoved her chair away with such force that she fell onto the floor.

Looking down on her he sneered. 'That's the way, and while you're on your knees you can pray to the Lord for forgiveness.'

Forsaken by Lindsay and grieving for Antoine, Kate sought solace more and more in aquavitae but its beneficial effects began to dwindle. The water of life gladdened her heart less and less and shrivelled her brain more and more. Cursed with constant visions and doited from lack of sleep, Kate staggered through the corridors of Craigmillar, plaiting and unplaiting her braids of golden hair and wailing the ancient dirge of the three ravens picking at the eyes of a new-slain knight:

She lifted up his bloody head
And kissed his wounds that were so red.

When she became feverish and her face and arms broke out in a rash, it was feared that Kate had fallen victim to the Black Death. For the young king's safety, she was banished from the castle to suffer the cruel treatment inflicted on those suspected of carrying the plague. Imprisoned in a cage in a field some distance away, with food and water to last a few days, Kate was left to her fate.

No-one from the court was allowed to go near, especially not the king's trusted tutor. For several long, lonely days and nights Kate cowered in the corner of her cage, open to the wind and rain. When no tell-tale swellings or black blisters appeared on her body, the royal physicians, after much anguished deliberation, allowed her back into the castle.

Her cruel quarantine had done nothing to cure her grief or guilt, however. Accursed Kate could not be at peace as she clawed at the rash on her skin and cried out in delirium that devils with whiplash tails and forked tongues were crawling all over her, jabbing her, tormenting her. Bloodletting was the only remedy the physician could recommend.

Kate's crazed eyes stared in horror at the tiny demons sucking her life blood: corbies picking at her blue een. She had to be tied to the bed with linen bandages to stop her plucking off the leeches clinging to her skin. When her eyes had sunk deep in her shrunken face and life seeped from her wasted frame, she begged for a priest to be given the last sacrament. Though loath to pander to such superstition, Lindsay gave in because, if nothing else, the blessed trinkets pacified her. With shining eyes, she grasped the crucifix with both hands, kissing it over and over again. The demons were fleeing her body, she was sure. Her soul felt lighter. Bring more holy relics, she pleaded, believing that only their miraculous healing powers could cure her.

As the rosy-cheeked Kate withered away to a skeleton, with a sacred scapular round her neck, the wishbone of an obscure saint in her hands and holy water dabbed on her lips she murmured, 'Forgive me, Lisbeth.'

Lindsay fell silent before murmuring, 'Those were Kate's last words.'

'So if Kate didn't die of the plague, was it the sweating disease, perhaps, or, God forbid, leprosy?' Elisabeth asked.

'If truth be told, Kate died of the pox,' Lindsay stated glumly and ran his free hand across his face, as if wiping away a bad memory. The physician had confided that this new affliction, becoming more common among courtiers, induced just such demonic delusions.

'The pox? But that is a disease of... debauchery and... degeneracy.'

Lindsay nodded. It was not a pleasant tale. The knight in shining armour had blighted those he laid siege to with the French disease. Kate died for love—but not for love of Lindsay—then again, neither had he loved her. He had felt a responsibility towards her: after all, it was he who had led her to the king's bed. King James was generous with his quines but he'd made no provision for her before he died. Out of a sense of duty, Lindsay had given her a home but not his heart. Perhaps if he'd been able to give Kate a child, her life would not have turned out so tragic.

'Everyone's life is tragic. All human lives end in tragedy.' Elisabeth fell quiet. Had fate turned widdershins on Kate for casting curses on herself and Meg?

'But you and I are fortunate, Lisbeth. We've been given a second chance.' Lindsay twisted round to face her. 'We risk flying in the face of fortune if we fling it away.'

He put his hand on her arm but she wriggled free and stood up. She had no wish to be wooed by his honeyed words.

'Remember our handfasting, Lisbeth?' he said quietly. 'When we swore to be true to each other until death? Thon night—as brief as a fire-flaucht—when we loved each other? If we can snatch that back again, then...'

'Then what Davie?' Her voice was sharp and edgy. 'We are no longer the same as we were then. We've grown older. We've changed.'

'Only on the outside, Lisbeth. You may be dressed in a nun's habit and I may wear a monk's robe, but that's not who we are. We're only playing these parts.' He raised himself up on his crutch to stand closer to her. 'For though the years may have left their mark on my body, in my very soul, deep in my heart, I'm the same man who loved ... nay ... ' he faltered, 'who still... loves you.'

Elisabeth shook her head. What was the point of declaring his love now? It was too late. The pocket of grief, so fastidiously sewn together, must not be ripped apart. She couldn't risk the life she'd carved for herself. In order to hold fast, to *endure fort*, she imagined her heart as the polished kernel of the St John's nut: her charm against witches. Or wizards.

'Forgive me, Lisbeth, if I am disrupting your quiet life.' The corners of Lindsay's mouth crinkled.

She threw her head back and laughed. 'For one thing my life is anything but quiet. Whoever thinks of a convent as a place of peace and quiet contemplation need only bide here for four and twenty hours. And for another, you disrupted my life years ago

—at the Tournament of the Wild Knight and the Black Lady. Making my head giddy and my heart thump with your birling.'

Lindsay's eyes twinkled. 'And your bold proposal that day captured my heart forever. I am not whole without you, Lisbeth. Like the lame man in the Scripture, I need faith in your love to heal me so that I can throw away this.'

As he raised himself up, the crutch fell from under his oxter and clattered against the bench. He gripped her shoulders with both hands and held her at arm's length, studying her face closely to read her thoughts.

Chapter Forty-Four
The Tragedy of the Papingo

Who climbs too high, perforce his feet maun fail.
—*The Tragedy of the Papingo,*
Sir David Lindsay, 16th Century

St Mary's Abbey, Spring 1528

As Sister Agnes cleaned out Papingo's cage, the bird roosted on the edge of the table, its head cocked in rapt attention listening to her crooning a French lullaby. When she came to an abrupt halt, Papingo flapped its wings.

'Wheesht! Wheesht!' the bird shrieked, urging her to continue, but Sister Agnes was blushing with shame. Was it not wicked to use her singing voice other than to praise the Lord? But perhaps the little bird was as nostalgic for her homeland as she was. She uttered a wistful sigh; with so many blessings to count it was sinful to feel so gloomy.

From the window, Agnes looked down on her potagerie where cold east winds had shrivelled her French-grown herbs and shrubs and was pleased to see tiny green shoots peeking through the clay soil. *Deo Gratias*, the onions, so necessary for cleansing the blood and warding off the plague, were at last thrusting their way through the foreign clay. Through trial and error and listening to Betsy, it had taken her some years to learn what would survive the harsh, fickle weather. In the orchard, sheltered by high walls, the fruit trees were beginning to blossom. Apples, pears and plums at least managed to thrive in this dour climate.

Though she longed for the warmth of the nurturing southern sun, was it sinful to admit that, more than anything, she missed the food of her native land? Would that be the sin of gluttony? The French nun was astounded at the humble fare the Scots seemed to survive on. Coarse barley bread! And oats! And everything salted—beef, mutton and herring—all washed down with barmie ale. Tired of chewing her way through the tough, leathery meat, she had sent to France for herbs, spices and olive oil to disguise the taste and soften the texture, and for good wine to help digest it. In season, there was plenty of fish and seafood—everything from tiny buckies and whelks to mussels and oysters—delivered fresh or 'caller' from the nearby ports. As well as laying hens and geese the convent had a large dovecot and a rabbit warren for year-round meat.

All in all, the weather may be foul but the fare was almost fair, she smiled at her little *bon mot* for, when she tallied all the benefits, her crosses to bear were flimsy indeed. What greater happiness and contentment could she have on this earth than to be among those she loved and who loved her?

Though of late she'd been concerned about Dame Elisabeth. Sensitive to the slightest shift of humour in the prioress, Sister Agnes had noticed that she seemed more agitated, more distracted, especially in Friar Lazarus's presence. With his glib tongue and teasing manner, he seemed too sophisticated for a religious man. Who was he? A feigning fox in their coop, false and dissembling, ruffling their feathers as he prepared to pounce?

Brushing the thought aside, she bundled up the debris from the bottom of the cage and went to the window to shake out the cloth. The bird hopped up and down a couple of times, trying out its wings, before perching next to her on the sill.

‘Ah, *ma petite* Papingo you have no desire to flee either, do you?’ The parrot clung on to the sill with its claws for dear life. ‘All your creature comforts are here.’

Sister Agnes leaned out to flick the cloth then suddenly drew back. As she brought her hand up to her mouth to stifle a startled gasp, her elbow knocked the little bird and propelled her out of the window into the wide blue yonder.

‘Mon Dieu!’ she shrieked, as the bird flapped its wings in a frantic effort to keep airborne. Agnes propelled herself downstairs, as fast as her long habit and heavy flannel petticoats would permit.

‘John! *Venez*! *Vite, vite*!’ she screamed.

Carrying a ladder, John struggled to keep up with Sister Agnes as she darted hither and thither. He trailed after her, leaning the ladder against one fruit tree and then another in response to her ever-changing directions.

‘No, not there. Here. There she is. No, not that one. This one. *Vens, ma petite. Ici.*’

After the initial shock, the cagebird revelled in the giddy sensation of flight. It circled round a few times before attempting to escape over the orchard wall, but that proved too ambitious. The plump, well-fed Papingo, unused to such exercise could only flit about in short bursts and a flash of colour revealed that it had come to roost high up in the branches of a tall apple tree.

Weary from all its efforts, the parrot snuggled down for an afternoon nap, savouring the warmth of the early spring sun on its feathers. Slowly, so as not to alarm the bird, John inched his way up the ladder, but it wasn’t long enough for him to reach it.

‘We'll leave her be for a while,’ he shouted down to Sister Agnes. ‘She'll come down in her own good time. When she gets hungry.’

‘It's not *her* appetite that worries me,’ Sister Agnes wailed, ‘I fear for her safety. Papingo never leaves her cage. She's not used to flying. Her wings are not strong. She'll be caught and devoured by a hawk. Oh, what are we to do?'

He could wing her with his bow and arrow, John suggested. That would force her down, but Sister Agnes threw up her arms in horror.

'Mon Dieu! Non! *Non*! You might kill her. Glory be to God! Oh, Blessed Virgin!' she wailed, making the sign of the cross over and over again. She'd never forgive herself for letting the bird go, but she'd been distracted. For, as she had shaken her cloth out of the window, she'd spotted Elisabeth and Friar Lazarus together by the dovecot near the boundary wall. From the way the prioress was shaking her head at the friar who was wildly gesticulating, it looked as if they were arguing. Her earlier sense of unease may not have been imaginary. And the way he suddenly, violently, laid hands on her, had made the nun gasp.

'*Que faire*? What are we to do?' She wrung her hands in despair. 'What will the prioress say? She'll never forgive me.'

'Agnes! Are you hurt?' Sister Katherine dashed from the infirmary: from the volume of Agnes's screams, someone must be seriously injured. Dame Elisabeth too, came running, followed by Friar Lazarus hobbling on his crutch.

'She'll come back down when she's cold and hungry,' John said. Having no head for heights, he didn't offer to clamber among the branches to coax the bird down.

They all craned their necks as the fugitive fluttered its wings but then folded them again to settle down for another little snooze. Just then a brisk breeze blew up, shaking the topmost branches and ruffling the feathers of the little bird, waking it up. Displeased at being disturbed from its reverie, Papingo gave a disgruntled squawk, 'Wheesht! Wheesht!'

Another blast, stronger this time, rustled the newly sprung leaves and it squawked again, more loudly, alerting birds of prey in the area. The sky darkened as a sparrow hawk glided silently towards it and hovered, poised ready to dive.

'*Mon Dieu*!' Agnes cried. Her hands clasped in despair, she stood looking upwards. While John positioned the ladder on one side of the apple tree Elisabeth was waving frantically on the other side to fend off the hawk. Stationed thus beneath the tree of knowledge, the trio of the grieving mother, the fearless Magdalene and the beloved disciple, formed a striking tableau of the crucifixion, Lindsay reflected.

'Papingo!' Elisabeth cupped her hands to call out as the sparrow hawk finalised its position. The little parrot tried to respond with a plaintive cry of 'Whee... whee... but the hawk swooped down on its prey and carried it off. Seconds later, startled by an arrow from John's bow, the hawk dropped its catch. After a pathetic attempt to flutter its broken wings, Papingo plummeted to earth. Elisabeth knelt down and carefully picked up her little pet bird. Its wings hung limp and its scrawny twigs of legs were gawkily splayed. Running her fingers along its tiny skeleton she could feel its bones—as fragile and frail as Meg's had been—and the appeal for help in its bead-like eyes squeezed her heart.

'I think her back and wings may be broken.'

'Then it would be more merciful to put an end to her suffering and wring her neck, Lisbeth,' Friar Lazarus said quietly.

'*Mais non, impossible*!' Meek, mild Agnes bristled at his cruel suggestion. 'We must do what we can to help her.' She glared at him angrily. Besides, how dare he address the prioress so boldly?

Elisabeth cradled the bird in her hands, cooing to it like a baby. Papingo gave a final shudder before its head sagged limply to one side. Elisabeth let out a plaintive little moan, and with a look of utter misery, turned to Friar Lazarus. Without a second thought, he drew her in towards him with his free arm.

'Wheesht, wheesht,' the friar murmured, ill-chosen words which set her off into further paroxysms of weeping.

Agnes could hardly believe her eyes. How dare he be so familiar with the prioress! Was he indeed a friar? His untonsured head had caught her notice but then, if not a friar, who was this interloper? Why had he come here? To lure the prioress from the nunnery? From her? Rather than wrench herself from the friar's insolent embrace Elisabeth had flopped shamelessly into his arms. Seeing their two bodies in such an intimate clinch, Agnes whimpered in pain, for an intense pang of jealousy, as sharp as one of John's arrows, had pierced her to the very core. Hearing Agnes's stifled sobs, Elisabeth disentangled herself and rushed over.

'Don't torture yourself, dearest Agnes. Our petite Papingo was getting old. But at least she had her moment of freedom. Flying in the sunshine. Who knows what happiness she found in her last moments?'

How sweet Elisabeth's embrace should have been, but Agnes shrank from those arms so recently entwining the friar. Her eyes welled up with tears. That it was her elbow that had nudged the Papingo, first into liberty and then into eternity, was unbearable enough but now, as she examined her conscience, she decided that the fall of the Papingo was a fable, a parable even. A warning and a punishment for her sins: self-pity, complacency, but most of all for jealousy and wicked thoughts. As she turned away in agony Sister Katherine's usually callous eyes gazed at her with pity.

John wrapped the Papingo in a linen cloth and, with all due ceremony, buried it in a deep hole in the orchard where its little corpse would be safe from disinterment by foxes and other wild animals.

'*Adieu, ma chère* Papingo. *Requiescat in pace,*' Sister Agnes wailed while Betsy shook her head, wondering what all the fuss was about.

'A burial for a bird! Whoever heard the like? What a waste of a plump-breastit chookie! Why don't we just put it in the pot? It would earn its keep at last.'

Chapter Forty-Five
Best Laid Schemes

Marriage, by my opinion, is better religion
As to be Friar or Nun.
—*Ane Satire of the Three Estates*, Sir David Lindsay, 16th Century

St Mary's Abbey, 2 September 1528

Betsy plonked her well-cushioned bottom on the rosewood kist to ease the weight on her arthritic legs and wiped away the tears rolling down her cheeks.

'Here was me thinking that I was one of them that had lived long enough to see the most.' Her shoulders were shaking with laughter. 'Who'd have thought it? And now you plan to run away together? To gang o'er the marsh as you yearned to do all those long years ago. I'm not sure whether to laugh or greet.'

Neither was Elisabeth, so taigled up and tapsalteerie were her feelings. 'Betsy, it's no jape. I truly believed I'd smoored my feelings but now ... ' She slid her hand into the deep pocket of her habit to make sure the velvet pouch was still there.

'I feel as if I've been awakened from a long sleep, Betsy, and now being in love why, every scrap of you comes alive. It consumes your whole being, stirs your blood...'

'And boils your brain,' Betsy scoffed. 'Look at you. As skittish as a sappie-headed kitty.'

And in truth Elisabeth was. After Papingo's sorrowful funeral she had parted from Lindsay, promising to meet later. Alone in her chamber she had taken off her wimple and shaken out her hair confined beneath the skull-fitting coif. Contrary to convent vows, she had let it grow—a minor infringement of the rules—and then set about grooming it to its former glory. After a great deal of brushing with long, hard strokes she was pleased to see the shine returning to her copper mane. Stripping off her nun's robes, she'd dressed in the only gown belonging to Dame Janet that fitted her—of blood-red satin. Then she dug out the velvet pouch, buried at the bottom of the kist, where she'd hidden the king's ring. When Lindsay arrived later that evening, they had closed the chamber door and slid the bolt home. From round his neck Lindsay unwound the lover's knot he'd worn since their handfasting and placed it gently round hers.

'Forgive me but I cannot give you mine in exchange,' Elisabeth had fretted, 'for Sister Maryoth had frizzled it in a candle flame.'

'It's of no matter,' Lindsay had whispered.

'But I have this.' She placed the king's ring in his palm. 'Its journey has been as fateful as ours,' she said. Wasn't it weird how John had found it in the vestry where it had lain hidden all these years and had then hung it on the Black Madonna's finger where, glinting, it had caught the Papingo's beady eye? Fortune's wheel had come full circle.

Awestruck, Lindsay listened 'And after all these years, here and now, in this moment, we're fulfilling our promise to keep our tryst.'

When his attempt to slip the ring onto her middle finger failed because but it was too tight, Elisabeth could only laugh. 'Are we doomed, do you think? It will have to fit on my pinkie.'

Forgetting the torment of their personal purgatory, the years spent apart—they were whirled back in time to the dizzy headiness of their young love to recreate their brief spell of happiness. Then, lying together, drifting in a drowsy limbo of love, they renewed their vows, pledging to be together. Forever.

After hearing about their tryst, Betsy heaved a great sigh. 'I mind fine the day of your handfasting when you thought you'd cheated fate, but the signs did not bode well and a lot of water has flowed under the brig long since. Forbye, the pair of you are gey old to go flitting round the continent like a pair of cooing-doves. Where will you live? How will you live? Lisbeth, my lass, have you thought this through?' Betsy's voice cracked with emotion. Struggling to stem tears, she twisted her apron round her fingers. 'You'll never come back here again. We'll never see you again. And I'll no live long enough to see you again on this earth,' Betsy predicted. She wiped her teary eyes with the corner of the apron.

Elisabeth fell to her knees and took hold of her gnarled hands. 'But, Betsy, I'd never dream of leaving you behind. You'll come with us.'

'Ha!' she cackled, showing a gummy mouth. 'And what would an old crone like me want with traipsing about foreign countries where they don't speak my tongue? Forbye, I'm too lang in the fang to learn new-fangled ways.'

'Nay, that's not true,' Elisabeth contradicted, at the same time noticing how tired and worn-out Betsy looked. How had she lost so many teeth? Since when had she become so breathless and wheezy as she hobbled about her chores?

'And how will you tell your holy sisters that you're about to run off with a man?' Betsy asked.

Elisabeth pondered for a moment. 'I'll say I'm going to Rome. On a pilgrimage.'

Rolling her eyes, Betsy chuckled. 'To flyte with the pope more like. And who'll look after the abbey while you're gallivanting across the continent?'

Elisabeth had thought it all through; while Agnes managed the apothecary and the hospice, Katherine would be in charge of day-to-day affairs. Doubtless that would please Davie Beaton who would rub his podgy hands in glee and gloat on hearing that his sister was in control of St Mary's—with all the monies pertaining to it—but Elisabeth had faith in Katherine's ability to slap down her brother's greedy paws.

‘And what about young John?’ Betsy asked. ‘He’ll be bereft. He worships you. You’re more than a godmother to him, you’re…’ she faltered. ‘Will you leave him to Beaton’s mercy?’

‘Why, no! He’ll come with us. To study in Rome. In the very heart of the Vatican.’

Betsy looked doubtful. ‘Catholic Rome. Is that what he’d want?’

Elisabeth groaned. ‘I don’t even know what *I* want. Oh, Betsy, what should I do?’

She began worrying at her hangnails, reverting to the bad habit a French education had stamped out, but when Betsy reached out to smack her down, she swiftly thrust her hands into her pockets.. Kneeling down in front of her old nurse, she held out her left palm.

‘Read my future, Betsy. Tell me what lies ahead.’

Betsy pointed to the ring on her pinkie. ‘You’re not needing my counsel. It looks as if you’ve already made up your mind.’

Elisabeth gave a nervous laugh. ‘Aye, and it’s a tight fit. It’ll need some softened wax to twist it off again. Tell me Betsy, have I chosen right?’

The old nurse heaved a sorrowful sigh. ‘Why ask me? What do you want to do? Unlock the gates to your heart to find the answer.’

‘I honestly don’t know, Betsy,’ Elisabeth shook her head. Hadn’t she just torn open the pocket of grief to allow love in once more? But was that what she wanted? ‘When I was a lass, I was so sure that all I wanted in life was to wed Davie Lindsay. That was my wish, do you mind, Betsy?’

‘Aye, and your wish was granted,’ she murmured, lightly stroking Elisabeth’s palm, ‘when you were handfasted. And Meg’s wish, too, came true, for she found the peace and quiet she craved while Kate was willing to sell her soul to become one of the highest ladies in the land.’

‘Aye, but Meg had no wish to die, nor did Kate desire to be a discarded mistress and an unloved wife.’

'Did I not warn you all to be wary what you wished for?'

Elisabeth sprang up, clasping her ringed hand to her heart. 'Then where's the use of wishing if everything that is to be, will be? But I'll not be a plaything of fate. I shall take charge of my own destiny. I'd fain be free of responsibilities. To cast off wimples and rosaries and live with my love—wouldn't that be paradise.'

'Life on earth can never be paradise,' Betsy said quietly as she stared into the fire burning low in the grate. Elisabeth followed her gaze and knelt down to rest her head in the comfort of Betsy's lap.

'There's aye something to gar you grue in this life, my thistledown,' Betsy whispered. 'And at the door, there's aye a shoogly stone waiting to stammle you.'

Chapter Forty-Six
The Return of the King

'What help,' quoth she, 'would that I ordain
To bring thee unto thy heart's desire?'
—*The King's Quair,* James I, 15th Century

St Mary's Abbey, 3 September 1528

The stealing sands of the hourglass numbered the hours of Lindsay's absence. Where was he? They had their future to discuss and their new life together to plan. Elisabeth paced anxiously up and down her chamber and then drew back the tapestry in front of the hidden door of the garderobe, stepped inside to listen for his footsteps. Friar Lazarus would use Dame Janet's secret passage from the chapel for their clandestine tryst.

Hearing hoofbeats and noises coming from the courtyard, she darted to the window. Mounted on horseback Patrick Hepburn was flourishing his bonnet and shouting, 'The king is free! Long live the king!'

As stableboys and servants rushed out to hear the news, John helped Earl Patrick dismount. From a corner of the courtyard, Betsy hirpled her crooked way towards them, but was swiftly overtaken by Friar Lazarus who tugged at the earl's dust-covered doublet. 'What's that you say? The king is free?'

'Aye.' The sixteen-year-old earl of Bothwell replied, with a look of disdain at the monk. 'He's escaped the clutches of Archie Douglas and he's on his way to Haddington.'

That was the good news, earl Patrick declared. The bad news was that preparations were being made for war and he'd been ordered to organise the muster at the abbey fields before the arrival of King James himself—this very Monday. Patrick was about to swagger off when he was stopped again.

'My lord, do you mind me? Do you mind your old nurse?' Tearful at seeing her wee laddie again, Betsy flung her arms round him. Self-conscious and fearful that his men would think him a milksop for being a hen-wife's darling, he tried to prise her arms from around his neck. Aware of the earl's embarrassment, John intervened to drag her away but she grabbed them both in a sturdy clinch, squeezing them for dear life. For such a small woman, Betsy was surprisingly strong.

'My two wee laddies. My bonnie blue-eyed bairns. Here you both are. The pair of you together.'

Anyone seeing them for the first time would have assumed that the lanky, fair-haired Patrick, with his rounded shoulders and pale consumptive skin, was the cleric and that stocky John Knox, with his thick dark hair and ruddy complexion must be the soldier. The Fair Earl gave his childhood companion a curt nod of thanks before disentangling himself from Betsy's embrace. He was on the king's business and had important, grown-up matters to deal with.

Elisabeth rapped on the window to attract Lindsay's attention. Looking up, he put his hand on his heart and mouthed what might have been an apology. From his hand signals she understood his meaning. Her heart shrivelled; he was off to find King James.

The Palace of Haddington

To get past the palace guards, the friar flourished his hand in an exaggerated blessing; they would think twice about hindering a holy man carrying out his sacred office. In the royal chamber the young monarch, arms outstretched in the crucifixion pose, was being tortured by seamstresses jabbing him with pins. Still a martyr to fashion, then, Lindsay mused.

James had grown taller and lankier since he'd last seen him, but there was an edgy restlessness about him, caused, no doubt, by being kept a virtual prisoner all these years. His pale eyes were no longer innocent but hardened with distrust. Years of court intrigue and being played as a pawn had made him suspicious but, on assuming command, he was quickly learning to play the imperious king.

'I have no wish to confess.' As James raised a sleeve to wave the friar away, pins tinkled to the floor.

The friar bent down to pick one up and held it up. 'Alas, I'm not even worth a pin to you, sire?' Placing his right hand on his heart he began reciting:

When thou was young I bore thee in mine arm
Full tenderly, till thou begouth to gang,
And in thy bed oft happit thee full warm
With lute in hand, syne, sweetly to thee sang.

James's brow furrowed as he delved deep into his memory and then his eyes opened wide with childlike wonder.

'Da Lindsay! Is that you!' He kicked away rolls of silks and satins to throw his arms round his old tutor's neck. Lindsay winced at the pinpricks but the easily shed tears pained him more. Though overjoyed to see his young master again, he was saddened to see that James hadn't cast off that fatal weakness of Stewarts—tending to be maudlin and sentimental.

Watching him grow up, Lindsay had feared that the young monarch was more alike in temperament to his grandfather, the ill-fated James III, than his father. When Archie Douglas took over his education, Lindsay despaired that James's weak nature would make him easy prey for the rapacious regent to manipulate him for his own ends. In his exile, he worried that all the hard work he'd put into the king's upbringing may have been ruined and now, meeting him again, it looked as if his fears had not been groundless.

Arms fluttering in excitement, James gabbled about how he himself had planned his own escape, how he'd dressed up as a groom to dupe the guards at Falkland, how he'd ridden to Stirling and claimed the Great Seal. From his account it would seem that he alone had engineered his flight. Lindsay's heart sank.

'Now I am king, I shall no longer be ordered about. I am the one who gives the orders.' James's mouth ached from the satisfied smile stamped on his face since his escape.

'Strip off that shapeless sackcloth at once, Davie! Not only does it not become you, but it offends the royal eyes. I'll have Jessie my wardrobe mistress sew a tabard of the finest brocade for my Snowdon Herald,' James said. 'You are friar no longer. I hereby command you to return to my service. And I shall dispatch you to the royal courts of Europe to herald my accession. Forthwith.'

Chapter Forty-Seven
The Lollard Oath

> He was a constant Catholic
> All Lollard he hated and heretic.
> —*Chronicle of Scotland,*
> Andrew of Wyntoun, 14th–15th Century

St Mary's Abbey, 1529

'What in heaven's name is Lollardy?' Elisabeth enquired. 'It sounds like some kind of wasting disease.'

'In a way,' Davie Beaton replied, 'but it is the worst kind of disease, even more odious than the French pox. While that may disfigure the body, Lollardy is an insidious heresy that damages the soul. The Lollards, or Babblers as they are sometimes called for the nonsense they babble, believe only what's written in the Bible. Since they deny the authority of the pope and condemn our whole ecclesiastical structure, you can understand how dangerous their ideas could be.

'So, since the Declaration of 1416, all students must take an oath to defend the Church against the insult of the Lollards and resist with all their power whosoever adheres to their sect. We thought they'd all been wiped out, but they are rearing their ugly heads again in the form of Luther and his ilk on the Continent. I'd assumed the examples of Patrick Hamilton and Henry Forrest would serve as a warning, but enemies of the faith, such as John Mair and thon blackest of Black Friars, Thomas Williams, continue to sow evil heresies in the minds of our impressionable youths. Perhaps the time has come for sterner measures.'

Since all of these misguided students couldn't be excommunicated, Beaton was putting pressure on their families to make them change their minds. If not, he would be prepared to overlook their youthful rebellion in exchange for a contribution to the university purse. However, for those intent on a career in the church, taking the oath was mandatory.

So far Knox had been an outstanding scholar at St Andrews and testimonials from his tutors reported that he had a promising future. However, before he would be allowed to graduate, he'd have to take the oath or face excommunication. As Knox's godmother, the prioress was responsible for his spiritual education and, if she wanted him to follow a clerical career, she must ensure that he took the oath.

But her thrawn godson was refusing to co-operate. Elisabeth tried to curb her temper as she cornered Knox in the vestry where he was tidying up after morning Mass.

'John, please tell me, why will you not take the oath?' she asked again.

He continued folding the linen altar cloths and arranging them in neat piles, his usually forthright eyes downcast, avoiding her gaze. Lately, he'd become so gloomy and morose, nervous and edgy, because of his age, Elisabeth thought. After all, he was already fifteen and growing into manhood, with tufts of hair sprouting from his chin and clusters of pimples dotted about his face. As he turned to put away the cruets in the cupboard, she picked up the gold-lined chalice to admire the intricate engraving. He spun round.

'Put that down. It's consecrated,' he said, his voice rising from a low growl to a high-pitched shriek. He snatched it from her hand and held it close to his chest. 'It's a sacrilege for a woman to touch the sacred vessels.'

'Only when you've taken holy orders will I take orders from you, John,' she retorted, startled by his rudeness. 'And afore that can happen, you must take the oath.'

'You're jeopardising your future, John. Abbot Beaton says...'

'Thon so-called priest has a concubine and a wheen of bastard bairns!' Knox spluttered angrily. 'Abbot Beaton has as much conscience as a border reiver, flouting the rules and stealing from the church. A bully, who slashes and burns his way through the truth of Christ's teaching. Have no fear, his time will soon be over.'

'The abbot has his faults, I have to admit, but ...' Her words tailed off. But what? What virtues could she point out to this youth seething with impotent rage? Defender of a Church the lad held in such low esteem?

'Friar Lazarus says...'

'Neither can you always believe what Friar Lazarus tells you,' Elisabeth retorted.

'When is he coming back?' Knox suddenly demanded. His angry stare as he pressed for the truth pierced her heart.

'I don't know if he will be coming back.' Elisabeth's eyes flashed with impatience. 'Unlike his biblical namesake, I doubt he'll be rising from the dead.'

'Aye, he will. He never bade me farewell, and he'd never leave without doing so.' His brow creased as his look of stubborn determination modified to one of doubt. 'Has Beaton arrested him? Is he going to burn him, too?'

His obvious concern and affection for the friar touched Elisabeth and, she was surprised to admit, stirred a pang of jealousy. She shook her head.

'Then I need to speak to him,' Knox said and glared at her, his lips tightly compressed.

Elisabeth fain would speak to him, too, but she hadn't seen Lindsay since the day he'd suddenly rode off with King James. Without bidding her farewell, either. Only a letter in which he poured forth his guilt at having broken his solemn promise—

not to her, but to the late James IV, for failing to take care of his precious son and heir. Stalked by unseen vipers lurking in the undergrowth, plotting and conspiring to wrest power from him, the young king was vulnerable, but fate had blessed Lindsay with a second chance to rescue him. Only he could counsel and shield him from faithless friends and hostile foes.

His loyalty to royalty had infuriated her. Had Lindsay forgotten that they, too, had been given a second chance? Twice she'd been willing to elope with him, and twice he'd let her down. Forever destined to be the faithful courtier, Davie Lindsay would always put the king's will first. He hadn't even mentioned John in his letter. Had he abandoned him, too?

Resisting the temptation to take one of the altar cloths and wrap it round his neck, Elisabeth tamped down her irritation to say, 'You can talk to me, John.'

Knox turned away to rearrange the sacred vessels. 'You're a woman. You cannot understand.'

Forbye, he was reluctant to confess his ambition of joining the Franciscans, the only religious order that vowed to be true to the teachings of Christ. Like Friar Lazarus, he fain would become a travelling preacher and reach out to the common folk.

'You disappoint me, John. Is that what those larbars are filling your head with? Turning you into one of those men who justify their scorn for women by insisting that we, weak-willed daughters of Eve, are lax and immoral and full of vice?'

Knox shot her an angry look. 'They're no larbars.'

'Why, then, do they closet themselves in a university with only other men and young lads? I'll tell you why. Because these impotent men are afeart of women,' she scoffed. 'Jealous and scared of monstrosities of nature as they dare to cry us.'

Knox shifted uneasily at the truth in her words.

'Consider this, John. Who stood by Christ in his hour of need? Not his cowardly apostles who denied him before fleeing, but his holy Mother and Mary Magdalene. And why did he choose to appear to Mary Magdalene after his Resurrection and not to his disciple Peter?'

Knox bowed his head and bit his lip. Because, his colleagues jeered, the news of his Resurrection would be spread the sooner. Christ knew a woman wouldn't be able to keep her mouth shut, though he dared not admit that to his godmother.

'Because Our Saviour held women in such high regard, your cowardly scholars attack us out of jealousy. For they ken fine that our minds are as strong as our hearts, yet we have to thole their lies and conceits. You say you want to be true to Christ's teaching, well that's one truth you can bellow from the pulpit.'

Taking his bowed head as a sign of submission, she dragged him from the vestry and into the chapel where she shoved him in front of the statue of the Black Madonna.

'Consider the Blessed Virgin, chosen by the Lord God himself to bear his only Son. Blessed is the womb that bore him and the breasts which he sucked.'

Knox flushed as she unashamedly touched on those parts of the female body that set them apart from men and which set his colleagues smirking and sniggering with guilty embarrassment. Though they claimed that women were feeble creatures, this didn't ring true with Knox. They underestimated the mysterious, contradictory powers a woman had in kindling strong desires in a man or reducing him to an impotent larbar. His face burned as he reflected that beneath the nun's habit lurked a woman's body. In an effort to purge his impure thoughts, he tried to think of her as pure as the Virgin: unsullied, immaculate.

'I fear your mind is being poisoned, John. Take heed of Patrick Hamilton's tortuous death,' she appealed to him. 'If you will not take the oath against Lollardy, will you give me, your godmother, your word that you will forsake all heresy and that you will be forever true to your faith?'

He squirmed uncomfortably, unwilling even to look on the silly, simpering face of the Black Madonna.

'For that is the Hepburn motto: *Keep Tryst*. For my sake, swear on your life in front the Blessed Mother and her beloved Son that you will keep the faith.'

'I swear,' Knox said, keeping his voice low and solemn while crossing his fingers behind his back, 'that I will: *Keep Tryst*.'

As she leant forward to kiss him gently on the forehead, the sweet womanly scent of French lavender oil wafted in his nostrils, making his knees quiver and testing his resolve.

'John, please don't consider us as monstrous creatures. It is my dearest wish that, one day, you will be our herald and trumpet to the world the worth of women.'

PART FOUR

Chapter Forty-Eight
Raggle Taggle Gypsy

As soon as they saw her weel-favoured face
They cast a glamour o'er her.
—*The Ballad of the Gypsy Laddie,* Traditional

Haddington, 1 May 1531

'All that lassies lack from head to heel,' the tinker bellowed as he stepped out in front of him. 'A bonnie wee fairing for your jo!'

Stumbling his way through the streets of Haddington bustling for the Beltane festivities, Knox cursed the chapman billies and tinkers raucously peddling their wares. The cacophonous din from pipers, minstrels and songsters all competing to be heard, hammered his reeling brain. Up ahead, Earl Patrick and his Hepburn cousins were lowping and jigging their way from stall to luckenbooth: knocking down pins at roly-poly, flinging the dice and losing on games of chance. Unlike them, he had no head for drinking bouts, nor was he in any mood to celebrate. Beaton had refused to register his graduation until he'd taken the Lollard oath and that he'd never do. Grabbing hold of a post, he leant his birling head against it to steady it.

'Beware of the bear, laddie!' the handler bawled. 'For he'll drive you berserk.'

Opening his dizzy eyes, he stared in alarm at the mangy brown bear being tethered to the stake beside him. The beast yelped in pain as its handler yanked at the chain, rubbing the iron collar against its raw inflamed neck. Tufts of mangy fur sprouted through patches of bare skin, covered in seeping sores, which never had a chance to heal. In his maudlin mood, tears of pity for the beast sprung to his eyes and Knox leaned over to stroke it. But misunderstanding his gesture, the maltreated beast gaunted toothless jaws and lashed out with its great paw.

'Bruin's no a dancing bear but you can teach him if you have a mind to, my bonnie lad,' the handler grinned. 'That's sure to draw a crowd.'

Already a small gang had gathered with brutal bulldogs and mastiffs straining at the leash. Unable to watch the bear being baited, Knox pushed his way past the jesters and buffoons waving their jingling sticks, tumblers and rope-climbers turning head over heels, and causey-paikers hawking their favours. Every so often the cry, 'Stop thief!' rang out as picky-fingered pursepikes weaved in and out amongst the crowd, helping themselves from the pockets of those too muddle-headed with drink to notice or care.

Catching sight of the Fair Earl's shock of blonde hair, Knox made his way in his direction. In a dingy corner of the marketplace, Bothwell and his cronies were taunting a lass pinned up against the wall. As dark-skinned as the Black Madonna, the swarthy gypsy lass gawped, bleary-eyed with drink at her tormentors. Her naked belly, big with child, swelled over the top of her skirt and from under her bodice.

'This gypsy besom tried to cheat us,' Bothwell slurred as he took a swig from a pewter flask.

'Aye, she's been demanding silver for reading palms,' his beefy cousin also called Patrick sneered. 'When everyone kens you can't sell spaecraft. That's robbery. Forbye, look how much this hizzie has pilfered.'

Burly Patrick and fat Patrick were two of the sundry bastard sons of Bothwell's dissolute uncle, Patrick Hepburn, Bishop of

Moray, who, confusingly and vaingloriously, called all his offspring, after himself. The greedy pair were sharing out coins she'd hidden in the pocket sewn inside her skirt.

'I'm no purse-pike,' the gypsy lass retorted. 'And I never ask for payment. Folk give freely for the good luck I bring.'

'And we'll take freely the favours you'll give,' the earl jeered, thrusting his leering face into hers. When a gob of spittle landed on the earl's velvet jacket, fat Patrick grabbed her by the wrists. 'This filthy wee trollop needs to be taught a lesson.'

'Let her go,' Knox barked. 'Can you not see she's far gone with child?'

'Meaning she's been well ploughed. It's best to work a mare when she's in foal.' The fat one licked his leering lips. Brought up by their depraved uncle, a lecherous pervert with nearly twenty bastard sons, the Patricks had carnal knowledge well beyond their years. As he thrust his hand between her legs, Knox growled, 'Leave her alone.'

The gypsy lass focussed groggy eyes on him. 'I ken those bonny blue een. I saw your future,' she mumbled and put up two fingers. 'Mind and choose aright.'

'Don't think you're favoured just because she's giving you the glad eye, priestie. I'm the one to yoke her up,' fat Patrick snarled.

Knox raised his fists to square up to him but a hard thump between the shoulders from behind hurled him headlong. Burly Patrick then heaved up the gypsy lass, threw her over his shoulders like a sack of oatmeal and lurched towards the river while she spewed a stream of vomit and ale down his back.

In the eerie May twilight, Knox trailed him down to the Tyne where he stopped underneath the span of the Nungate Bridge and dumped his load onto the grassy bank. After the muggy warmth of the day, an ethereal mist rose from the river, wreathing the bank and distorting everything familiar. A sudden flash of light burst in front of him and then just as suddenly dimmed. He watched it flickering and flitting hither and yon, now near, now just out of reach. The twinkling, twirling will o' the wisp was a bad omen: a malign spirit that presaged a tragedy or led the unwary to their death. Always one to dismiss superstitions, Knox couldn't ignore the tiny hairs rising on the back of his neck.

Alarmed, he turned to go but tripped over a boulder that gave a low, aggrieved moan as it lurched sideways. He squatted down beside the hunched form of Bothwell who thrust a flask under his nose. Through the wispy trails of mist Knox discerned shapes stirring under the bridge. The fat lad's bare hurdies the glimmered like pale moons in the gloaming as they heaved up and down. With a last strangled gasp he collapsed on top of his victim, threatening to squash her to death, until the burly one shoved him away to straddle her. Her warped cry—like a wild animal in pain—split the night air.

'Wait!' Knox yelled as he struggled to his feet. 'Stop!'

'Dinnae meddle in their roistering Johnnie,' Bothwell slurred. 'You'll only come off worse. Here, a swig of this'll quicken your pistle.'

Knox knocked the flask out of his hand and stumbled across the bumpy ground.

'Go on, priestie,' the burly one dared him. 'One more will no matter to her, but I wager it's the first time for you.'

They had pulled her skirts up, exposing the swollen mound of her belly and the dark triangle beneath. Blood was oozing from the split between her splayed legs. Tears dribbled from beneath her closed eyes and she was breathing heavily. Knox crawled over and knelt in front of her, intending to pull down her petticoat to cover her nakedness.

Her eyelids flickered. 'You, too, changeling,' she burbled and puckered up swollen lips to spit at him. Stung by her words, Knox fell backwards onto his haunches.

'The devil swarbit on you all,' she growled. 'As for you,' she panted, lifting her head to fix her dark eyes on Bothwell, 'your lecherous loins will spawn devils that will bring shame on any woman they touch.'

As Bothwell's pale complexion tinged green, he took another gulp from the flask.

'Witch,' burly Patrick muttered as he kicked her stomach.

'Carlin,' the fat one growled as she rolled over hugging her belly in pain.

'Let's see if she is,' the burly one said, looking round. 'We need a douking stool. A plank of wood will do. If she sinks, she's the devil's own and if she floats, she isn't.'

Knox shook his head to clear his befuddled wits. Was that the test for a witch? Or was it the other way round? Surely with her womb so swollen, she wouldn't drown. He grabbed the flask from Bothwell.

'You are their liege lord. Call off your henchmen,' Knox hissed, shaking him by his humpit shoulders.

Bothwell tried to focus his sozzled eyes on him. 'She's just a gypsy lass, Johnnie. A pagan. She doesn't have a soul like us Christians. If she is a witch, she deserves to die.'

Knox half-crawled down to the riverbank. The two Patricks had abandoned their search for a douking stool and were lifting the girl by the arms and legs.

'Nay!' Knox screamed out as he stumbled towards them.

'Heave ho!' They swung her once, twice and thrice before hurling her into the water. The Tyne was in full spate from the spring rains and swarms of May midges jittered above the ripples where she'd vanished.

Knox peered into the cold, greenish-brown water where he'd caught a glimmer of limbs and the sway of the black fronds of her hair undulating under the surface. He blinked to clear his vision. If he dived in, he could grab hold of her but the thought of being submerged in the dank river-water paralysed him. He stood rooted to the bank, as numb and wooden as a statue as the strong undercurrent carried her away. He wiped his clammy brow and turned to her tormentors.

'You'll hang for this!' he growled.

'And who's going to clype on us? You, priestie?'

While fat Patrick gripped him by the arms, burly Patrick punched him hard in the belly, knocking the wind out of him. Dragging his limp body by the legs they set off back down to the riverbank, chanting, 'One less priestie to mar our fun.'

'Leave him be!' Bothwell struggled to his feet to block their way. 'Here, take this!'

Dropping their burden to the ground with a callous thump, the two Patricks wrestled with each other for the purse of silver he'd thrown at them.

Chapter Forty-Nine
The Thirling of Bothwell

To the great God Omnipotent
Confess thy Sin, and sore repent,
And trust in Christ, as writes Paul,
Who shed his blood to save thy soul:
For nane can thee absolve but he,
Nor take away thy sin from thee.
—*Kitty's Confession,* Anonymous, 16th Century

Edinburgh Castle, August 1531

As the warder unlocked the studded iron door, a sickening sour-sweet stench belched out from the cell. Knox screwed up his nose while Elisabeth covered her mouth with her wide sleeve and tried not to gag. They both hovered in the low doorway, waiting till their eyes adjusted to the dimness. A chink of light through the narrow slit in the far wall was enough to show a bedraggled figure cowering in the corner. He was curled up into a ball, his head resting on knees tucked into his chest, his feet shackled in chains. His flaxen hair was leaden grey and lank with grease and straggled untidily over his hunched shoulders.

'Get up onto your feet to greet your holy visitors.'

The prisoner flinched at the warder's voice, his frightened eyes squinting in the unexpected light. As he stumbled to his feet, the stink from his soiled breeches grew sharper.

'They can't cut my head off,' he snivelled, sniffing back the snot hanging from his nose. His eyelids were encrusted with pus and inflamed from hours of weeping. 'I am the earl of Bothwell,' he maintained, though his voice was squeaky with fear.

'You don't seem to have learnt your lesson, Patrick. You've been charged with treason,' his aunt said impatiently.

He lowered his head and howled like a fox caught in a trap. For this wasn't the first time that he'd been imprisoned for giving protection to robbers in Liddesdale. His failure to oust Angus from his coastal eyrie of Tantallon, even with the promise of the castle as a reward, was another black mark against him. Looking at him as he sat in his own mess, a midden of his own making, Elisabeth despaired of ever inducing him to take responsibility for his actions. Bothwell blew with the wind, like one of God's fools, above the common law—or so he liked to think.

'This is far more serious: a hanging offence. Take heed of how the reivers Johnnie Armstrong of Gilnockie and his henchmen were strung up.'

'Am I to die? Don't let them hang me, Johnnie,' he snivelled while Knox hunkered down beside him. 'You've always stood by me. Stay with me. Don't leave me now. Hear my last confession.'

Patrick's jaw slackened, his lips trembled, and his eyes began to water. Please don't weep, Elisabeth begged silently. The cringing wretch appeared to have none of the traits of his father—if indeed he were his father's son—or even his grandfather. The first earl, Patrick, had earned his title; the second, Adam, had given his life for his country, and now, the third earl had been found guilty of betraying his monarch.

What a great pity Adam had been slain. He'd never have allowed his son to grow into this petulant milksop, his shoulders stooped under the weight of all his perceived grievances. Nevertheless, however much her nephew deserved punishment, however much he'd weakened the Hepburn line, she couldn't allow it to die out.

If only Davie Lindsay were her she'd ask him to petition the king for Bothwell's release but he'd been sent on a diplomatic mission to Denmark. Before he left, he'd promised to send for her—urging her to be like her Papingo, to stretch her wings and fly off across the seas to far-flung places to be with him, but the Snowdon Herald had only got as far as the English court to spy for James.

Leaving the prisoner to stew, Elisabeth begged an audience with King James and knelt before him to grant mercy to Patrick and plead for his life.

'I've shown great forbearance with your nephew, Dame Prioress, but the Fair Earl has overstepped himself with this.' James unclenched his fist and thrust a missive into her hands.

Quickly scanning it Elisabeth shook her head in disbelief. 'There must be some mistake.' Could it be true that Bothwell was offering to bring six thousand commoners and one thousand gentlemen to the service of Henry VIII, should the English monarch wish to invade Scotland?

'No mistake.' James jabbed his finger at the foot of the document. 'There, do you see?'

There was no doubting the distinctive flourish of the Snowdon Herald's signature.

'Sir David Lindsay sent me this missive or I wouldn't have believed it otherwise. Bothwell is one of the three lords I trusted to sit upon my secret council, but Lindsay is my eyes and ears at the English court. Would that he were here now, for I am surrounded by traitors. Who am I to trust?'

The king's breaking voice sounded tetchy and insecure, as if he were on the verge of tears. And then he began to pad about restlessly, nervously stroking his wispy beard as if willing it to grow more profusely for a lush growth would be a visible sign of manhood, a symbol of strength to all challengers. Another young lad with too much responsibility. Not yet twenty years of age but with all the worries and concerns of the kingdom on his narrow shoulders. A puppet king manipulated by the lairds for their own ends. Elisabeth could only feel pity for him, but would he feel the same for Patrick?

'Your grace may take into account the earl's youth. And the fact that he lost his father at a young age,' she began, hoping to evoke some fellow feeling for an orphan.

'He wasn't the only one,' James snapped.

'But the Fair Earl was then abandoned by his mother when she took another spouse.'

'Aye, as I was too. But chancy for him, he didn't have Angus as his stepfather: a mishanter and milygant, in league with Auld Nick himself. Are you saying that Bothwell has fallen under his evil spell?'

More likely beglamoured by gold, Elisabeth thought. Patrick's peerie heid, easily swivelled by the promise of money, made him easy prey.

But these were not just glib, toom–tongued words. James truly believed that Angus had learnt the black arts from his mother, Lady Douglas, and knew how to cast cantrips to bewitch his allies and curses to menace his foes. To forestall this, he'd asked Beaton to use bell, book and candle to excommunicate Angus but with no authority to do so the abbot had refused. Instead, he'd issued a decree denying the holy sacraments to all the Douglas kith and kin.

Being refused baptism, matrimony and Christian burial, however, was having less effect on the heathen Douglas tribe than the cancellation of their grazing rights on the vast church lands and being refused access to the monastic mills to grind their grain. Spiritual deprivation might have little effect on their immortal souls but leaving their unharvested grain to rot in the fields and imposing increased tithes and payments, would starve out the Douglas clan.

'But unlike you, the Fair Earl lacks a mother's love,' Elisabeth said. Despite Margaret Tudor's past misdemeanours, James seemed to have been genuinely fond of his mother for he'd not only sanctioned her divorce from Angus but also given her new husband, Henry Stewart, the title of Lord Methven. Meanwhile, Bothwell's mother, the flighty Nancy Stewart, wed for the third time to Lord Robert Maxwell, had well and truly flown the coop. To Thrieve Castle in the far south west of Scotland.

Seeing James stroke his beard as he considered this, Elisabeth went on, 'Forbye, neither has my loveless, luckless nephew been gifted with your wisdom or wit, sire. Nor has he been blessed with such a wise guide and prudent guardian as Sir David Lindsay.'

The king's boyish face lit up at Elisabeth's words.

'Aye, indeed, my faithful tutor. Only Da Lindsay is true to me.'

How she wished she could say the same. She'd always known that his first loyalty was to the king. Once this difficult period was over, and life settled down then perhaps...

James was now frowning. 'Da Lindsay, too, tries to convince me the earl is a victim of circumstances. But what am I to do with him? If I don't execute him, my lords will think me weak.' His voice rose to a petulant whine.

Sensing from James's crestfallen face that he was swithering, she hastened to say, 'May I remind you that you and the earl are bonded by blood, your grace. You share a half-sister, Jenny. You and Patrick are kin.'

Perhaps a sense of kinship would soften his heart. As he shaped his scraggy beard into a point, she was struck by the likeness between the king and the earl: fatherless bairns with absent mothers, both lads sullen and resentful. Could the rumour that James IV had sired Patrick by Nancy indeed be true?

'*Treat ilk true baron as he were thy brother*,' she started to say, '*Which must at need thee and thy realm defend.*'

This quotation captured the king's ear, which he inclined towards her, listening intently as she went on:

'When suddenly one doth oppress one other,
Let justice mixed with mercy them amend.
If you have their hearts you have enough to spend...'

'Ha, these are Da Lindsay's words, no? He's aye scrieving lines like that for me. Never gives up advising, counselling. Aye, and complaining.'

'Aye, indeed,' Elisabeth said. 'They're from his poem, *The Tragedy of the Papingo*. The death of my pet bird inspired him to write these lines advocating mercy and I'm sure, if he were here now, Sir David would have wise advice with regard to the wanwittit earl.'

'So, what would his counsel be?' James asked plaintively.

Knox sighed and heaved himself up from the dank floor of the cell. He was about to call for the warder to be let out when Bothwell yelped, 'Don't go, Johnnie. Stay and tell me, what sin must I confess? What have I done wrong?'

Being urged to confess, Bothwell had, with prompting, owned up to some minor, venial sins. 'Maybe I've swyved with a lassie or two but they were willing enough. And maybe I've taken the Lord's name in vain but then who doesn't?'

'And the gypsy lass. What about her?' John asked.

'Oh, aye, that still tortures me.'

'Then confess. Make an act of contrition and you shall be absolved.'

Bothwell gave him a blank, glaikit stare. 'Confess? For doing what? I've done nothing wrong. She's to blame for all my bad luck. Didn't she put a curse on me? May she rot in hell.'

Knox took a deep breath. Years of being tutored by his reprobate Uncle Patrick had cleansed Bothwell of any conscience. He had no concept of sin for, if he could justify any of his actions or pass on the blame, then they were not, to his mind, sinful.

'It is what you did not do, my lord. You could have stopped your kinsmen from flinging her in the river. A sin of omission is just as venial, or as mortal, as a sin of commission.'

Bothwell furrowed his brow. 'I'm no scholar, Johnnie, as you well ken. I trauchled with Latin and so I cannot understand all yon flumgummery. But I wasn't to blame. I'm the one who was accursed when that heathen put her damned spell on me. Forbye, did I not save your life? And that cost me dear. A whole purseful. We're brothers in blood, now. So, since you're in my debt, you can cast out the gypsy's spell for me with your priestly blessings, Johnnie. Banish the evil eye that has blasted my life.'

Knox sighed. The earl was as contrite as the fox in Henryson's Tale. In the Tod's confession to Friar Wolf his only regret was that he'd slain so few sweet hens. Further theological discussion would be pointless, Knox thought. After instructing the penitent to repeat the *Confiteor* in Latin, he left him to dwell on his sins.

On the way to the king's stables Knox, too, reflected. What could be done with a penitent who showed neither understanding nor remorse for his sins? Should he have absolved Patrick after his empty act of contrition? But then how many of his congregation were ever truly sorry for their sins? When Knox had finally said, *Et dimissis peccatis tuis,* Bothwell seemed reassured that these magic words would exorcise his demons. Was that all they were? A magic spell?

Dame Elisabeth was more satisfied with her morning's work. After they had picked up their horses and they were riding down the Lawnmarket she said, 'Dame Fortune has smiled on the Fair Earl. King James has shown mercy. He is to bide in Edinburgh Castle as his ward.' Only after she'd agreed to pay a substantial bond as guarantee of his good behaviour. 'And when he comes of age, he'll be married. If we can find a suitable wife,' she added with a sigh of sympathy for the woman doomed to marital thirling with Patrick.

'Earl Patrick has aye been pompous and vain but his nature has been further spoilt by his uncle,' Knox said grimly.

Glancing at his face, stern as a judge, Elisabeth was pleasantly surprised at his readiness to forgive human failings. Justice mixed with mercy: Lindsay's influence hadn't been totally harmful. Knox would make a good notary apostolic, she decided, and that would help further his career in the Church.

Reaching Holyrood Park, Knox snarled. 'Wantonness has weakened the earl's wits. That well-knit lecher and whoremonger, the Bishop of Moray, has taught him to value gold over goodness and the flesh over the spirit. But never fear. His like will burn in the flames of hell,' he spat out angrily as he spurred his mount into a canter.

Chapter Fifty
The Royal Hunt

> 'Away, away, thou traitor strang!
> Out of my sight soon may'st thou be!
> I granted never a traitor's life,
> And now I'll not begin with thee.'
> *The Ballad of Johnnie Armstrong,* Traditional

Meggetdale, August 1531

The royal hunting party had left Traquair House at daybreak and ridden through the Ettrick Forest with little success. Cursing the thieving poachers, the master of hounds was calling in his pack of fallow hounds and buckhounds scampering among the underbrush on the scent of deer.

'The men will be grouching,' Margaret Erskine whined. 'They loathe losing the chance to smear themselves with stag's blood after the gralloching. Nor is it the poachers' blood they should go after but the Hepburns'. It's no secret they're in league with them.'

The king's favourite mistress had shaved her hairline and plucked her eyebrows to create a fashionably high forehead. Her eyebrows had arched even further on being told that a prioress would be joining the royal hunt. Shouldn't she be praying in her cloister? she'd said within Elisabeth's hearing. And then shot up again on scrutinising the tight-fitting jacket and leather breeches specially made by the court tailor so that Elisabeth could ride astride a saddle.

Margaret Erskine was peeved because the king had shown favour to the prioress who had then invited the royal party to hunt on Bothwell land. Now Mistress Erskine was seeking to discredit her by blaming Bothwell for the lack of game because he'd had been laggard in another of his duties—routing the poaching reivers in the Meggetdale.

'The Fair Earl was lucky not to lose his head, only his freedom. He should be grateful to his grace for showing mercy,' Lady Margaret declared. 'Treason is a hanging offence.'

Elisabeth held her tongue, resisting the temptation to answer back. If that was the price to pay for hunting with the royal party, it was worth it. To be back in the saddle galloping across open ground, breathing in the sharp, crisp moorland air was exhilarating and made her feel alive.

Gradually the trees began to thin out to scrubland where black cattle grazing amongst whins and lichen-covered rocks scattered as the riders trotted by. By mid-morning they were galloping across the wide swelling hills clothed in purple heather and brown bracken. Their horses flew over the drystane dykes and splashed through sparkling burns that tumbled down mossy banks into black pools. High above the hawks circled then hurtled down at great speed to snatch their prey—blue hares and rabbits Elisabeth was glad to have leave the deep dark forest for the wild open moorland so that she could indulge in her favourite sport—hawking.

They stopped at midday beside a burn for the horses to drink the peaty water and for the heavily pregnant Margaret Erskine to rest.

'Is it not time to be in your lying-in chamber?' Elisabeth asked. 'Your bairn must be due very soon. Forbye, are you not feart that riding might harm the unborn babe? Does your husband allow you to be out and about in your fragile condition?'

Margaret's expression soured. It was no secret that despite being married to Sir Robert Douglas of Lochleven the king's favourite mistress was carrying his child. Nevertheless, considering James's roving eye and wandering shanks and penchant for seducing unsuspecting maidens dressed as the Gaberlunzie Man, her situation was by no means secure. She dared not absent herself from the king's presence in case he forgot about her.

'That is none of your business, my lady prioress,' she retorted and turned way to chatter to her ladies.

Elisabeth left them to their gossip to join the falconers to do some hawking. She held out her left arm encased in a leather gauntlet to let the peregrine falcon alight on her wrist. Its hard yellow eyes fixed her with a look so akin to her Papingo that it made her heart jolt. Once the falcon had caught its share of prey, she covered its piercing eyes with a hood and cautiously transferred the falcon to its keeper. She positioned herself on a rug near the ladies to hearken to their gossip. Who was their prey now?' she wondered.

'She's still a Douglas. And with those skellie eyes what's to stop her casting a hex on His Grace? Or withering my womb with her evil eye?'

Elisabeth pursed her lips. They were tearing to pieces Jinty Douglas whose husband, Lord Glamis, a friend and supporter of King James had died suddenly. Jinty had been accused of poisoning him, though why she should murder her beloved husband was never explained. Elisabeth wouldn't be surprised if the malicious Margaret Erskine were behind the rumours. She could hold her silence no longer.

'But the charges against her were dropped, were they not?' Elisabeth dared to point out, though she didn't dare say it made more sense for Lady Erskine's husband to be poisoned, leaving her free to marry the king. While the position of queen consort was vacant, Margaret regarded any unwed lady of rank with jealous suspicion, and Jinty, a young widow with a rare kind of glamour, was now a potential rival.

Beneath the arched eyebrows Lady Margaret's eyes smouldered with spite as she said through clenched teeth, 'The trial collapsed because the jurors failed to appear. Why, pray tell me? Because they were bribed to do so, by Angus himself no doubt, to save his own sister. Thon Douglas tribe will do anything to gain power. Who's to say that Angus isn't now plotting to put his sister Jinty on the throne? That she did away with her husband so as to be free to wed his grace? And that, with thon squinty eyes, she uses witchcraft to beguile men?'

Meddlesome minx, Elisabeth thought. Had she conveniently forgotten that she herself was married to a Douglas? Jinty may have kept her skin this time but, with Lady Erskine ruffling a whaup in the nest, she wasn't out of the woods yet.

When the horn signalled the start of the hunt they rode off in the direction of Caerlanrig, where the fledgling monarch had ordered Johnnie Armstrong and forty of his men to be executed without trial. Hempen ropes had been slung over branches of trees, nooses placed round their necks and their horses shooed from under them. Tales were told that, since then, the trees had withered and never flourished again, leaving the site abandoned and godless. Despite the warmth of the day and the heat worked up by the hunt, Elisabeth shivered. Not from dread of catching a glimpse of shrivelled corpses dangling from wind-twisted hawthorns but in sympathy for the ghosts of those who'd been unjustly jettisoned into the next world.

'That's how a Stewart deals with his enemies,' Lady Margaret declared proudly, with a warning glance at Elisabeth. 'Keeping true to his motto: *Wha daur meddle wi me*. A lesson his son will be well taught,' she said patting her womb.

On the way to Melrose, they crossed over the Eildon Hills where Thomas the Rhymer had descended into Fairyland. Elisabeth hummed the ballad to herself quietly while she cantered along, wondering which of the hillocks might be the fabled fairy mound.

> He heard the trampling of a steed,
> He saw the flash of armour flee
> And he beheld a gallant knight
> Come riding down by the Eildon tree.

They were about to crest the hill when a scout reported sighting a small group of horsemen making its way along Tweed valley. An English raiding party, perhaps? Or marauding border reivers? Or a plot to ambush the king? They reined in their horses and waited for the order to flee. Once the horsemen were identified they were taken to the king who engaged them in a brief discussion. The horsemen, a weary band of Scots returning from the English court, were then free to fall in beside the hunters.

Despite his face being streaked with dust and grime from the long journey and his beard being grey and stubbly, Elisabeth had also identified one of them. 'Have you come all this way to blow your horn for the hunt, Lyon Herald?'

Lindsay stared at her in surprise. 'What are you doing here, Lis... Dame Prioress?'

'You didn't recognise me in my new riding gear. A gift from King James himself. Though I drew the line at any plumage.' She touched her velvet bonnet. 'No ridiculous feathers adorning my *chapeau*. Only the best cloth for the hunting-coat and the supplest of leather for my breeches. Made for me by the finest seamstress in the land...'

He looked abashed, Elisabeth thought, and so he should. She couldn't resist a smug smile as she went on, 'Mistress of the king's wardrobe, no less—and, it would seem, even more.'

Lindsay reined his horse round so that they could ride side by side.

'You've met...' he hesitated before saying, 'Mistress Jessie.'

'A fine seamstress. Yet, now with her elevated status, has she not become even more...' she searched for an appropriate word, 'alluring?'

She looked at him askance pondering how long to keep Lindsay dangling before reeling him in. During the fittings, Jessie had confided in Elisabeth her fear that her new husband was finding her a tiresome auld scrag of mutton. Jessie's long face had drooped even more as she explained how she'd tried every auld wives' remedy to make her bonnie. In vain, for no amount of bathing her face in the May morning dew had smoothed away the scarring left behind from smallpox. Then she had dropped her voice to a confidential whisper to ask about the nun at the abbey who had found the elixir of beauty and could work miraculous cures. Or so the court ladies had gossiped. Poor glaikit unloved Jessie, Elisabeth had thought and, in gratitude for her painstaking tailoring, had given her some of Agnes's salves to slap on her plook-ridden skin. What a surprise that would be for her husband when he came back, Jessie had exclaimed. Surprise indeed, Elisabeth now thought.

'Alluring?' Lindsay asked, puzzled.

'Aye, marriage ofttimes does that to plain women.' Elisabeth brought her horse to a halt and wheeled it round. 'Do you see those braes over yonder?'

Lindsay's gaze followed her gloved hand pointing at the purple misted Eildon Hills.

'Yon is where Thomas the Rhymer disappeared for seven long years, forsaking his loved ones to bide with the Queen of Fairyland. He came back with two gifts. One was the gift of prophecy: and the other, a tongue that could never lie. Since I doubt you have the second sight, Davie, will you now tell me the truth? About Jessie—your wife.'

Chapter Fifty-One
Twice-Marrit Lindsay

'Away wi your former vows,' she says
For they will breed but strife;
Away wi your former vows,' she says,
'For I am become a wife.'
—*The Ballad of the Demon Lover,* Traditional

Stirling Castle, 1521

'Da Lindsay, you shall wed Nurse Marion. You'll be my father and Marion will be my mother. And then you can both look after me,' the boy king decreed as sat on his hunkers to survey his army of toy soldiers lined up across the floor.

'If she were willing, I would consider it an honour to take Nurse Marion as my wife.' Lindsay winked at her behind the young monarch's back. 'If she'll have me.'

'Me? Your wife? I'm o'er auld to marry,' she hooted in reply. A stout, motherly woman in her early fifties with an easy-going, kindly nature, Marion Douglas had been the king's nursemaid since his birth. 'Sir Davie needs a younger and bonnier lass, no an old wizened crone like me.'

'I'd rather have you any day than some of those painted floozies that decorate the court.'

'You're aye the gentleman, Sir Davie. I can see that it would take more than a pretty face to turn your head. Now, my kinswoman, Janet that we cry Jessie, would make him a good wife, sire.'

The boy king's expression was serious as he contemplated this.

'She's no so bonnie but she's no flibbertigibbet either. She's a couthy, canty lass, steady and hardworking. And there would be no harm in marrying one of us.' Marion cast Lindsay a meaningful glance.

It was no secret that, as soon as Regent Albany returned to France, Angus would attempt to seize power to prevent his estranged wife, Margaret Tudor, holding the reins for her son. Nor did Angus hide his jealousy of Lindsay's influence over the young monarch and desire to be rid of him. Being married to a Douglas might mean a stay of execution for Lindsay.

Jessie Douglas came from an impoverished scion of the family but her legendary skill with a needle had earned her a place at court as seamstress. Not only could she sew a fine seam, with the tiniest stitches invisible to the naked eye but she had a way of cutting cloth to drape so elegantly that veiled defects of figure.

While her skills were much sought after, she herself was not. With neither beauty nor dowry, Jessie expected to go to her grave an old maid, and so a proposal of marriage from the king's own gentleman usher and tutor was most unexpected and most welcome. Flushed and flustered as a young maiden, she accepted, and when, in honour of their marriage, James elevated her to Mistress of the King's Wardrobe, she was overjoyed. Despite reaching the dizzy pinnacle of her career, Jessie remained a douce, simple soul who resisted all her husband's efforts to teach her to read and write.

'Such learning is not for the likes of me! A gowk with no head for letters,' she'd said.'

Yet, Lindsay would point out, she could measure up to within a twelfth of an inch, calculate exactly how many yards were needed for a garment and judge the quality of a cloth by its weight, but it made no difference. His praise made her blush with embarrassment and tilt her head to one side with a coy smile. She was quite content to listen to Lindsay reading out his poems while she plied her needle.

While her meekness may be commendable, it hindered her from being able to gainsay the young monarch in any way. His royal wish was her command and his first, on coming of age at twelve years old, had been to burn all his childhood clothes. Those practical woollen garments of grey, russet and black were far too drab and mundane for a monarch, he had decided. While James jigged and reeled about the bonfire, screeching encouragement, Lindsay looked on aghast as his wife flung them onto the flames.

Not even given away to the poor, he complained. Though the virtue of humility seemed beneath the monarch then at least James might have acquired that of charity. Instead, Jessie was pandering to his vanity, turning the monarch into a manikin by choosing the most sumptuous fabrics and extravagant trimmings for his new clothes; breeches of crimson satin, doublets of plush velvet, bonnets trimmed with outrageous plumes, robes of cloth of gold embroidered with pearls and encrusted with precious stones. James V had inherited his Tudor mother's love of finery.

'Forbye, he's the king. It's his right to be clad in the best,' Jessie said to excuse him.

'But not to be pricking and prinning himself like a pensie princess,' Lindsay grumbled, shaking his head, as James strutted about proudly showing off each new lavish costume: with rings on his fingers and bells on his toes.

When Lindsay was dismissed from court along with all the other members of James's childhood entourage, Jessie was spared. Not for being a Douglas, though that was the whisper, but because of her sewing skills. Keeping the vain boy king amused with clothes of wondrous splendour and extravagance left Angus free to pursue his political joukerie-pawkery.

After listening to his tale, Elisabeth looked at him askance. And did the twice-marrit Lindsay—thrice-marrit, if their handfasting counted—ever intend to tell her that he had taken yet another wife? she enquired.

'Lisbeth, you must believe me. I never meant to mislead you. It's hardly a marriage. We haven't lived as man and wife for years. While Jessie may be my wife in law, she has never been my soulmate.' He frowned, the lines on his face deepening to accentuate his look of utter dejection.

'You've been most ill-fated in your selection of wives, Davie Lindsay. It makes me question your taste in women.'

As they trotted along, he held the reins in one hand and counted his fingers on the other, enumerating the various grounds he had for an annulment. There had been no issue from their marriage that, if truth be told, had never been consummated. They had been separated for several years. And most importantly, if their handfasting were acknowledged, then he was already married—to Elisabeth.

'At least we have a witness in Betsy. And King James will show favour. Then you can accompany me to foreign courts.'

She gazed ahead, blinking rapidly to clear the tears that threatened to mist up her eyes.

'Oh, Davie, what a buttery-lippit hunker-slider you've proved to be. Your poet's tongue can beglamour with all kinds of dreams and fancies.' She turned in the saddle to glare at him. 'Whatever tales you spin me, you must tell John the truth. For some reason he reveres you—or at least he's put Friar Lazarus on a pedestal. Forbye, his ambition is to become a Franciscan, like the blessed friar.'

Lindsay's face twisted in pain, wounded by the scoffing sarcasm he knew he deserved.

'Lest I forget, take this.' Elisabeth tore off her gauntlet and pulled the ring from her finger. 'Put this ring back on your finger where it belongs. You're wed to the king, Davie Lindsay.'

Pressing the ring into his palm, she spurred on her horse and rode off to join Margaret Erskine's cavalcade.

Chapter Fifty-Two
The Pardoner's Tale

My patent pardons you may see
Come from the Khan of Tartary
Well sealed with oyster-shells;
Though ye have nae contrition
Ye shall have full remission
With help of books and bells.

—*Ane Satire of the Three Estates,* Sir David Lindsay, 16th Century

Haddington, 1536

Knox left the courtroom in a foul temper. At the age of twenty-three, with Prioress Elisabeth's intercession, he'd at last been ordained a priest by the Bishop of Dunblane. But because of Beaton's intervention, he'd not been assigned a parish. Instead, the prioress had suggested he train to become a notary apostolic, a position that would appeal to his innate sense of justice. While the legal work veered from the boring and mundane—drawing up and witnessing documents, dealing with disputes between neighbours—it was court business that roused his blood.

That day Knox had faced yet another flagrant flouting of the law. A blacksmith who'd lent his neighbour a horse that had then drowned in a quarry was seeking compensation. Totally bewildered by the Latin legal terms, the illiterate blacksmith had failed to pay his court fees on time and was being forced to pay 'sentence-silver'. Daring to challenge this unfair verdict,

Knox had been overruled. Now, as he made his way back to the abbey, he strove to curb his anger at this latest example of injustice.

A fine drizzle was falling, mingling with the dung and muck chucked onto the street and leaving the cobblestones dangerously slippery. An elegantly clad young woman, had hitched up the front of her skirt to avoid the swill, unaware that her stylish petticoat tails were leaving a snail's trail through the sludge at her back. Knox shook his head in disapproval. These young kitties would never forfeit fashion for forethought: they'd rather be dead. This new French style that was literally sweeping the streets had inspired at least one poet to ridicule the folly of it.

I ken ane man who swore great oaths
How he did lift ane kittock's clothes
And would have done, I know nocht what,
But soon remeid of love he got.
He thocht nae shame to make it witten,
How her side tail was all beschitten.

When the kittock turned and winked at him, Knox fled across the market square. He elbowed his way through a rabble of drink-fuelled young bucks whose entertainment consisted of tossing bawbees into the gutter and jeering at the miserable beggars scrabbling for them. In the midst of this heaving mass of desperate paupers, a scrawny lad and scraggy lass were being trod on and kicked as they grappled for a groat. When at last the lad grasped a coin, a heavy boot ground down to crush his fingers, but he wouldn't let go.

Knox waded in to pull the lad and lass from the scrum and thrust some coins into their skinned hands. While wiping down his mud-splashed hose he noticed the look of cold fear erasing the gratitude on their shrunken faces. The other beggars were skulking round them with darkly envious glances: as soon as he'd gone, they would ambush the miserable mites. That could not happen, Knox thought, who ambushed them instead.

In the abbey kitchen, Sister Agnes gazed with pity at the two winsome waifs ladling broth into their mouths. Tattered rags hung from their skeletal bodies and stinking mud splattered their barefooted legs. Clarty streaks ran down the lass's hollow-cheeks as she licked her bowl clean while her brother's hungry eyes pleaded silently for more.

'I'll look out some warm clothes for them to wear home,' Sister Agnes said.'

'They have no home to go to,' Knox replied. 'Neither mother nor father, nor even a merciful church father. They've walked all the way from Tranent. Father Cadell should be black affronted.'

Hardly was their father cold in his bed when the buttery-lippit corbie had flapped down to get his claws into the corpse-present: his coat, the quilt and his best cow. When their mother, a wretched widow, died not long after, the predatory priest had returned to take the other cow, condemning these bairns to destitution and beggary.

'Hanging by the neck is the penalty for a paltry pickpocket, but there's no such punishment for the grasping clergy who besiege the beds of the dying to extort bequests for themselves or the Vatican on pain of hellfire,' Knox snarled. 'The bishops have thumbed their noses at the king's request to forbid the exaction of the corpse-present as a death-due to the church.'

While Knox railed against their plight, Sister Agnes could only reply, 'In the words of Christ Our Lord, the poor will always be with us, John.'

'Aye, but that need not mean that the very people who should be showing them charity, the clergy, should trample them further into the dirt with their swinish trotters. Where's the justice in that?'

Sister Agnes sighed. 'Don't fret, John, they will face divine retribution on the Day of Judgement.'

Not soon enough for Knox who stomped off to Tibbie's Tavern to sluice out the anger rising in his gullet. Inside, a crowd had gathered round a trestle laden with knick-knacks, a tinker's stall, he assumed, until he caught sight of Father Cadell presiding over it.

'Ah Master Knox, have you come here to seek out an indulgence? The pardoner here has sacred relics that will lessen your soul's stay in purgatory.'

'It's you who should fear eternal damnation, Father Cadell. For pocketing the widow's mite and stealing from two orphan bairns.'

The priest held out his arms in supplication. 'Is the law sinful? You cannot accuse me of theft. I only ever take what is my due: Render unto Caesar, saith the Lord.'

Knox took a deep breath to curb his anger. It may be true but it was not right. Since the church connived in the parish priest's greed, there was nothing he could do, not even as notary apostolic, to bring him to account. And, if the shameless priest could stand behind a stall, brazenly selling false promises to poor, guileless folk, then the villain had no conscience.

A skirmish that had broken out at another stall in the tavern distracted Knox. A hired man in ragged nicky tams was shouting and waving a shard of bone at a man dressed in a long black coat and a wide-brimmed hat.

'My cattle are all dead!' the hind was screaming. 'This bone of St Bride you said would cure them is of no use. I gave you my last groat for this shard of shit! I demand my money back!'

The man in black shook his head, the smile on his lips patronising. 'Nay, nay! I cannot return your money, for that would break the sacred contract. But I tell you what I'll do. I'll bless it again. Free. Gratis. *Deo Gratias*.' He took out a phial of holy water and sprinkled it over the bone. 'And this time your pardon will last a thousand years.'

'A thousand years? I'll no live that long. I crave no pardon. I want my last groat back.'

The pardoner chuckled as if at a secret joke before addressing the crowd who had gathered round the disaffected hind.

'Take heed while I explain.' Which he did, slowly and deliberately, as if speaking to a dullard or a simpleton. 'When you die and are condemned to purgatory, say for a thousand years, then you'll be able to redeem this pardon and go forthwith to paradise.'

'Not till I die? Not till then? And what if the good Lord condemns me for more than a thousand years?' the hind asked.

'In that case your sojourn there will be cut short by that time.'

'But what if I end up in hell? How shall I redeem my pardon then?'

When the pardoner raised his eyes and extended his arms as if to say, O Lord, grant me patience, Knox grabbed one of his arms.

'Give him back his money,' he snarled. His blue eyes flashed with barely controllable anger. 'Your kind are nothing but blood-sucking leeches. Even the most sleekit tinker bearing tawdry wares is more honest than you. Swindling honest, simple folk into parting with money for a bogus promise. Hanging, drawing and quartering is too good for cozeners such as you.'

The pardoner feigned an ingratiating smile as he shrugged off Knox's grasp. 'I see that you're a man of the church. My work is sanctioned by no less an authority than the Vatican itself,' he started to protest, 'as Father Cadell will verify.'

Knox clenched his fists, digging his nails hard into the palms of his hands to stop himself from hitting out at the sacrilegious scoundrel.

'Peddling dead men's bones for pardons. Defrauding the faithful with the false promise that "*As soon as the coin in the coffer rings, so the soul from purgatory springs*,"' he trilled with undisguised sarcasm. 'These so-called indulgences are just another ruse to fill the papal coffers and build fabulous Vatican palaces. Why do you line the pudgy paunches of Romish cardinals when the bellies of our own folk are squashed flat against their spines?'

Knox cast a scornful eye over the table where the charlatan had laid his god-forsaken gew-gaws and then, filling his lungs, he heaved it up and tipped it over. In a frenzy of anger, he trampled on the so-called relics; crushing bones of martyred saints, scattering splinters of the True Cross and smashing to smithereens phials of the Virgin Mary's blood which splattered the floor with ruby-red tears.

Blinded with rage, he stumbled outside where someone grabbed him by the arm.

'Well done, John,' Friar Lazarus said with a smile. 'Well done.'

Chapter Fifty-Three
Ordeal by Fire

Thou shalt not suffer a witch to live.
—*Exodus* XXII:18

Edinburgh, July 1537

'I hear they are preparing a pyre on castle hill,' Abbess Joanna Seton said.

Elisabeth joined her sister to gaze out of window of her chamber in St Catherine's Convent. Situated on high ground to the south it offered a panoramic view of the city dominated by Edinburgh Castle squatting like a toad on a rock.

'For a reformist martyr?' Elisabeth asked.

Joanna gave her a stern look. 'Nay, not for any *heretic*,' she said spitting out the hateful word. 'A witch.'

'So some poor lass, then,' Elisabeth said sadly.

Now that both sisters were mother superiors of convents, they should have more in common, she thought. Nevertheless, the severe black habit of the Dominican Order matched Joanna's stricter, more orthodox views—her support of the campaign by the Archbishop of St Andrews and his nephew, David Beaton, to burn out heresy, for example—whereas Elisabeth's cream-coloured Cistercian robes reflected her more tolerant outlook. The difference was also manifest in the way they ran their convents. The refuge of St Mary's welcomed hopeless cases—fallen women, wretches wasted with *aquavitae*

—while St Catherine's 'City of Ladies' preferred pious penitents and paupers with a prospect of salvation.

'Poor lass or not,' Joanna said, 'she's one of the Douglas tribe, found guilty of conspiring to kill the king. Lady Glamis that was, Lady Campbell that is, or Jinty Douglas as she's better kent.

Then she would go immediately to plead for mercy, Elisabeth decided, with or without Joanna's blessing.

At the gate of Edinburgh Castle, a grisly, blood-spattered head impaled on a stake brought her up sharp. This gruesome caricature of its owner had belonged to the Master of Forbes, a guard informed her. The skull of Jinty's son-in-law leered at her like the one in her nightmares. She hurried on past and into the castle to request an audience with King James. Instead she was confronted by Margaret Erskine. His grace had gone hunting and would be gone for a few days, his mistress informed her with an insincere smile.

'Hunting you say, my lady. Chasing for another bride in France, perchance?

Lady Margaret's lips compressed into a sphincter and her high drawn eyebrows fused as she glared at Elisabeth. The prioress need not await the king's return since he would be deaf to any defence of a Douglas.

'If indeed that is so, Lady Douglas, then you, too, must be cautious.'

.My husband has aye been a faithful friend to his grace.'

So faithful that the gallant Douglas of Lochleven had turned a blind eye to his wife's infidelity, Elisabeth thought.

Besides, Margaret Erskine continued, the prioress's intercession would be futile for Jinty's servants had already confessed that her family had been plotting with Angus to organise a coup. And hadn't her churlish brother George threatened to tear the young king to shreds when he'd tried to escape his gaolers? James had never forgiven this terrible show of *lèse-majesté*.

More seriously, Jinty, her husband and young son had been found guilty of conspiracy to poison the king. His grace could not turn a blind eye to high treason, Lady Margaret said in her haughty tone, and reminded her of the fate of the reiver, Johnnie Armstrong of Gilnockie, hanged from a tree in Liddesdale.

Elisabeth took her leave to seek out Jinty's cell in the castle prison. The grimy jailer could not refuse a holy woman's request to save the witch's soul but he stood by the door, watchful that nothing passed between them. Feeling all of her thirty-five years, she went down on creaking knees to crouch beside the captive. With manacled feet and wrists, poor Jinty was in extreme pain.

'And tomorrow I'm to be burnt on the pyre...' Jinty moistened her lips with her tongue, then gazed skellie-eyed at Elisabeth who tried to focus on the gap between her eyebrows. The disconcerting cast in her eyes, more pronounced in her grey, grief-stricken face, gave Jinty a fey, demented look.

'... as a witch.' She chewed the dry, cracked skin of her bottom lip until she drew blood. 'But there may still be hope,' Jinty went on. 'If I throw myself on the king's mercy, perhaps he will show clemency. He must.' Her voice rose to a desperate squeal. 'I'm the mother of young bairns. If he will not pardon Campbell or me, for the love of Christ, will he not spare Johnnie! Oh, my poor bairn!'

Tormented by the image of her sixteen-year-old son being hanged, drawn and quartered, she rocked to and fro. It would be no comfort to tell her that all the confessions had been extracted by torture, Elisabeth decided. Knowing that her son's youthful bones had been broken and mangled on the rack, his flesh ruptured and screws driven through his thumbs, would be more than a mother could bear.

'They say I poisoned my own dear husband! And now that jury of craven henchmen has found me guilty of plotting to poison the king himself!'

Aided and abetted by the earl of Huntly. Whether or not he lusted after Jinty, whose skellie eyes seemed to inflame passion in men, Huntly definitely lusted after her lands. In order to lay his hands on the Glamis estate, he'd bribed witnesses to give false evidence as well as the jury to deliver a guilty verdict.

'They cry me a witch. They say I have the sleekit eyes of a grimalkin. That I learnt my powers at my mother's knee.' As she laboured to breathe, her speech became jerky, coming in short spurts.

While Jinty and her family were undoubtedly martyrs in the bitter feud between Angus and James, they might also be victims of Margaret Erskine's bitterness, Elisabeth jaloused. The pope's refusal to grant her a divorce had quashed her twin ambitions—to become queen and to legitimise her son—and then, stoking her black-affronted fury even further, King James had gone in chase of a royal bride in France.

Pale and frail with feverish eyes, Princess Madeleine, the delicate daughter of King Francis, had to be carried off the boat at the port of Leith. The two bright spots on her porcelain cheeks—tiny ripe cherries and a sign of good health, James affirmed—had spread rapidly, like sparks from a bonfire inflaming her whole body. When the damp, smoky air of Auld Reekie finally stifled the last of the breath in her weakened lungs, James was inconsolable, tearing his hair out, beating fists against his breast in grief.

The rumour mill churned faster: thon witch, Jinty Douglas, must have put a hex on her. Wasn't her own sister wed to the Wizard of Goblin Ha'? Hadn't her mother been knacky in the black arts? Lest James turn a glad eye on her, Margaret Erskine was dripping poisonous tittle-tattle into his ear, Elisabeth suspected and, in his misery, he believed her. Someone had to be blamed for his misfortune. Since the other Douglas sisters were too well-connected to be persecuted, Jinty was to be the scapegoat. Her blood sacrifice would serve as a warning to Angus.

There was a faint chance that the flichtersome James might have a last-minute change of heart. The monarch's capricious behaviour, veering from the weepy sentimentality of the Stewarts one minute to the harsh brutality of the Tudors the next, was evident in his reaction to his beloved queen's death. No sooner had Madeleine's body been shrouded in her wedding dress and nuptial bells tolled as funeral knells than James dispatched the two Davids, Beaton and Lindsay, to France to negotiate for the twenty-one-year-old widow of the Duke of Longueville.

If only Lindsay were here to intercede—the king would listen to him, surely—but, in his absence, Elisabeth could only hope that gralloching a few deer might drain his bloodlust enough for James to grant mercy to Jinty.

'And I am to be executed!' Jinty cried. 'Not by a swift blow of the axe or a sudden jerk of the rope but cleansed by fire so that not one single hair on my head remains to sully God's earth.'

She gazed up at the iron-barred window where a sliver of sky could be seen.

'Oh, Lisbeth, how I wish they'd fling me off the topmost tower of Tantallon! Do you mind the time we stood there together? I'd rather be dashed to my death against the rocks than have my flesh roasted and my blood slowly broiled.' She leant her cheek against her knees and closed her eyes. 'And then, while my body plummets into the depths below, my soul will be lifted high above the waves, up into the heavens.'

Her body shook with the sobbing spasms juddering along her spine. Elisabeth put out her arms to console her, but the jailer chided her.

'No touching,' he barked, for he had orders to make sure that the prisoner had no chance to take her own life or be given any help to do so.

'As a sister of mercy, it is my calling to comfort the afflicted,' Elisabeth pleaded, 'and to pray with her. Would you deny her that consolation in her last hours?'

The jailer shrugged his shoulders. Prayers could do no harm: nor any good, for a hellbent carlin such as yon.

Hugging her tightly, Elisabeth could feel Jinty's heart flip-flapping wildly like a scary doo fluttering to break free from its cage. As her sobs quietened down to pitiful whimpers Jinty whispered, 'Soon I shall be able to beg Meg's forgiveness. Dame Fortune is punishing me, Lisbeth. My soul has never been easy not since...' She trailed off, her voice fading. 'Meg's death hangs heavy on me.'

'Meg's death was tragic but you were not to blame. It wasn't your fault.'

If anyone was responsible it was Angus whom Elisabeth had cursed at the time.

Jinty shook her head from side to side. 'But it was. Mind how you and I used to have fun playing tig together at Tantallon? One time, I was playing hunt the gowk with the maids. We were chasing each other round and round when I saw Meg standing at the top of the stairs. She must be feeling better, I thought. She was smiling. She must want to join in. So I threw the veil over her and shouted: Hunt the gowk! But she was so frail that she toppled over and tumbled down and down.'

Jinty had hovered on the top step of the staircase watching helplessly as Meg's arms flailed at the air in a futile attempt to fly. She pressed her eyelids tightly with manacled fists, as if trying to gouge the memory from her skellie eye.

'Perhaps I am evil,' Jinty sobbed, breaking the silence. 'Perhaps I deserve to die.'

'Nay,' Elisabeth replied, shaking her head. 'And neither did Meg.'

It pained Elisabeth to leave Jinty but a messenger arrived at the dungeon to summon—her to the king she assumed. In spite of Margaret Erskine's meddling, perhaps James would hear her mercy plea. She was shown into a chamber, lit by many candles and heated by a coal fire burning in the grate. Though it was past midsummer, the warmth of the July sun hardly penetrated the thick stone walls of Edinburgh Castle.

'Take a seat, Dame Prioress.' The voice, high-pitched with an English twang, was not that of the king but his mother, Margaret Tudor.

Seated at a writing desk, the squat figure was no longer the princess praised by poets as being *most pleasant and preclare.* If she ever had been, for Elisabeth hadn't believed it even when she first set eyes on her at the Tournament of the Wild Knight. Now, in late middle age, the Tudor Rose had lost her bloom. A bout of smallpox had scarred her complexion leaving it pockmarked and sallow and a French hood concealed her once luxuriant flaxen hair. Her face had become puffy, threatening to obscure her small, froglike eyes—eyes that still flashed fiercely when aroused. Elizabeth's impression of the innocent English bride all those years ago was reinforced. At nearly fifty-years-old, the royal princess had transformed into a puddock.

The queen mother put down her pen. 'I hear you've come to plead for Jinty Douglas. Don't look so surprised, prioress, I know everything that goes on in this godforsaken castle. Despite everything, I'm still the queen mother and retain my own loyal retinue.'

And still the proud Tudor princess, Elisabeth thought.

'But Margaret Erskine will have the last word in this sorry case. Whatever arts that shameless harlot uses to keep my son in thrall, I dread to imagine. Like his father before him, my son has a string of mistresses but this wily wanton is getting too bold. She has what you Scots call a guid conceit of herself,' the queen mother said, trying to mimic a Scots accent. 'But as she wangles her way to the throne, *she* is the witch, I wager, not hapless Jinty.'

'But Lady Margaret is already married to Douglas of Lochleven,' Elisabeth said. 'And His Grace's ambassadors are at this moment negotiating for a French bride.'

'There's many a slip betwixt cup and lip. And divorces can be as bought as easily as fish at the market nowadays—and smell just as high. That wasn't the case in my day. I would have done anything to break free from Angus. Nothing but anguish he gave me,' she whined, her voice rising to a resentful wail. 'I should have bided my time and married Albany. He was very fond of me.' Her froggy eyes misted up at the memory. 'But his French manners were too sophisticated to put up with our boorish, uncouth Scots. And so he left, more's the pity, leaving us all to the mercy of Angus.'

Had she been called to the royal presence only to hear Margaret Tudor's confession? Elisabeth wondered. Or would she be offering to support her mercy plea?

'Sadly, I can do nothing to help Jinty.' The queen mother was shaking her head. 'I no longer have any influence over my son. He has surrounded himself with fools, not least my Lord Muffin,' she gave a contemptuous snort. 'My nickname for my errant husband,' she explained, 'the noble Lord Methven who has tired of me and taken a younger mistress. And they say that women are weak, inconstant creatures! Humph. Like all the men in my life, Henry Stewart is proving to be false and fickle.'

She snatched up her pen and waved it. 'To that end I've petitioned the pope for a divorce and I'm now writing to my brother Henry the heretic to see if that hypocrite can help me. But I imagine he's created himself the Supreme Head of the Church in England only to justify his own divorce.' She gave a snort of contempt and then her expression softened to one of self-pity. 'All I crave now is to be free of men and their machinations,' she whimpered. 'You see, Dame Prioress, I envy your reclusive life of peace and tranquillity. My life has not been a bed of roses, but strewn with thorns and thistles,' the Tudor Rose whined. 'My health is not good and I may not have many years left. I have fond memories of my short stay at St Mary's Abbey on my way to wed the king. Now I hear that St Mary's has a reputation for being a haven for distressed gentlewomen. It's my wish to enter your City of Ladies.'

But not my command, if I can help it, Elisabeth thought, rather taken aback. Recovering her self-composure, she said, 'If and when your divorce is granted, your grace, then by all means you will be at liberty to seek out the destiny you deserve. But perhaps the regime at my sister's convent, St Catherine's, here in Edinburgh would better suit your royal temperament.'

Castle Hill, Edinburgh, 17 July 1537

The mood among the spectators at the execution was subdued, Elisabeth sensed. Any sporadic jeers and heckles, mainly from drunken youths, were swiftly shooshed into silence.

'That might be your own ma up there,' a matron scolded, deeply affected that a mother of poor bairns should be sent to such a cruel death. 'And that might be you up there.' She pointed up at the tower where Jinty's second husband, Archibald Campbell, and her son John, the Master of Glamis, had been dragged from their dungeon to watch her die.

As Jinty was led to the pyre, her fey eyes, pools of black ink in her sunken face, had a vacant look and she seemed unaware of the tarred barrels and oiled faggots being piled around her. Her squint eye rolled in its socket, seeming to search out the crowd, but her good eye was directed upwards, beyond the parapet where her husband and son were being forced to watch. She'd been locked in the darkest dungeon for weeks, poor lass, the bruit ran through the crowd, so that her blinded eyes could hardly see.

Thank goodness, Elisabeth sighed. Under the jailer's gimlet eyes she'd been unable to pass on the phial of belladonna she'd smuggled in for Jinty but, at first light, she'd waylaid the priest on his way to give the condemned prisoner the last rites. The bejewelled silver casket contained a communion wafer, freshly made that morning by the nuns of St Catherine's Convent, she explained, already blessed with Christ's blood by the archbishop himself. And, of course, the reverend father could keep the casket for his pains.

The holy wafer had indeed been anointed—with enough drops of the drug to numb Jinty's senses and dull the pain—and, if she remembered Elisabeth's instructions to inhale deeply when the first smoke scorched her lungs, she would suffocate long before the flames consumed her. Judging by her vacant expression, Jinty had managed to take the drug.

As she was being tethered to the stake, the executioner, his head eerily shrouded in a hood, knelt to beg her forgiveness. Jinty blinked and gave a cursory nod. And then, before putting the noose round her neck, he asked if she wanted a hood to cover her eyes.

'To play hunt the gowk?' she replied, a fey smile playing on her lips, and shook her head. The executioner turned one last time to the captain of the castle guard who bowed his head. There would be no reprieve. As the hangman pulled on the rope to fasten her head to the stake, Elisabeth prayed that he would be merciful and throttle her. Jinty gazed skywards to where her spirit would be soon soaring, up and away into Meg's forgiving arms.

The reprieve for Jinty's husband and son came the next day: too late for Campbell. The night before, while lowering himself down from the castle, his escape rope ran out and he fell to his death. His body was dashed to pieces against the volcanic rocks, freeing his spirit to join his jinxed Jinty.

Chapter Fifty-Four
Dramatic Interlude

Famous people, tak tent and ye shall see
The Three Estates of this nation
Come to the Court with a strange gravity;
Therefore I make you supplication
To keep silence and be patient, I pray you.

—*Ane Satire of the Three Estates,* Sir David Lindsay, 16th Century

Linlithgow Palace, 6 January 1540

The two mistresses stood together, eyeing each other with sidelong looks, as they waited for the royal procession. When Margaret Erskine extended her short neck as far as she could above the ermine collar of her gown and adjusted the necklace of Scottish seed pearls to show them off, Marion Ogilvie threw her sideways look. The flesh of the concubine's ample bosom, mottled blue with the cold, did not display this expensive gift from the king to best advantage. With a shudder, Lady Marion pulled her own fox fur collar more tightly round her neck, for even the finest Flemish and French tapestries covering the bare stone walls and windows failed to keep out draughts in the Great Hall. To retain heat, the fourteen small apertures in the high window in the eastern wall had been glazed so as to keep the richly painted ceiling illuminated.

'Those are bonnie.' Lady Marion pointed to the French hangings she knew to be part of Queen Marie's dowry.

'Not as fine as the ones his grace has commissioned for Stirling Castle. All to his own design, they depict the hunting and capture of a unicorn,' Lady Margaret boasted. 'Since he hasn't stinted on gold and silver thread, they sparkle and shimmer like illuminated manuscripts in the candlelight. And here, under the king's direction, our own guildsmen have carved all the woodwork.' Indicating the intricate intertwining of the crown, thistle and *fleur-de-lys,* she added, 'Even the French craftsmen cannot match that.'

'That's as may be, but is the Great Hall not over-vaunting?'

'In what way, my lady Marion?' Elisabeth had already circled the hall to admire the tapestries before coming to join the two matrons.

'For one thing, these pillars and porticoes may suit a grand palace in Rome with its warm climate but they make a Scottish castle such as this far too cool and draughty. Though some may beg to differ,' Lady Marion remarked, looking pointedly at Margaret Erskine.

But the royal concubine's attention was drawn elsewhere. Her eyes had narrowed beneath the arched eyebrows and were darting a look of such malevolence that Elisabeth was startled. Was this the powerful evil eye that had wrought so much havoc on Jinty and her family? She followed her gaze towards James Hamilton who was dashing about as if his life depended on it—which it probably did.

For failing to persuade Pope Paul III to grant Margaret Erskine a divorce, this erstwhile minion of the king had fallen out of royal favour. The royal mistress had seen to that. She would never forgive the Bastard of Finnart, as she insisted on calling him, for robbing her of the crown. Let him rush hither and yon in a desperate bid to wean himself back into favour, but she would make it her business to ensure that he did not.

Lady Margaret crooked her finger to summon the Bastard. In a loud, commanding voice she demanded to know whether the waterways and drains had been checked. Also, had the chimneys stopped reeking? And what about the *pièce de resistance,* she snorted in parody of a French accent, would it be flowing freely with French claret?

Finnart frowned. Overseeing the building programme started by James IV, now carried on by his son to impress his French queen, was a thankless task. While Falkland Palace was being refurbished for his private pleasure, Linlithgow was to be the setting for grander, public entertainment. The *pièce de resistance,* the courtyard fountain, was being decorated in the classical style, with all manner of ornate carvings, including naked musicians, but those idle masons had downed tools. The stone was too hard to work with, they complained and were demanding more money to finish it. Finnart jaloused that, forewarned of his weak position, those mowdieworts, the masons, were holding him to ransom. There were many who would rejoice to see him fail.

'There may be no whimsical whinstane whistlers but at least there'll be warm-blooded, well-wetted pipers playing in the gallery for your entertainment. And a banquet fit for a Queen Real.'

The royal mistress glowered at this jibe. On the king's orders, the rarest delicacies had been kept back from the yuletide tables to be served up on Twelfth Night; goose, swan, peacock, sturgeon and porpoise would surely satisfy the greediest of pudding fillers and titillate the pickiest of palates, as well as impress his French bride. At the blast of the trumpet, the chattering courtiers fell silent. As the heavy oak doors creaked open to admit the royal procession, a young lad broke free and scampered over to show off his new plaidie to his mother.

'Jamie!' She hissed. 'Get yourself back there! Mind who you are!'

Margaret Erskine shooed her son away. At her insistence James Stewart was always to be included in any formal ceremonies. A bastard he might be but regardless of what anyone said, this trophy of her womb, his father's eldest son, had a royal birthright. The ill-begotten lad pouted and grudgingly slung the plaidie over his shoulder. The queen mother would have been affronted at the royal mistress's audacity to flaunt her bastard at court, Elisabeth thought, but Margaret Tudor was afflicted with the palsy and not expected to live.

Frolicking beside the procession, waving his stick and bell, the court jester, Cacaphatie, teased the royal party, even daring to mock King James himself in his multi-hued highland garb, specially made for him by Jessie Douglas. James, however, took it in good humour for it drew attention to his intent to 'daunt the isles' and challenge the authority of the rebellious highland chiefs.

Catching Elisabeth's eye, the king asked her to sit with Queen Marie. Being able to converse fluently in French, she'd become not only an invaluable counsellor to the queen, guiding her through the mire of Scottish affairs, but a valuable confidante and friend. Elisabeth settled her on an upholstered chair, plumping up soft cushions at her back and resting her swollen ankles on a footstool. One of the first to learn of her pregnancy, Elisabeth had offered the services of Sister Agnes and Betsy in her confinement. Pleased to have the experienced Scots midwife as a buffer against the self-important physicians as well as the French-speaking sister for spiritual comfort, Queen Marie had gratefully accepted. Besides, she felt comfortable in the company of nuns.

Before being married off to Louis, Duc de Longueville, she'd shared the ascetic life with her grandmother who had retired to the convent of the Poor Clares. Now she sat with her arms folded protectively over her swollen belly, trying to rein in her resentment at hearing her husband's mistress gurgling laugh and seeing her bastard son being treated like a prince. In his wedding speech David Lindsay had pointedly reminded the king of the marriage vow—to forsake all others—but sadly this had fallen on deaf ears.

'If only I could have remained with my dear grandmother in the convent but my family had greater ambitions,' the queen whispered. 'A woman is merely a pawn in men's affairs and, I must admit, the prospect of being bundled off to Scotland and abandoning my three-year-old son did not fill me with joy. My compatriots warned me that Scotland was a country of wild savages with a primitive culture and even more inclement weather. It is little wonder that poor Princess Madeleine perished here.'

'And are we, your grace?' Elisabeth enquired.

The queen smiled before responding tactfully. 'Compared with the English—no. At times I give thanks that I wed the King of Scots and not that Bluebeard, Henry of England. Just imagine! When he expressed interest in *une grande dame* like me, I let it be known that, though I may be big in person, my neck is far too small!' She trilled, patting her throat. 'I thank God for my lucky escape and pray that the Scots do not follow the English custom of beheading their queen.

'Nevertheless, though I keep my head, I do not have my husband's heart,' she lamented, her gaiety changing to sadness. 'He is fond of me, as he is of his pet dogs, but I know he does not love me as he adored the Princess Madeleine,' she declared. 'That was *une alliance d'amour*. I still recollect how his eyes sparkled when he first beheld her. *Fou d'amour*, we all agreed. But then, I must confess, I do not love him the way I loved my dearly departed Louis, or my son. *Mais, malgré tout*, I have fulfilled my obligation,' she said, patting her protruding stomach. 'Though it is not easy when he comes to me still warm from his mistress's embraces.'

Margaret Erskine must have sensed her resentful glance, for her head swivelled round. The malevolent glower she darted so alarmed Elisabeth that she leant forward to shield the royal womb from her green-eyed jealousy. Just then the jester leapt before the queen, jiggling his bell and pointing his stick at her.

'What grows in its neuk and swells up under the firm grasp of a cocky young bride?' he said with an impudent leer.

While the queen coloured and turned away, Margaret Erskine let out a gleeful screech at his bawdy riddle, loudly whispering the answer in the king's ear.

Meanwhile, Cardinal Beaton came sauntering down the hall, cricking his craig to look upwards, before seating himself beside his mistress. Resplendent in cardinal red velvet, with an enormous bejewelled crucifix dangling on a gold chain round his neck, the flamboyant cock robin overshadowed his dowdy female, dressed modestly in russet silk.

'Where are the carvings his grace has commissioned?' he asked. 'Thon likenesses of well-kent figures of our time? Mine will doubtless be among them.'

Lady Marion patted his arm. 'For one thing, thon whittled heads are to be raised to the rafters at the Great Hall in Stirling Castle, not here. And for another it would take a muckle block of oak and a wheen of paint to render your grand visage, Beaton o' the *Ceann Mhór*,' she quipped.

He looked askance and feigned offence. No kind words then from his lady fair whose Scotch love could be relied upon to cut him down to size.

'My dearest lady, with your lacerating tongue you rival Cacaphatie,' Beaton retorted. 'Or even the makar himself. No doubt Lindsay will present us with some seasonal anarchy. A witty Epiphany from his well-inked quill,' he said with a smirk.

A flourish of trumpets heralded the start of the spectacle and the audience hushed as a cloaked figure stepped on to the dais. He pulled down his hood and introduced himself as Diligence, the narrator, who would relate how the Vices who held King Humanity in their evil grip at his court would be overcome and driven out by the Virtues.

'Saints and sinners alike, tak tent to me,' he bellowed before announcing that the yuletide reign of misrule was now over. This provoked disgruntled jeers and hisses from the spectators who'd been expecting the anarchic Abbot of Unreason and his unruly mob. They were in the mood for entertainment, not a sermon, and certainly not the morality play this was turning out to be. The comely figures of King Humanity's dissolute courtiers, Wantonness, Placebo and Solace in various states of undress appeared to appease the audience. But appreciative whistles greeted the entrance of Dame Sensuality who shimmered onto the dais, swaying sensuous curves discernible through her gossamer gown.

At first the flame gold hair and the knowing smile playing on the luscious lips of this Dame of Vice, made Elisabeth sit up. That can never be Nancy. Her brother Adam's widow would now be in her mid-forties, she calculated. No, if it couldn't be Nancy, it must be her daughter Jenny, now wed to Lord Fleming. La Fleming, as they cried the king's half-sister, oozed with the same kind of voluptuous desire and promises of sensual pleasure as her mother. As this lusty lady and her maidens took centre stage, King Humanity's adviser, the virtuous Good Counsel, was hustled out.

'*Qu'est-ce que dire?*' the queen whispered, her eyebrows furrowed in confusion. 'They speak too quickly for me.'

It wasn't only the fast-spoken language that prevented her from enjoying the spectacle: the sight of plump Margaret Erskine, wobbling in paroxysms of glee at the king's side and hugging their son in her copious lap, grieved her. Well acquainted with the agony of being the short side of an unequal triangle, never to be foremost in your lover's heart, Elisabeth sympathised. At this very moment, behind the scenes, Jessie Douglas would be fussing with costumes and acting as Lindsay's helpmate. She sat up and straightened her back to concentrate on the play.

Dame Sensuality had moved on from the first estate—the court of King Humanity—and was now seducing the Abbot and Friars of the spiritual estate. Driven out of the monastery, one of the Virtues, Chastity, in a long white flowing robe was appealing to Dame Prioress for sanctuary in her convent, but the Prioress, who was learning to dance a *pavane* with the Abbot, shunned her, saying:

Pass hind, Madame, by Christ you come nocht here!
You are contrary to my complexioun.
Gan seek lodgins at some auld monk or friar
Perchance they will be your protection.

Saying so, the rôle-playing Prioress pulled off her wimple and shook out her hair and then lifted up her habit to reveal a kirtle of red silk. While the audience howled with laughter, nudging each other and exchanging knowing glances, the real-life prioress blushed with embarrassed indignation. 'The flighty nun' was no better than a common cow-clink, they whispered behind her back. Elisabeth knew that her habit of following the king's hunt had earned her this nickname but there was no need for Lindsay to reinforce it. None of the three estates was spared his merciless satire, but surely he could have forewarned her that she, too, would be ridiculed.

Stricken by this cruel caricature her mouth became too dry to translate for the queen, Elisabeth squirmed uncomfortably in her seat. Swithering whether or not to flee the hall or give Lindsay a hard slap, she felt a sympathetic pat on her hand. Queen Marie raised her chin to stare proudly ahead and lifted the corners of her lips into a strained smile. Aware of being dubbed the 'French mare'—a *sobriquet,* probably started by the spiteful mistress—the queen was demonstrating her way of coping with derision by putting into practice her motto: *Endure Fort.*

After a short interlude for refreshments, the play began with a warning blast from the character of Divine Correction clad in black. Before he'd uttered a word, his stern countenance was enough to silence the mocking laughter from the spectators, now even more inebriated.

‘I am an judge richt potent and severe,’ he cried, his bass voice resounding throughout the Great Hall. Imperious and mighty in his robes, he glared at the audience and waved an admonitory finger at them all, while accusing them of every possible vice. No estate was spared his censure. Courtiers were arraigned for their shameful wickedness, the lords for selfishness, the burgesses for greed, the church for immorality and sensuality and the monarch for lethargy.

As the Three Estates—the clergy the nobles and the burgesses—entered blindly led by their Vices and walking backwards, he raged at them. With their backsides foremost, how could they know where they were going? Commanding them to turn and face King Humanity, he bellowed,

‘Get up, Sir King! Ye have sleepit enough into the arms of Lady Sensual.’

While the audience gasped at his audacity, Margaret Erskine’s high brows furrowed in anger as Divine Correction continued his tirade. He reminded King Humanity of one of the lessons of Sodom and Gomorrah: how King Sardanapall who had spored his lust among fair ladies for so long was overthrown by rebellious lieges. Although the actor was heavily disguised, Elisabeth recognised the candid blue eyes glinting above the theatrical bushy black beard as he boomed:

I have power great princes to down thring
That lives contrair the Majesty Divine
Against the truth which plainly does malign
Repent they nocht I put them to ruin.

Unnerved by his vehemence, Queen Marie clutched her belly with one hand and gripped Elisabeth’s arm with the other. Then Divine Correction fixed his eyes on the leader of the clergy, Cardinal Beaton to warn:

I will begin at thee, which is the head,
And make on thee first reformation.

Lindsay had trained Divine Correction well, too well perhaps, in his rôle as avenging angel, Elisabeth thought. For John Knox was not play acting, she feared, but meant every word he uttered.

Chapter Fifty-Five
Indictment

Then Patience says, 'Be not aghast:
Haud Hope and Truth within thee fast
And let Fortune work forth her rage
Whom that no reason may assuage.'
—*Meditation in Winter,* William Dunbar, 15th–16th Century

St Mary's Abbey, June 1541

'He's been waiting for you to come hame, as fidgety as a fiend in the inferno,' Betsy said as she helped Elisabeth off with her riding cloak. 'Says it's important but won't tell me what it is.' She gave the cloak a good, hard shake. 'I've telt him to wait until you've had your supper or caught your breath at least but he says he can't put it off.'

Trauchled after a fifteen-mile ride from Edinburgh, Elisabeth's only desire was to fall asleep in her soft feather bed. Instead she flopped down onto the settle and closed her eyes.

'Let's put him out of his misery,' she muttered. 'I'll hear what he has to say.'

After placing the paradise bird cushion behind Lisbeth's wimpled head and a pitcher of weak ale on the table, Betsy folded her arms and glowered. 'And then you'll have your supper,' she stated and hirpled off to the kitchen.

As Knox gazed down at the prioress, her care-worn face smeared with dust and grime, a sharp pain stabbed at his heart: *Stabat Mater dolorosa.* The lustre may be fading from the radiant Queen of Heaven but her innate beauty was still intact. In those few moments of contemplation her face was impressed upon his memory, as that of Christ had been embossed forever on Veronica's veil. Loath though he was to add to her sorrows, the document he was holding was so inflammatory it seemed to scorch his fingers. The accusation should be doused at once.

'While you were away this came, Dame Elisabeth.'

'You are the notary, John. Surely you can deal with it,' she said, keeping her eyes firmly shut.

'It concerns you personally, madame. It appears to be an indictment.'

'An indictment?' Her eyes flew open and she raised her head from the cushion. 'Who has served this on me?'

Knox quickly scanned the parchment. 'One John Hay, 3rd Lord of Yester.'

'Lord Hay! The Wizard of Goblin Ha'! How dare he! No doubt he's acting out of spite because of the case he lost against me years ago. That devil incarnate would haggle the breeks off a beggar. Why, he even sued his own grandmother.'

It was true. When Hay had reneged on an agreement to manage her estates, his grandmother, Lady Belton, had obtained a decree appointing her other son, his uncle, as factor. Not to be outdone, Hay had declared that she was illegally occupying Belton Castle. From the goodness of his heart, however, he'd allow her to bide there if she allowed him to continue to factor the lands. The wrangling dragged on for years and, while the Wizard seemed to thrive on it, his grandmother finally gave up her broken spirit.

'He haunts the courts like a demented demon. Do you ken he sued the earl of Arran for pulling down eighty yards of a boundary dyke! Eighty yards! Forbye, a man who would pursue his own grandmother to an early grave for the sake of a groat is not to be trusted.'

'But what does he hope to gain by this?' Knox frowned.

'Thon miserable lickpenny would fley a louse for its skin to sew a purse for his scrimped savings. Hay covets lands at Nunraw bestowed on the abbey by our founder, Countess Ada. I jalouse the warlock has conjured this up out of thin air to blackmail me, hoping that, in return for his silence, I will hand over the lands to him. Burn it.'

With an impatient sigh, she rested her head again and closed her eyes. Knox picked up another document, no less damning than the indictment. He pulled up a stool and sat down to steady the tension in his shaky legs.

'There's also a statement from his aunt who claims to have been a witness at the time.'

Elisabeth blinked. 'His aunt? Who might that be?'

'It would appear that a certain Sister Maryoth Hay was once a nun here. Do you remember her?' Knox asked.

Remember her? How Elisabeth wished she could forget her. So that's where all this was coming from. She sat up and rubbed her eyes. There could be no rest for her now.

'Sister Maryoth and her brother have borne malice towards me ever since I was appointed prioress in her stead. No doubt thon warlock is kindling his clyping aunt's grudges to fan the flames of his case against me.'

Knox waited until she'd calmed down. 'She swears by Almighty God and His Holy Mother, that,' he paused to take a deep breath before reading from the witness statement, 'the accused, Elisabeth Hepburn, has not preserved a wholly unstained character these many years. Namely, that her unseemly conduct and past misdemeanours render her unfit to be a prioress of the church.'

'Nothing more than clash and clatter,' Elisabeth sneered. 'The vindictive tittle-tattle of a serpent so full of venom and hate for me that it has poisoned her soul and shrivelled her senses.'

'More seriously,' Knox began, but his tongue kept sticking to the roof of his dry mouth. And when a fit of coughing couldn't clear his constricted throat, she poured him a tassie of weak ale. With a nod of gratitude, he drained it before carrying on, 'More seriously, Sister Maryoth claims that the child you were carrying, the fruit of this liaison, was done away with in murderous fashion.'

A noise made Knox look up. The prioress had slipped from the settle and was standing over him, eyes blazing in her ashen face. He shifted nervously from one buttock to the other.

'What malicious slander is this? What precisely is the accusation?' she fumed.

Knox gripped the parchment with trembling hands and began to read. 'On the Second Day of June in the Year of Our Lord 1541, this Indictment to be served on one Elisabeth Hepburn, Prioress of St Mary's Abbey,' he broke off, 'an accusation of...', he swallowed hard before continuing, 'Carnal Dalliance.' In his rush to finish reading, his voice had ascended from a sombre bass to a high-pitched squeak.

'Carnal dalliance? Is that what they cry it? Fyking in other words!' the accused spluttered. 'And who, if anyone, is cited as my partner in this crime of carnal dalliance?'

Her intense stare was causing beads of prickly sweat to break out on his forehead. Knox moistened his dry lips before pronouncing, 'One Harry Cockburn, brother of Patrick Cockburn of Newbigging.' He kept his head down, his eyes fixed on the document, for he could not face her. The idea of his prioress engaged in the act of carnal dalliance was making him feel uncomfortable, even queasy. After a brief, unbearable silence, she suddenly burst out laughing.

'Harry Cockburn, you say? Harry Cockburn indeed!' Still shaking with laughter, Elisabeth picked up the witness statement. 'Here's what we do with this festering filth from that old witch, that accursed crone.' She held it up by the corner as if it were soiled. 'Purification by fire.' Despite her creaking knees, she knelt down and placed it on the glowing embers of the log fire.

Knox didn't try to stop her. Once flickers of flame had licked its edges, she slowly fed in the rest of the indictment and the witness statement. In silence they watched the black ink gradually turn grey, the corners of the parchment slowly curl up and shrivel into a heap of ash.

'There.' Elisabeth wiped her hands and rose from her knees. 'There's an end to that. Harry Cockburn indeed,' she snorted. She crossed to the cupboard and took out a bottle of French cognac to pour them each a generous dram. She took a long swig and lay her head on the cushion tilting her starched wimple askew. 'Who do they take me for?' she said, her laugh heavy with scorn. 'The Abbess of Unreason?'

Sipping his cognac, Knox seemed uneasy: he didn't share her joke, rather his frown deepened.

'I fear it may not be the end,' he began tentatively. 'Lord Hay has sent copies of these papers to the diocesan commissioners in St Andrews. The board plan to discuss it when they attend the half-yearly session here at the abbey next week. Cardinal Beaton is coming with them. He's taking a personal interest in the case.'

'Indeed? Then we can rest easy. Davie Beaton and I may be auld enemies but we're also auld friends. He'll make sure this scurrilous scandal is scrapped.'

Knox squirmed on his stool. 'Perhaps. If so, then why has his uncle, Archbishop Beaton, granted Sister Maryoth a special dispensation to break her silence? She is prepared to give testimony.'

Coldingham Priory, April 1541

'What do you want with me?' Her voice, brittle from lack of use, cracked through the grille in the cell door. 'And speak up,' Sister Maryoth demanded, cupping her good ear with her hand. 'Who did you say you were?'

'John Knox. Notary apostolic. I've come to inscribe your testimony.'

'Nay,' she shrieked loudly in the way of deaf people. 'Parchments can be burned, or torn up or lost, perchance. My testimony shall come from my own tongue. I will trust no-one with it, far less the godson of the prioress. Oh, aye, my memory hasn't deserted me yet. You may not remember me, Johnnie Knox, but I mind you.'

She tapped a bony finger against the grille for him to come closer but her rancid breath made him turn his face away. 'Carnal dalliance is venial compared to the gross sins committed by that woman. Their dallying had been going on for some time. I should know. I kept close watch on them. Let her say that Harry Cockburn snatched her from the abbey and then violated her, but I tell you, I saw her jump up behind him of her own free will and ride off with him for three days and three, long, nights.'

Sister Maryoth broke off, wheezing with the excitement of telling her tale. After years of incarceration in a closed order—at John Hepburn's insistence so as to gag her errant tongue—she was now being given the chance to break her silence and she wasn't going to waste it.

'And when she came back, she was heavy with sin and heavier still with child. She will deny it, but I saw her swelling belly with my own eyes. She left the abbey to have her bairn and, for all I know, thon pagan, Betsy Learmont, slaughtered the innocent to protect the reputation of that Jezebel. I was sworn to silence, but I did so, not on the Holy Bible, but a book of false images for all I ken. My time in this vale of tears is nearly up and I cannot go to my Maker without seeing justice done to that whore of Babylon.'

Listening to these slurs on the prioress's reputation, the easily riled Knox had to clench his teeth to keep his temper. 'If what you say is true, sister, then Harry Cockburn would have been charged with...' he paused to draw breath, since the scurrilous words were searing his tongue. 'Abduction and ravishment.'

Sister Maryoth cackled in glee. 'He was never found.' She had made sure of that—plying the old watchmen with strong drink and then setting Harry off on a horse from the abbey stables. 'While *she* escaped her punishment,' she said bitterly.

A cloistered life of prayer and abstinence had clearly not filled her heart with peace and love but addled the wizened old crone's wits.

'You may think I'm doited, but I tell you my mind is as clear as my conscience. But what about hers?'

When, once again, her skeletal finger dunted against the grating, Knox had to fight a strong urge to grab hold of if it, twisting it until it cracked. Instead, he took a deep breath before attempting to reason with her.

'If what you say is true, sister, then why not leave the prioress to divine retribution? Is it not written: Vengeance is mine, sayeth the Lord? Like us all, she will have to stand before Almighty God to be judged and punished.'

'It's not vengeance I demand, but justice,' she cried, rattling the grille with both hands. 'Forbye, when she's sent to hell, I shall not be there to see her suffer!'

Knox winced before taking another tack. If she would not listen to reason, perhaps an appeal to her better feelings would melt her hardened heart. 'Did not Our Lord, Jesus Christ exhort us to turn the other cheek?' he reminded her. 'Let he who is without sin cast the first stone.'

Sister Maryoth puckered her thin, withered lips up to the grating and rasped.

'Turn the other cheek? Show mercy to a shameless sinner? By Christ's sacred blood, I'm prepared to cast the first stone. If it's the last thing I do. Only then will I rest in peace.'

St Mary's Abbey, 12 June 1541

When Beaton arrived in full cardinal pomp, Elisabeth looked him up and down, noting his four-neukit cap and voluminous scarlet cape of watered silk trimmed with ermine that needed to be supported by a trainbearer, an acolyte in a pure white lace surplice.

'An avenging angel come to give judgement, Davie. You may have gained the long-coveted cardinal's hat, but I think your peacock-feathered bonnet suited you better.'

With a huffy harrumph Beaton, now a fully-fledged prince of the church, straightened his biretta and dangled his podgy hand adorned with the cardinal's ring for her to kiss: like a remorseful collie dog offering its paw, seeking forgiveness. For she was infuriated that he'd taken the indictment seriously enough to bring to court. As *Legatus a latere* to the Vatican, he could easily have used the papal plenary powers to trample it underfoot. To squash it, by hook or by cardinal's crook.

Lamentably he couldn't do so, he'd explained, lest he be accused of turning a blind eye to a serious case of veniality. Furthermore, a bride of Christ, especially a prioress, like Caesar's wife, should be above suspicion. However, he did hint that Hay might be prepared to drop the case in return for the lands of Nunraw.

Elisabeth was unyielding. 'Since you, as cardinal and so-called champion, seem loath to defend my honour, I shall have to contest this case to clear my name. And, if anyone should be charged with carnal dalliance, it should be you, Davie Beaton.'

With a curt bow he replied, 'Let battle commence.'

At the high court battle lines were drawn up. On one side two independent commissioners were flanked by the prosecuting notary and his team and on the other by a detachment of notaries apostolic for the defence and their scribes. The preliminary bout opened with a request from the defendant to hear the case in private, behind closed doors, but Lord Hay objected and threatened to appeal to the Archbishop of St Andrews.

Claiming superior authority as cardinal, Beaton immediately overruled it. If nothing else, the abbey's champion would ensure that the prioress's honour would not be subject to public scrutiny. Nor would she be called to give evidence before the other party cited in the indictment.

It had taken four men to haul Harry Cockburn out of the alehouse where he spent most of his time and money carousing with his cronies. Now an aging, battle-scarred border reiver gone to seed, his burly frame swayed unsteadily in front of the bench, yawning and clawing at the beasties that were gnawing at his nether parts. Though coarsened with war and bleary-eyed with drink, the fright at seeing the assembled might of the Roman Catholic Church went some way to sober him up.

Fear was replaced by bewilderment when the charge of 'carnal dalliance' with Prioress Elisabeth Hepburn was read out. His legs buckled underneath him and he clung on to the back of a chair for support. Carlin dancing? Dancing with witches? That would be serious. Folk were burnt for less.

'Or to put it more simply, that you have lain with the prioress,' one of the commissioners helpfully explained.

'Lain with the prioress?' Harry's red-flecked eyes narrowed as he tried to concentrate. 'What sort of carlin would I need to be to have done that? Auld Clootie himself couldn't lowp o'er yon nunnery wall. Though the monks o' Mains might manage it.' When his inane, black-toothed grin was answered by scowls, sweat broke out on his forehead, for he may well be digging his own grave—if not lighting his own funeral pyre.

'No cursing and no calumny in court,' the prosecutor reprimanded him. 'We're speaking of the time before she became prioress and you were employed as a stable lad at the abbey.'

'Thon was auld lang syne.' Harry rubbed the sweat running into his eyes with a clarty hand. 'I cannot mind what I did yesterday, never mind when I was a lad.' Again he pulled an idiotic grin.

'Answer the question or you'll be put in the stocks for contempt. Is the person with whom you've been accused of committing said carnal dalliance present in this court?'

Clearly confused, Harry was clawing his scalp and rubbing his dirt-streaked face as he scanned the courtroom. Just then, Elisabeth, who had been sitting with her head bowed, looked up and beamed an encouraging smile. Lady Lisbeth. Harry blinked a few times to clear his bleary eyes. From deep within his drink-sozzled brain a memory surfaced and with it a promise that never, as long as he lived, would he ever betray Lady Lisbeth.

'Aye, I think so, but no I didnae...'

'Which is it?'

Lord Hay tugged at the prosecutor's sleeve. 'You may have to use more persuasive means to extract a confession from him,' he said in a whisper loud enough for Harry to hear. 'A night in the dungeon would not go amiss with...' He mimed twisting the thumbscrews.

Harry's eyes bulged in terror at the threat of the pilliewinks. He clung to the back of the chair to steady the quaking in his knees that rapidly spread upwards until his whole body was trembling. Whether the waggling of his head was voluntary or involuntary; whether he was nodding or shaking it, Elisabeth couldn't tell. She braced herself for what he might say.

'It wasnae me. I never touched her. Maybe I did try to kiss her—for yon Sister Maryoth told me she was keen on me—but Lady Lisbeth was having none of it. Aye, I did ride with her but only to take her to Hailes...to see her brother...'

As he began gibbering incoherently, Elisabeth clasped her hands tightly together in silent prayer. Please stop, Harry. Stay silent. Don't say any more.

'I need to piss,' he whimpered, hopping nervously from one foot to the other.

'Then piss in your breeks,' the prosecutor grumbled. Which Harry did, letting the stream run down his legs to form a puddle on the flagstones. The sour smell, mingling with his sweat and rancid body odour, wafted towards those on the bench who pinched their nostrils.

Knox stepped forward to object—the prosecutor's question was clearly confusing the witness. Then, with the court's permission he asked, 'Harry Cockburn, you only have to answer one question. Have you ever lain with Dame Elisabeth Hepburn? Aye or nay.'

'Naaay!' Harry's long drawn-out wail deafened the court.

'That was not a denial but the braying of a donkey,' Lord Hay protested. Beaton, however, swiftly overruled him and signalled to the guards who heaved Harry out of the chamber, dragging his feet along the flagstones.

Tap-tapping her walking cane before her, Sister Maryoth shuffled into the courtroom. Now in her late sixties, she was shrunken and shrivelled from years of fasting and denial of the flesh. Though cataracts veiled her eyes, rendering images fuzzy and blurred, her sense of smell wasn't impaired. As she was led to her place, she sniffed the air, screwing up her nose in disgust.

'Is this a courtroom or a pigsty you have brought me to? Hogs on the bench with their swinish snouts in the trough,' she muttered.

When informed that Harry Cockburn had denied the accusation of carnal dalliance, her withered lips tightened. 'He would. The Jezebel beglamoured him.'

'Are you now accusing the prioress of witchcraft?' Knox asked.

She crinkled up her cloudy eyes to peer round the room before pointing her cane at Elisabeth. 'All I ken is that she learnt weirdly ways at her heathen nurse's knee.'

When Knox called Sister Katherine as his first witness, Beaton immediately raised an objection. Because she was not at the abbey when the events on trial took place, her testimony was not relevant. Because her evidence would shed light on the character and disposition of the accuser and would dispute the validity of the indictment, Knox argued, she should be heard. The acid malice in the cardinal's withering look momentarily unsettled him, but he would not be intimidated. Nor would he yield to his morally corrupt demand.

While the commissioners listened with considerable interest to Sister Katherine's testimony, Beaton couldn't decide who had angered him more; Knox—for calling on his own sister as witness, thereby signalling his defiance—or Katherine, for agreeing to testify. Coldly and dispassionately, she described the scene at the election for the new prioress when the intoxicated sisters had been asked to pray for inspiration from the Holy Ghost.

'May I suggest,' Knox was saying, 'that the potion was hexed and that it wasn't the Holy Ghost but Satan himself who was called down to inflame their minds.'

Then, when asked if Lord Hay had been a frequent visitor to the abbey, Katherine nodded. 'Aye, and he always left with a laden cart or two.'

Again, Hay leapt up to object, but once again was ordered to sit back down.

'Weighed down with goods and monies misappropriated by his sister which he then misused to indulge his necromancy,' Knox declared. 'The Wizard of Goblin Ha', as Lord Hay has become known and not without reason, was accused of practising sorcery and cavorting among the legions of Lucifer. His sister Maryoth was banished from St Mary's, not only for unlawful election, but for swindling the abbey finances.'

Turning to the commissioners' bench, Knox continued. 'I contend that it is Sister's Maryoth aim to besmirch the good character of the prioress and bring about her dismissal, not only to wreak personal revenge, but to arrange for the lands at Nunraw to be awarded in compensation to her nephew, Lord Hay. In doing so she has concocted this story to dishonour the prioress. However, the question now arises: if the witness's intention is morally corrupt, can the court trust her testimony?'

Realising that the trial was turning against her, Sister Maryoth uttered a strangled squeal.

'What about the bairn! That wanton had an ill-begotten bairn! I saw her swollen womb with my own eyes! Then she cast it out! She's a murderess!'

When the commissioners looked baffled by this disclosure, Beaton called Knox over. Why had this been withheld? he demanded to know. If it were true, such an outcome would be undeniable proof of the crime of carnal dalliance. Indeed, Knox agreed, and begged permission to call another witness.

Over the years Betsy's hirpling gait had worsened as both hips had become rickety. Leaning heavily on a crutch, she limped into the courtroom, stopping for a moment in front of the old nun before taking a seat directly opposite her. Sister Maryoth's milky eyes blinked in terror and a chill ran through her bones. She fumbled for her beads and began mumbling prayers.

'Aye, Dame Elisabeth did indeed bring a wean into this world,' Betsy began, sending a *frisson* throughout the court, 'when she helped me deliver it. After a lengthy struggle, the bairn had no strength left to take his first breath. When Dame Elisabeth here blew life into his weak lungs, the mother asked her to stand as godmother. I mind it as if it was yesterday. For the bairn she gave life to was you, John Knox. Aye, and you wouldn't be here today if it wasn't for the prioress,' she said, waggling her head at him. 'But auld age doesn't come alone and, if it's no the body, then it's the mind that weakens. I'm thinking that Sister Maryoth's brain may be wasted and her memories all taigled up.'

There was silence as the court digested this information. Positioning himself in front of Sister Maryoth, Knox asked, his voice low and threatening, 'How do you respond to this, Sister? Or has the grimalkin got your tongue?'

She had indeed been struck dumb, not only by the evil eye of that heathen, Betsy Learmonth, but the ghost of Bishop Hepburn, whose voice—deep and resonant enough to fill a cathedral—rumbled like distant thunder in her deaf ears. But when Knox leant forward, those same piercing blue eyes speared into her very soul, seeking vengeance for breaking her sacred word. She squirmed in her seat, jerking her legs and sending her stick clattering onto the tiles. Bending down to retrieve her cane to fend off the fiend, her head began to whirl. She opened her mouth to speak but her face had drooped into a one-sided grin. No words came from her lolling tongue, only slavering drool as she slumped sideways.

The men in the court gawped in helpless horror while Betsy and Elisabeth rushed to Maryoth's aid.

'Is she dead?' Elisabeth asked.

Betsy shook her head. 'Nay, there's life in the auld bird yet, but I fear she's been blastit. Struck by what we cry the apoplexy,' she explained. 'She might live for a while but her tongue will never clatter again.'

As Lord Hay scooped up his aunt's crumpled body and carried her away, Betsy squeezed Elisabeth's arm and whispered in her hear. 'That will teach her to cry me a witch.'

When the commissioners dismissed the case, Elisabeth gave her nurse a grateful hug. Though found not guilty, Harry still had to be cleared of any accusation or suspicion of carnal dalliance with Elisabeth, Prioress of Haddington. Willingly he agreed to purging by oath rather than purging by ordeal. Repeating incomprehensible words was preferable to being locked in the stocks and pelted with keech or whatever muck the mob would fling at him.

The verdict did not please Beaton, however. 'Two fools in one house is a couple o'er many,' he remarked through gritted teeth. 'And I jalouse there may be yet another who thinks himself smart.'

From the black glowering looks that Beaton hurled at him, Knox knew that his future in the Roman Church was doomed. Before the trial, the cardinal had taken Knox aside to hint that, if the case against the prioress were proven, he'd be well rewarded. Not only would he overlook his refusal to take the oath and award him his degree but would assign him a lucrative parish. The prioress's dismissal would mean the end of her monstrous, irreverent regime that was harming the church's reputation, Beaton maintained but Knox was not deceived.

The end of Hepburn reign at the abbey would leave the cardinal free to exercise his right to appoint her successor and, by filling the vacancy with one of his cronies, he would then gain control of the abbey's considerable finances. Instead of defending the prioress, Beaton was scheming behind her back. That this Judas had been prepared to sacrifice her to cram pieces of gold into his fat paws only stoked Knox's contempt for the cardinal. His defiance tolled the death knell in their troubled relationship.

Chapter Fifty-Six
St John's Vigil

See, I have this day set thee over the nations and
over the kingdoms, to root out and
to pull down and to destroy.
—*Jeremiah* I:10

Haddington, 23 June 1541

From the Nungate Bridge, Knox watched dark figures whooping and whirling in and out of the shadows cast by the huge bonfire burning on the haugh by the Tyne. On this, 'the merriest of nights', the mob were celebrating midsummer as they had always done, by flagrantly flouting the church's attempt to usurp the pagan festival with their own feast day—the Vigil of St John the Baptist. His gaze searched out the spot where the gypsy girl had cursed them all.

When her drowned body had been washed up at the weir further down the river, Knox gawped along with the other ghouls. He should have come forward, perhaps, but given the verdict—that, being drunk, she'd fallen into the river—he decided to say nothing. Nor had he said anything at the time to prevent her brutal murder. Should he have confessed? For a sin of omission was just as venial as a wicked deed. Though the gypsy girl's blood had long since been washed away, he fretted that it tainted his soul with mortal sin, like an inkblot seeping into a parchment. Head down, whipped by the lash of conscience, he was scurrying down the bridge ramp when he heard his name being called.

'Hey! It's Johnnie Knox! Are you going awa?'

Others took up the refrain, their raucous voices jarring in the still, midnight air.

'To tell your ma? Then who's your ma?'

'Naw—a hoore's your ma! Your ma's your holy sister.'

'And where's your ma, your holy ma?'

'In the hoor-hoose, behind the priory wa.'

Nuns and priests would aye be the butt of jokes even so these jibes at the prioress wounded Knox. The recent indictment against her for carnal dalliance, even though disproved, had further stoked the fire of innuendo against her. And Sir David Lindsay's cruel and public mockery of her in his *Satire* hadn't helped.

As he fled from the pagan rabble down the steps of the bridge, Knox recalled that crossing water warded off evil spirits. Some superstitions were as deeply ingrained in him as catholic doctrine.

Hurrying along the bank of the Tyne Knox cast his mind back to Friar Lazarus's sudden disappearance all those years ago that had left him bereft, even though he understood his reason: a friar with his reformist beliefs would not be safe from Beaton's persecution. In Nungate he came to a halt outside Tibbie's Tavern, the spot where he'd bumped into the friar. Overjoyed at seeing him again, he'd invited Knox to Garleton Castle to meet a good friend of his. Intrigued, Knox had accepted.

There the friar left him to wait in the oratory while he sought out his friend. The summer sun streaming through the stained-glass window lit up the shelves of books, many of them poetry, but Knox was surprised to see laid out on the table works by reformers such as Luther, Melancthon and Erasmus. Who would dare to read such prohibited books?

'I see you're admiring my collection.'

It had taken Knox a moment to recognise who stood before him. Friar Lazarus had swapped his monk's habit for the ceremonial tabard of the Lyon Herald. Sir David Lindsay was not only a skilful playwright but consummate actor.

'Forgive me for deceiving you, but I had to do it, John,' Lindsay explained. 'At the time I feared for my life.'

He'd been on the point of freezing to death on the cliffs near Tantallon that January night in 1526, when he'd been arrested by Angus's men posing as the royal guard. After leaving him on the cliff-top, Harry Cockburn had come back and taken him to the Franciscan Friary in Haddington. Disguised as a Greyfriar he'd avoided recognition and arrest until King James seized power and recalled him into his service as ambassador. During his travels on the continent, he'd met many reformist sympathisers and had managed to smuggle in these inflammatory works. For no-one—not even Beaton—would dare challenge the king's trusted envoy, the Lyon Herald.

'I've seen exciting new dramatic forms that have inspired me to write a play criticising corruption in the church. Not a blundering charge with the heavy-handed cudgel,' he explained, seeing Knox's horrified face, 'but swift, stinging cuts with the sharp rapier of satire. Folly, not reason, John, is the governing principle of the makar's world. The conceit centres round a satirical parliament of bishops, knights and burgesses, to where the Poor Man brings his complaints. I have a rôle in mind for you, John, if you're willing to take part in the performance at court.'

Far from disappointing Knox, the transfiguration of the monk into the makar had given him new heart, and he'd readily agreed. The scathing criticism couched in poetic imagery of Sir David Lindsay's, *Ane Satire of the Three Estates,* should certainly make them sit up and take heed, though Knox was uneasy with his cruel condemnation of Prioress Elisabeth.

'*Mea culpa,*' Lindsay had beat his breast, 'but only because I deem it a sin against nature for women to be closeted away, imprisoned behind the walls of a nunnery. They should be wives and mothers. Nor, for that matter, should priests remain celibate.'

'No doubt the cardinal and most of his bishops agree with you,' Knox scoffed, 'but the hierarchy will only change the rules again when it suits them.'

'But they will have to. There is change afoot, but small steps at a time, John, for long strides risk leaving the faithful too far behind.'

Now, years later, time had disillusioned Knox. Nothing would change the minds of those gross ignorant sloths: the glimmer of hope kindled by Lindsay's play had been extinguished. Although it had stirred King James into issuing a decree for holy scripture to be translated into the vernacular, the bishops had immediately objected, a meaningless protest since few people could read anyway.

He'd been so wrapped in thought, that he was caught off guard to find himself at the abbey chapel where he'd served as an altar boy. He knelt down to pray for guidance but almost immediately leapt up again. This was not how the Lord should be worshipped, subserviently on the knees, mindlessly mumbling incomprehensible litanies. He settled on a bench at the back of the chapel, as far away from the altar and the tabernacle lamp as possible and bowed his head to examine his conscience.

There was no future for him in the church of Rome. He'd hammered the final nail in the coffin. Not even the prioress would be able to save him from Beaton's flames of persecution. Knox's heart constricted. She was the only reason he hadn't already left the priesthood. He was beholden to her for everything—his upbringing, his schooling, even his very existence, for had she not breathed life into his failing lungs?

Let them mock her, but she was one of the few heads of a religious house who used the benefices of the abbey for the common good to support the apothecary and infirmary. Though the prioress struggled to understand his theological concerns, she'd tried to channel his rebellion and listened to his dream of establishing a school for the sons of the poor. So when he was asked to tutor the sons of local lairds at Samuelston village school, she agreed, on condition that he also served as priest at St Nicholas's Chapel. Not without criticism, however, he thought, recalling how she'd challenged him.

'Only the sons?' she'd asked, eyebrows raised.

'Forbye, you already have a school for girls here,' he'd replied.

'Aye, for the daughters of those brave gentry who do not fear that straining their brains will make them unbiddable and unbeddable,' Elisabeth had said.' A school for poor lasses would be of more worth—like Isabelle. What would have become of that wee orphan if you hadn't brought her here? She'd have ended up a strumpet on the streets. Thanks to you, she's under Sister Agnes's benevolent wing and not only learning the mysteries of the alphabet but the secrets of the physic garden.'

Now his conscience pained Knox for he hadn't confessed that he was teaching his pupils reformist doctrine and that it stuck in his craw to celebrate mass. With its incense, bells, and extravagant vestments, holy mass was nothing more than an elaborate ceremonial, a smoke screen designed to mystify the faithful. And to insist that, at the eucharist, the bread and wine was transformed into Christ's body and blood to be devoured by the worshippers, reeked of cannibalism. As for baptising newborn babes in arms who had no inkling of the solemn pledge being made on their behalf—that was plain dishonest. Better to wait until they were of an age to decide for themselves. That thought made him sit up on the bench : he was nearly thirty years old. The same age as John the Baptist and Christ had been when they started out on their ministries. Neither of them had baulked at leaving home. The time had come for him to follow his conscience.

Striding down the aisle he shook his fist at every plaster saint and graven image, cosily ensconced in its niche. Idolatry. The worship of false gods. Only when he stopped at the statue of the Black Madonna draped with offerings from the desperate and destitute did he remember the promise he'd made to Elisabeth: *Keep Tryst*. Could an oath he'd made to a false idol with his fingers crossed be binding? He would indeed keep faith. By keeping true to his own conscience.

'You no longer have any hold over me. I refuse to prostrate myself in front of you.' He lowered his voice and sneered. 'Look at you! Bedecked with baubles like the whore of Babylon.'

He stripped off the rags and trinkets and tossed them onto the floor. Indulging in prayers and offerings to the saints was no different from believing in spells and incantations to the gods. He wagged his finger in front of her face as blank and unfeeling as the plank of wood she was carved from.

'Never again will I worship a graven image. May God strike me down if I do!'

And for good measure he tugged at the rosary beads dangling from her hand, hung there by some misguided soul. The Black Madonna teetered for a moment on her pedestal before crashing face down onto the flagstones. With a woeful crack her right arm splintered and sent her infant flying across the aisle. On the way out he passed the missal still open at the order of mass for the Vigil of St John the Precursor. He was about to smite the book from the lectern when the words from Jeremias caught his eye:

> *The word of the Lord came to me, and his message was: I claimed thee for My own before ever I fashioned thee in thy mother's womb; before ever thou camest to the birth, I set thee apart for Myself I have a prophet's errand for thee among the nations.*
>
> *And with that the Lord put out his hand and touched me on the mouth.*

Chapter Fifty-Seven
The Madness of King James

Bewailing in my chamber thus alone,
Despaired of all joy and remedy
Worn out with thought and woebegone.
—*The King's Quair,* James I, 15th Century

St Mary's Abbey, July 1541

'Where is Agnes? Is she not with you?'

With alarm in her voice and distress etched on her face, Sister Katherine greeted Elisabeth struggling to dismount after a wearisome journey

'I, too, would wish Agnes were with me. And Betsy for that matter,' she replied archly, rather peeved at receiving no warm words of welcome after her long absence. 'What would I give for one of Betsy's remedies to soothe this pounding in my head and Agnes's healing hands to ease my aching back,' she groaned, leaning back and forth to stretch her spine, 'but the queen has the greater need. Do not fret. Agnes is well and you will see her soon enough.'

'Surely you didn't ride all the way from Stirling?' Sister Katherine shook her head in disapproval.

'Aye, and my creaking old bones are also showing their displeasure. But think of Agnes's pain. Our pitiable pilgrim is at this moment tramping her way to Musselburgh with King James. To the shrine of Our Lady of Loretto, where he means to pray for peace in the realm and his own wits, and the queen, the health and strength to bear another heir.'

Queen Marie had already given birth to two sons. The French doctors and apothecaries officially in attendance had condescended to let the French speaking Sister Agnes and Betsy the Scots skeily wife do the messy work while they pontificated about how the royal sons should be cared for.

When Prince James, a fine thriving child until his wet nurse's breasts ran dry, mewled and whined at the breast of the new one, Betsy suggested that her milk may be too sour and was upsetting the infant's digestion. Only when the queen threatened to feed him herself did they agree to replace her.

During her next pregnancy when the queen became very heavy and lethargic the learned French physicians in their wisdom prescribed daily purging. Betsy shook her head for it sapped her strength even more. Left to deliver the bairn after a long travail, Betsy was troubled to see that the listless newborn's skin was an unhealthy yellow pallor. The archbishop was immediately called to baptise Prince Robert. Their twofold joy, however, changed to twofold grief when the prince died within hours, followed a few days later by the heir, Prince James.

'It's a sair fecht. The wee mites have quit the womb only to be buried in the tomb,' Betsy lamented. What other ways would fortune find to skelp their unfortunate queen?

Rumours ran amok that the bairns had been poisoned by ruthless enemies, but Betsy blamed overzealous French doctors. Tripping over themselves to show off their high-flown ideas—to justify their high fees, no doubt—they ended up falling flat on their faces. All theory with no practice was the problem: barking orders without getting blood on their hands. If only they had let her and Agnes get on with it, the bairns might have survived.

The double death of his heirs had greatly troubled the king and his erratic behaviour was unnerving Queen Marie. Taking

Elisabeth into her confidence she described how, one evening she was greatly affrighted when her bed-curtains were suddenly drawn back. She'd sat bolt upright in bed as a tall figure loomed before her in the darkness. Not her lady of the chamber, then. And since the king preferred to share his bed with Oliver Sinclair, his current minion, probably not her husband.

An interloper then. As she let out a scream, the figure began hopping up and down by her bedside reciting:

> And sometime, like a feind transfigured,
> And sometime, like the grisly ghaist of Gye,
> In diverse forms oft times disfigurate
> And sometime, disguised full pleasantly.

The madman was tearing wildly at his hair and beating his chest. 'It has come true!' he shrieked. 'My nightmare has come true! The grisly ghost of Gye is none other than James Hamilton. The Bastard has cut off my two arms. Slain my two bairns,' he wailed and loomed in closer, his mad eyes rolling with terror. 'And he shall come back for my head. For me. Oh, what have I done? What have I done?'

'Wheesht, wheesht!' The queen tried hushing him in the Scots way to quieten him. 'There is no sin that cannot be forgiven and absolved. Besides, we are young enough to have more children.'

Saying that, she pulled back the bedcovers and tried to persuade him into her bed but James waggled his head. 'Nay, there will be no more children. We are undone. The evil eye is upon us.'

For the Stewart curse was falling heavily on him. Hadn't his father James IV killed his father, James III at Sauchieburn and then been slain at Flodden as punishment? And now he, too, was guilty of beheading, the Bastard James Hamilton. He should never have listened to his lords of council. Jealous of his close relationship with his minion and kinsman they had convinced him that the Bastard was plotting to assassinate him.

Was it even true? He didn't know what to believe any more. There were too many whispering voices, too many conspiracies. He could trust no-one.

Listening to the queen's tale of woe, Elisabeth had commiserated. James was afflicted by the Stewart curse, she'd explained, when the greatest glee was followed by the deepest gloom. Queen Marie had agreed. She feared his rapid changes in mood. After a bout of high spirits when he hardly slept, he'd lie listless, heavy-lidded and hollow-eyed for days. His mind, already raddled with fear and mistrust of everyone around him, was becoming more and more unhinged. During his descent into the depths of despair, the king accused the queen of adultery, his lords of treason and his courtiers of cheerfulness.

'What am I to do?' Queen Marie wailed. 'He accuses me of being the cardinal's mistress.'

Elisabeth shook her head. 'He should close his lugs to all that clatter and clack about the Carnal Cardinal and his myriad mistresses. Havers and nonsense. Tell him that any woman, no matter who she was, even you, madame, would have to vie with Lady Marion Ogilvie.'

When neither the expensive receipts that Sister Agnes had ordered from France or Betsy's more homely remedies had been effective, Betsy decided the cause lay in the king's belief that he'd been curse by the evil eye. 'I fear he may not be cured till the spell has been lifted' she'd said.

At this suggestion Sister Agnes had signed herself with her crucifix but had then offered her own. If the king were indeed possessed by demon then exorcism by the cardinal would be the only cure.

Lindsay was furious when he heard 'Nay,' he roared. 'There shall be no cantrips and spells to cast out any evil eye or demonic power. I this superstitious gobbledegook just as evil as sorcery.' Nor would he allow Cardinal Beaton to splash holy water and wave his magic wand of a sceptre to gain power. He did, however, agree to a pilgrimage to the shrine of Our Lady of Loretto in Musselburgh.

Chapter Fifty-Eight
Widow Ker

All the days ordained for me were written
in your book before one of them came to be.
—*Psalm* CXXXIX:16

Samuelston, 1542

Swirling and twirling its grotesque, tumescent tail the dragon flirted and flounced with the whore of Babylon. The harlot whipped up her scarlet petticoats as the loathsome serpent flicked its tail between her legs in a monstrous act of fornication. The dragon reared its head with the bloated bulbous face of Beaton while the whore leered at it with the face of...

Knox woke up swathed in sweat, a milky flux oozing between his legs and trickling onto the bed sheet. The whore of Babylon, the daughter of Eve, the mother of God had all transmogrified into one creature, the horror being that it had the face of the prioress. Despite studying late into the night to tire himself, this recurrent dream troubled his sleep.

He sprang out of bed as if chased by a ghoul and tore off his nightshirt. He filled the basin from the pitcher and splashed cold water on his face and onto his groin. Opening the shutter, he stood in front of the window to let the fresh morning breeze dry him. Once dressed, he cast his eyes over the lines he'd written the night before and could not help sniggering like one of his schoolboys.

And meikle Latin he did mummle
But I heard nocht but hummle-bummle.

What had started as a dull re-writing of the Calvin catechism for his pupils had, when he'd given his imagination free rein, turned into a satire, a scathing parody of the clergy who used the confessional for sexual voyeurism. The rather ribald, *Kitty's Confession*, owed a large debt to Lindsay's *Satire* and would not only amuse his pupils but have a deeper impact. Nevertheless, however amusing, his censure of the church was as dangerous and heretical as the protestant tracts, smuggled in from the continent that he spent long nights studying. If he were caught with these, the penalty wouldn't simply be excommunication—a fate he didn't fear—but death, which he did. He'd stowed away his treasured copy of the forbidden, *Patrick's Places*, that had sent its author Patrick Hamilton to the pyre.

It was true: words were more powerful than swords. The belief that everyone should be taught to read so as to experience the beauty of evangelical truth in the Bible now fired his ambition and his preaching. His sermons at Samuelston and Longniddry were gradually converting many to the reformed faith. He slipped the manuscript of *Kitty's Confession* between the covers of his copy of Lindsay's poems and went down to breakfast.

The housekeeper, Widow Ker, was a small compact woman, as plump as a dumpling yet who carried herself daintily on tiny feet as she went about her domestic chores. A safe type of woman, soft and warm, like Betsy, he remembered fondly. A maternal Martha rather than a demanding Mary Magdalen, whose comfortable presence made him feel lazy and drowsy. Following her generous figure as she bustled about, he felt his eyelids droop and a warm glow, like melted butter, seep through his veins. If she were to stroke him, he would purr like a cat. How would it feel to nuzzle up to her generous warmth, bury his head in her soft bosom and be caressed by her strong hands? Feline feelings, he murmured, rousing himself from his lethargy.

Sloth might be making him smoulder like a smoored fire, but at least it was not the lust aroused by those shameless hussies of his parish who, with their brazen, forthright looks, lured their menfolk to sin. Who, in turn, stumbled shamefully to confession to receive absolution from Knox who, in his turn, felt ashamed—of the very voyeurism he'd denounced in *Kitty's Confession*. Such scarlet harlots, however, did not kindle any carnal desires in him. Kindred sisters of the gypsy girl, they used their charms to beguile unwary men. Nay, if truth be told, the type of woman who quickened his loins was the young, innocent maiden with downcast eyes, demure, unsullied, unknowing of the ways of men. He gave a sudden start as Widow Ker plonked his bowl of porridge in front of him and stood beside him with her plump arms folded.

'You should take care, young master.'

He gave a start. Had she been reading his sinful thoughts? She looked around furtively before delving into the pocket of her apron. 'And be wary of leaving such as thon lying about. Some would deem it downright heretical.' She slapped down one of the reformist pamphlets he must have left lying about.

'You can read, Widow Ker?' he asked.

'Aye, that I can,' she replied. Her brother-in-law, James Ker, who'd invited Knox to lodge in his house, sympathised with reformist ideas. Along with Hugh Douglas of Longniddry and John Cockburn of Ormiston, he'd hired Knox to educate their sons in the new evangelical thinking: to discuss and debate the Bible for themselves.

Washing up at the sink, Widow Ker looked over her shoulder. ' And I can write as well. My father made sure of that. He believed that everyone should be able to read. Even women.'

Her father, she confided, was a descendant of Adam Reid of Barskimming in Kyle. In the Ayrshire hills the spirit of Lollardy was kept alive. Evangelicals, the people of the Book, swore by the Holy Bible as their only guide and rejected the vast religious edifice of formal priestly religion that centred upon the outward temple.

Now that the synagogue of Satan, Roman Catholicism, was under threat, Widow Ken wasn't afraid to voice her ideas. For too long the Anti-Christ in Rome had usurped the teachings of the Saviour and warped them for his own ends. For too long her kind had been lurking in the shadows. Now was the time to abandon the darkness and light the lamp of faith.

'I mind my father telling me about how his grandsire was charged by Bishop Blackadder for denying that God is in heaven. And what did Adam Reid respond?' Widow Ker drew herself up to declaim, 'Whereas I believe that God is both in heaven and on earth, you, Bishop Blackadder don't even believe that God is on this earth. Otherwise, you wouldn't be playing the proud prelate and neglecting the charge of Christ when you preach the Gospel.'

Her plump shoulders heaved as she wiped away tears of laughter with the hem of her apron. Widow Ker exuded the quiet confidence of one who knew herself to right and therefore could do no wrong. To be one of the elect, she explained in her slow, languorous tones, was to be one of the righteous, chosen by God for salvation. For those who receive the gifts of faith and divine grace there would be no eternal damnation, even if they sinned.

'Even a mortal sin?' Knox queried.

'For his elect, God puts aside his wrath as judge,' the widow replied. 'He that believeth in him shall not perish. As long as they forsake evil and keep true to the light.'

Knox furrowed his brow. 'How can you be sure you're one of the chosen? And how can you know that Satan is not sowing doubts?'

'Because I have faith, Master Knox.' Widow Ker raised her eyes to heaven. 'As it is written: The Just shall live by faith—and faith alone. And being justified by faith, we have peace with God.'

Her eyes took on a faraway look as she explained how, once the gracious gift of faith had taken root in her soul, she had experienced a sense of mystical peace and spiritual security that released her from anxiety. Knox envied her placid tranquillity.

'Except a man be born again he cannot see the kingdom of God. Not by entering his mother's womb a second time, but through the spirit.' Her words sent a slight shiver up his spine and elsewhere. When she placed a hand on his shoulder he was alarmed at the sinful stirrings it aroused in him.

'Faith is all, John. Faith alone.'

Chapter Fifty-Nine
The King is Dead: Long Live the Queen

Ladies no way I can commend
Presumptuously which doth pretend
To use the office of ane king
Or Realms take in governing.
—*The Monarch,* Sir David Lindsay, 16th Century

Linlithgow Palace, 27 November 1542

'And I am to have my hair cut short and wash it once a month. For greasy hair gives rise to croup and an unhealthy mother will give birth to an unhealthy son.' A wry smile curled Queen Marie's lips as she considered her mother's latest advice. She passed over the long, solicitous letter for Elisabeth to translate.

'She seems certain you're carrying a lad,' Elisabeth noted.

'God willing, her prayers, and mine, are answered,' the queen replied before turning to Betsy. What are your thoughts, dear Betsy?'

'Every land has its ain law,' the humble Scots skeily-wife muttered, though she didn't agree with all the French ways. Whenever she'd tried to put in her ha'penny worth, the physicians had turned up their hoity-toity noses at her. Hell mend them, she'd thought, and then gone behind their backs to follow her instinct. But she was getting too old to put up with all their cocky chicanerie. This would be her last royal birth.

And now the grand French Duchess Antoinette was poking her neb in —with advice that might even be the death of her daughter—for Betsy's dreaded that the queen would catch a chill. Let French women hack at their hair and boil their heads for all she cared, but it would be perilous for a pregnant woman to do so at any time, far less in the midst of one of the bleakest winters Betsy had ever lived through.

Great billows of immaculate white snow drifted high up against the palace walls. Wells and water courses were frozen and not only icy water, but all meat and victuals had to be thawed. High in the north-west corner of Linlithgow Palace, where they were preparing the chamber for the queen's confinement, Betsy made sure the fire was stacked high with logs day and night. She wouldn't allow coals to be burned; to her mind, there was the whiff of the devil about the reek from thon hellish black stones mined from the depths.

Swathed in a fur-lined cloak, Queen Marie peered intently through the thick, greenish window glass. Below, the ice-covered lochan shimmered in the last rays of the low November sun, before it disappeared over the horizon. This would be her last glimpse of daylight for a few months. She dreaded the perpetual night of the sealed chamber, the womb-like existence she'd have to endure until the birth. Shuttered windows were hung with heavy curtains to blank out the light; every possible opening—every chink, crack, or keyhole—was plugged with straw and cloths to block perilous cold air from seeping in.

Cocooned like a grub in the tightly curtained four-poster bed, the queen would not be allowed to stick out an arm or even her nose in case she caught cold. Smothered in blankets, choking on the reek of tallow candles and smoke from the constantly blazing log fire, she was more likely to suffocate and precautions would be even stricter this time. With the deaths of two sons, no chances could be taken with this birth. Little wonder she yearned to postpone her incarceration as long as possible.

She wiped her frosted breath from the glass pane and gazed at children screaming excitedly as they slid down the brae on their hurley-hacket, whizzing past servants dragging up sledges.

'See how the foraging worker bees bring supplies to their queen cloistered in her hive,' she quipped.

'While the drones are dismissed having done their duty,' Elisabeth said in response.

Queen Marie chuckled and rubbed her very rounded bump. '*Oui, c'est vrai!* Oh, how you lift my spirits, my lady prioress.'

A sudden draught of cold air as the door curtain swung open made them shiver and then a chilly voice cut through their mirth. 'Why are you laughing?'

Swaying unsteadily, the king staggered over towards them. 'Why are you merry when my heart is full of misery? I look around for pity, where pity is none: for comfort, where no comfort is to be found. And my own dear Oliver is fled,' he wailed, doubling over in pain. 'Oh, Oliver is taken! Oliver is fled!'

The queen looked nervously at Elisabeth. The rout of his army by the English at Solway Moss seemed to have unhinged the monarch. His bloodshot eyes blazed at his wife. 'And your accursed Cardinal Beaton is to blame for this catastrophe. Spurred on by your faithless De Guise brothers. Guisers each and every one of them, masquerading as cardinals and dukes.'

Beaton had discovered that a belligerent Henry Tudor had instructed his archbishop to comb through every possible document for proof that he was overlord of Scotland. Since only a show of force would prevent Harry Coppernose from seizing control, Beaton had badgered James to declare war on England. However, overcome with a mysterious malaise, the monarch had been unable to lead his troops into battle and had sent his favourite, the young and inexperienced Oliver Sinclair in his place. Resenting the minion's incompetent command, his cringing lords had thrown down their weapons and surrendered.

'My lord,' Queen Marie began hesitantly, 'I am about to be brought to childbed. Does that not fill your heart with joy?' Hoping that the imminent birth of an heir would rouse him from his deep melancholy she leant forward to place his hand on her bump but he lurched backwards, as if she were putting a hex on him. His eyes burned with a weird glint and his gaunt, twisted face grimaced with pain.

'How do I ken that it's my own bairn lying in your belly? Lying and false.'

Aghast, Queen Marie hugged her womb. 'My lord! Have you no faith in me? Do you suspect me of infidelity? Do you accuse me of...' she hesitated before daring to utter that perilous word, 'adultery?' However reluctantly she may have had to take care of his bastards, the queen knew better than to risk carrying one.

Gripping his side, the king slumped down onto the settle. He grabbed a cushion and cradled it on his stomach, his tongue lolling idiotically as he rocked back and forth.

'What does it matter? Any son you bear will only become a vassal of Henry of England.' A shadow of pain darkened his face.

'You are weary, my lord. Stay a while and rest,' the queen coaxed. 'Let Betsy bring you a comforting posset.'

'No more potions. No more sorcery. No more bloodletting. No more blood.'

He rolled his head from side to side then sat quietly for a while, his glazed eyes staring into the middle distance. He leant forward, hunched over the cushion. 'They're poisoning me,' he muttered. 'The Douglas witch and the Hamilton Bastard are plotting against me. From the fires of hell, spurred on by Satan himself. I can hear them whispering constantly. Conferring. Conniving. Conspiring.'

Throwing aside the cushion, he stood up abruptly like a startled hare, his ears on the prick. 'Here they are...' His eyes widened. 'One here,' he yelped, glancing over his right shoulder, 'and the other, there,' glancing over his left. 'By Christ's blood, they will be the death of me,' he howled and ran off as if chased by a pack of hellhounds.

Once the queen was sealed safely in her chamber, James set off around his kingdom like wildfire to escape his demons. Lindsay kept Elisabeth informed with alarming reports which she dared not show to the queen.

> *The king veers from lying flat on his back to running round in a feverish frenzy. His physicians believe that an internal wound is the cause of his frequent vomiting but he resists all their attempts to investigate. He doses himself with regular swigs of cognac from his pewter flask to dull the pain in his side. He is jittery and edgy and we, his courtiers, can hardly keep up with him.*
>
> *First, he made us ride to Edinburgh to make an inventory of all his treasures and jewels, and then we sailed to Hallyards in Fife to consult with this treasurer. After a long conference with Sir William Kirkcaldy of Grange, James sank again into deep melancholy. The canty lady of the house endeavoured to rouse him, wishing him good cheer for the merry season of Yule about to begin. His Grace gawped at her as if she were a simpleton or a fool. 'My portion of the world is short,' he answered with a sneer. 'Ere fifteen days are past, I will be gone from this wretched life.'*
>
> *I fear for his wits. Though growing weaker by the day he has given orders to set out for Falkland. I had thought it would be his desire to return to Linlithgow to be near the queen who is soon to be delivered of an heir. 'You choose where you want to be,' he said with the secretive smile that has become a habit now, 'but this I can tell you. On Yule day, you will be masterless and the realm without a king.'*

Linlithgow Palace, December 1542

After braving the blizzard that had blasted their craft in the stormy waters of the Firth of Forth, the royal messengers then had to trudge knee-deep in drifting snow to Linlithgow to deliver the tragic news. 'The king, my lady, is dead.'

The official statement from David Beaton, Cardinal of Scotland declared: On the fourteenth day of December in the Year of Our Lord 1542, James V of Scotland, in his thirtieth year, had passed from this world: *Requiescat in pace.* In his missive the Lord Lyon King of Arms, Sir David Lindsay, expressed his deep-felt condolences and offered his loyal services. The queen said a silent prayer and made the sign of the cross. She looked towards the cradle where her newborn infant lay quietly sleeping and asked, 'Was he told of the birth of his daughter?'

'Aye, your grace.'

'Had he any words for her?' Queen Marie asked, her voice tinged with hope.

Furtively Elisabeth fingered Lindsay's letter hidden up her sleeve, willing the courier to be silent.

He hesitated before shaking his head. 'Nay, your grace.'

Elisabeth breathed out. The queen had enough to grieve her and the disturbing details of the last few hours of the king's life would only distress the new widow. After many days of delirium, James had come round, and had lain motionless, a rapt expression on his face, as if listening to an inner voice. The joyous news that the queen was lighter of a child seemed to rouse him from his languor but when told he had a bonnie daughter, his spirits sank again.

'A lass! Alas a lass! It came with a lass and it will gang with a lass,' he'd murmured, before falling into a dwam, his glazed eyes focussed on the world beyond. Not long before midnight, a faint smile had flitted across his face as if he were glad to be departing this vale of tears. Better that the queen heard no more portents, no more prophecies.

Hearing the infant cry, Betsy carefully lifted the precious bundle from the cradle and placed her in her mother's arms.

'Long live the queen,' Marie de Guise whispered into the tiny buckie-shaped ear of the eight-day-old Queen of Scots as she snuggled into her mother's breast.

She'll have a sair fecht with our dour and fickle folk, Elisabeth thought sadly.

Holyrood Abbey

The walls of the Dolorous Chapel in Holyrood Abbey were covered with black buckram hangings fringed with black silk. Black velvet draped the catafalque on which the cast lead coffin would rest, covered in the cloth of state. Lindsay could feel a lump choking his thrapple. He'd never thought that in his lifetime he would witness the death of another monarch. At fifty-five, it should have been him in the coffin, not the thirty-year-old king. And then, the night before the funeral, he'd sat with his wife Jessie until she passed away.

As he watched the life-size effigy of his beloved monarch being dressed for his last state engagement in his royal robes of purple velvet lined with ermine, the twice bereft Lindsay fought back tears. Despite the pain in her gnarled, misshapen fingers, the strain in her eyes weakened by years of working by candlelight and the canker devouring her, Jessie had been determined to make sure that the king's grave clothes—every stitch of which she'd sewn for Queen Marie's coronation—would fit his shrunken frame.

Betsy had kept her going, dosing her with enough arrows of hemlock, as she called them, to deaden the pain but, when Jessie finally put down her needle, she gave Betsy a meaningful look. Now that she had fulfilled her last royal task, Jessie surrendered to the canker's final, fatal onslaught. While the ground was frozen, her body would remain unburied until

Lindsay could take her on her last journey to Garleton. Lindsay swallowed hard. Tumbling swiftly to the foot of life's hill, he may not be far behind.

To the mournful sound of trumpeters rehearsing the doleful dirge, Cardinal Beaton strode into the chapel and shoved a parchment under Lindsay's nose. The Last Will and Testament of His Grace, James V, Beaton assured him.

In the gloom, Lindsay screwed up his eyes to peer at the signature scrawled at the foot of the document. 'This doesn't look like the king's hand.'

The funereal torches flickered eerily across the cardinal's inscrutable face.

'As you well ken, his grace was in great distress before he passed away. His confused wits would affect his hand,' Beaton declared.

'Then even more reason to discount his so-called last wishes.' Lindsay pondered for a moment before saying, 'As you well ken, I've been King James's closest friend and trusted confidante since the day and hour he was born. It seems very odd that he didn't inform me of his intentions.'

Beaton drew himself up and puffed out his barrel chest. 'His grace confided in me during his last confession. While I was administering the sacred sacrament of Extreme Unction.'

'If that is true, is it not then a sacrilege for a confessor to betray what should be known only to God?'

Beaton bristled. 'Of course, that's why I beseeched the king's permission to put it in writing for him to sign. To make it a lawful document.'

Lindsay quickly scanned the provisions of the Will, one of which specified a regency council for the infant queen to be set up—with the cardinal as chief governor and ruler of the council. 'I doubt whether this document is legal. I see no notary's signature as witness.'

Beaton jabbed his finger at the bottom of the parchment. 'See here the Great Seal. That is sufficient authorisation.'

‘Ah, the Great Seal,’ Lindsay harrumphed, ‘which rests in your safekeeping as chancellor. This is o’er ambitious, even for you, Beaton. The lords will not take kindly to a man of the church o'erstepping himself. Nor will they be so easily deceived. I would advise you to destroy this.’

Fearful that Lindsay would tear it up, Beaton snatched the precious document from him and narrowed his eyes. ‘Tell me then, Lord Lyon, who will take charge of this godforsaken kingdom which has been malgoverned for so long? Who is capable of taking the reins? Certainly not the fey earl of Arran, the most inconstant man under the sun. In thrall to the reformed religion, Hamilton will hand over the infant sovereign to that murderer and heretic, Henry of England.’

‘Perhaps now is the time to negotiate with Henry Tudor,’ Lindsay said wearily. ‘His son and heir would make a good match for our queen.’

‘What do you say?’ As Beaton fumed, spittle spluttered from the corners of his mouth. ‘These words are not only treacherous, Davie Lindsay, but blasphemous. Our future is wedded to catholic France, not protestant England. Keep out of politics, Lyon Lindsay, and see to your mournful duty. You have a royal funeral to arrange; I have an unruly kingdom to rule.’

Chapter Sixty
The Queen's Suitors

My clear voice and courtly carolling
Where I was wont with ladies for to sing
Is rawk as rook, full hideous hoarse and rough.
—*The Testament of Cresseid,* Robert Henryson, 15th Century

St Mary's Abbey, August 1543

Elisabeth twisted round on the low stool, cricking her neck to see what was happening. The rope tying her arms behind her back and securing her to the bedpost rubbed against her wrists.

'You'll find no money here,' she grumbled. The lid of the kist was open and, while one of his henchmen flung the silk and satin gowns on to the floor, another slashed through them with his dagger in case gold or jewels were hidden in secret pockets or pouches.

'Where is it then?' the Fair Earl of Bothwell demanded.

'You receive the amount due to you as baillie of the abbey, Patrick,' she replied, striving to keep her voice calm, though inside she was fuming.

'One hundred pound Scots. God's troth, that is hardly enough to mend my boots!' Patrick raged and stomped his foot. 'You can well afford to settle more than that on me. The abbey is richly endowed with lands and moneys.'

'As prioress it's my responsibility to see that it remains so and not become a pot for you to dip into whenever it pleases you. Forbye, if you prefer to squander your money on drinking and gambling, rather than repairing your boots, then that is your choice.'

He tilted her chin upwards with the tip of his sword and glared at her. 'I am the earl of Bothwell and your liege lord. You shall obey my orders.'

'And I am a nun in thrall to no man: I answer only to God,' Elisabeth shot back. 'And in return for these generous endowments we sisters pray for the souls of our patrons in perpetuity.'

'Aye, and they're all on their knees in the chapel at this moment,' he jeered, 'paying tribute to my men.'

'If any of my sisters are harmed, you will hang for it, Patrick, and you'll have to plead for mercy yourself, for I'll no be doing so again,' Elisabeth warned.

What a traitor the Fair Earl had turned out to be: he could no more keep tryst than tell the truth. His boyhood mischief had matured into malicious self-interest and now, through his own fault, Bothwell was seriously in debt. Because of his repeated disloyalty and inconstancy, King James V had eventually banished the flichty earl and confiscated his lands. Had his experiences taught him nothing?

Clearly not, for now, on the king's death, he'd deemed it safe to return and had arrived at the abbey demanding funds. Frustrated by her obstinacy, Bothwell had instructed his men to comb through the abbey, leaving nothing unturned. To work unhindered, he'd ordered them to round up the nuns and servants and imprison them in the abbey dungeon.

'And you shall join them unless you give me my due. I am the earl of Bothwell, mind, the leading noble of the land! I cannot attend court dressed as a shabby commoner.'

Why, then, he need look no further than Hailes Castle where there was a kist of fine garments belonging to his late father. Sadly, the twenty-one-year-old Adam had never had the chance to wear them out.

He railed against her suggestion saying, 'Dead man's duds! Moth-eaten and outdated!

'That may be so,' she replied keeping her temper, 'but neither do you deserve to don his garb. Clothes do not make the man and you will never be the brave man your father was.'

She felt the tip of steel against her chin as he said, 'Forbye how would I win the queen dowager's hand dressed as a bogle?'

So that was his intention. She might have jaloused as much. Now that the official mourning period was over, many thought the widowed queen mother should take another husband to shoulder her burden. As the foremost earl in the land, Patrick Hepburn ranked his chances very highly, and why not? Had not all his ancestors courted queens? Aye, thought Elisabeth, it was indeed a sorry trait in Hepburn men to be dintit with the king's women. And had it slipped his feeble mind that he was already married?

'Agnes Sinclair has been a devoted wife to you and mother of your two bairns.'

Patrick swatted away her objection as if it were a pesky fly. Forbye, since they were cousins, he was pursuing an annulment of their marriage on the ground of consanguinity.

'Had there been any suspicion of madness or any other serious affliction that might weaken the bloodline, then you wouldn't have been allowed to marry in the first place. And your union has produced a sturdy son and a healthy daughter,' Elisabeth reminded him. 'Forbye, you risk raising the hackles of all those nobles who, like you, were granted a papal dispensation to marry their cousins.'

Curses on the whole clamjamfrey: Bothwell didn't fear their contumely. Divorce Agnes he must in order to stand any chance against Matthew Stewart, 4th earl of Lennox. Unmarried, with royal blood and a valid claim to the Scottish throne, Lennox was the firm favourite. He also had the backing of Cardinal Beaton who had lured him back from France with the double promise of the queen dowager's hand and the regency of her infant daughter.

Appealing to his vaulting ambition, Elisabeth said, 'Your brutal ill-treatment of our sisters and insolence to me will hardly win you the favour of my dear friend, the queen, who greatly values our abbey's charitable work. If you seek to raise yourself in her esteem, you'd better untie me now and release my sisters. And, if you do so with good grace, I may even smooth the path of your rough wooing,' she added.

The sullen earl pondered this for a few moments, stamped a shoddy boot and then called off his men.

Stirling Castle, 9 September 1543

It didn't augur well that the date chosen for the infant Queen Mary's coronation had been the 9th of September, the thirtieth anniversary of Flodden. However, with the royal bairn being used as the ball in a game of kick the ba' by Beaton, Arran and Henry VIII, it was lucky to have taken place at all, Elisabeth thought. The ceremony in the chapel of Stirling Castle had been a frugal affair, and once the nursemaids had put the queen to bed the nobles were keen to celebrate.

Elisabeth was sitting on the royal dais with Queen Marie to watch the merriment, when a courtier whispered a request. The Earl of Bothwell sought permission to entertain her grace.

'Is the earl singing in Scots?' The queen dowager was perplexed. 'For I cannot catch any of the words.'

Elisabeth covered her mouth with her hand to smother a giggle. No, this mangled doggerel, delivered in a quavering falsetto punctuated with guttural catches in the throat, was Bothwell's attempt to impress the queen with his poetic prowess in her own tongue. He'd spent hours with Sister Agnes who'd done her best to teach him endearing words and phrases in French so that he might compose *verses de amour* inspired by the *Song of Roland*.

‘Hark at the screeching from his thrapple. Like a peacock afflicted with rheum.’ The waggish lord’s cruel barb prompted other courtiers to erupt into unashamed jeers. The battle between two young bucks vying for the favours of a widow queen was beginning to cheer up the court in mourning. Ignoring their heckling, Bothwell finished his *chanson* and then bowed low to present the queen with his poetic composition, flamboyantly tied up with red ribbon and sealed with the Hepburn crest*:* Keep Tryst.

‘Weigh well these verses that I write for your grace,’ he whispered, ‘for they express the secrets of a heart that is subject, bound and in thrall to your governance.’

Graciously Queen Marie thanked him and promised to read them in private.

When Matthew Stewart took the floor, the courtiers listened in hushed and attentive silence. Newly arrived from France, the twenty-six-year-old earl of Lennox who had carried the sceptre at the coronation was still a novelty at court. How would this brave peacock perform? No worse, surely, than his tuneless rival. From the first notes on the lute, it was clear that Lennox was an accomplished musician and when, in his strong tenor voice, he sang the latest song from France—in perfectly pronounced French—the audience was enchanted.

Elisabeth glanced over at Patrick whose round shoulders slouched even more. Dark spots of rage flushed the Fair Earl’s cheeks and his watery blue eyes were pink-rimmed with petulant tears. As soon as the musicians struck up a gavotte, the brazen Jenny Stewart whirled Lennox onto the floor. Despite being well married to Lord Malcolm Fleming, Jenny was determined to shine in the reflected glory of this handsome and fashionably dressed gallant.

Not to be outdone, the gangling Bothwell shuffled clumsily into the throng and attempted to follow the steps but kept treading on toes with his shabbily shod feet and knocking into everyone with his knobbly elbows. Finally cast out from the dance for tripping up Jenny, Patrick loitered on the side, gawky and gauche in the expensive ribbed velvet doublet that his handsome, broad-shouldered father had worn to great effect.

'The earl seems most disconsolate,' the queen remarked.

As well he might, Elisabeth thought. Bothwell glanced up at the royal dais and glowered at his aunt. If looks could kill... She knew of old he would be blaming her for his humiliating trouncing by Lennox.

'Spare no pity for my nephew, madame, for he deserves none,' Elisabeth murmured. 'But take care not to cross him. He could be a dangerous enemy.'

Though amused by their contest, Marie de Guise's strong head was not easily turned. However persuasive Bothwell's poetry may have been, written in his spidery scrawl it was unintelligible and, however tall and splendidly built Lennox may be, his weak chin hinted at an inner, spiritual frailty. Too vain, she pondered, too proud perhaps. Nor was she in any hurry to marry again. To do so would not only lose her the regency and control of her daughter but stir up dissent amongst her nobles. Taking a lesson from Margaret Tudor's ill-judged experience, she would devote herself to her daughter's present wellbeing and future prosperity.

In the meantime, too worldy-wise and tactful to make her true feelings known, Marie de Guise continued to play off her two suitors against each other. This way she could count on their loyalty—for a while, at least. Until Bothwell started boasting that the queen dowager had promised to marry him as soon as he had secured an annulment.

Crichton Castle

Furious at his foolhardiness, Elisabeth rode to Crichton to seek out Bothwell's lair. Lacking the funds to pursue his suit of the queen, he'd slunk away to his favourite castle south of Edinburgh to think again. A woman of her age should not be tackling such a lengthy ride across a bleak landscape in wet weather, Betsy had warned her but needs must.

The Fair Earl was slumped in a chair by the fire, scruffy and unkempt as he drowned his sorrows with a flagon of wine. Elisabeth groaned. Patrick's wits were addled enough without their being sozzled. Was the thick-headed dolt wanting in wit by angering and insulting the queen in this way?

'Nothing but fair words she offers,' Patrick whined. 'If I don't force her hand, she'll keep me dangling and give Lennox time to worm his weaselly way into her favour.'

'You may think so, but if your act of bravado were taken as an attempt to abduct the dowager queen, you could be charged with high treason. And the punishment will not be a term languishing in jail but the loss of your block head.'

He scratched his scruffy beard to consider this threat. 'Aye, that's very true,' he said before sitting upright as if struck by a lightning bolt. 'I'm chasing after the wrong queen. Why should I waste time wooing the dowager when I can have her daughter? She may be an infant but in time Queen Mary will be the greater catch.'

Taken aback Elisabeth spluttered. 'What? *Who climbs too high perforce he must fall.* You must banish such grand ideas, Patrick. Forbye, neither the queen dowager nor the queen of Scots would countenance marriage to a man who has put his lawful wife away.'

Cursing him for his arrogant presumption, she left him to stew in his own juice.

Hailes Castle

Deaf to all advice and blind to all the scandal, Bothwell exulted in being granted a divorce from the mother of his children. His long-suffering wife must be distraught, Elisabeth thought, and set out to lend her support. Yet Agnes Sinclair seemed quite light-hearted, as if a great burden had been lifted from her shoulders. No longer thirled to the flighty earl, she was planning a new life with her daughter, Jean, at Morham, lands he'd gifted to her as part of the divorce settlement. Meanwhile, Bothwell had taken custody of his son and heir and was sending him into the care of Bishop of Moray at Spynie. With a sinking heart Elisabeth dreaded what kind of moral and religious instruction the nine-year-old James would receive from his dissolute uncle Patrick along with his innumerable ill-begotten offspring.

His education was to include the French language, the art of good handwriting and dancing lessons, Lady Morham as she styled herself, informed her. Bothwell may have scuppered his own chances of a royal marriage but he clearly nurtured hope for his son. Work hard at your lessons, he'd told the young James, so as to be worthy of winning the hand of a queen. Afore long, Queen Mary Stewart would be in need of a consort.

'For a Hepburn shall sit on the throne of Scotland one day. That is our destiny.'

PART FIVE

Chapter Sixty-One
The Abbot of Unreason

At the end of the Holy Days called Yule,
in a most vehement frost...
—*The History of the Reformation in Scotland*
John Knox, 16th Century

Haddington, December 1545

'Tak tent to me while I make a proclamation! Hark at my ordinance!' the Abbot of Unreason bawled as he struggled to keep his balance on the cart. He kept tripping over his cope of office, fashioned out of canvas and embroidered with curious signs and symbols, while his mitre, made of leather and studded with tawdry trinkets of tin, kept falling from his head. But he'd never think of letting go of his tankard of ale to steady himself.

'Hark at *his* ordinance! *You* maun take heed of *our* ordinance, you feckless friar!' a protester shouted. Reaching up, he tugged at the hem of the cope, causing the mock abbot to wobble. His mitre fell off and the tankard flew out of his hand, splashing over the folk at the front, to cheers from the rabble at the back. The Monk of Misrule, his friar's paunch well stuffed with a cushion, waddled over to give his superior another tankard.

'This'll help to loosen your tongue.'

The abbot took a grateful swig and wiped his mouth with his sleeve. 'I proclaim that from henceforth ...' But his words were drowned out by the mob.

'Steek your gabs and muck out your lugs o'er there. Hear what the unholy abbot has to say,' the Monk of Misrule yelled.

'Auld Nick has dryted on his tongue. Make way for one whose lips drip honeyed words,' an odd-looking fellow in motley butted in.

'What din-raisin Gilmoubrand dares to make a bauchle out of the abbot?" the Monk of Misrule challenged.

'Call me Cacaphatie, for my foul speech may offend your lugs.'

The crowd cheered as their late monarch's favourite jester scrambled onto the cart. His choice of outfit—a woman's sark that was too tight and too short and showed off his hairy shanks, combined with his manly beard—provoked jibes and jeers questioning his gender. Jigging up and down and jingling a bell on the end of a stick, the jester heckled the abbot. Vexed that his homespun banter couldn't keep up with the jester's sharp wit honed at court, the abbot attempted to pull rank on him.

'Be mindful that I've been elected the Abbot of Unreason, the master of these revels, and not you. By decree of the burgh councillors themselves I have command of the proceedings.'

'Aye, but in these daft days any command is to be defied, even yours,' Cacaphatie countered. 'The order of all things is tapsalteerie; the maid is to be served by the mistress, the laird must bow down to the soutar and the clergy must give ear to the laity. And all must heed the fool. Let the ranting and raving begin!' the jester bellowed.

Enthusiastic cheers demonstrated unequivocally whose side the crowd were on. The Abbot of Unreason retired, but not before making rude gestures behind the fool's back.

'Aye, and about time, too. Now get on with it,' an impatient onlooker demanded.

‘Preen back your lugs,’ Cacaphatie called out. ‘I have made a new rule. From henceforth all prelates, clerics, monks and abbots shall have not one whore ...’

‘There’s nothing new about that rule,’ the abbot piped up triumphantly. ‘They do that anywise. Keek into the lemand Lamp of Lechery and you’ll see the Franciscan friars fyking with their lusty concubines.’

As his brethren whooped in delight at his flyting, the abbot’s face broke into a self-congratulatory smile—soon wiped away by the jester’s retort.

‘Nay, I say not one whore…’ Cacaphatie yelled, ‘but two, or three. Or more to their loins content!’

The noisy rabble roared with laughter and cried out, ‘Another law, another law.’

‘Wheesht! Have I not been elected abbot?’ the deposed abbot reminded them. ‘Fairly and squarely? Would you heed a buffoon’s banter?’

‘Aye, they would! For you, Abbot of Unreason, are using good sense to win them over and your subjects will have no sense!’ The jester grabbed the abbot’s crosier and plonked the crudely made mitre onto his own head. ‘As the Right Reverend Abbot of Unreason,’ he called out, waving his crook, ‘I now ordain the First Estate to gang backwards—and widdershins round the cart.’

‘Gangan backwards? And widdershins? By the holy Mass, that's the way of Auld Nick himself,’ the usurped abbot retorted. ‘I'll have no dealings with the devil.’

‘Then you'll have to shun the demon drink! Do as you are bid or you’ll be tossed into the milldam for a douking!’

The milldam? The rabble became more subdued and less cocksure, for that ill-fated spot was where the gypsy lass had been found drowned. Reluctantly, the abbot obeyed but, as he waddled backwards round the platform, he puckered his lips and a deep ruckle came from his throat. Tottering unsteadily, he turned to spit forth his retort at the jester who nimbly sidestepped the gob of spittle that splattered into the crowd.

'No more of your proclamations, Cacaphatie! Gie us a song! Gie us a song!'

'Fill up ma shoon with sil'er first and then I'll gie you a song.' The fool took off his shoe to be passed among the crowd. Then, brandishing the crook in one hand and his bell on a stick in the other, he began to sing:

With a hey and a ho and rohumbelow,
Let some drink ale and some drink claret wine,
Michtie drink comforts the dull ingyne.

At the same time rubbing his groin and thrusting his pelvis he roused shrieks of delight from the womenfolk. Then, as he raised his sark to unfasten his underbreeches, the crowd clamoured for more to be revealed.

'Take a keek at this hellish horde,' he cried, 'leaving no place for me to pish but my ain shoe.' So saying, he pissed into his other shoe and held it up. 'Here's something sweeter than ale. *In nomine domini*, I baptise thee,' he intoned, splashing the crowd with its contents. While the first few rows ducked, two passers-by clad in clerical black weren't quick enough to avoid the unsavoury shower.

The jester jumped into the mob to retrieve the shoe filled with coins. 'And now I restore to you your rightful abbot,' he called out, ramming the tawdry mitre back on the abbot's head and thrusting the crooked crosier into his hand.

The ridiculed Abbot of Unreason, smarting with hurt pride, caught hold of him.

'For your brazen cheek you must now kiss my arse,' he grumbled before flipping up his cloak to expose his behind.

Cacaphatie screwed up his nose. 'I'd rather kiss a bullock's buttocks than a bishop's behouchie,' he scoffed. 'And you should take heed before baring your arse. Pride gangs afore a fall.' He winked conspiratorially to the crowd before landing a hefty kick on the abbot's generous hurdies. The jester then pranced off, followed by a swarm of admirers howling for more entertainment.

'So that is how I'm welcomed by Haddington. Pissed on from a great height.' The tall preacher clad in black calmly wiped his face, but his companion's short temper was inflamed.

Shaking his fist, Knox called out after the jester. 'How dare you soil the garments of this holy man of God!' He would have run after him and boxed his ears but the preacher held him back.

'I've had worse flung at me, John. Forbye, mark my words, yon fool's drowned body will be washed up in Lochleven ere long.' As he took off his French cap to shake it dry, Knox gawped at him. It wasn't like his master to bring down curses on those who crossed him.

George Wishart jammed his round velvet cap firmly back on his head and added, 'But it doesn't augur well.' Shivering, he wrapped his black frieze mantle more tightly round his gaunt frame. Knox led him to a stall where, despite his protests, he thrust a cup of hot, spiced ale into his white-knuckled fingers. He knew better than to believe Wishart's assertion that he never felt the cold.

'Yet there are more words of truth being spoken here in jest than in much of Catholic doctrine,' Wishart remarked, blowing onto the sizzling ale. 'If only we could harness the common folk's instinctive distrust of the hierarchy to topple the church of Rome. Sadly, the popish church knows only too well how to distract folk from engaging with scripture and the word of God,' he went on. 'To check him from champing at the bit, the Vatican unbridles the humble workman to let him to frolic with mindless merrymaking one day then brings him sharply to heel the next.'

Knox heartily agreed. Hardly a week went by when there wasn't some kind of elaborate ceremonial. Every possible feast day and obscure saint's day was observed by a procession and, with pageants at *Corpus Christi* and miracle plays at *Pasche*, it was a wonder that the local craftsmen got any work done. And now the Daft Days at the tail end of the year marked the end of the yuletide festivities. Knox was disgusted. What impression was this gallimaufry of pagan saturnalia in his hometown making on his master?

Lamentably, the infestations of the Roman Church in Haddington—one abbey, two monasteries, three churches and three chapels—were no longer houses of God but palaces of sumptuous splendour. Quantity did not signify sanctity. Was it not sinful and corrupt that so much wealth had been accumulated here and misdirected into endless erections of ecclesiastical edifices?

Now that the spiced ale had warmed their bellies, Knox tried to tempt his companion to eat something nourishing. The appetising smells from the abundant stalls selling all kinds of festive food—stuffed pies and sausages, mussel brose and howtowdie broth, mealie dumplings dripping with fat—were assailing Knox's nose. Ravenously hungry, he wolfed down a mutton pie, the grease dribbling down his chin, while Wishart only pecked at a bannock and a sliver of cheese to satisfy his modest appetite. While admiring his master's temperate habits, Knox was finding it difficult to emulate him.

Wishart ate skimpily, often skipping meals, and could lay his head on a bed of prickly straw. The one comfort he couldn't do without was a regular bath, daily whenever possible, a habit those who bathed once a year, whether they needed to or not, found most idiosyncratic. A monk's life would have suited Wishart, in a strict ascetic order, as long as he could indulge his weakness for frescoes. Though he disdained the crude decoration of Scottish churches, he'd admired the frescoes in Italian churches. So much so that, in his native parish of Fordoun, he'd painted the walls of his dwelling with his humble attempts. Knox had frowned when he saw them but said nothing. It was a small fault in a great man he decided. For, despite the adulation shown him wherever he preached, Master

Wishart was the least vain and least covetous man he had ever met.

He was also the most charitable. At some point during their wanderings, he would give away his cloak, along with other items of clothing, to the poor. Everything, that is, except the precious cap he'd bought as a scholar in France and which would be difficult to replace. Faithful to true Christian principles, Wishart desired to do good to all men and to harm no one. Besides, knowing that his every action, every movement was being scrutinised, both by his enemies as well as his friends, he resolved to teach by example.

The two men left the yuletide fair and took the high road to Ormiston where they would lodge for the night. The tall, gangly Wishart loped along in great strides, leaving the shorter, stockier Knox, weighed down by the hefty sword, struggling to keep up.

After a while Knox deliberately slowed down. 'We're being followed, master,' he said in a low voice.

Wishart seemed unperturbed. 'I ken.Those sergeants of Satan have become our constant shadows.'

As Knox swivelled round again, two hooded figures faded into the gloom. 'Grey Friars,' he muttered. 'What if they try to make another attempt on your life?'

In the plague-stricken city of Dundee, a Roman Catholic priest had attacked Wishart—at Beaton's behest Knox guessed. When the enraged congregation began tearing the priest to pieces, Wishart bade them to stop and sheltered his assailant in his arms. Such a response was so different, so contrary, to his own, Knox reflected. He'd have been the first to rip the murderous priest limb from limb with his own bare hands. He feared his fiery temper would never let him live up to such high standards, but then scolded himself for envying his master's cool self-possession.

'But you too are in danger,' Wishart warned.

‘Aye, I’m already in Beaton’s black books,’ Knox said, his lips frozen into a tight grimace. as they trudged, heads down against the sleet.

The rumour that the cardinal had drawn up a blacklist of heretics whom he proposed to eliminate one by one was probably true and Knox could no longer count on his godmother to protect him. Nevertheless, since the attempt on Wishart’s life, a faithful follower always carried a two-handed sword in his defence and now it was Knox’s honour to be entrusted with this task. When he gripped the sword with both hands, making ready to strike, Wishart laid a steadying hand on his shoulder.

‘Nay, John, I ken that I shall finish my life in that bloodthirsty man’s hands, but it will not be in this manner.’ Then, gazing wistfully ahead, he added in a sad whisper, ‘But it might be easier on me if it were.’

Chapter Sixty-Two
Wise Heart

Two women shall be grinding at the mill;
the one shall be taken and the other left.
Matthew XXIV:41

St Mary's Parish Church, 15 January 1546

Every blasphemous utterance stabbed mercilessly at her heart; every sacrilegious statement wounded her soul. Sister Agnes longed to jab her fingers in her ears to deafen the stream of evil heresy gushing like bile from the heretic's lips.

'The Holy Scripture is the highest and, indeed, only authority for my teaching,' the iconoclast claimed. On and on he went, attacking every belief that she held sacred. Ransacking the holy sacraments, destroying the creed, tearing apart her beloved church limb from limb.

Sister Agnes kept her head bent, forcing her beads between her fingers and burbling *Ave Marias* to drown out the blasphemous torrent flooding from the pulpit, for she feared she was committing a grave sin by her very presence. But curiosity had overcome her misgivings.

He'd recently preached a sermon outdoors under yew tree at Ormiston, but at John Knox's suggestion, David Forrest the infidel provost of Haddington had invited him to St Mary's. Yet another lance in his godmother's blessed heart.

She wouldn't have had the courage to come but for Sister Katherine who was eager to hear this devil's advocate. What would her dear friend, a stern authoritarian, be making of this? When the devil incarnate in the pulpit paused for breath, Sister Agnes took the opportunity to whisper:

'He'll burn for this. If not in this world then surely in hell.'

When Katherine turned her head slowly, Agnes stared at her in surprise. Despite the gloomy darkness of the church, a radiant glow shone from her friend's face. She seemed transformed. Transfigured. The harsh lines of her face had softened and the deeply etched line on her puckered brow had smoothed out. Her lips were slightly parted and her eyes dreamy. Katherine made no sign that she'd heard her friend but turned away again to gaze, enraptured, at the heretic.

'Wise Heart,' she whispered. 'He has come as I knew he would.'

Chapter Sixty-Three
The Sermon on the Tyne

> The voice of him that crieth in the wilderness.
> Prepare ye the way of the Lord, make straight...
> a highway for our God.
> —*Isaiah* XL:3

Haddington, 16 January 1546

The windows of Lethington Tower, the home of Sir Richard Maitland, were ablaze with light and the strains of music and singing rang clearly through the frosty air to the cottage. After Wishart and Knox had spent the night at David Forrest's house, the provost had got wind that Beaton's men were on their scent and found them a cottage on the Maitland's estate.

'They're wetting the head of Sir Richard's new-born,' the cottager explained. 'Another wee laddie for the laird. Thomas he's to be christened.'

'May the Lord grant him a long and prosperous life,' Wishart said. 'The frosty weather hasn't prevented his guests from attending the festivities,' he added morosely, an uncharacteristic hint of peevishness in his voice: for that was the reason Knox had given to explain the sparse audience at his sermon that afternoon. A lame excuse, Knox knew, for the truly committed would struggle through hell and high water to hear him.

Only a few days ago, Wishart had preached to capacity in the parishes of Inveresk and Tranent, but that afternoon only a humiliating smattering of souls, mostly beggars and vagabonds taking shelter, were dotted about the cavernous nave of St Mary's. 'We can only pray that word will spread and that tomorrow the kirk will be full. Forbye, my loyal Ayrshire brethren have promised to come. The Lollards will not let me down.'

The next morning, Widow Ker was waiting for them outside the huge oaken door of St Mary's. Her hand trembled as she handed Wishart a letter, from the Lollard brethren in Kyle, she muttered. As he read it through, his melancholy face became ashen and his long thin fingers trembled.

'They're not coming,' he said quietly, crumpling the letter in his fist. He breathed a long sigh and his eyes dulled as he stared along the riverbank. Light shone through the windows of the choir in the Franciscan Friary where the Greyfriars chanted their plainsong. The Lamp of Lothian was a rookery of spies for Beaton, Provost Forrest had warned him.

'You ken why, don't you?' Widow Ker folded her plump arms across her bosom. 'They've heard that your Longniddry brethren are plotting against the cardinal and are afeart the finger will be pointed at them too. I'm heartsick and sorry that my cringing countrymen have let you down. They should all be black affronted.'

'So, then, I am on my own?' Wishart's long face drooped even more.

'Nay, you are not alone.' Knox snatched the crumpled letter, tore it up and scattered the scraps over the bridge. For a few seconds he watched them flutter down into the Tyne and float along towards the accurst milldam. He touched Wishart's sleeve. 'I will never abandon you.'

'May God bless you, my faithful disciple,' Wishart said softly, though his watery smile hid a deep foreboding.

St Mary's Kirk

At the side door where the commonfolk entered St Mary's Kirk, the earl of Bothwell was giving orders to his troops with his customary arrogant swagger.

'No-one is allowed to enter the kirk,' he proclaimed, 'on pain of... er .. On pain of death... of their er... immortal souls,' he added hesitantly, his grasp of religious dogma as hazy as his sense of loyalty. The soldiers had been ordered to mount up so as to appear more menacing to the congregation; the breath from the snorting, whinnying horses steamed in the frosty air.

'Halt!' he yelled to a group of women who were trying to sneak past him into the church.

'Come down from your high horse, Patrick.' Elisabeth drew back the hood of her cloak. 'I need to speak with you in private.' Beckoning him to follow her behind a buttress, she confronted him. 'On whose orders are you prohibiting us from attending the sermon?' she asked, barely concealing the anger in her voice.

'His eminence, the cardinal's. He forbids the folk to hear this dangerous heretic.'

'And the queen mother? What are her orders?' she queried.

'The queen? Aye, well, I've been commissioned to arrest them,' he boasted, puffing his chest out proudly. 'As the sheriff of Lothian I have that power.'

'I see.' Elisabeth paused before asking, 'Them, you say?'

'Aye,' Bothwell replied rather sheepishly, avoiding her eyes, 'Wishart and one of his disciples. But we're not to arrest them till later—after his sermon. The cardinal doesn't want the flichty mob to turn against us and bring the wrath of the people down on us. And then I've to take them to the cardinal at Elphinstone. Forthwith.'

At the mention of Beaton, one of Elisabeth's group withdrew quickly and left.

'Patrick,' Elisabeth moved in closer to whisper, 'you ken I have the queen's ear. And I can tell you all is not lost for your heart's greatest desire. Now that Lennox is safely married to

Margaret Douglas and Arran's flimsy wits are befuddled, the way is clear for you.'

Hope lit up his pale blue eyes. Bothwell had lost a great deal in his fruitless contest with Lennox. Not only time, money and his reputation but also his wife, two children and, of course, the dowager queen Marie who had snubbed his advances. No wonder he was peeved, but now that his rival had flounced off to the English court and married the daughter of Margaret Tudor and Angus, he'd been thrown another chance.

'You may think the queen is in glunders with you,' Elisabeth continued, 'but she's even more scunnered with Cardinal Beaton. She wants no more bloodshed. If Wishart and his follower are taken to Elphinstone, Beaton will send them to the stake. And you know who his disciple is, don't you?'

Dull-witted Patrick looked down, avoiding her gaze. 'John Knox was aye a good friend to you, was he not? He always took your part when you were bullied. Whatever his beliefs may be now, he would never, ever betray a friend. And,' she added confidentially, 'I can assure you that Queen Marie would look kindly on you if you ... took your charges to Hailes rather than to Elphinstone.' She'd almost suggested that he 'lose' the prisoners but stopped herself in time. Bothwell might take it ill to be reminded of his punishment for 'losing' Archie Douglas when ordered to capture him at Tantallon. For that he was kept locked up in Edinburgh Castle and only after her appeal, was he thirled as king's ward till his 21st birthday.

The Fair Earl shrugged his rounded shoulders. 'But those are my orders.'

'From the cardinal perhaps, but the queen's wish surely carries greater weight.'

Bothwell furrowed his brow as his slow wits considered the options. Well aware that his own rough wooing of Queen Marie, had impoverished her fickle nephew, Elisabeth surreptitiously slipped a packet into his hand.

‘Here,’ she said. ‘Perhaps this may help you make up your mind.’

Inside St Mary’s Kirk, Wishart was pacing up and down behind the high altar, in and out of the shadows cast by the great pointed east window. Before preaching, he usually spent some time quietly absorbed in prayer and meditation but now he was too tense. His Lollard friends had forsaken him. Haddington had forsaken him. Had God forsaken him? Was this a sign that he was losing his gift?

Knox placed a hand on his sleeve. ‘Master, the time of your sermon approaches. You must calm your mind.’

‘And how many have braved the elements today?’ Wishart replied with uncharacteristic sarcasm before ascending the pulpit.

‘O Lord,’ he began, his voice echoing through the nave to be heard by the few intrepid souls who had sneaked past Bothwell’s guards. ‘I’ve heard that in Haddington, two or three thousand people would attend one vain clerk’s play, and lately I’ve seen for myself the multitude cheering on the Abbot of Unreason at the yuletide fair. Yet now, in all this town and parish there cannot be numbered a hundred persons to hear the messenger of the Eternal God. Men of God from Troon to Tranent have heard me gladly, but not the people of Haddington.’

Gazing up at the rafters, he continued his bitter complaint, sparing no scorn. ‘How long shall it be that Thy holy word shall be despised, and men shall not regard their own salvation?’ Then, digressing wildly from his prepared sermon, Wishart began to rant and rave at his sparse congregation, warning them of the wrath to come.

At the back of the church Elisabeth looked round for Katherine who had persuaded her to attend. Wishart was a true man of God, she’d said. She’d never encountered anyone with such conviction in his beliefs and, however wrong they might think him to be they should hear his message, if only to understand the reasons why Knox had abandoned the church. Listening to him now, Elisabeth was puzzled. Was this the man who was either revered or feared? She wasn't the only one to be perplexed.

'This is not the sermon he preached yesterday,' Sister Agnes murmured.

Underneath the pulpit, Widow Ker fidgeted uneasily on her stool. 'What is he saying? Perhaps we should stop him?' she whispered to Knox. But he paid her no heed, leaning forward on the hilt of his two-handed sword, listening intently. This was more like it. This fire and brimstone sermon echoing the Old Testament prophets or even Bishop Hepburn's tirades would stiffen the sinews and stir the blood.

After an excruciating hour and a half, Wishart reached the climax of his sermon. As if infused with some supernatural force he drew himself up to his full height and, waving his lanky arms madly, he began raining curses and prophecies down on them all.

'For your contempt of God's messenger, strangers shall possess your houses, chase you from your habitations and set upon you with sword and fire,' he predicted, smiting the air with his hand. 'Pestilence and famine shall afflict you. And the walls of this rose-red kirk by the Tyne will be open to the skies.'

Sitting upright, terrified by this tirade, Sister Agnes whispered anxiously to Elisabeth. 'He's not well, I fear.'

Indeed, despite the freezing temperature of the cold stone church, his usually pale complexion was flushed and beads of sweat trickled down his brow. His fist thumped down on the hard stone of the pulpit, making Elisabeth squirm for the pain it must have caused him. His blazing eyes scoured the church, seeking out sinners and ingrates. Then he bowed his head to say, his voice breaking with unbearable sadness, 'I am weary of the world because the world is weary of God.'

Knox laid aside the sword and joined Widow Ker to push through the small group of followers who, alarmed at his performance and concerned for his wellbeing, had gathered at the foot of the pulpit. After being helped down the steps, Wishart slumped onto a bench. The sermon had exhausted him. While Knox shooed the onlookers down the aisle and Widow Ker went to fetch some water for the preacher, Elisabeth crept up quietly behind Wishart and stood in the shadow of a pillar.

'Listen to me. Please.' She spoke in an urgent whisper. 'There isn't much time. Bothwell and his men have surrounded the church. You are to be arrested tonight.'

Without turning, Wishart stared straight ahead and nodded wearily. He had no need to be told: he had foreseen it.

'But don't worry. You won't be taken to Beaton—I give you my word on that—but to Hailes Castle. From there you will be freed.' How, she was not yet sure, but for now it was important to wrest Wishart from Beaton's clutches and gain time.

'But I have one thing to beg of you. Please don't take John with you. Order him to stay behind, for he won't leave your side otherwise. Please, as his godmother...' her voice trailed off and she slipped back into the shadows as Knox approached.

'Whatever will be, will be,' Wishart muttered. 'My travail is at an end. One is sufficient for a sacrifice. *Alas! he said and woe is me*!' he cried out and then went on:

I trow my deed will work me woe:
Jesu! My soul commend I thee,
Wheresoever my body go!

Alarmed by his master's haverings, Knox's voice wavered. 'What are you saying? Who were you talking to?'

'Fate,' Wishart replied, his eyes staring into the gloom. 'Destiny. Fortune. Whatever you like to call it.' He gave a long sigh. 'My mother was a Learmont, did I ever tell you? A descendant of True Thomas the Rhymer. Given two gifts by the Queen of Fairyland... '

‘Aye,’ Knox interrupted, ‘a tongue that never lies and the second sight.’

Wishart nodded. ‘Though I fear my inheritance has been more of a curse.’

He’d always been true to his beliefs, had never compromised, even when his life was at risk, as it surely was tonight. But it wasn’t difficult to foretell his future. From the day and hour he’d turned his back on the Roman Church, his destiny had been decided. Yet, he wondered sadly, had he had any choice? Had it all been predestined?

It was a mirk and starless night when they left the kirk. Thick frost was beginning to settle, they could see their breath on the freezing air and, since the frozen road would be too slippery for horses, Wishart’s small party prepared to set out on foot for Ormiston. When Knox appeared, wielding the two-handed sword, Wishart took him to one side.

‘Nay, John, stay with your bairns. Take the lads safely back to their lodgings.’

‘And then I shall follow you.’

Wishart nodded. ‘Aye, John, you shall follow me, but promise me this:

If thou wilt spell or tales tell,
John, thou never shall make lee:
Whereosever thou go, to firth or fell,
I pray thee never speak no ill of me.

And, kissing the mystified Knox on the cheek, he murmured, ‘One is sufficient for a sacrifice.’

Chapter Sixty-Four
Last Supper

Moreover, if thy brother shall trespass against thee, go and tell him his fault between thee and him alone.
Matthew XVIII:15

Elphinstone Tower, 16 January 1547

Sister Katherine had fled from St Mary's Kirk to hasten along the high road to Elphinstone. Faith in Wishart was giving her wings but her strength was threatening to run out. She'd stopped to catch her breath when a farmer, merry from market day, offered her a lift on his cart. While she gave thanks to God for sending this guardian angel, the boozy farmer, oblivious to her vocation—or perhaps not—carried on warbling bawdy bothy songs.

At Elphinstone Tower she ignored the warnings from astounded guards and burst into the chamber where her brother was taking supper. Her breath was ragged from running in the freezing night air. Frost had formed a silvery halo round her starched wimple making her eyes glint and her cheeks glow crimson.

'Davie, you mustn't arrest Wise Heart,' she blurted. 'Wishart is a man of God, his wise heart full of grace and goodness.'

She shook her head, spraying him with tiny flakes of melting frost. With a scowl, Beaton put down his goblet of wine and wiped the drips from his darkening face.

'Wise Heart? Is that what you cry him? Am I hearing aright? My devout sister is begging for mercy to be shown to a heretic? Has the devil's disciple bewitched you, too?'

He stood up and, resting his knuckles on the table, he leant forward. His hooded eyes narrowed to peer intently at her flushed face. 'Or have you fallen in love with him? Is that it? Then that is further proof he must be stopped. If Wishart's sleekit tongue can beglamour my pious sister so easily, think how he could dupe weaker minds.'

'You cannot say he's feeble-minded when John Knox has chosen to follow him,' she retorted.

Beaton snorted. 'That may be true, but perhaps his weakness lies in thon part which responds neither to reason nor religious conviction. Prioress Elisabeth has good cause to be concerned about his being in thrall to the zealot. I whiff something unhealthy, if not unnatural between the pair.'

Sister Katherine bristled. 'What do you mean by that?'

Slowly and significantly Beaton picked up the wishbone of the woodcock he'd been devouring and balanced it on his pinkie.

'Celibacy seems to be scant sacrifice for Knox who has never, to my knowledge, sought comfort in tail-toddle, at least with women. Which makes one suspect that he may satisfy his base cravings by other, how shall I put it? More perverse means. A monastery would suit him better; where he can associate with those who prefer the company of men. While for women who favour their own...' He curled the wishbone round his finger, all the while looking pointedly at his sister.

His lewd innuendo was not lost on her. 'What are you saying?' Her flushed cheeks deepened to a darker shade of crimson.

'It isn't uncommon for close friendships to thrive between young men who have shunned the companionship of women. Nor indeed among women who spurn men.'

Katherine's whole being was now aflame. She longed to fly at him and gorge out those scornful eyes. What was he insinuating?

'Whereas you've aye condemned me for my relationship with Marion, whom I consider my lawful wife in all but name,' Beaton went on, 'I have turned a blind eye to your *amitié* with the French nun. Pray, sister, where is your tolerance of human failings? Your much vaunted Christian charity?'

His words made her gasp for breath. How like her bullying brother to locate a skelf and then squeeze on it mercilessly until it throbbed. She grabbed the wishbone and snapped it in two, letting the splinters fall to the floor.

'You are no brother to me, Davie Beaton. May you rot in hell.'

Ormiston Hall

Faint with fatigue, Katherine leant against the wall outside the gates of Elphinstone Tower. The sleety rain helped to douse her burning indignation and wash away the tears smarting her cheeks but it could not wipe out the humiliation from her brother's sneering insinuations. How dare he pervert her innocent friendship with Sister Agnes or blight her admiration for Wishart. As her boots started slipping in the slush, her back began slowly sliding down the wall. What did she care if she sank down into the mud and never got up again? Her failure to plead for Wishart's life left her feeling weary unto death.

From out of the darkness, a hand touched her elbow, 'Come with me, sister. I'll take you to the master,' he whispered and led her to the house in Ormiston where Wishart was lodging.

Willie Brounfield, a groom at Elphinstone and reformist sympathiser, had been spying on Beaton and had overheard the siblings' heated confrontation. Reaching Ormiston, Brounfield stopped underneath an enormous yew tree just outside John Cockburn's house.

'This is our cathedral,' he declared. Within the canopy formed by its falling branches Wishart had held his open-air services. There was standing room for up to two hundred people, he told her proudly. Katherine laid her head against the trunk and said a silent prayer for her Wise Heart.

Ormiston

'Deliver me from mine enemies. O my God: defend me from them that rise up against me. Deliver me from the workers of iniquity and save me from bloody men. For lo, they lie in wait for my soul: the might are gathered against me ...'

Wishart was leading the small company in the 51st psalm when loud banging at the door interrupted their prayer. All but Wishart stiffened in their seats, fearful and alert. The arrival of the traitor Judas leading the multitude held no surprise for him and he began calmly reciting the Lord's Prayer. He was, however, caught unawares by the bedraggled nun who had pushed past Cockburn to hurl herself at his feet. On Brounfield's reassurance that, though she might be a holy sister and Beaton's sister, she was no spy, the small flock welcomed Sister Katherine into their midst. Widow Ker made them all shift round to give their new recruit a place by the fire to warm up and dry off.

As she glanced at their rapturous faces glowing in the firelight, enthralled by Wishart's readings from the Sacred Scripture, Katherine experienced both deep joy and heavy sorrow. Overjoyed to be among folk who shared this new and wonderful wisdom, knowing the fate awaited their master deeply saddened her. The worshippers kept watch until midnight when the Fair Earl surrounded the household with a troop of cavalry. While Cockburn stood his ground, refusing to surrender Wishart without a guarantee of his safety, the preacher slipped past him to address his captor.

'I praise God that so honourable a knight receives me this night,' he said, fixing Bothwell with his forthright gaze, 'for I'm assured your honour will not permit anything to be done to me against the order of the law. Forbye, I fear less to die openly than to be murdered in secret.'

Bothwell glanced shiftily from one to the other before addressing the floor. A flush of colour spread upwards from his throat to infuse his pale cheeks as he stuttered over the words he'd been rehearsing under the prioress's instruction.

'Not only shall I protect you from violence but I promise upon my honour that neither the governor nor the cardinal shall harm you. I shall keep you in my own power till either I set you free or bring you back here.' So saying, he was satisfied he'd honoured his promise to his aunt.

'Don't believe him,' Sister Katherine whispered to Wishart. 'Bothwell cannot be trusted. He sways with the wind. This Judas has been paid his thirty pieces of silver by my brother, the chief priest.'

Wishart inclined his head towards her and shrugged his shoulders. 'My hour has come,' he murmured in fatalistic tones that alarmed her. 'It is written,' he said then gave an ironic laugh. 'I maun dree my weird.'

Chapter Sixty-Five
The Trial

Greater love hath no man than this,
that a man lay down his life for his friends.
John XV:13

St Andrews, 28 February 1546

The noise was deafening. A ceaseless booming, relentlessly pounding against the hold of the ship. Bodies unsteady on their feet battered against each other. Slop buckets rolled about, sloshing out their squalid contents and stinking the already foul air. The booming grew louder and louder. The ship must be under attack. Every time a cannonball hit the side, the ship shuddered, planks creaked and cargo exploded.

When the smell of smoke stung their nostrils, the prisoners in the hold panicked, scrambling over each other to get to a source of air. Rats were scampering up the ropes but the hatches and portholes had been closed. Some tried to knock holes through the sides. From above they could hear sailors shouting, 'She's on fire,' and calling for water. From out of the depths they cried, 'Open the hatches! Let us out! Save our souls!' Briny seawater was seeping upwards from the bowels of the ship and lapping round their ankles. His lungs were burning. He gasped for air.

Wake up! A voice shouted. In an effort to move his cramping limbs Wishart realised he was shackled to the wall. In the perpetual darkness, he couldn't tell whether it was day or night and, despite the eternal booming and the chilling dampness in the unlit Sea Tower of St Andrews Castle, he must have dozed off. The unexpected light from a candle thrust in his face made him blink.

'What day is it?' the preacher enquired.

Stepping out from behind the warder a Franciscan friar said, 'The final day of February.'

So, the twenty-eighth day of February: an ominous date. Fourteen years to the day since Patrick Hamilton's execution. Twice seven long years. Is that why he'd dreamt of fire? And, with the waves battering his ears, hardly surprising that he dreamt of the sea. Fire and sea together, his mother would have avowed, were powerful portents of disaster. Predictably enough, he thought wryly.

And predictably enough, Bothwell had proved false, moving Wishart from pillar to post in a macabre parody of Hunt the Gowk. The privy council had ordered Bothwell to take him from Hailes Castle to Governor Arran in Edinburgh. He in turn had been commanded by the dowager queen to surrender his prisoner to the cardinal in St Andrews who then locked him up in the Bottle Dungeon.

He was to appear before the lord cardinal the next morning, the Franciscan, John Winram, informed him. 'To give an account of the seditious and heretical doctrine you have been teaching. But beforehand, I've been asked to preach.' He paused before continuing. 'And I'm taking as my text the parable of the sower in St Matthew's Gospel, with which you're well acquent.'

Wishart gave a slight nod of acknowledgement. The sub-prior of St Andrews had chosen the very text he'd used in his Christmas sermon at Leith when he'd dared to liken the clergy to the thorns among which the seed of truth was sown. 'And some fell among thorns and the thorns grew up and choked it and it yielded no fruit.' Saying this, he scrutinised Winram's face for any sign of sympathy, but the Franciscan remained inscrutable.

St Andrews Cathedral, 1 March 1546

On the grassy knoll in front of her brother's grand house, soldiers were piling up logs and timbers. Horror-struck, Katherine stopped abruptly: such a huge pyre would not be for roasting the fatted calf. So even before the trial, the Bloody Cardinal had already judged Wishart and found him guilty. Other soldiers were training the castle cannons onto the execution pyre while an armed force of one hundred men lined up to escort the prisoner on his last journey.

'Your brother must be afeart that we'll try to rescue our Wise Heart.' Taking her by the hand, Widow Ker hauled her away. 'Come on, there's no time to stand here and gawp. We'll no get a place otherwise.'

Outside the cathedral, the cardinal's men, emboldened by liberal tots of French brandy, were haranguing the large crowd of spectators seeking entry. There were no places left. The cathedral was packed. Go home.

Widow Ker nudged Katherine. 'Tell them you're the cardinal's sister.'

Katherine glanced down at the scruffy woollen skirt and clarty pinny, which barely skimmed her ankles. 'They'd never believe me. An Anstruther fishwife is better clad than I am. Forbye, I'm ashamed to call him brother.'

Widow Ker grunted and together they inched their way round the cathedral to a narrow door guarded only by a gnarled old porter who barred their way.

'Take pity on us,' she moaned, 'for I'm the prisoner's poor widowed mother and this is his beloved sister.'

The porter swithered before whispering confidentially, 'If it's any comfort there's many here in Fife who say it's the wrong man on trial and that Beaton will rue this day.' He beckoned them to follow him along a dark, musty passage into the nave.

High up in the chancel, the hierarchical rivals, Cardinal Beaton and Gavin Dunbar, the Archbishop of Glasgow, famous for his great cursing against the border reivers, headed the tribunal on the specially constructed grandstand.

In the pulpit, the Franciscan Friar Winram had begun his sermon but, listening to his opening words, Katherine could hardly believe her ears. He seemed to be accusing the hierarchy of sacrilege and criticising bishops for failing to be faultless, sober-minded and holy. He even decried them as thorns among the seeds of truth. Was he not meant to be defending the Church? What would her brother, the cardinal, think of that?

Katherine stretched up on tiptoe, craning her neck, hoping to glimpse her brother's face—furious indignation, no doubt from, Winram's reaction. Faltering, he seemed to lose heart. then he changed tack and was calling for heretics to be cut down. Head downcast he descended the pulpit where Wishart was waiting at the foot. After exchanging a few words Winram shook his head while Wishart patted him on the shoulder in a sign of forgiveness.

The crowd were reluctant to let the pair claiming to be the prisoner's widowed mother and sister cut a swathe through them, until Katherine pulled back her shawl. On her head she'd squashed the French cap Wishart had gifted her on the night of his arrest.

Hovering in the shadows like a helpless guardian angel, Katherine had followed the martyr on every station of his *via dolorosa* to his final Golgotha—the place of the skull.

'Aye, that's the master's hat all right,' a sympathiser stated. 'He never took it off, not even in his bed. God's blessing on you ladies.' With that, the crowd parted to let them through.

When Wishart knelt to pray in the pulpit, Katherine bowed her head. Instinctively, she began fumbling for her rosary to join him but she'd flung her beads away with her nun's habit. She would not be lost for words, however. What better time to discard her Latin prayers and appeal directly to God in her own tongue to come to the aid of her Wise Heart?

When she raised her head again, the cardinal's secretary was standing in the opposite podium, drumming his fingers impatiently on the battery of case papers piled up in front of him. John Lauder. A powerful prosecutor: a pitiless persecutor. By force of habit she raised a hand to sign herself with the cross to ward off Satan but stopped short on seeing Widow Ker's disapproving frown.

In a quiet, determined voice, Wishart requested permission to summarise his doctrine: so as not to be judged unjustly, he explained. Lauder's screech of derision skirled throughout the cathedral.

'If it were not lawful for you to preach without any authority of the church, then it's certainly not lawful for you to preach now,' he bawled and then went on to spit out a list of accusations:

That it was vain to build costly churches.

That the eucharist was only common bread and wine.

That a priest saying mass was like a fox wagging its tail.

Dear God in heaven! Katherine squirmed. He's hammering in the nails. He'll crucify him ere long.

'My lords, I did not say so. What I did say was that moving the outward body, without moving the inner heart, is like an ape playing, and not the true serving of God.'

While Wishart nimbly defended himself against all the charges with admirable self-control, Katherine couldn't stop the violent thrumming in her breast. If only she'd thought to bring a stool like others in the congregation, but then scolded herself for her weakness. She must stand firm. When Widow Ker linked a comforting arm through hers, Katherine strained to smile her thanks but her mouth was frozen in a rictus of fear. By way of consolation, Lauder, too, was finding it difficult to maintain his composure.

'You deny that there are seven sacraments?' he snarled.

Whether there were seven or eleven sacraments Wishart couldn't say since he taught only what was in scripture.

‘So, in your humble opinion, neither confession nor baptism is a sacrament?’

Since God alone could grant forgiveness and absolution, confessing our sins needed no intermediary, Wishart argued. And as for baptism: how could an infant make a promise before God without understanding the conditions?

Ignoring these replies, Lauder continued. Did he not say that every layman was a priest and that the pope had no more power than any other man? From the grandstand the clergy greeted these accusations with howls and snorts of derision. Meanwhile, in the body of the kirk, amongst the lay folk, Katherine was pleased to notice many nodding heads and lips mouthing agreement.

‘And you deny the existence of purgatory?’ Lauder continued questioning.

‘I’ve read the Bible many, many times, and to this day I have never yet found such a term in any place of scripture,’ Wishart admitted, before throwing the question back to Lauder. ‘Can you prove any such place?’

Lauder spluttered before spinning round to seek guidance, but no-one from the humming and hawing ranks of the highest clergy was prepared to do so.

As for the practices of fasting, not eating flesh on Friday and the use of holy water, Wishart dismissed them as sheer flummery, conjured up by the Roman Church to mystify their flock. Faith, not the routine of rituals, was the way to God.

‘You must be in league with Lucifer to teach such lies—or Luther, as the wily archfiend guises himself. This Luther-Lucifer is but a scurrilous servant of Satan, spouting forth skaiths and curses on the one true Church,’ Lauder blustered, finally losing his temper.

If his teachings were being condemned as the work of the Evil One, then Wishart knew he was doomed. Weighed down by weariness and dejection, his shoulders drooped as he shrank to a shadow of himself. He clutched the edge of the pulpit for support awaiting the next onslaught.

Just then from behind Katherine a voice yelled out, 'The devil cannot speak such words as yonder man speaks.'

Murmurs of agreement among the lay folk, rankled by John Lauder's abrasive manner, began to ripple through the nave and rose to a crescendo. Wishart gave a wan, grateful smile because this surge of sympathy showed that ordinary folk had come, not just to gawp at the heretic, but were listening and taking heed of his defence.

And there, near the front, he could see his French cap bobbing up and down. Katherine was here. If he could convert a devout catholic nun, Beaton's own sister, then all was not lost. From that moment he perked up. Making the most of his last chance on God's earth to preach, Wishart roundly ignored Lauder and directed his replies at the congregation. The exasperated cardinal beckoned to his prosecutor.

'Read out the remaining articles,' Beaton rasped, crooking his chubby finger at him. 'And, if you cherish your life, make sure he has no chance to reply.'

The doomster would formally pronounce sentence after a break for dinner, the clerk of the court announced. Since Beaton had already passed judgment before the start of the trial, the tribunal of the cardinal's chosen colleagues was free to enjoy the lavish dinner in his private chambers. They were licking their fingers and patting their well-filled paunches when the episcopal guard announced the queen's herald.

'Ah, the post-prandial entertainment is here. The court jester has come to amuse our little gathering,' Beaton quipped.

Lindsay, however, was in no mood for jests. He'd only found out about the trial after returning from a diplomatic mission abroad. Whatever judgement may have been passed on the accused, he reminded Beaton, the law demanded that Governor

Arran supply a criminal judge, not a clerical one, to act as doomster.

Mellow with cognac, the cardinal continued to taunt. 'Arran! That witless fool's authority is of no consequence. If we were to await a decision from that swithering dolt, Wishart would die a slow, lingering death in the Bottle Dungeon. Our way is more merciful. I shall be his doomster on earth; let him face Divine Judgement ere the day is out.'

'You're making a grave mistake,' Lindsay snarled. 'You'll only make a martyr out of Wishart. Followers will rush to his cause and instead of stamping out heresy, you'll be dealing the church a deathblow. Do not uproot the whole tree for the sake of a few rotten branches. Whereas if you set Wishart free...'

Beaton raised a beringed finger and gave him a scathing look. 'Have no fear, the rantings of Luther and his loathsome lackeys cannot topple the Holy Roman Church with one thousand five hundred years of tradition and truth behind it. Why should I liberate this English spy in the pay of Henry Tudor? If not for heresy then your saintly Wishart would be on trial for treason.'

'Nay!' Lindsay interjected. 'You mistake him for Wishart, the Baillie of Dundee, who is indeed a spy and a traitor. Set the preacher free and events will take their natural course.'

Beaton sneered. 'Their natural course? You mean a reformation in Scotland paid for by English gold? Do you not see how Henry's rough wooing is laying waste to our land? An alliance with the cruel and merciless English king would be the deathblow to Scottish independence. It is far better that we ally with France and Rome.'

'Mark my words,' Lindsay warned. 'The time is ripe for reform but it must be properly directed, without bloodshed...'

'Properly directed! Hark at the minstrel playwright! Harp and carp, Lindsay! Harp and carp! You are an idealist, Lyon Herald, forever playing the role of John the Commonweal.'

'And you, Cardinal Beaton, are a self-important pragmatist who fears not so much the rise of heresy but the loss of power: any power, however petty. Was it really worth brawling with your sainted colleague there,' he pointed to Gavin Dunbar, 'over who should head a procession in his own cathedral? Have you mended your crosiers yet?' Lindsay snorted, whipping up gales of laughter from the other bishops.

Once the hilarity had quietened down, Lindsay continued, 'I'd be wary, Beaton, in case thon archbishop calls down a curse upon you. But here's a prophecy.' Lindsay's tone became serious. 'Mind what was said about Patrick Hamilton? That the reek of his burning would only fuel the fires of reformation, not put them out. If you burn Wishart I can predict, without a word of a lie, that your blood will be splattered next, Davie Beaton,' he warned. 'Now will not be too soon to start writing your obituary.'

Chapter Sixty-Six
Burnt Offering

For thou desirest not sacrifice;
else would I give it:
Thou delightest not in burnt offering.
—*Psalms* LI:16

St Andrews, 1 March 1546

The crowd of onlookers—ghouls in her mind—was so dense that Katherine couldn't get near the pyre, nor could she see above the jiggling heads and shoulders.

'Let me through. For pity's sake, let me through. I am his sister.'

Charily at first, the ghouls stepped aside and jostled her up to the front. When Wishart was brought out, his hands tied behind his back and an iron chain fastened round his waist, Katherine went weak at the knees. Would she be able to thole it alone? Widow Ker was heartily sorry, but she had no stomach for the burning. If only Sister Agnes were here. Her heart clenched as she recalled how she'd left her dear friend without saying a word. No explanation, no word of farewell for her dear friend *Agnus Dei*.

A noose was hanging loosely round his neck. Perhaps they would hang him instead. That way, at least, his agony would be over sooner. Friar Winram was by his side, ready to hear his confession if he changed his mind at the last minute. Wishart had already dismissed the two friars Beaton had sent and had asked for Winram. Not to shrive his soul but to thank him for his sermon and to consider his own future.

'Do not fear the truth, my friend. There's no middle way. One day you'll have to decide. And may the Holy Spirit come down on you.' Before kneeling to pray, he shuffled forward to address the crowd, his eyes swiftly scanning the jumble of spectators. 'Because I am about to suffer this fire for Christ's sake, do not turn against the true religion. You must keep on learning the Word of God which I have taught you.'

At the front of the throng, Katherine took off the French cap and waved it frantically in the air to catch his attention. He glanced towards her and as he inclined his head, a smile flitted over his lips, for those standing next to her were staring in surprise at her shorn head.

'Behold my face,' he declared to the ghouls, keeping his eyes fixed on Katherine. 'You shall not see me change my colour. I fear not this grim fire. Weep not for me.'

Biting into her bottom lip to quell the tears, she drew blood, but Wishart remained calm, even forgiving the hooded headsmen. As he kissed them on the cheek, one of them dropped to his knees. His unexpected declaration—that he didn't will the death of so holy a man—provoked a chorus of *Amens* from amongst the crowd. Nevertheless, he joined his colleague in stuffing bags of gunpowder into the pockets of the buckram coat, tying more under the condemned man's oxters and then buckling the coat with straps.

Though every inch of her being yearned to flee from his suffering, Katherine braced herself to stand firm. When they chained him to the stake, she willed him to look her way and see that she, too, would not flinch. She would share his suffering: no matter what. When Wishart twisted his head, she followed his glance to the window where her brother, the cardinal, and his bishops were viewing their victim's final agony.

The treacherous high priests, their plump behouchies seated on cushions embroidered by nuns at the abbey—including herself—were callously laughing and joking as if at a fool's play and not a tragedy. She wanted to spit. Wishart's lips were now moving in prayer, she presumed, but the bruit flashing amongst the crowd was that he'd uttered a prophecy.

'Whereas I expect to sup with my Saviour before the night is spent, he who feeds his eyes on my torments in a few days shall be hanged at the same window.'

To the piercing blast of trumpets, the headsmen circled the giant stook of the pyre, setting it alight at various points. A gasp ran through the crowd as the captain of St Andrews Castle suddenly leapt up on to the scaffold. Katherine held her breath. Would he offer a last-minute reprieve? Would he wrench the martyr from the stake and carry him off? But no, the captain had only braved the blaze to wish him good courage.

At first, as the flames from the kindling lapped gently at his feet, it looked as if Wishart were paddling in the shallows of a fiery sea, but then they crackled into life and spiralled upwards into a blazing tower, hungrily devouring his hose, peeling the blistering skin from his legs and sizzling through to the bone. Blood oozed from the corners of his mouth as he sank his teeth through his tongue to silence his scream of agony.

As the stench of his roasting flesh punched the pit of her stomach, Katherine gulped hard to keep from retching. Those sadists, anxious not to miss a moment of the martyr's torment, wafted away the scorching air and smoke, only backing off, choking and coughing, when the pungent reek hit their throats. With loud bangs, the bags of gunpowder began to explode, spurting blood and spewing flesh, bones and offal into the crowd. Those blood-soaked slivers splattering her cap and shawl could have burst from his liver, spleen or even—may God have mercy—his heart. His Wise Heart.

When a halo of flames encircled his blackened head, instinctively she recoiled in horror, but then steeled herself.

However harrowing it was to witness the intense heat melting his skin through to the skull, transforming his features into the ghoulish grin of a neep lantern, she *would* behold his face. Only when a last blast blew his head from his shoulders, leaving it to dangle by a sinew, did her eyes close as she slumped to the ground.

Chapter Sixty-Seven
Murder Most Foul

As for the Cardinal, I grant
He was a man we weel could want,
and we'll forget him soon.
And yet I think that, sooth to say,
Although the loon be well away,
The deed was foully done.

—*The Tragedy of the Cardinal,* Sir David Lindsay, 16th Century

St Andrews, 29 May 1546

Lady Marion Ogilvie sat in the gloom of the hovel willing the old woman to quicken up as she slowly stirred a spurtle in the simmering cauldron on the swey hanging over the fire. Wood smoke stung her eyes and offensive smells assaulted her nose. A cluster of kittens scampered about the floor watched over by their mother, a tawny she-cat with luminous green eyes. Stout-hearted she may be but Lady Marion was scared of cats and started in terror when a sooty black cat leapt onto her lap, digging its sharp claws into her flesh, fixing her with its evil eyes. An ominous sign. A shudder ran through her but she was more afraid to shoo the crone's vile creature away.

She was beginning to regret coming but the potions prescribed by Sister Agnes had run out. The wise wife had listened, head cocked to one side, eyeing her up like one of her chookies, as she read out the ingredients of the French sister's receipt.

'That's as may be, but I'll use my own home-brewed remedies, not any fancy foreign ones,' the auld wife declared, and began dropping powders and dried leaves into the cauldron.

Lady Marion wished the old crone would hurry. She'd left Davie Beaton propped up in bed promising that she wouldn't be long. He'd had another restless night, kept awake not only by stomach-wrenching pains from his bilious liver but also the nagging fear of assassination. Ever since Wishart's execution, the mood of resentment against the cardinal had intensified and plots against his life were rife. He'd stubbornly refused her suggestion of seeking refuge at their newly built castle at Melgund near Forfar. It would be safer to remain in St Andrews Castle, which was being fortified against attack.

Clad from head to toe in black so as to move unnoticed among the clerical populace, Lady Marion had slunk out through the postern gate at daybreak. Herring gulls swooped in and out of the skeleton of wooden scaffolding erected around the castle for the army of workmen. She had passed the drawbridge where the porter, old greybeard Ambrose Stirling, was remonstrating with a group of masons about the work not being carried out fast enough for the cardinal. The labourers hung about idly chattering and loitering but straightened up when a Franciscan friar approached them.

Now, impatient to leave the roach-ridden hovel, Lady Marion paid the crone the extortionate price she asked for, without any haggling, much to the old hag's surprise. Clutching the precious flask and treading cautiously so as not to slip on the cobbles, she made her way back to the castle. The din of the skirling gulls had been replaced with that of a yammering crowd gathered at the edge of the castle moat. Workmen were fleeing in panic over the drawbridge and yelling that a monstrous deed had taken place.

She joined a small group of townsfolk gathering about the provost who, with his hands cupped round his mouth, shouted up at the castle.

'What have you done with my lord cardinal? Where is he? Have you slain him? We shall ne'er depart until we see him.'

Alarmed by the hubbub near the castle drawbridge, Lady Marion darted over to a small group huddled tightly in a circle. She edged her way through, her heart battering against her ribs. A body had been tossed over the walls and was lying splayed on the strand. The back of the skull had been crushed, splattering the brains like skirlie across the sand. Lady Marion strove to stem the bile gathering in her throat as they turned the body over. The face, smashed to smithereens, was unrecognisable.

'Nay, it's not the cardinal. It's the porter. Poor old Ambrose Stirling. Never did anybody any harm.'

Hearing shouts and screams from the east blockhouse, she ran back. Something was being lowered slowly down the wall of the tower. Her hand shot to her mouth. It can't be. They wouldn't. She prayed her eyes were deceiving her. A man's naked, bloodied corpse , with one arm and one leg tied to a makeshift rope of the best linen sheets, bumped and battered against the stone wall until it dangled in mid-air. Between his legs a gaping wound was encrusted with dark purple blood where his genitals had been hacked off before being stuffed crudely between his lips.

Lady Marion shoved her fist into her mouth to stifle the scream of despair that threatened to alert everyone around her. If they realised who she was, she'd be hoisted up there beside him. One of the assassins had tottered unsteadily along the ramparts and was now untying his breeches. As it dawned on the crowd what he was about to do, they began to jeer.

'Pishing is too good for the likes of him.'

'Aye! Keech on him from a great height.'

Waving his free hand in the air in a triumphant gesture to the cheers of some of the spectators, the desecrator of the murdered cardinal toppled backwards as he was hauled off the rampart.

'First they desecrate now they defecate. *Sic transit gloriae mundi,*' a voice from behind Lady Marion muttered. As she swivelled round the Grey Friar pulled his cowl over his head and scurried away. It crossed her mind that, in this city sated with ecclesiastics, he had been the only cleric she'd seen that morning. She left the crowd yelling insults at Beaton's mutilated body and slipped round to the postern gate, unsure what to do. It would be foolish to try and go in. What could she do? Beaton's murderers might turn on her, leaving eight children orphaned. She'd kept her promise to be faithful unto death. Now her duty was to look after their family.

She was about to turn away when a young lad sidled through the gate. A velvet bonnet with a bedraggled feather bobbing at a jaunty angle was pulled down over his eyes and under his arm he was carrying a box. He hesitated for a moment, his frightened eyes darting hither and yon.

'Charlie!' She beckoned to him. 'Over here.'

As Beaton's chamber-child, Charlie Baxter's chores included emptying the cardinal's chamber pot, tending to the fire, keeping his bed warm in winter and carrying out other menial tasks. After Lady Marion had left that morning, the lad had been about to set the fire to heat water for the cardinal's ablutions when he heard a clamour outside.

'What was that?' Startled from his doze, the cardinal had stumbled to the window.

'The castle has been taken,' a voice shouted.

Tripping over his nightclothes, Beaton hurried to the postern gate. On his orders, this exit was always kept open, not only for the free wayleave of his mistress Lady Marion but in case he ever needed to escape. The gate, however, had been secured and a guard stationed. He fled back to his chamber where he ordered the terrified Charlie to steek the door and pile up kists and settles against it. Then he hastened to conceal a casket in the coal box and laid coals on top. When they began to ram the door, Beaton took up his two-handed sword and bellowed, 'Will you spare my life?'

'It may be that we will,' was the answer.

'Nay,' the cardinal replied. 'Swear to me by God's wounds and I will open unto you.'

This time there was no response, only the sounds of mutterings and scuffling from behind the heavy oaken door. Charlie sniffed the air. Was that burning he could smell? He keeked through the keyhole: a chamber pot filled with burning coals had been placed against the door.

'Fire!' the terrified lad screamed. 'Fire! They're going to burn us out!'

That might signal an appropriate end for the Bloody Cardinal but it was not Charlie's choice of exit from this world. He scrambled over the kists and boxes, knocking them over in his haste to open the door. Beaton had braced himself to confront his enemies face-to-face but cramping pains in his belly forced him to sit down. When two men rushed in, daggers drawn, he clutched his stomach and cried out,

'I am a priest. I am a priest, do you hear. You will not slay a man of God!'

'For that very reason we shall!' Howling with laughter they slashed their daggers through his flimsy nightshirt.

'Haud your hand!' a commanding voice bawled.

The slayers halted to stare at their captain. Sickened and disgusted by the cold-blooded murder of the porter William Kirkcaldy of the Grange wanted no more slaughter.

'Aye, he's right,' the usually mild-mannered James Melville said. 'The work and judgement of God ought to be done with greater gravity.' Saying so, he forced Beaton to his knees and pointed his sword at him. 'Repent of your wicked life! And of shedding the innocent blood of George Wishart that demands vengeance afore God!'

Without giving Beaton time to repent, the murderer ran his sword through his body once, twice, thrice, splattering the walls red with martyr's blood.

'Fye, fye! All is gone!' The cardinal spluttered his last words before slumping forward in the chair.

While the rest of the conspirators tumbled over each other into the room, squabbling about what to do next, Charlie swiftly retrieved the casket. From behind one of the kists, his eye caught sight of a bonnie velvet bonnet with a fine feather. Picking it up, he crept out of the chamber.

'Good lad, Charlie. You keep the bonnet, I'll take this. While the lad adjusted Beaton's hat on his head, Lady Marion took the casket of gold coins from him and tucked it under her cloak. 'This will pay our way to Melgund Castle. No good can be done here.'

Chapter Sixty-Eight
Armistice

Wherefore I counsel everyilk christened king
With in his realm mak reformation
And suffer no more rebels for to ring
Above Christ's true congregation.
—*The Tragedy of the Cardinal,* Sir David Lindsay, 16th Century

St Andrews, 16 December 1546

Light snow was starting to fall and the weak December light was already fading as Lindsay crossed the drawbridge to St Andrews Castle for the second time that day. Once again a trumpet heralded his arrival as the Lord Lyon King of Arms, but this time the Castilians, as the reformist rebels called themselves, agreed to speak with him. Passing through the courtyard, he had to scramble past piles of rubble from buildings bombarded by Governor Arran's artillery.

Arran, however, was in a quandary. Beaton had kept his eleven-year-old son captive in the castle to secure his father's loyalty and now the Castilians were holding him to ransom. James Hamilton was dear to him; he had high hopes of marrying him to the young Queen of Scots. He'd swithered between starving them out—but he feared for his son's life—and blowing them out, but he hadn't enough guns. One of his dafter ideas had been to hew a passage through the solid rock to rescue him. In the end he'd ordered a cannon to be discharged sporadically to remind them of his presence.

The courtyard was littered with snow-covered humps. Could they not at least shovel up their dead and store them away until the frozen ground thawed? At his approaching footsteps, some of the corpses roused from their slumber and struggled to their feet: so, not dead then, but dead drunk. The ragged urchins rummaging among the rubble and poking around the debris and detritus were skinny, undernourished and sickly looking. Lindsay sniffed deeply at the posy Elisabeth had thrust into his hand: dried cinquefoil to ward off infection from the deadly disease raging through the garrison. With luck the freezing temperature would kill off the plague.

'Is the cold skrinking your cockles? I can warm them up for you.' The thin, pinched face of the woman accosting him was covered in suppurating pustules. 'Whatever it pleases you to give, kind sir, I'll take.'

'But I won't take what you'll give me,' he muttered, waving her away.

'Anything,' she pleaded, trying to link her arm in his, unwilling to part with this visitor from the outside for a well-fed, well-dressed gentleman must have something. Lindsay brushed her off, striding out at a pace too fast for her half-starved body to keep up with him.

He'd been assigned a difficult mission. The deadlock had to be broken. On the one hand, Marie de Guise was anxious to send for French help but Arran was unwilling. Never decisive at the best of times, twa-fangelt Arran swithered and dithered, relying on others to make his decisions for him. Then Sir David Lindsay of the Mount would be the man to negotiate with the Castilians, advised the Fife gentry, the very lairds behind the murder of Beaton. Lindsay was not only an experienced diplomat with kin in Fife but known to be sympathetic to their cause. Despite this, the Castilians had been in no hurry to grant him admission to the castle.

'We're expecting Henry of England to send aid at any moment,' Kirkcaldy explained.

'You may have a long wait. The English king is bloated and cunt-bitten from the pox and is in no state to help,' Lindsay informed them. Nor was Henry keen to buy any more skittish Scots who swayed with the wind. Assured they were assuredly not, the exasperated king had said. With no help forthcoming from the auld enemy they agreed surrender on certain conditions, the first of which surprised Lindsay.

'A papal dispensation for the murderers of Beaton? Why?' Lindsay was bemused.

John Leslie dropped his gaze. 'We fear for our immortal souls,' he said. 'For if we die in a state of mortal sin, we'll go straight to hell.'

Lindsay snorted in disbelief. 'But you are followers of the reformed faith, are you not? Evangelicals such as you do not recognise the authority of the pope. You answer only to Almighty God Himself. Surely only He has the power to pardon you?'

Leslie shifted uncomfortably. Like most uneducated laymen whose beliefs were based on a mixture of superstition and hearsay, he barely understood Roman Catholic dogma far less the arguments of the new, reformed faith.

'We also demand a pardon from the governor. And his assurance that we will be allowed to go free,' Kirkcaldy stated.

'And unpunished,' Leslie added.

Lindsay could see the strain of the long siege in their gaunt, haggard faces and the desperation in their eyes. It was clear they were floundering in a mire of their own making and were looking to him to pull them out. They should be willing to barter.

'The pope will not grant absolution while the body of the cardinal lies unburied,' he claimed.

Beaton's mutilated corpse had been stowed in a lead-lined vat of salted water at the bottom of the infamous Bottle

Dungeon in the Sea Tower. If it were up to Lindsay he could languish there, unblessed and unburied, until Judgement Day, but he would keep his promise to Elisabeth and Lady Marion.

Distraught that there could be no eternal rest for the soul of her beloved Davie, until a requiem mass set it free Lady Marion was anxious to arrange a Christian burial. Only then could she, too, rest in peace. Queen Marie sympathised. She, too, was bereft after the savage slaughter of her trusted counsellor but with no influence over the Castilians, she'd sought advice from her herald. Lindsay had been reluctant to intervene—until Elisabeth cornered him.

'Whatever else he may have done in his life, he was a good father to his bairns,' Elisabeth stated, 'and Lady Marion was eternally grateful that he'd given her a life as mistress of her own household when no-one else would have her. And he was a faithful spouse, Aye, it's true,' she added in response to his sceptical look, 'for ever since their first, fateful meeting, Beaton never cast lustful eyes at any other woman. Rumours grew wings and lies long legs where Davie Beaton was concerned. How dare they decry him as a butcher of hundreds when he was guilty of only seven executions? Why, your beloved King James had far more blood on his hands. Not least that of an innocent young mother burned as a witch.'

That was not one of his most triumphant moments Lindsay had to admit and regretted not being around to persuade the king to show mercy to Jinty.

'And Lady Marion is prepared to pay in gold if necessary. That's how much she loves *her* Davie,' Elisabeth had reproached him. 'Aye, there were times when I would have gladly throttled Beaton myself. However, I knew it was his deep desire to save our church from heresy that drove him, but what about you, Davie? Tell me truthfully, did you have a hand in Beaton's murder?'

Lindsay shrugged. 'The Bloody Cardinal signed his own death warrant. Every time he signed his name to an execution order.'

'That is the answer of a courtier and diplomat. And makar. You may not have struck the deathblow but you've aye been skilled as the master of revels, planning and directing the actions of others. I only ask because of something Lady Marion mentioned. That all the clerics seemed to have spirited themselves away that fatal day except for one Franciscan friar. Did Friar Lazarus resurrect himself?'

Lindsay gave a wry laugh. 'All I will say is that thon friar was as much a monk as Beaton was a cardinal.'

That evening the Castilians invited him to their meagre supper. He chewed through the beef or horse or whatever flesh it was that had been heavily seasoned with salt and vinegar to disguise the rank smell and brackish, bitter taste. As he picked at his meat the image of Beaton's unburied body, pickled in salt, came unbidden to Lindsay.

'How long do you intend the corpse of the corrupt cardinal to rot in the cellar?' he asked his dining companions.

'Until the day of doom,' John Leslie asserted.

'Until hell freezes over,' William Kirkcaldy maintained.

'Ah!' Lindsay muttered, 'Then you are braver men than me. For while the cardinal's body lies unburied, you'll never be at peace. His restless spirit will haunt you for ever more.'

He lowered his head to attack his meat, letting the superstitious rebels digest his words,

'Aye, you may be right,' John Rough, the Ayrshire preacher, as rough as his name, was quick to agree. 'For I believe that the foul fiend of hell, Auld Nick himself, may have us in his evil clutches.'

Since the siege had begun, more than one hundred and fifty people had entered the castle. Some were dedicated to their cause, but many were hangers-on: beggars, vagrants and the like who had heard that the English were supporting the rebels with money and supplies.

'They have come, not for the glory of God but for English gold,' he complained. And when Lindsay remarked on the drunken bodies littering the streets, Rough exclaimed, 'Drinking is the least of it. Debauchery and whoring are weeding us out. The dreadful disease that has befallen us is not the plague, but the venereal pox. Something has to be done,' he bellowed, thumping the table with his fist. 'If word gets out that St Andrews has become the Sodom and Gomorrah of our age, our cause will be lost.'

Appealing to Lindsay his fierce eyes misted over as he. 'Our ship is rudderless. Without guidance, this ship of fools will lose its way and sink fast. Sir David, you are the very man to lead us. Join us now and steer the reprobates in the right path. You have condemned the corruption of the Roman Catholic Church in your *Satire*. Denounce the depravity here too. They will listen to you.'

Lindsay pointed to his hoary head, 'I'm gey old for grand gestures. I'm not the one to lead you forward but, if you'll trust my judgment, I ken the very man who can.'

Chapter Sixty-Nine
A Dolent Death

And see ye not that bonnie road,
That winds about the fernie brae?
That is the road to fair Elfland,
Where thou and I this night maun gae.
—*The Ballad of Thomas the Rhymer,* Traditional

St Mary's Abbey, 21 March 1547

The flickering candles at the base of the icon cast an eerie light on the Black Madonna. The infant that had been wrenched from her arms was now clumsily bound against her chest with a hempen rope. Elisabeth had drawn up a stool, more comfortable than kneeling at the *prie-dieu,* to pour her heart out to the Virgin. She'd never disciplined herself to learn prayers by heart for, if truth be told, she had little faith in their magical power. She'd seen little evidence of heaven ever paying heed to their endless chants in Latin.

At times Elisabeth envied the certainty with which the pious Sister Agnes practised her faith, but then unlike Agnes, she had not chosen the religious life. Besides, if the all-knowing, all-seeing God had already determined everything that would ever happen, where was the use in praying? All her struggles to impose her will, to change the course of her life, had been thwarted; whereas Betsy's simple belief in destiny that you maun dree your weird was proving to be true. What will be will be. What's for you will no go by you.

Forbye, Betsy wouldn't thank her for her prayers. Knowing her time was up she was undaunted about passing over into the twilight world of the spirit. She'd left instructions as detailed as the Roman Catholic last rites for dealing with her death. No priest, no prayers and no pity. Her last wish was to bid farewell to her loved ones but would John Knox come in time?

If she couldn't pray for Betsy, then Elisabeth would strive to pray for Knox. Implore the Mother of Christ to lead him back to the fold. Divert him from the road to perdition. But the ballad of True Thomas kept trespassing into her *Pater Nosters*.

And see ye not that braid, braid road,
That lies across that lily leven?
That is the path of wickedness
Though some call it the road to heaven.

Elisabeth pressing her eyelids against her eyeballs to concentrate all her thoughts on Knox For a few moments there was nothing but darkness, endless black. Then, as the gloom slowly cleared, a tiny white figure appeared, floating away from her along a tunnel, receding into a distant radiance. As the weird feeling engulfed her, she knew that once he reached that eerie luminescence, he'd be lost forever, never to return.

With all her strength, she urged him to turn round and come back to her, but another, stronger power was drawing him towards the light. In this struggle of wills she felt as if her head would burst, but she couldn't let go: Come back! Come back to me, John! Don't go! A flash of light seemed to explode in her head. Colours flashed in front of her eyes. Suddenly there was no opposition, no resistance. She'd lost sight of him. He was gone. All went black.

'Lisbeth! I'm here! Can you hear me? Wake up!' a voice from afar was calling out.

Dazed and breathing heavily, she strained to raise her eyelids. As the mist slowly cleared from her eyes, she realised she'd toppled from the stool and was lying on the cold stone floor. Lindsay was kneeling over her and splashing her face with fusty smelling water from the font. His worried face was sepulchral grey as he hugged her close. The holy water might have revived her but she crinkled her nose when he tried to make her drink some. How many filthy fingers had been dunked in it?

'Have you brought him?' she murmured.

'Aye, he's here.'

Elisabeth heaved with a grateful sigh. 'Thank you for that, Davie.' Drained and wabbit, she nestled in closer to his embrace and closed her eyes.

In the corner of the outer chamber, Betsy lay cocooned in her cot. Over the last year or so she'd shrunk to the size of a wizened waif with weakened legs and a humpit back. Her auld bones were crumbling away and there was no cure for that. Dust to dust she'd remarked, a wry smile flitting over her desiccated lips. Her wrinkled hands were parchment thin and spotted like the paper of ancient books. No longer able to swallow, she licked the diluted aquavitae that Sister Agnes had dabbed on her lips to moisten them. Incense burned in holders to keep away the smell of death.

'She'll have no priest, John,' Sister Agnes said, wringing her hands. 'Nor the last rites.'

Then, bowing her head she whispered a guilty confession; she had taken the liberty of baptising her with holy water. The thought that Betsy would depart this world unshriven, in a state of original sin was too much to bear but what about other sins?

She lifted her distraught face to plead, 'John perhaps you could say even a short prayer to release her soul?'

Knox considered the dilemma. He no longer believed in purgatory, where sinners languished till Judgement Day unless released by prayer and indulgences, nor limbo, for unbaptised bairns and heathens, but the fate of Betsy's soul troubled him. If anyone deserved God's grace, it was Betsy who should be destined for eternal salvation, no matter what—baptised or unbaptised.

'I'll stay with her now. You have some rest.'

Sister Agnes gave a thankful nod before asking, 'Have you any word from Sister Katherine? I, that is we,... we've heard nothing.'

Neither had he. And it shamed him that Katherine, a mere woman, had shown far more courage than he had. She'd stayed with Wishart until grim death whereas he'd slunk away like a wounded, fear-stricken bear, spending the long, lonely dark winter hiding in safe houses all over the Lothians. His time in the wilderness was not a worthy episode.

'Is it true,' Sister Agnes's voice constricted as she went on, 'that she has fled for safety to Ayrshire,' she hesitated before adding, 'with Widow Ker?' A painful notion, judging by the frown on her flushed face and the tears welling in her eyes. 'Tell me, John, please. Will she ever come back?'

Knox was unable to console her for he didn't know. Deep sorrow etched Sister Agnes's as she crossed herself and slipped out.

As he bent towards the cot, Betsy's eyelids flickered.

'Is that you Meg?' she muttered.

He followed her gaze towards the Orkney chair by the fireside. Meg's chair, that Betsy had retrieved from Hailes, was empty but were her eyes, clouded to the present world, already seeing beyond to the next?

'No, it's me, Betsy. It's John Knox.' With no belief in the Romish last rites, what succour could he offer his beloved Betsy in her final hours? How to soothe kindly, warm and comforting Betsy, who'd loved him with a mother's unconditional love. He could only think to stroke her forehead.

'Johnnie,' she murmured. 'My wee laddie.'

Her clawlike hand grabbed his finger and held on to it. Her puckered lips twitched restlessly as if recounting a long tale.

‘I’m here, Betsy.’ His voice was husky as he choked back tears.

‘Don’t greet any tears for me, son. It’s my time.’

Betsy Learmont, whose stories of the past were so scrambled with ballads, tales and superstitions that the truth was obscured, was facing the final reality. Did she hold the secret? Could she see beyond the veil?

‘Betsy,’ he whispered, anxious for some guidance, ‘what am I to do? What is my fate to be?’

Knox feared the future. Wishart had bidden him lay down his two-handed sword and take up the torch; there must be one who would keep the flame of enlightenment and reform alight. Come with me to share my fate and it shall be extinguished, he’d said, but what should he do? Remain in Scotland and risk being burnt at the stake? Flee to Germany where sympathisers would shelter him until it was safe to return? Would that be seen as the coward’s way out?

‘Words no swords.’ Betsy squeezed his finger tightly and began to mutter the words of the Fairy Queen:

O see ye not yon narrow road,
So thick beset with thorns and briars?
That is the path of righteousness,
Though after it but few enquires.

Gasping for breath, Betsy broke off and then said, ‘Tell it to me, Johnnie. True Thomas, tell it to me, laddie.’

Hesitantly at first, Knox took up the lines of the legend, with Betsy filling in when he stumbled or forgot.

My tongue is mine ain, true Thomas said:
A goodly gift ye would gie to me!

‘That is your gift, John, and your fate,’ Betsy mumbled.

In the abbey chapel, Elisabeth gave her head a good shake, adjusted her wimple and pushed back the strands of hair that had escaped. The jaggy thistle was back to her prickly self.

'It's a blessing that Wishart is dead, for now we can pick up where we left off.'

'A blessing?' Lindsay blurted. 'How many people did Wishart burn at the stake?' He tried to calm the irritation in his voice. 'Surely it's an even greater blessing that Beaton is dead.'

She gave him a long, hard look. 'Did he have a dolent death?' she taunted, her words carefully chosen to let him know that she'd read his poem. *The Tragedy of the Cardinal* expressed no sympathy for Beaton's assassination; not only did it absolve the murderers but judged them to be divinely inspired.

Lindsay inclined his head. A shadow of a smile passed over his face lined with worry and age. 'And now that his reign of terror is over, it's crucial for us to carry on making reforms within the church.'

'For you, perhaps, but not John.' Elisabeth pursed her lips. 'I forbid you to take him back with you. You're to blame for his abandoning the priesthood. Ever since yon *Satire* of yours, he's fancied himself as Divine Correction, doughty Diligence or some such other daft conceit. It's high time he dropped the play-acting.' Reinvigorated with colour flooding back into her cheeks, she was ready to wrestle for Knox's immortal soul if necessary. 'He needs time to clear his dirling head of these dangerous ideas. Heresy is hearsay! He's become so fey, as if he's been blasted by a fairy wind. He can bide here until all this... mayhem blows over.'

Lindsay snorted. 'Play-acting! Mayhem! Is that how you see the most important reformation taking place in the church in all its centuries of history! You want to pull John back towards the dying church and I'm pushing him towards ideas which will breathe new life into its sluggish soul.'

'Is that how *you* see it?' Elisabeth sneered. 'I won't let you do it, Davie,' she declared, for only she could save Knox from this pernicious path that would lead to burning at the stake or the gallows. 'I shall send John to France. To Cardinal de Guise.

Under his guidance, John will be made to see sense. He shall become a bishop and then—who kens?—even a cardinal one day, and then John will have *real* power to make those changes you're so keen on.' She turned to go but he grabbed her arm.

'Listen to me, Lisbeth. John is a man of what, thirty years? Old enough and wise enough to make up his own mind, and here we are squabbling over him as if he were a three-year-old bairn.'

His words stopped her dead. Still feeling giddy from her recent dwam, she began to sway. As Lindsay caught hold of her, she gazed at him, desperation in her eyes.

'But Davie, you don't understand. To me that's what he is. My bairn. John is not just my godson.' Her voice became ragged as she forced out the words. 'He's... my... son.'

The light of life was fading fast from Betsy's befuddled eyes but, seeing her lips move, Knox leant in closer to hear her.

'Lungs fit for a preacher,' she muttered mysteriously.

Uncertain how to reply, Knox tried to recall more lines from the ballad:

Betide me weal, betide me woe,
That weird shall never daunton me.

His stammering recitation seemed to please her, for a dim smile flitted over her blue-tinged lips before Betsy closed her eyelids for the last time. With tears clouding his eyes, Knox kissed her gently on her cooling forehead. He watched her chest rise and fall, lower and lower each time, as her breathing become more and more shallow. Whenever there was a long pause, he considered calling for Sister Agnes, but Betsy clung on with surprising strength to his finger. The candle spluttered and guttered. Sitting in the gloaming, he could hear voices coming from the prioress's chamber next door.

Elisabeth and Lindsay had left the chapel by the secret passageway to her chamber. She leant against the stone mullion to cool her flushed cheek, as he poured her a good measure of cognac.

'So,' Lindsay began, 'Sister Maryoth's story was true? That you were with child?'

'Aye, I had a bairn, Davie,' she began warily, her shoulders curved, her arms tightly crossed over her chest as she strove to keep the polished nut of grief intact in its neatly sewn pocket. 'A wee laddie. A son.' Unspoken for all this time, these words, soaked in tears came spilling out, burning her cheeks. Lindsay hesitated, yearning but not daring to place his hands on her shoulders. 'But I thought you said you'd lost him.'

'I have, Davie, but not in the way you think. It's time you heard the truth.'

St Mary's Abbey, 1528

Nearly twenty years ago, when hearing about Elisabeth's plan to elope with Lindsay, Betsy had kept her head bowed, twiddling her thumbs nervously in the lap of her apron. There was aye a shoogly stone at everybody's door, she'd said and what she was about to tell her might change her mind or it might no.

She'd taken a deep breath that whistled in her throat. 'I've borne this secret like a skelf in my side for many a year, thinking whether I should tell you, or take it with me to the grave.'

But now if Lisbeth was leaving and she might never see her again, it was time to tell her the truth. Elisabeth's memory of the birth was hazy: she'd made sure of that. As soon as her waters had broken, Betsy had given her a potion that dulled the pain and made her drowsy. Not even the ferocious yell her laddie gave as he tumbled into the world roused her from her drugged doze.

'Lungs fit for a preacher,' Betsy had mumbled cheerlessly. She'd been sorely aggrieved that Prior Hepburn had made her promise to do away with the bairn as soon as it was born.

Baptise it with a splash of water or some morning dew, he'd said and then do the needful. The easiest and quickest way to do away with an unwanted or sickly wean was to press on the bone at the back of its neck and pull the head back swiftly. But she had no heart to throttle this braw wee fighter and send him prematurely to kingdom come. God's heavenly choir would have to wait for its divine trumpeter.

'So I gave him to Maggie Knox to suckle. The widow was rich in milk but poor in silver and so was glad enough to take in him.'

''Btu what happened to her bairn? The one we delivered?'

'The poor wee mite you breathed life into was a changeling. I should have snapped its head off there and then or just let him die for want of breath but for your pleading and the promise you made to his mother. Pity that thon scarth had ever seen the light of day.'

'Scarth?' Elisabeth queried.

'That's what we cry those creatures that are neither one thing nor the other, neither lad nor lass. He'd been shrivelled by the fairy blast, afore he even took his first breath so your blast of air couldn't save him. He failed to thrive and so it was a mercy when he slipped away a few days after his christening.'

Elisabeth could hardly believe what Betsy was saying: it sounded as fanciful as one of her tales.

The effort of telling the truth brought out beads of sweat on Betsy's brow. 'Aye, Maggie Knox kept your son and brought him up as her own until she passed away, poor lass. She never got o'er her man's death at Flodden.'

Elisabeth leapt to her feet, too quickly, for the sudden rush of blood to her head made her feel giddy. Tapsalteerie! Whigmaleerie! 'Betsy! What are you saying?' she yelped.

'What do you think? John is your own son. With his mother's thrawn head and his father's glib tongue. Aye, and Hepburn lungs,' she said nodding her head. 'Fit for a preacher.'

Throughout her confession, Elisabeth had stood with her back to Lindsay, sipping her cognac.

'So, then, it was true that Harry Cockburn,' he broke off, 'that he ravished you?'

She drained the goblet before answering. 'That's what I let them think when they found out I was with child,' she began. A glimmer of a sarcastic smile skimmed her lips, 'in order to save *your* skin that my enraged uncle was ready to flay and to wipe that smug smirk off Maryoth's scheming face. What a naïve creature I was. Nay, you may cast me as being as wanton or as sensual as one of your dames, but I'm sorry to disappoint you. The only man I've ever lain with, the only man I've ever had carnal dalliance with, is you, Davie Lindsay.'

'What?' he pressed his fingers against his temples to ease the crushing thought. 'So what are you telling me...?'

'That John my son,' her voice wavered, 'is also your son. Our son.'

Lindsay fell quiet as he took in this news. 'And you never told me, Lisbeth? Why?'

She sucked in her breath. 'I was going to tell you. After I learnt about it from Betsy, when we were planning to elope. Again. At the time I thought we'd take John with us so that we three would be together. Our wee family. An indivisible trinity,' she scoffed. 'That was before I learnt about Jessie and before I realised that you'd already made your choice. Since King James would always have first claim on you, I made *my* choice and kept John for myself.'

Lindsay nodded. Her accusation was justified. 'And have you told him?' he asked.

'Nay, and now I'm thinking perhaps I should have. But the time never seemed right. After you left, he became so thrawn and bull-horned that I feared he might hate me, blame me, if I told him. I didn't want to lose his respect, his love.' She gave a little laugh. 'I was his Madonna but he didn't know he was my child! And I made him solemnly swear that he wouldn't follow the path of heresy. The one you, his own father, are determined to lead him down. If he's taken from me…' she tailed off, unable to bring herself to admit that her life, her future would have no meaning. 'Mind the grief that engulfed you when you lost your beloved monarchs? That's how I feel now. Bereft.'

'Lisbeth, I'm sorry,' was all Lindsay could manage to say. Lost for words, the silver-tongued poet kept shaking his head and apologising. 'So sorry. If only I'd known. If only you'd told me. No wonder you can never forgive me.'

He moved towards her and, as their eyes locked, he caught a fleeting glimpse of her pent-up pain, a fleck of grief in her ferny green eyes. For a split second it seemed possible that, by holding her close, he could breach her defence wall and share her sorrow. Even start again where they always seemed to be leaving off. Now that he was free, of both monarch and wife, they could spend their remaining years together, with John, their son—their future.

Just as he was about to say all this, Elisabeth blinked and looked away. She threw back her shoulders and straightened up to confront him: once more the efficient, capable prioress.

'What's done is done, Davie Lindsay. No use picking over old scabs, as Betsy would say.' Feigning a cheery smile, she licked the salt tears collecting at the corners of her mouth and poured another cognac.

Lindsay ran his fingers through his greying hair, still struggling to come to terms with this startling revelation. 'But what is to be done, Lisbeth?'

'All I ask, Davie, is that you don't take John away from me.'

She stood facing him, arms crossed, waiting for him to give his consent. The tense pall of silence was becoming unbearable until the heavy curtain between the two chambers was drawn back.

Knox seemed hardly aware of their presence as he moved between them like a wraith towards the window. 'Betsy asked me to open all the doors and windows,' he said bleakly, tears staining his cheeks. 'To let her spirit gang free.'

Chapter Seventy
Gethsemane

O my Father, if it be possible,
let this cup pass from me.
—*Matthew* XXVI:39

St Andrews Parish Church, Ascension Sunday 1547

Shameless snores reverberated throughout the nave of St Andrews Kirk from those in the congregation who had nodded off. Knox didn't blame them. He, too, was finding it difficult to keep awake as the preacher rambled on, dropping his listeners off along the way. At his side, his three lads yawned and fidgeted on their stools, unable to follow John Rough's lengthy, convoluted argument. Rough by name and rough by learning as he'd be the first to admit, the Ayrshire preacher was a man of the heart not of the head. He knew only too well that his unpolished sermons failed to command the crowd's attention and had pleaded with Knox to preach, but he'd always refused. He'd only agreed to come to the besieged castle of St Andrews to continue educating his pupils.

As his attention wandered away from the sermon, he wondered if it had been the right thing to do. After Beaton's murder the new archbishop of St Andrews was hunting down Wishart's disciples and Knox was on his list. He'd considered fleeing to Germany, but Hugh Douglas and John Cockburn were loath to lose their sons' tutor.

'Why not join the Castilians in St Andrews? Lindsay had suggested. 'You'll not only be safer there, but your presence will help to quell the anarchy that's threatening to overwhelm their cause until the English army—expected any day—arrives. And take your lads with you.'

Late on Maundy Thursday evening, their band of fugitives had huddled in a cove near Aberlady, waiting for the boat to ferry them across to Fife under cover of darkness. When a rough fishing coble emerged from the mist, they took off their shoes and waded through the shallows towards it.

'Welcome aboard, Johnnie.' The burly skipper slapped him on the back and shook his arm firmly.

It took Knox a few seconds to recognise the full-bearded, weather-beaten sailor as his brother whom he hadn't seen for many a long year. William dragged a deckhand by the scruff of the neck saying, 'Do you mind this braw laddie? Jamie's got a sturdy pair of sea shanks,'

The waif Knox had rescued with his sister Isabelle gave a shy smile before William sent him away with a smack on the back of the legs.

'I'm only a humble fisherman, Johnnie, but I hear you're to become a fisher of men,' William went on. 'So never fear. Now you're one of our select band, we'll aye be behind you.'

Towards midnight Skipper Will lowered the sail. 'It's bad luck to sail on Good Friday,' he told him, 'but seeing we've sworn to get you there somehow, needs must. '

As he and his bosun took to the oars, he signalled for Knox and his lads to take up the spare ones. 'The more the merrier and the swifter the sooner,' he grinned.

Early on Good Friday morning, they landed near Earlsferry where a cart was waiting to transport them overland. Knox held out a blistered hand to his brother. 'I pray I never have to pull an oar again. May God be with you, brother.'

Skipper Will gave a deep, throaty laugh and hugged Knox in a manly embrace, bidding him God speed.

Very early on Easter Sunday morning, a builder's cart carried Knox and his bairns into the castle. It was then going to smuggle out the salt-sodden corpse of Beaton, the carter confided. A fitting end for the proud Romish potentate, steeped in the puddle of papistry, Knox had sneered.

After only a few days in St Andrews, Knox regretted having brought his lads to this city of sin where sloth, drunkenness and fornication were rife. This Sodom and Gomorrah was no place for young men. To keep his lads away from temptations of the flesh, he'd established a rigorous regime in the parish church that served as his schoolhouse and had invited anyone wishing to learn to come along to his lessons.

'You are clearly called by God.' Henry Balnaves was impressed, not only by Knox's expositions of the scripture and Calvin's catechism, but his teaching of Latin and Greek authors. This experienced civil servant, a procurator in the consistorial courts, had plans to establish a religious settlement of the type being set up in England. Knox would be a valuable recruit.

Painfully aware of his inadequacies, John Rough had begged Knox to take to the pulpit in his place. 'You have a voice for preaching, not me,' he said, 'and a gift for putting in plain words the message of the gospels.'

Knox could not agree. It was one thing to teach Calvinist doctrines to the few, but another to take on the more responsible rôle of preacher to the many. At the very least t would lead to persecution and exile and, at worst, to an agonising death like Wishart's. Nor did he wish to appear presumptuous. But then, he fretted, was he being deliberately deaf to his call? And how would God communicate his will? With a hallowed whisper in his lug?

Now the sudden change of pitch in Rough's tone from a dull drone to a thunderous bellow startled Knox and all those around him. Those who'd dozed off shook themselves awake and looked up in astonishment at Rough who seemed to be raising a lather about the power of the congregation to elect ministers of the church.

'Brother, be not offended!' he bawled. 'In the name of God, and of his Son, Jesus Christ, and in the name of these present, I charge you not to refuse this holy vocation.'

His lads were squirming on their stools, stifling sniggers as Knox turned to see where the pointing finger led.

'Hearken to the very last words of the Blessed Christ on his Ascension: Go out into the world and preach the gospel to the whole of creation: he who believes and is baptised will be saved; he who refuses belief will be condemned...'

Realising that Rough was directing his words at him Knox felt a spine-chilling wave of fear flooding through him. Cold sweat soused his forehead, his palms became clammy and the blood roared in his ears. He blinked away unwelcome tears, dangerously welling in his eyes and, opening his mouth to answer, found he could not speak. Despite swallowing hard and moistening his lips, his voice sounded strangely muffled as he addressed the congregation.

'Truly, is this your charge to me? And do you approve this vocation?'

'Aye, and we approve it,' they answered with one voice.

His eyes darkened as the pillars of the nave closed in on him and Rough's gruff voice echoed as if from a deep chasm. He could feel fiery flames lapping his ankles and licking his legs. Rising to his feet, he struggled to steady himself and, before his shaking legs could crumple beneath him, he hurtled down the aisle, past David Lindsay and Henry Balnaves, their mouths agape.

For several days Knox endured his personal agony locked in his room but, as he did with Christ in the Garden of Gethsemane, God remained silent. He heard no reassuring call, no response to his prayers. Answer came there none. Only the voice of his own conscience tormented him, taunting him for being a coward, a feardie-gowk. He, who had been so proud to bear the two-handed sword, threatening to smite anyone who dared to harm his master, had then dropped it at the first sign of trouble. In the footsteps of the apostle Peter, after his brave show of cutting off the soldier's ear, he'd also gone on to deny his Lord thrice.

He recalled that fateful night outside the kirk in Haddington where, petrified by a deep sense of foreboding—or was it cowardice?—he'd watched the swirling January fog swallow up the tall, stooping figure of his master. The spot on his cheek where Wishart had kissed him farewell, burned with shame, an eternal stigma that would never wash away. Then again he'd abandoned him at his trial and crucifixion in St Andrews.

And now the third and final betrayal: refusing the call to take up the torch for his master. In this he was even more blameworthy than Bothwell, labelled Judas Iscariot by many for delivering up Wishart to Beaton. But, like Judas, weak-willed Bothwell could be forgiven for doing what had to be done whereas Knox was being weighed in the balance and found wanting. He wasn't brave enough to die for his faith: *Timor mortis conturbat me.*

Outside his door, David Lindsay had set up camp to wait.

'John,' he called through the keyhole. 'Do you mind when we first met? The long hours we spent discussing how to reform the church? You said that preaching was vital to teach the lay folk. For few can read but all might hear, isn't that what you said?' When there was no reply he went on. 'I jalouse you're praying for guidance, for a sign. But think on this. Does God not make use of unlikely messengers?'

Knox listened in silence, willing him to go away. Lord I am not worthy: Father, take this chalice from me.

'The time has come, John. The folk are waiting. Your life's journey has led you to the steps of the pulpit. You cannot flee your fate.'

Ascension Sunday, the time for death and mourning was making way for the season of resurrection, rebirth and renewal of the spirit. What were Betsy's last words? Lungs fit for a preacher. Well, then, Father, not *my* will, but thine be done. He unsnecked the door to give entry to Lindsay.

Chapter Seventy-One
Nunraw

Choose thy counsel of the most sapient,
Without regard to blood, riches or rent.
—*The Testament of the Papingo,* Sir David Lindsay, 16th Century

St Mary's Abbey, May 1547

'The English are coming! The English are coming!'

Jean Hamilton's high-pitched shrieks as she sped about the courtyard threatened to spread panic and mayhem. 'We will be murdered! Raped! Roughly wooed!' she bawled.

On her next turn of the courtyard, she ran full pelt into Elisabeth who grabbed her firmly by the shoulders. Glaikit Jeanie had inherited the Hamilton slack jaw and thick drooling lips which could make her look fey or daft or sleekit or all three: living proof that years of interbreeding produced unhealthy offspring.

'Now, now Jeanie, no need for false alarms,' Elisabeth said.

Waving a pamphlet above her head, she lisped, 'But it thays tho here!'

A claim the prioress found hard to believe for, whatever cant the pamphlet was promoting, unlearned and unteachable Jeanie wouldn't be able to read it.

'But we will be! The English are pagan heathens! They want to grab the queen. And she's promised to my brother.'

'Mind, your father is in command of the soldiers, Jeanie. He shall see that no harm comes to us.'

Jeanie thought for a moment her thick lips slowly broadened into a self-important smile.

'Aye, and he will thave uth from the English for the Lord ith on our thide.'

'If that is true, Jeanie, then all the more reason to stay calm. Be brave and your father will be proud of you.' How she would love to slap her silly face, but she dared not incur Arran's wrath. Instead, she prised the pamphlet from the girl's sweaty grasp, tucked it into her sleeve and went to meet her guest.

In the guest chamber, the Lord Governor of Scotland was savouring their hospitality, munching on dainties and slurping one of Sister Agnes's famous liqueurs. He twirled the empty goblet in his fingers, squinting his eyes to examine it.

'My Jeanie is used to eating with the best cutlery from the finest crockery. She has complained that you won't let her use the gilt knives and silver forks I sent her,' Regent Arran whinged.

'Your gifts, however generous, my lord, are much too extravagant for a fourteen-year-old. May I remind you, lord governor, that this is a Cistercian nunnery in Haddington, and not the de Medici court in Florence.'

Though spoilt Jeanie Hamilton strutted around the cloister as if it were a Renaissance palace, drawing envious glances from the other girls at her expensive velvet cloak trimmed with gold thread that trailed behind her sweeping the cobbles. Chattering like a nest of fledglings they huddled together and clyped about her kists full of costly clothes and jewellery and other expensive gifts from her indulgent father.

'Nothing is too good for my bonnie Jeanie,' Arran replied, his eyes dewy with adoration. 'Whatever her heart desires she shall have.'

But not out of his own pocket, Elisabeth was tempted to add, for it rankled that he blatantly funded his generous gifts to his bonnie wee Jeanie from the Scots' public purse and English gold. For twa-fangelt Arran had changed sides more often than his clothes and Queen Marie no longer trusted him. In her view, he was to blame for not stopping Hertford's troops as they laid waste and set fire to all towns and villages along the coast on their way to Edinburgh. Not satisfied with looting, pillaging and raping the capital, they then destroyed Holyrood Abbey and desecrated the tomb of her husband, James V, and her sons much to the shock of the unshockable 'cock of the north'. George Gordon, earl of Huntly greatly disliked the rough manner of Henry VIII's wooing and bristled at being bullied into love.

Now, in exchange for money and advancement, Arran was conspiring with Somerset to snatch the young Queen Mary and send her to be married to his heir, King Edward. If that fell through, Arran proposed to betroth her to his own son.

'Without more ado, let's get down to business. It has come to my attention that, er... as prioress of St Mary's Abbey, you are under an ancient engagement to keep the fortlet of Nunraw from the auld enemies of England and er ... all others ... er... ' Arran peered through shortsighted eyes as he ran a sticky finger down the tattered parchment. 'And that you shall not deliver er... said place to any manner of persons than me as lord governor, or cause it to be razed to the ground, so that no habitationer may benefit from er... that time forth er... ' he stuttered with a tongue too big for his mouth.

Elisabeth raised her eyes to heaven. And I am to take orders from this flichty birkie of dubious birth, she thought resentfully. A weak, silly man who hid his stupidity under the mangled language of officiousness but who, nevertheless, could be dangerous.

'Pray tell me, my lord governor,' she opened her arms in a gesture of supplication, 'how would you advise us, weak, defenceless sisters of religion to defend this important fortalice and then—God forbid that the English attack us—to destroy it? That is, of course, if they do not rape and murder us first.'

Arran's brow furrowed as he struggled with her question. 'You must remove yourselves to Nunraw, Dame Prioress. Forthwith. It is an ancient ruling.'

If he were planning to requisition the abbey for his troops, she'd rather he spat it out, for then she could negotiate conditions.

'Furthermore,' Arran stuttered, 'I need to ensure the safety of my daughter. I have no wish for another of my bairns to be seized.'

She bristled. So that was it. The selfish hypocrite was prepared to gamble with the queen's life but would move heaven and earth—or the nunnery at least—to safeguard that of his spoilt darling. She pressed her hands together, seemingly in a gesture of prayer but in an effort to curb her anger.

'I understand your concern, but surely Jeanie will be safer here, at St Mary's, where you and the brave Scots army can defend us.' She feigned an innocent smile. 'Forbye, the fortlet of Nunraw is nothing more than a primitive keep. We will not only be isolated there but without supplies, without water, without defence.'

Arran frowned as he considered this. His bonnie Jeanie would not fare well without her comforts. Sensing his uncertainty, Elisabeth's voice brimmed with helpless pleading.

'And will you, as our governor and chief lord, help us, weak sisters in Christ, to arrange our flitting?'

He nodded hesitantly, wary of what he might be agreeing to.

'Let me see,' Elisabeth began, 'how many horses and carts will we need? The bedridden and the lame will have to be moved and, of course, our sisters, and then all maids and serving lasses and scullions.' Elisabeth began counting on her fingers. 'And our young maidens with all their baggage. We cannot expect genteel daughters of the gentry, such as Lady Jean, to leave behind their belongings,' she added with a sideways glance, 'and of course an armed guard to escort us.'

As the list grew, Arran's slack jaw sagged even more.

'At such a perilous time,' she went on, 'when danger threatens the whole nation, it is most generous of you to spare soldiers and transport. However, the greater sacrifice lies in your willingness to place the safety of our little community above the well-being of your troops.'

A baffled frown creased his brow as he struggled to follow her reasoning.

'For, if we are to be moved to Nunraw, our sisters will not be on hand to nurse and tend your wounded soldiers.'

Chapter Seventy-Two
The Paraclete

And they were all filled with the Holy Ghost
and began to speak with other tongues.
—*The Acts* II:4

Pentecost Sunday, 1547

Knox hovered at the door of the vestry and fumbled in the pocket of his gown for the phial. Lindsay's gift—the power of speechmaking—could only be activated he believed, by these precious drops.

'As soon as you open your mouth you will know whether or no God has chosen you,' Lindsay had declared, 'and to fan the flames of divine inspiration, sip this to loosen your tongue.'

Since anxiety rather than fear was crippling Knox, Lindsay had been prescribing a tincture of arcanum. A few miniscule drops at a time were enough to stave off an attack of the cringes and allay his gnawing doubt that Satan was puffing him up with self-pride. Lindsay had come across Paracelsus's remedy In Denmark. He'd found it beneficial for calming down anxiety before confronting an audience. Knox clearly suffered from the same frailty. He was his father's son, after all.

Over the past week, the makar of plays had been helping Knox to write and rehearse his sermon.

'Think on how I taught you to act as Divine Correction in my *Satire*. Now you are no longer John Knox the Catholic priest, but John Knox, preacher and reformer. This is the rôle you must play from now on. Leave your past behind.'

At Lindsay's cue, Knox inhaled deeply and mounted the steps to the pulpit. Wasting no time, he launched into a tirade against the false teachings of the Romish Church, denouncing the pope as the Anti-Christ and Whore of Babylon and roundly condemning the doctrines of clerical celibacy, fasting, purgatory and the Mass. His powerful sermon, endorsed with references from the Book of Daniel and the Epistles of St Paul, pleased many of the congregation.

'Master George Wishart never spoke so plainly, and yet he was burnt. And so will this one be,' John Leslie feared.

'This is even more successful than we'd hoped,' Henry Balnaves remarked. 'Your playwright practices have paid off, Sir David.'

While both men were thrilled at his performance, Lindsay was less so. In spite of Elisabeth's wishes he had gone ahead and lured Knox to the pulpit. On his advice, Knox had taken the Book of Daniel as his inspiration, condemning pilgrimages, pardons and priests as being wicked and unnecessary trappings, but then he'd gone on to argue that good deeds did not guarantee eternal salvation: that Christ's blood purged all our sins and that man was justified by faith alone. He had gone too far.

Lindsay had assumed he could direct Knox's thinking and divert his radical ideas into reforming the Roman Catholic Church but Knox had seriously deviated from the script. It was clear to Lindsay that, while he was still clinging desperately to the branches of the withered fig tree, Knox was hacking at the roots. He had a mind of his own. Like someone else he knew. Lindsay was crushed.

Taking the congregation's positive reaction as the sign he was looking for, there was no holding Knox back. He had found his voice: and not only lungs fit for a preacher but those of a thundering prophet of the Old Testament. From then on, Knox preached a sermon every Sunday, filling the kirk not only with those cooped up in the castle, but with folk from the city and university of St Andrews and beyond. Until his heterodoxy reached the ears of the church authorities.

Early on Sunday morning, on entering the parish kirk, Lindsay was puzzled to notice that the saints' statues were still covered in the purple cloaks of mourning for the crucified Christ even though Passiontide and Holy Week were long past. In the centre of the nave, Knox was laying out goblets and plates on a white cloth spread over a trestle table.

'What are you doing?' Lindsay asked.

'This,' Knox explained, 'is the Lord's table. Where priest and layman, noble and commoner, stout citizen and broken man shall break bread together and pass the common cup from hand to hand. Unlike the papish church, we evangelicals shall welcome John the Commonweal to the Lord's table and treat him as an equal.'

Lindsay nodded slowly. He could hardly disagree with his own words. 'They mean to silence you, John.'

Knox looked up from laying his holy table. 'How so? Condemn and burn me? Like they did to Master Wishart?'

'Nay,' Lindsay replied, 'not so drastic. To make sure you've no opportunity of spreading heresy beyond the castle walls, they're going to prevent you from preaching on Sundays. Dean Annan is making arrangements for clergy from the abbey and the university to occupy the pulpit every Sunday from now on.'

'I shall not let them gag the true word of God,' Knox retorted. 'Sunday may be dedicated to God Almighty, but every day is the Lord's Day. I will preach on every other day of the week.'

Lindsay shook his head. 'You won't be allowed to, John. To expose the heresy of your propositions, you're to be challenged to a religious duel.'

Knox snorted. 'A duel! Against whom? Dean Annan?'

'Nay, he dares not joust with you. He's sending in his champion, that doughty debater, sub-prior Winram.'

'Then I shall win,' Knox declared confidently, his dark blue eyes gleaming. Not only because his training as a notary had equipped him to argue and dispute every point of an argument but because as, one of God's elect, he had unshakeable faith in his convictions. Unlike Winram who, since meeting Wishart, had been wavering in his beliefs. The truth for the friar, once so crystal clear, was becoming murky.

Thus, when called before the convention of Dominican and Franciscans in the yard of St Leonards, Knox refused to defend himself against thon grey friars and black fiends. Instead, playing devil's advocate he asked, 'Can any person here prove that any one of the nine articles was inconsistent with the truth of God?'

Annan hissed at Winram, 'Go on! Trounce the heretic.'

With great reluctance the sub-prior stuttered and stammered his points, becoming more and more dispirited as Knox outwitted him at every turn. Aware that he was beaten, Winram called on one of the other Franciscans to carry on the dispute. Friar Arbuckle, too, was soon outsmarted, being driven to the astounding statement—as heretical as any of Knox's own —that the apostles had not received the Holy Ghost until after they had written their epistles.

'Hark at the learned theologian,' Knox taunted. 'Hoisted with his own petard. I fear Friar Arbuckle is so wandered in the mist of his own arguments that he's fallen in a foul mire,' Knox scoffed. 'The Abbot of Unreason in the season of misrule has more coherent arguments than these so-called learned minds of the catholic church.'

Chapter Seventy-Three
Black Saturday

Though love be hot, yet in ane man of age
It kindles nocht so soon as in youtheid.
The Treatise of the Twa Marrit Women and the Widow
William Dunbar, 15th–16th Century

St Mary's Abbey, 8 September 1547

Wheesht! Wheesht! Haud yer wheesht! Elisabeth silently pleaded as the peal of bells from St Mary's Kirk jangled in her skull. She sank her head into the soft pillow, pulling it round her ears to muffle the scunnersome sound. But the carillon persisted, not only in honour of St Mary, but as a call to arms for the townsfolk, warning them that the English forces were on their way. There would be no procession for the Miracle of the Flood today. Instead, the Black Madonna had been taken for safekeeping to St Mary's Kirk where a mass imploring Our Lady's intercession in the coming conflict would be celebrated.

Elisabeth would not be joining them. Vivid nightmares had brought on a pounding migraine. At the mirk hour of the morning, the macabre procession of hamstrung corpses jigging their dance of death had tormented her sleep, with the leering skull at its head jeering:

At Pinkie Cleugh there shall be spilt, much gentle blood that day.

Let the quick of the earth live in hope but they will die in despair.

She must have cried out for Sister Agnes came running. After changing Elisabeth's sweat sodden nightdress, she'd prepared a tisane of feverfew to soothe her thudding head. Fluttering anxiously like an agitated mort-heid moth at a taper, she'd been loath to leave her, but Elisabeth was glad to be left alone.

'Go and sing your praises to the Madonna, Agnes, and ray for victory over the heathen English.'

'And for our young queen to be delivered safely to France,' Sister Agnes added and left.

Whether through prayer or witchcraft, Catherine de Medici, queen of France, had, after ten fruitless years of consulting doctors, astrologers and even sorcerers, at last given birth to her first son in January 1544. Though delicate and undersized because of the gruesome potions the Italian witch had taken or the pox, the puny prince had managed to survive to the age of four. King Henri was gallantly offering this precious prize, the dauphin, to the Queen of Scots.

Not without a fight from his rival, the nine-year-old King Edward, under the Duke of Somerset's protection. Even more determined to enforce the Treaty of Greenwich, his manner of wooing was proving more sophisticated than that of Edward's recently departed father. Not content with attacking on several fronts, Protector Somerset was waging a war of words in a series of epistles and proclamations. Almighty God had come down firmly on the English side, so claimed the pamphlet that Elisabeth had confiscated from Jean Hamilton.

Had the Lord not manifested his divine will in the deaths of King James and his two sons, leaving a girl queen so perfect a match for England's boy king? And such a union would not only divert the Scots from following a false religion but would free them from false friends, their so-called ancient allies, the villainous French. Elisabeth's first instinct had been to consign the polemical pamphlet to the flames but had kept it—just in case.

Elisabeth pulled the bed curtains together to shield the light slicing through her eyelids, and then slipped off her muslin cap to massage the deep crease in her forehead left by the starched linen wimple. Smoothing her hair, she noticed that not only was it losing its lustre—no wonder, being forever crushed beneath the tight-fitting cap—but that it was now spun through with silver. No point in denying or regretting it—she was growing old. Now that the tight band crushing her scalp had eased, she hoped to doze off.

A soft click alerted her. The panel of the secret entrance in the garderobe was opening and a slight draught stirred the bed-curtains. She lay quietly, holding her breath. All the sisters had gone to mass and the scullery maids would be gossiping idly in the kitchen. She was alone. The English wouldn't have appeared so silently. They would have rampaged their way through the abbey running amok, breaking down doors, looting and pillaging. Thieves, then, assuming the abbey to be deserted, but how could they have found the secret passage? She had nothing to defend herself: not even her wooden crucifix. Better to lie still and feign sleep. With luck they might not notice her. She clasped her hands together on top of the coverlet and let her breath slip softly through parted lips.

A chair shoogled and then the bed-curtains twitched, letting in a chink of light. She took a deep breath. It might be her last. Sensing someone standing over her, she fought the desire to open her eyes but, raising her eyelids ever so slightly, she could peek through from underneath her eyelashes. Holding her breath, she lay as rigid as a corpse.

But when the shadowy figure leant over, first stroking her hair and then brushing her forehead with his lips, she gave an astonished squeal. As the Grey Friar sprang backwards, his cowl slipped down.

'Davie Lindsay, you ghoul! You scared me half to death!'

'Lisbeth! It's you! And you're alive!'

'No thanks to you. This trick of yours is becoming a habit. Twice in a lifetime is two times too often.'

'And you affrighted me. Lying there as still and pale as a corpse with your hair spread out on the pillow like that, I thought you were dead.'

In his friar's guise, Lindsay had sneaked in unseen along the secret passage from the chapel for he needed to speak with her. The shock of seeing her like this, however, was making him tremble and he gripped the bedpost to steady his shaking hands. Seeing his face as grey as his monk's habit, she patted the bed beside her, inviting him to join her. They lay quietly for a while, like two figures carved on a marble sarcophagus, only the rise and fall of their chests revealing signs of life.

'Here we are, lying together like a lang-marrit couple,' she sniffed. 'Me an ancient crone and you an auld birkie.'

'Or even a larbar. Ever the jaggy thistle, but I'll not take offence now,' he sighed. 'Not after all this time—how long has it been?'

She began counting up. 'Why, this will be thirty-four years almost to the day of our handfasting! The year of Flodden! When we plighted our troth and promised to keep tryst. Do you mind, Davie?'

He minded only too well. The spectre of Flodden raised painful memories of that tragic time and now, with the English army at their gate, the country was under threat once again. 'And I fear that once again we will be crushed,' he said morosely.

Elisabeth could not disagree, for her nightmare had left her with a deep sense of foreboding. The lines from her dream about blood being spilt at Pinkie Cleugh bothered her. 'One of True Thomas's prophecies that Betsy once told me.'

Lindsay shook his head. 'Let's be done with portents and omens for I have some news.' He raised himself up onto his elbow to gaze down on her.

'Tidings of joy, I hope,' she said but his furrowed brow told her otherwise.

'From St Andrews.'

When his hand sought hers, she didn't pull away but held onto it tightly, bracing herself to hear the worst.

'John has been taken captive,' Lindsay said at last.

'Oh!' Elisabeth let out a little sigh of relief; at least he was still alive. 'How did that happen?' she asked.

Worn down after long months of plague, hunger and constant bombardment the besieged Castilians had surrendered to the French under the command of Admiral Leo Strozzi, Prior of Capua and cousin of Catherine de Medici. After agreeing to their conditions, the treacherous Italian had immediately broken his pledge. Nothing Lindsay could say, not even appealing to his sense of honour, could change the admiral's mind: in fact, his pleas had been met with scornful guffaws. 'We do not barter with godless heathens,' he'd replied sternly before throwing back his head and laughing. 'If this new religion makes men so naïve and soft-headed, then I doubt we will have much to fear from them.'

Not only the Castilians had been duped. Furious for being a fool to trust the perfidious French, Lindsay was ashamed to tell Elisabeth that the rebels had given themselves up—on his advice. So far Strozzi had spared their lives but could they now trust him to honour his promise to show mercy?

'When I last saw him, John was being bundled off to the galleys with the other Castilians.'

She'd been lying still, but then her eyes flew open and she slapped a hand to her splitting head. 'The gallows? What? To hang him?'

'Nay. The galleys. We must be thankful for small mercies,' Lindsay said, as much to reassure himself as Elisabeth. 'At least Strozzi hasn't handed them over to the Scots to be burned at the stake. Instead, they will be shipped off to prison in France and remain in captivity while we negotiate to exchange hostages.'

Seeing her face light up, he shook his head. 'But there may be scant hope for John. Being a priest and scholar and of low birth, then...'

'Then we must acknowledge him!' Elisabeth said sitting upright. 'We must tell them who he is. That *we* are his parents. John is as noble as any of the Stewart bastards or the spawn of spineless Arran. I'm not afeart. Are you? I shall confess everything to Queen Marie. She'll understand. She knows well enough what it is like to lose a son.'

The look of intense determination on her face made him waver. He lowered his gaze, unable to meet her eyes shining with hope. A pang of regret gripped his heart and sweat dampened his brow as he said, 'But not, alas, one who is a known heretic and traitor. The queen mother is unlikely to show him mercy.'

'If John is in France then I will go to him,' Elisabeth replied. 'Nay, we will both go. You have his ear, Davie. He will listen to you. Talk him out of this reformist nonsense. He may be more willing to hearken to us after a spell in prison has tempered his zeal.' Though the thought that he'd be shackled in a dank, dark dungeon like Jinty and Bothwell chilled her.

Her false hope made Lindsay feel the worst possible hunker-slider. Being a heretic and a hostage of little worth, Knox's punishment would be to toil at the oars as a galley slave. He pulled her in closer, his lips gently caressing her ear as he whispered, 'There's nothing we can do, Lisbeth, except watch and wait.'

Vexed, she broke away from his embrace. 'Nay, nay! We cannot let him fall foul of such a fate! You must do something! You're to blame for all this!' Just how much of a rôle had Lindsay as *eminence grise* played in all the plots and intrigues over the years, she would like to know.

He held her firmly while she shook her head to and fro. When she had worn herself out, he released his grip and fumbled in his pouch. 'Lisbeth, will you take this?'

She flinched as he held out his pinkie encircled by the ring she'd thrown back at him.

'Not for yourself, for I know fine you'll refuse it, but to keep safe for John until he comes back.'

The engraved skull on the gold ring glinted in a beam of sunshine as it birled round the tip of his finger. The king's ring that had circled so many hapless fingers had proved to be no lucky talisman. She shook her head. 'Misfortune has befallen all who've worn it, Davie.'

'That's if you believe in auld wives' tales, Lisbeth. Our fate isn't shaped by baubles and bangles.'

'Then give it to him yourself. You're his father.'

'If God spares me, I will, but I'm no longer young and God alone knows how long I have left.' From his pallid countenance she couldn't tell whether he was being sincere or playing for sympathy. Davie Lindsay had aye been a skilful performer.

'Enough of the doom-laden blethers, you auld larbar. I'll keep it safe till the day we can both give it to him. And tell him the truth. Together.'

Chapter Seventy-Four
The Galley Slave

Priesties content you noo, noo,
Priesties content ye noo.
Norman and his company
Have filled the galleys fu'.
—*Song,* 16th Century

A French Galley, Autumn 1547

Would he never escape the clutches of St Mary? Knox frowned. Fate was playing a malicious trick on him, imprisoning him in a vessel named *Nôtre Dame.* On board the two-masted French galley 180 forsairs took it in turns to toil relentlessly at the oars; their sails were of no use in the lashing seas of the Bay of Biscay. Because the equinoctial gales threatened to drive them inshore, the awnings that screened the galley slaves were also furled, exposing them to merciless hammering by the Atlantic waves. Nor did the uniform, a sleeveless brown jerkin, give much protection against the elements or the knout. Sodden with sweat and briny sea water, the coarse canvas cloth clung pitilessly to their cracked peeling skin, rubbing salt into the running sores and weeping weals that never healed.

When first put to the oar Knox, the smallest and weakest, had toiled to keep time with the other four forsairs chained by the leg to their bench. His small stature placed him at the outboard end of the oar so that he didn't have to heave himself up on tiptoe to take his stroke like those at the inboard end. At least he was further away from the dreaded comité. The overseer strode up and down the central coursier that ran from stem to stern of the ship wielding a whip ready to lash any laggards for a steady rhythm of rowing had to be maintained at all times.

After months at the oars, his arm muscles had strengthened but thick calluses covered his scholar's hands and Knox worried whether he'd ever be able to pick up a quill again. He had to drive out despairing thoughts and remain resolute, not only for himself but also for his fellow Castilians. Fearing that losing track of time would mean losing his mind he started keeping a rudimentary diary, scratching a notch each day on his oar.

Crack! The force of the blow propelled him forward and he struck his forehead against his oar. He nearly blacked out but the tip of the knout whipping sharply across his back and his bare arms roused him.

'My God, my God, why dost thou forsake me?'

Wearily Knox lifted his head. James Balfour, a fellow Castilian was bent over his oar, his spine racked by sobs. His bench-mates were cussing and swearing at him for lagging at the oar, because they, too, and anyone else who got in the way of the whip, were being flayed unsparingly by the overseer. Knox put out a hand and patted his shoulder.

'Never abandon hope, lad,' he urged, his voice thick from the lash.

'Even Christ on the cross lost hope,' Balfour sobbed.

Their overseer, a muscular Moor, leant over and grabbed Balfour by his matted, stringy hair and pulled his head back. Stinging tears flowed down the runnels of the cracked skin of his shrunken face.

'Which would you sooner have? Your unwashed corpse thrown overboard or fed to the rats down below?' the overseer threatened, letting go of his head to thud against his oar.

Down below, the bowels of the ship housed the hospital, ostensibly for the recovery of those stricken with disease or weakness but in fact a filthy hole where the afflicted were thrown, often never to come out again until dropped over the side. Since the slaves were either criminals or heretics, their lives were expendable. When galley fever was rife, many victims preferred to die toiling at the oar than be hurled into the charnel house where the ship's rats scampered over the bodies sniffing out weakness. Then they would begin gnawing at the eyes, it was said.

'Keep in mind Christ's suffering and passion, my lad,' Knox wheezed. 'Consider this agony to be your *via dolorosa*. The oar is your cross and with each pull of the oar... another step on the long road to...'

'Golgotha and death!' Balfour wailed in despair.

'Nay,' Knox panted with the effort of speaking and rowing, 'to resurrection... of the spirit. Never forget Wishart and Patrick Hamilton,' Knox urged him. 'Our suffering is as nought compared to the final agonies of those martyrs for the faith.'

After another lash of the knout, Balfour heaved himself up and pulled down on the oar. Once they were swept into the rhythm of rowing, Knox chanted psalms to keep their spirits up. The mindless repetition of the rosary or endless litanies might have brought comfort, but no such popish profanities would ever pass his lips again.

By the end of September they had reached Nantes at the mouth of the River Loire where they were to moor for the winter: the shallow freeboard of the galleys rendered them unsuitable for voyages in high, wintry seas. Until their winter quarters on shore were ready, the slaves were kept on board, chained to the oar, their only shelter against the chilly night air being underneath the awnings used to protect them against the harsh summer sun. Though most of their time was spent mending ropes and sails and carrying out essential repairs,

Knox was surprised when the Scots were allowed pens and paper. Some concession must have been reached. Fortunately, his hands were not so mangled that he could not correspond with Henry Balnaves, confined in comparative comfort in the Castle of Rouen, and those Castilians incarcerated on Mont Saint-Michel. The knowledge that he was not a lone voice crying in the wilderness inspired Knox and spurred him on to hone his thoughts and compose religious tracts and letters.

Though the Castilians had survived their baptism of fire that did not prevent the French crew from trying to convert the heretics back to the Roman faith. On Saturdays, they lined up the Castilians with the other Christian galley slaves, to sing the *Salve Regina* in front of *Nôtre Dame,* an image of Our Lady crudely painted on a rough board and nailed to the mast. The Scots, however, steadfastly resisted her charms and turned their backs on the idol, drawing their hoods over their heads and covering their ears. On Sundays, they refused to attend mass, and on Mondays they were flogged for it.

'Do you not worship the prophet Christ?' the Moor asked, mystified as to why the Scots were being ostracised. Being told that, indeed, they were followers of the true teachings of Jesus Christ, he was still confused. Surely there could be no questioning the word of the prophet?

'His Word has been corrupted,' Knox explained, 'and in our struggle to find the way back to the true path we are being tested. God is pushing us to the limit of our physical endurance so that, once delivered from this bondage, we shall be invigorated with renewed will and strength to carry out his purpose. Of that I have no doubt, for it has been ordained. And God's will *shall* prevail,' Knox assured him.

This the Moor did understand. To him, all Christians were infidels, yet in Knox's fatalism and capacity for suffering, he recognised qualities that he'd believed peculiar to his own, Islamic faith. Everything is ordained. Everything is as it should be. By the will of Allah.

8 December 1547

'Kiss her, hérétique,' the argousin bellowed. 'Save your damned soul, you son of Satan and kiss. For this is Our Lady's Feast Day.'

The French sailors had burst into the Castilians' bagne, a crudely built barrack on the riverbank where the forsairs were quartered for the winter. After an all-night drinking spree the comité and his crew were seeking more fun. In the early dawn mist, they forced the Scots hérétiques onto the foredeck to pay their respects to the image of *Nôtre Dame*. The argousins took particular delight in tormenting Knox who, thanks to Sister Agnes's tuition was a fluent French speaker, and was always ready to answer back. Now the comité removed the painted icon from the nail and thrust it into the heretic's face.

'Trouble me not,' Knox said, shrinking away from his brandy breath. 'For I will not worship a graven image.'

'You shall pay due honour to Christ's Blessed Mother,' the comité insisted and forced the icon between the heretic's manacled hands. A triumphant cheer rose from the rest of the crew. 'Now kiss her, you spawn of the devil.'

For a moment it looked as if the heretic were praying to the idol between his hands. As the crew fell silent waiting for him to obey, Knox suddenly swerved sideways and pitched the icon overboard into the Loire as if it were a burning skivet.

Then he turned to address his companions in Scots. 'Let Our Lady now save herself,' he jeered. 'Being so holy she should sink, but since she's light enough, she'll swim.'

The Scots tried to hide their sniggers for, if the French understood that a 'light' woman meant one of easy virtue, a slattern, Knox would be severely punished for his blasphemy. From then on, however, the comité and his crew left the irredeemable Scots infidels to their own damnation.

Chapter Seventy-Five
The Treaty of Haddington

What is fortune, wha drives the dett so fast?
We wat there is baith well and wicked chance.
—*Fickle Fortune,* Henry the Minstrel, 15th Century

St Mary's Abbey, 4 July 1548

The two girls stood on tiptoe, fingers gripping the edge to peer over the parapet of the abbey belltower. All around and as far as they could see the countryside was ravaged: black gaps in woods slashed for timber gawped like an auld crone's toothless mouth; deep trenches gashed long, vicious scars in fields and meadows while fortifications and ditches steadily encircled the town like a noose. The English were digging themselves in well and truly. From the lofty bastion of the garrison's headquarters being built nearby, a soldier waved to them.

'Douk doon!' Isabelle shouted. 'For if thon English devil sees us, he'll cast his evil spell o'er us and turn us to whinstane.'

Jeanie hunkered down and stuck her thumb in her mouth, her eyes widening in terror in her doughy face. Whatever Isabelle said must be true for she knew everything. Brought to the abbey by Knox, the penniless orphan lass had been named and claimed by Sister Agnes who had taught her all about plants and herbs and healing and let her help out in the infirmary. Isabelle could not only concoct poisons that could kill folk, she could also cure them with magic potions. And she could speak French and even understand Latin, languages which were just gibble-gabble to Jean. Isabelle was wise beyond her years.

'The English are heathen devils,' she continued to torment her, 'with horns and tails and cloven hooves!' From the corner of her eye, she could see Jeanie's bottom lip trembling and, though Sister Agnes had taught her a chant to ward off evil spirits—something like *abominomalo diabolo*—she wasn't going to use it to console the earl's vauntie daughter.

'Hearken!' she shrieked as Jean clapped her hands over her ears and jolted at a thunderous explosion from the English cannon. 'That's their fiendish mouths spouting fire and brimstone. But you're surely not afeart, Jeanie Juniper? You're the brave governor's daughter.'

'And he will thave us,' Jean lisped, whey-faced and quaking. 'He'll be here thoon. He gave his word. I shall go and find him.' With that she scrambled to her feet and twirled off down the turnpike stair.

Elisabeth only gave her a cursory glance as she watched her scampering off followed a few minutes later by Isabelle. Playing a game of tig, she assumed.

'Whatever else is happening lassie will be lassies,' Queen Marie said as they walked their mounts along the riverside to survey the troops setting up camp.

'As daft as her father, thon lass,' Elisabeth replied. 'Had Errant Arran stood firm on the field of Pinkie Cleugh, all this could have been avoided,' she blurted, unable to conceal her bitterness.

So much for the confident governor, gloriously arrayed in gleaming new armour, who'd ridden out to lead one of the largest hosts in Scottish history: so much for his well-prepared trenchworks and well-oiled field artillery train: so much for the priests and monks, geared up and armed for battle, who strode among the ten thousand men mustered along the banks of the River Esk, spurring them on to fight the devil's own: for the legions of hell, their number swollen with experienced mercenaries and highly trained cavalry, had might on their side.

If the constant gunfire from the English fleet in the Firth of Forth could split ears in Haddington, then it swiftly shattered the brains and the resolve of the Scottish host. When the foot soldiers, fleeing a shock charge by heavy horse, had dashed for the safety of the marsh or of Arthur's Seat only to be ridden down and slaughtered, Arran had panicked and fled the field. On Black Saturday, while the Esk ran red with the gore of ten thousand Scots, the streets of Edinburgh flowed with the seventy tuns of beer Somerset had ordered for the victorious English troops. Thomas the Rhymer's prophecy had come true.

'And then our bold lord governor was forced to flee again—from the wrath of Edinburgh wives who vowed to stone him to death,' Elisabeth sneered. 'How I wish I'd been there to cast the first stone.'

'Only those who are without sin may do so,' Queen Marie said quietly.

'Oh, for the pleasure of pelting errant Arran's hide, madame, I would brazenly deem myself to be unsullied.'

'I fear your heart is desperately wicked, *ma chère amie*,' the queen laughed. 'Or at least *très méchant*.'

'Or, as the Scots would say, madame, as mischant as Auld Mischanter.'

The queen stifled a giggle before heaving a sigh. 'I should be grateful that Governor Arran has persuaded the stubborn Scots lairds to sign our Treaty.' Regret tinged her voice, for it meant she would have to bid farewell to her beloved daughter. While the Scots had at last agreed to Mary's betrothal to the dauphin, she was to be kept safe in France until her marriage, far away from the thieving English heathens.

'Only because of the rewards your King Henri has offered our brave governor; the promise of a wealthy French bride for his son, Lord James, and, more importantly, the Duchy of

Châtelherault and a generous pension for himself,' Elisabeth reminded her.

Before they changed their minds, parliament had been summoned to the abbey at Haddington to ratify the Franco-Scottish Treaty.

Elisabeth drew up her mount. 'What are our wranglesome lawmakers squabbling about now?' It looked as if representatives of the three estates were coming to blows over who should be assigned the largest, most lavishly equipped tent. Thon master of diplomacy, David Lindsay, should be here to placate them, Elisabeth thought, but his valuable skills were being put to use in Denmark where, as a member of the Scottish embassy, he was ostensibly negotiating a trade treaty but, in reality, requesting assistance against attack from the English.

Before they could intervene, Sister Agnes stepped in to harangue the group of clergy, lords and burgesses. The diminutive nun wagged a finger at them and ordered to them lay aside their pride and vanity. The biggest tents would be needed for a makeshift infirmary to tend the wounded, from the inevitable conflict of your making.

'Good for Sister Agnes,' Elisabeth said as they dismounted at the edge of the camp.

Seeing the fluttering flags and pennants of the gaily-coloured tents and pavilions—used in times of peace for spectacles and pageants—brought memories of the Tournament of the Wild Knight flooding back. Closing her eyes, Elisabeth savoured that moment when Lindsay had whirled her high in the air. Never again would she experience such giddy excitement. No more wheeling and whooping. No more birling.

Perhaps it would have been safer to retreat to Nunraw, she thought, giving herself a shake, but the English had seized all the strongholds in the area including Yester, Hailes and Nunraw. Queen Marie was also concerned. Although French troops had landed at Leith in over a hundred vessels and were on their way to Haddington, she feared there would be too few men and not enough provisions. The siege would be a long one.

That, however, should not affect her daughter. As soon as she had signed the Treaty, Queen Marie would set out for Dumbarton Castle where Queen Mary was waiting. Galleys that had dropped off the French troops at Leith were now sailing round the north coast of Scotland to the Clyde estuary to pick up the young Queen of Scots and take her to France.

'How furious Protector Somerset will be when he finds out his precious prize has been snatched from under his nose.' Queen Marie gave a quiet chuckle.

'And we shall miss you too when you leave, madame,' Elisabeth said sadly.

Marie de Guise furrowed her high, noble brow. 'I'm not leaving,' she declared. However strongly her De Guise relatives had urged her to abandon the wild Scots to their own devices, however much she pined to return to her motherland and however many torments lay ahead, she would remain in Scotland. 'I must safeguard my daughter's inheritance at all costs. If I leave, the Scottish lords will be easily won over to the protestant cause. Not for any religious conviction, but for English gold,' she added ruefully.

'Prioress! Wait!' a voice shouted. Sister Agnes came stumbling over the uneven ground towards them. Clinging onto her skirts, red-faced Isabelle seemed about to burst into tears.

'Lady Jeanie has disappeared!' the nun gasped.

Isabelle bowed her head as she explained how she'd scoured the abbey for Jeanie. Too ashamed to admit that it might be her fault for filling her simple soul with dread, she sobbed out her fears that the feckless lass might have fallen down a well or into the river.

'We shall have to call out the guard,' Sister Agnes said, gathering the weeping orphan lass in her arms.

'Not yet,' Elisabeth replied. The fewer who knew about it the better—so as not to alert the English who might scoop her up and hold her for ransom—and certainly not her father who'd never cease casting their carelessness up to them.

Crowds were streaming through the streets of Haddington where a barricade had been put up round the market square. There was almost a carnival atmosphere as musicians, tumblers and assorted street entertainers, taking advantage of the impromptu audience, began to perform under the cautious eye of English soldiers on patrol.

Jeanie had come to a standstill. Sucking her thumb and twirling a lock of hair into a ringlet, she balanced on one leg, for she had lost one of her calf slippers and her pretty lace-trimmed bonnet. Barefoot urchins in filthy rags were pointing at her and daring each other to run up and tug at her satin skirt with their clarty hands. She glanced around, terrified in case one of the horned English devils leapt out at her. Tears welled in her eyes. Where was her father?

Across the street an important looking man in a smart uniform sat astride a snorting stallion. She began to limp towards him when a stout woman caught hold of her arm. The sharp, acrid smell from her clothes stung Jeanie's nostrils but the woman had a kindly smile and sparkling eyes.

'Come away here, my bonnie lassie. Have you lost your mother?' she whispered in her ear. Her sour breath stank of ale.

Jeanie wrinkled her nose. 'I'm looking for my father. He's the governor.'

'Is he, indeed, my bonnie bird? Well, thon's the English governor up there. You don't want to get trampled under his hooves.' Jeanie shuddered, not daring to look and see if they were cloven or if fire and brimstone were spewing from his great gob.

'Don't fash, lassie. Rosie here will take care of you,' she wheedled, rubbing her satin gown between her forefinger and thumb to check the quality while casting a calculating eye over her expensive calf slipper.

'And I've lost my shoe,' Jeanie whined.

'And I wager it cost a pretty penny. I should ken, for I'm a tanner's wife. Come, my lass, I'll help you look for it. And to sweeten our search, I'll buy us a dainty or two.'

As Rosie lured her away, the crowd suddenly surged forward and pushed them up against the barricade. In the makeshift ring, two soldiers brandishing swords and bucklers were circling each other. As the first clang of sword clashing on sword rang out, the tanner's wife asked, 'What's going on?'

'Two of our lads stationed at Yester,' a spectator replied. 'Grey could have had them both hanged and that would have been the end of it, instead he's putting on a show for us. To make us think the English believe in fair play.' He hawked up a gob of spittle that narrowly missed Jeanie's one remaining slipper. 'Thon foul-tongued Newton was caught cussing the King of England's blessed name but, instead of crawing about it, the cowardly poltroon's putting the blame onto his mate, Hamilton.'

Jean's ears pricked up. Hamilton? Did that mean her father was here? She clung onto the barricade, resisting the tanner wife's attempts to prise her knuckles away.

Unable to push their way through, Elisabeth and Agnes were circling the densely packed mob, hoping to catch a glimpse of Jeanie's stylish lace-trimmed bonnet. A sudden hush fell over the raucous rabble as the falsely accused Hamilton finally forced the false-tongued Newton against the flimsy barricade. The crowd held their breath, not daring to distract their champion as he drew his sword back ready to slay the sleekit slanderer.

'Thlay him, brave Hamilton! Thlay him!' a shrill, girlish voice piped up from behind the barricade.

For a split second, Andy Hamilton hesitated and, turning his head slightly in the direction of the cry, presented his exposed thrapple to his opponent. In a trice, Newton plunged his sword into Hamilton's windpipe, piercing right through to the back of his neck, and then wrenched it out to sink it deep into the stricken man's chest.

Jeanie Hamilton's wide eyes gawped as the blood spurted like a fountain, spattering her satin gown and splashing her calf leather slipper and white stockings. She stood petrified, spittle drooling from the corners of her mouth as she sucked on her thumb. Sensing that the furious mob might turn on them, the tanner's wife slunk off through the crowd, muttering that the sappie-heided lass was fey.

But the rabble was baying for the blood of the sleekit Newton, who was cowering on his knees before the English Governor Grey, claiming the right of the law of arms to be set free. A barricade of English soldiers, arms linked, held back the outraged mob to let Newton mount his horse and ride off. Only when Grey gave an imperceptible nod to three mounted knights who set off after him did the crowd calm down. Justice would be served after all.

Elisabeth pushed her way through the mob to drag Jeanie away. Blissfully unaware of having caused a man's death, she was engrossed in rubbing at the bloodstains on her pretty gown. How Elisabeth longed to shake the gormless lass until her bones rattled and her teeth clattered, but what would that serve? That a man's life could depend on the whim of a capricious wee lass leading everyone a merry dance, only confirmed the fickleness of fate.

Chapter Seventy-Six
In the End is my Beginning

Farewell, ye lemand lamps of lustiness
Of fair Scotland, adieu my ladies all.
—*The Testament of Squire Meldrum*
Sir David Lindsay, 16th Century

A French Galley, July 1548

Sweating and straining at the oars, the rowers listened, ears on the prick, for the crack of the whip that signalled the end of their shift. Then they flopped across their oars, too exhausted to be irritated by the flapping wings of gulls diving into the slops and splattering them with guano. Before he could rest, Knox used his ragged thumbnail to scratch out a mark on his oar. Another notch, another day over. In late spring the galleys had been fitted out, French soldiers had trooped on board and they had set sail once again into the turbulent Bay of Biscay. To where, they were not told.

He slumped over his oar, wrinkling his nose at the foul stench from the sludge sloshing about under his feet, and shut his eyes to blot out the sight of it at least. When he'd enquired where he might relieve himself, the Moor had laughed gustily as if he'd never heard anything so drôle in all his life.

'Unless you've brought your own chamber pot, you'll piss and shit where you sit.'

Young lads scuttled like cockroaches under their benches to sluice away this bree of urine, faeces and vomit. Today the stench curdled his stomach and he wanted to retch. The thought of food made him feel sick but he took his scran bowl when it was passed along: he wasn't ready to donate his rations to his starving mates yet.

Thankfully today's offering wasn't gruel, a greasy sludge of oil and beans that stuck in his craw and which even the sour, brackish water couldn't sluice down. It was a thin watery skiddle boiled up from scrapings and peelings, which, if nothing else, would slake his drouth. He nibbled round the dry, fusty biscuit, spitting out weevils that had wormed their way into it. To force the crumbs down his gullet, he had to keep gulping and when the ladle was passed round, he slurped at the musty rainwater until it slittered down his chin. He had to eat and drink otherwise he risked being flung into the hospital. He would not die in harness.

The next morning he could hardly raise his hand, never mind lift his arms to row. The smell of vomit clogged his nose and his face was swathed in sweat. All night a constant flux—spewing up green bile at one end and dribbling a skittery mess from the other—had sapped his strength and left him steeping in his own stinking midden. When he tried to stand up, he blacked out, falling forward and hitting his head on the oar.

The Moor overseer unchained him, eased him onto the gangway and slapped his face a few times to revive him. He summoned the French surgeon who, on seeing who it was, just shook his head and left. The Scotch hérétique was already dead in his eyes and deserved no treatment. Knox was lowered down into the dreaded hospital from where no-one came out alive. In the cramped space around him emaciated bodies writhed in their death throes, calling out to their various gods for mercy: Allah. Jehovah. Almighty God.

The galley glided silently along, enshrouded in a thick, impenetrable mist that muffled the sound of the creaking vessel. He was utterly alone in the eerie silence. The sea and the sky had blended into a mirky greyness but then, as the hazy outline of the Craig of Bass loomed out of the haar, his spirits lifted. North Berwick must be nearby, and soon they would be within reach of Aberlady.

Unseen in the mist, he slipped his scrawny leg through the leg-iron and slithered quietly into the icy waters of the Forth. The coldness knocked the breath out of him. He plunged deeper and deeper beneath the waves, spinning and spiralling downwards towards the darkness. Desperate for air he flailed out with his arms and legs upwards before his lungs burst. Opening his mouth he retched out briny seawater and bilious green gaw. He grabbed hold of a piece of flotsam floating past and gratefully wrapped himself around it.

How long he dozed bobbing on the waves, he couldn't tell, but when he came to, he was no longer clutching a plain board but the statue of the Black Madonna. Ferny fronds of maiden's hair caressed her simpering lips and slimy bladderwrack coiled around her crudely painted face. The hard wood slowly yielded becoming as soft as womanly flesh under his fingers. The Madonna was changing into a mermaid before his eyes, with a long, lewd figure and fish tail. With a shudder of disgust, he thrust away the profane icon and then kicked and splashed his way towards the wide bay of Aberlady. As he waded through the shallows to the shore, he could see the familiar outline of the Garleton hills in the background: a light breeze carried the sounds of a welcoming peal from St Mary's Abbey. A short walk home and freedom.

The rays of the morning sun burned through the haar and lit up a figure coming down the brae towards him, arms beckoning. But when he tried to move, it was as if lead weights were dragging his legs down. His breath came in jerks and his ears felt as if they'd burst. He couldn't lift his feet out of the quicksand that was swaddling his feet. He threw up his arms in a vain attempt to slow the swamp that was swiftly sucking him down. Then he saw her face.

The Queen of Heaven, radiant and divine, her face shining with her beatific smile, her arms outstretched in a gesture of compassion. Gratefully he reached out, but as he clasped her blessed hand, the slender fingers blackened into writhing tentacles. Her compassionate smile twisted and warped into the lecherous leer of the gypsy girl and then the gruesome grimace of the Black Madonna.

As if bitten by the serpent, he dropped her hand and opened his mouth to scream, but thick evil-smelling slime slid down his throat and squeezed against his eyelids. With a slurp he slipped into the smothering darkness. A wave of cold seawater suddenly splashed across his face.

'Master Knox!' Master Knox! Wake up! You must wake up!'

With great effort he opened heavy-lidded eyes and blinked a few times. James Balfour was kneeling over him, wiping his face with a cloth.

'Forgive me, but you were so feverish, the Moor told me to douse you with water.' Appalled at the surgeon's lack of compassion, the Moorish overseer had released Balfour from his chains to tend to his compatriot in his last hours.

So he was still here. Lying on a bare board in the stinking hold of the galley with only a threadbare blanket to cover his nakedness: Jonah in the belly of the whale.

'We've passed North Berwick and we'll be within sight of St Andrews ere long,' Balfour said, trying to sound optimistic.

'Aye,' Knox mumbled. 'I can hear the bells.'

'Bells? You must still be dreaming.'

'Aye, well, whatever nightmare was tormenting me, it's over now,' Knox replied. 'Thanks be to God.' Raising himself up onto his elbows he tried to get to his feet. Every bone ached and his head dirled but he was desperate for at least a glimpse of St Andrews, perhaps his last. Balfour asked the Moor if he could take Knox up on deck. To see, St Andrews, a holy city he explained.

'As Mecca is for us. Allah Akbar.'

Knox struggled up the rope ladder with the help of Balfour pushing his legs and the Moor pulling his arms. Never a tall man, he seemed to have shrunk. Scranky-shankit and bow-backit—could this gaunt, shrivelled old body be his? Streaks of grey in his straggly hair and unkempt beard daubed him as brockit as a badger. The sun and wind had etched deep lines on his face and hunger had scooped hollows in his cheeks. He had descended into the hellhole as one man and come out another.

The first blast of the bitter east wind nearly blew the frail Knox over and the salt spray stung his eyes. Craning his scrawny neck, he could just about make out the spires of St Andrews rising out of the Scottish mist, and yonder the steeple of the church where God had first opened his mouth in public.

'And you shall do so again,' Balfour declared.

His eyes watering from the salt spray, Knox bowed his head. Aye, he would that. Confirmed as one of God's elect, he wouldn't depart this life until he had preached there again. Deemed unfit to take up his oar, Knox was given respite and allowed out on deck during the day to take fresh air and regain strength. Meanwhile, the galley had sailed round the north coast of Scotland and would be setting anchor ere long.

'I've heard we're taking on a most precious cargo,' the Moor told him. 'Of utmost secrecy. Your Scottish gold, perhaps, or your crown jewels.'

At Dumbarton harbour, it was no easy task to coax daft Jeanie Hamilton onto the gangplank to board the galley as she wriggled in Elisabeth's hand like a squirming tiddler. If children from noble families were to accompany the young queen, then the earl of Arran insisted that his son and daughter be among them. But the fushionless lad was too unwell to travel, while the spoilt lass was digging her heels in at the end of the pier, snivelling that monstrous sea creatures dwelling in the deep would drag her down.

'Come on.' Lady Fleming grabbed Jeanie by the shoulder and gave her a good shake. 'No more girning. You're not a bairn. See how her grace, your queen, so bravely trotted up the gangplank and she's only five. Set an example to the younger lassies.' She tilted her head towards a group of girls in matching costumes and bonnets, chattering excitedly.

Jenny Stewart, with her mother Nancy's flaming hair and her father's fiery Stewart temper, stood no nonsense. Widowed after Lord Fleming was killed at Pinkie, Jenny was to travel to France as chaperone to the toddler queen and her attendants, the four Maries, one of whom was her own daughter.

After successfully herding them up the plank she turned her Stewart charm on the French skipper. On hearing that unfavourable winds would delay their departure for days, she begged leave to go back ashore. But the skipper was unyielding: all passengers had to stay on board.

'He's a true sailor, thon tarry breeks,' she grumbled to Elisabeth. 'No doubt the auld sea dog favours heaving his mast with his bosun's mate,' she sneered and flounced off to supervise her charges. The five-year-old Queen of Scots and her new playmates were chasing each other in a game of tig round the narrow gangways that ran round both sides of the ship from prow to stern.

Elisabeth edged her way to the forecastle where sailors were loading supplies into the cabins underneath. On the foredeck, Margaret Erskine, another Pinkie widow, was bidding farewell to her seventeen-year-old bastard son being sent to study at the Sorbonne in Paris. The morose-looking James Stewart stood stiffly, averting his eyes as his mother harangued him in a quiet but firm voice. Never forget whose son he was, never forget that he was the queen's elder brother and never let himself be pushed aside by the bullying French. And be prepared for the day when his sister had need of him, for that day would come, Margaret Erskine was certain. Then, pinning his arms to his side, she pressed him roughly against that oft-admired bosom.

A sudden pang of envy struck Elisabeth as she witnessed this brusque hug between mother and son. Squalls of wind intensified the pitch and yaw of the boat making her feel queasy: the murky water lapping the sides of the shallow boat seemed to be welling up. She grasped hold of the rail and focussed her eyes on the landmark of Dumbarton Rock to steady her reeling head. From the castle, unable to bear protracted farewells from her daughter, Marie de Guise would be watching and waiting.

'*Vous êtes malade, Abbesse*?' The skipper was gazing at her with concern. Elisabeth shook her head. She only wanted to look round the galley. 'To make sure your royal passenger travels in comfort?' he said. 'Never fear, Abbess. Your precious child queen, our dauphin's betrothed, will be well sheltered from any storms.' He pointed to the stern of the ship where sailors were erecting a tent on the captain's deck. The other passengers, he explained, would berth under awnings on the gangways during the voyage.

What about the sailors? There didn't seem enough space for the jostling crew.

'There are cabins—but not enough for all the mariners—but since they work in shifts, they can share a berth or bed down wherever they can. The forsairs have to sleep at the oar. That's all those murderers and heretics deserve so don't waste any prayers on their damned souls, Abbess,' he said by way of farewell.

Elisabeth thanked him and then began to grope her way along the rail. The sour stench rising from the lower deck stung her nostrils: she wished she had a nosegay or a muslin cloth to cover her nose but she forced herself to look down. She scanned the scraggy, gaunt bodies of galley slaves slumped over their oars or sprawled across their benches. Was this the miserable existence Knox had to endure? she was thinking, when a sudden, sharp noise made her jump. A strong-armed Moor had cracked a whip to rouse the dozing forsairs. She flinched. A barefooted lad, wearing only a pair of tattered breeks and a red cap came out of a cabin underneath the foredeck, struggling to carry a pail. He thumped it down and began ladling slops into wooden bowls, passing them among the slaves who slurped greedily at the pigswill.

The Moor laid down his whip and, balancing like a tightrope walker, edged his way along the corsair between the benches. With both hands, he heaved at an iron ring and yanked open a hatch in the deck. Then he knelt down and positioned his strong arms underneath the oxters of a captive to pull him out of the lower depths. Blinded by sunlight, the slave staggered for a moment before the Moor led him, stumbling over his shackles, along the gangway. Then he propped him up against a coil of ropes in front of the cabin. With a weary nod of thanks, the captive stretched out his legs, raised his face to the sun and gulped down lungfuls of fresh air.

Elisabeth's heart squeezed in pain: she felt a sickening lurch in the pit of her stomach. The weird feeling of foreboding that had haunted her all her life now threatened to overwhelm her. She clenched her fingers round the rail to keep herself from fainting. Now was not the time to fall into a swoon for, despite the scraggy beard and the matted hair, she recognised him. Sunk deep into their sockets Knox's unmistakeable blue eyes shone out more intensely against his weather-beaten skin.

A sharp stab of pity for the torture he must be suffering pierced her heart, but that would all end soon. She would go immediately to Queen Marie and petition for his release. Then she would take John home and nurse him back to health—salve his wounds and heal his scars—but most of all she would give him the love she'd kept back all these years. A mother's love. Witnessing Margaret Erskine with her son had taught her that. Whatever her faults, the royal mistress had never deprived *her* son of his birthright.

John Knox had a right to know who his parents were, however upsetting it might be. She wouldn't wait—like her father had—until *her* deathbed to tell him the truth. And he should be given the chance to decide his own future. With no wish to be a prioress, had she not railed against her fate? She, of all people, should have realised all this. Who was she to accuse Lindsay of sending Knox down the path of perdition, when she was no less guilty in her determination to manipulate his destiny? Knox may have been coerced, rather than forced, into Holy Orders but he'd been given few other options: bishop or cardinal were hardly choices.

That that would all change now. Let him leave the church if he wished—she would seek a papal dispensation for him—but not to follow a false path. He should start a new life: marry a loving wife who would bear him children; live the life she'd been denied. Placing her hand on her chest, she could feel, underneath her sark, the king's ring pressing against her heart.

'John!' she called out.

Knox blinked a few times before looking up at a dark figure silhouetted against the sky. The woman clothed with the sun; the Queen of Heaven, her face forever imprinted on his memory. But now, in his dreamlike state, he saw her as she was when she first appeared to him with the multi-hued Paraclete perched on her arm. Once more he experienced an intense desire to touch her soft hands, smell her lavender oil and sense her warm, sweet breath as she placed a tender kiss on his cheek. A great weariness overwhelmed him as his spirit weakened and his resolve melted away.

'John!' she called out more urgently. 'John! Recant now and you can go free!'

He stiffened at her words. This woman clothed in the sun was not a vision, but a delusion. Not the Queen of Heaven but the Queen of Elfland, tempting him away from the right path:

For that is the path of wickedness,
Though some call it the road to heaven.

The Whore of Babylon in the guise of the prioress was trying to seduce him with her feminine wiles and he had almost succumbed. For, Almighty God, in his infinite wisdom, knowing full well the love that Knox still harboured for his godmother, had set him one last trial. But Knox would prevail, vowing to harden his heart against such temptation. He would never recant; he would aye *Keep Tryst*.

Elisabeth clambered onto the ladder leading to the lower deck but, on reaching the bottom rung, muscular arms the colour of burnt chestnut overpowered her. Waggling her head from side to side, straining to see over his shoulder, she grappled with the Moor in a macabre dance.

Knox's eyes narrowed to needle points of piercing blue. He raised his shackled hand not in blessing but in warning. He pursed his lips and mouthed the words: Go. In the name of God, go. And then he pressed his eyelids tight shut.

As her legs buckled beneath her, the Moor threw her over his shoulder and carried her up the ladder. When she made to turn back, he picked her up again and swung her round. For an instant she was the thirteen-year-old Lisbeth again, being whirled round by Lindsay, the world and her future whirling in front of her eyes. Tapsalteerie. Whigmaleerie.

As the Moor urged her towards the gangplank, she kept looking back and calling out plaintively, 'My son! That's my son!' But her words were borne away by the breeze.

7 August 1548

With favourable winds at last, the fleet of galleys lifted anchor and prepared to leave the Firth of Clyde. Three mothers stood on Dumbarton pier, gazing out to sea and clinging on for a last glimpse of the galleys: *Stabat Mater dolorosa*. Standing well away from Margaret Erskine, Marie de Guise stood firm by Elisabeth's side, steadfastly refusing to show tears in front of her auld enemy. Only when they left the pier did she share her grief with the prioress.

'Shall I ever see my beloved daughter again?' she said softly. 'If only...'

'There's no sense in wishing that life could be otherwise, your grace. What will be, will be,' Elisabeth replied in an effort to comfort the desolate queen mother, but that was not what she believed. Although Knox had dismissed her this time, she would not give up hope. For the day would come when he would turn to her again and she would regain his trust. But until then she must: *Endure Fort*.

The queen mother was nodding, 'Wise words, *ma chère soeur*. And what is that saying the Scots are so fond of? About submitting to fate?' She pondered for a moment before moistening her lips to pronounce in her best Scots tongue, 'You maun dree your weird.'

The End

Author's Note

Nearly all of the principal characters in this novel existed in real life, apart from a few who are fictional: Betsy Learmont, Kate Hepburn, and Sister Agnes. The events are mostly based on historical fact with a liberal use of artistic licence in their interpretation.

The main liberty is taken with the central relationship of John Knox, Elisabeth Hepburn and Sir David Lindsay, which, although a matter of conjecture, is not beyond the bounds of possibility.

Knox was notoriously reticent about his early life and he first appears in the written records as a Notary Apostolic on 13 December 1540. While some of his biographical details have been disputed, it is now accepted that he was born in Giffordgate by Haddington in 1513 or 1514, but his parentage remains obscure. He and his brother William were orphaned at an early age and, while Knox described himself as 'a man of base estate and condition', some biographers consider that his family must have had reasonable financial resources to send him to St Andrews University. Knox also mentions strong kinship with the earls of Bothwell—the Hepburns of Hailes Castle—but, as far as he was concerned, he was born again when the reformist preacher, George Wishart, pulled him from the 'puddle of papistry'.

Elisabeth Hepburn appears in the records as Prioress of St Mary's Abbey from around 1520 till 1563. Described in one document as the daughter of an Augustinian canon and in another as the kinswoman of John Hepburn, Prior of St Andrews, she is assumed to be the prior's natural daughter. Hepburn requested from Archbishop Forman her appointment as prioress—at the very young age of twenty-three—overruling the election by the nuns of their own nominee, M. H., presumed to be Mariota, or Maryoth, Hay. In an entry in the Haddington Protocol Books of June 1541, Elisabeth is accused of 'carnal dalliance' with one Harry Cockburn. She is also recorded in the Accounts of the Lord High Treasurer of Scotland as riding to the hunt with the court of James V.

The young king's tutor, Sir David Lindsay of the Mount and Garleton, who later served at court as herald and diplomat, was a renowned poet and playwright. His famous work, *Ane Satire of the Three Estates,* is a scathing attack on the corrupt practices of the Roman Catholic Church and, singled out for scandalous behaviour, is a Prioress. She then defends herself by cursing those friends who compelled her to be a nun and 'would not let her marry'. Did he base this character on the free spirited, real-life prioress Elisabeth Hepburn? And could Knox have inspired—or even played the part of—Divine Correction, God's avenging angel, sent to instigate reform, and John the Commonweal, who takes up the cause of the Poor Man?

Lindsay certainly encountered Knox in St Andrews Castle in 1547 when he encouraged him to preach against the antichrist of Rome, and the parallels between the imagery of this sermon and Lindsay's poem, *The Monarch,* are too striking to be simply coincidental. While it has been acknowledged that Knox appears to have exerted a decisive influence on Lindsay's reformist ideas, it is also likely that theirs was a close, mutual relationship that began much earlier, with the older poet inspiring the younger cleric.

All three could have met around 1527 when Lindsay was exiled to his property at Garleton near Haddington where Knox was a pupil at the grammar school and Elisabeth was prioress at St Mary's Abbey. These coincidences form the springboard for a plot that interweaves documented fact with inspired guesswork. This novel is an attempt to shed light on the early, formative years of one of the most influential figures in Scottish history, John Knox.

About The Author

Marie Macpherson

Hailing from the historic town of Musselburgh, six miles from Edinburgh, Scottish writer Marie Macpherson was brought up on the site of the Battle of Pinkie and within sight of Fa'side Castle where tales and legends from the past haunted her imagination. Inspired by the film *Dr. Zhivago* to read the works of the Russian literary giants in the original, she left the Honest Toun to study Russian at Strathclyde University. She spent a year in the former Soviet Union to research her PhD thesis on the 19th century Russian writer Mikhail Lermontov, said to be descended from the poet and seer, Thomas the Rhymer. Though travelled widely, teaching languages and literature from Madrid to Moscow, she has never lost her enthusiasm for the rich history and culture of her native Scotland.

Having taken early retirement, she has found her niche in writing historical fiction which combines her academic's love of research with a passion for storytelling. Her inspiration comes not only from historical records and documents but also from the landscape of the Scottish lowlands where she attempts to conjure up what life was like for the inhabitants of those now ruined castles and deserted abbeys. Exploring the personal relationships and often hidden motivations of historical characters drive her curiosity.The Knox Trilogy is a fictional biography of the fiery reformer, John Knox, set during the 16 th Century Scottish Reformation

Prizes and awards include the Martha Hamilton Prize for Creative Writing from Edinburgh University and *Writer of the Year 2011* awarded by Tyne & Esk Writers.She is a member of the Historical Writers' Association (HWA), the Historical Novel Society (HNS) and the Society of Authors (SoA).

BETWEEN TWO KINGS

BY

OLIVIA LONGUEVILLE

Anne Boleyn is imprisoned in the Tower of London on false charges of adultery, high treason, and incest on the orders of her husband, King Henry VIII of England. Providence intervenes – she escapes her destined tragedy and leaves England. Unexpectedly, she saves King François I of France, who offers her a foolhardy deal, and Anne secretly marries the French monarch.

With François' aid, she seeks vengeance against the English king and all those who betrayed her and designed her downfall in England. Henry must face the deadly intrigues of his invisible enemies, while his marital happiness with his third queen, Jane Seymour, is lost and a dreadful tragedy also strikes the king. The course of English and French history hangs in the balance.

From the gloomy Tower of London to the opulent courts of England, France, and Italy, brimming with intrigue and danger – Anne Boleyn survives, becoming stronger and wiser, and fights to prove her innocence. Her hatred of Henry is inextricably woven into her existence.

THE ALTERPIECE

BY

SARAH KENNEDY

It is 1535, and in the tumultuous years of King Henry VIII's break from Rome, the religious houses of England are being seized by force. Twenty-year-old Catherine Havens is a foundling and the adopted daughter of the prioress of the Priory of Mount Grace in a small Yorkshire village. Catherine, like her adoptive mother, has a gift for healing, and she is widely sought and admired for her knowledge. However, the king's divorce dashes Catherine's hopes for a place at court, and she reluctantly takes the veil. When the priory's costly altarpiece goes missing, Catherine and her friend Ann Smith find themselves under increased suspicion. King Henry VIII's soldiers have not had their fill of destruction, and when they return to Mount Grace to destroy the priory, Catherine must choose between the sacred calling of her past and the man who may represent her country's future.

PENMORE PRESS
www.penmorepress.com

ASSASSINS OF ALAMUT

BY

JAMES BOSCHERT

An Epic Novel of Persia and Palestine in the Time of the Crusades

The Assassins of Alamut is a riveting tale, painted on the vast canvas of life in Palestine and Persia during the 12th century.

On one hand, it's a tale of the crusades—as told from the Islamic side—where Shi'a and Sunni are as intent on killing Ismaili Muslims as crusaders. In self-defense, the Ismailis develop an elite band of highly trained killers called Hashshashin....whose missions are launched from their mountain fortress of Alamut.

But it's also the story of a French boy, Talon, captured and forced into the alien world of the assassins. Forbidden love for a princess is intertwined with sinister plots and self-sacrifice, as the hero and his two companions discover treachery and then attempt to evade the ruthless assassins of Alamut who are sent to hunt them down.

It's a sweeping saga that takes you over vast snow-covered mountains, through the frozen wastes of the winter plateau, and into the fabulous cites of Hamadan, Isfahan, and the Kingdom of Jerusalem.

"A brilliant first novel, worthy of Bernard Cornwell at his best."—Tom Grundner

PENMORE PRESS
www.penmorepress.com

The King's Corpse

By

M J Jones

Medieval Saint relics stealing.

MJ Jones brings a hilarious detective story from the Dark Ages into the light of day. Our disreputable hero following his grubby profession leads us on a merry chase around the English and Welsh countryside.

His name's Tryff, he comes from Wales, and he steals saints for a living. Used to, anyhow. But everybody in England's got to have a lord, so Tryff's become radman, mounted protection (and general dogs-body) for the abbess of a little country convent. She sends him to find the missing body of her cousin Edward, the probably murdered king of England. It's a nigh on impossible job, but he takes it because he needs the money to buy his mother out of slavery.

Tryff's confronted with a vicious royal court, a double-crossing bard, and a revolting waker-of-the-dead. They rout him completely. Now he must look for the king's body in Wales. With but three English nuns for help, Tryff sets off to track down not only the king's body but also his mother, the Great Harp of King Arthur, and love besides. island.

www.ingramcontent.com/pod-product-compliance
Ingram Content Group UK Ltd.
Pitfield, Milton Keynes, MK11 3LW, UK
UKHW041302040525
5756UKWH00020B/98

9 781946 409508